STIRRED & SHAKEN

TWISTED
FOX
SERIES

BOOKS 1 & 2

USA TODAY BESTSELLING AUTHOR
CHARITY FERRELL

Editor: Jovana Shirley, Unforeseen Editing, www.unforeseenediting.com

Proofreader: Jenny Sims, Editing4Indies

Cover Designer: Opulent Designs

Stirred

Cohen

"JUST FOR A MINUTE," I plea, rocking my newborn son in my arms. "Hold him for one damn minute."

It'll change your mind.

It has to change your mind.

Heather sneers, refusing to look at us, and crosses her arms, as if she's scared I'll push him into them.

I count to ten, my jaw clenching harder with each number. Ten hits and I blow out a series of calming breaths.

Not that it works.

I'm fighting to keep my cool.

For him.

Not her.

Fuck her.

"Enough is enough, Heather," I say.

Her green eyes, void of emotion, narrow when they meet mine. "I told you, Cohen, I wanted out. I can't do this—"

"You decided out of the fucking blue that you wanted out *two months ago.* A little too late to change your mind about having our baby."

"I don't want him. You agreed to accept all responsibility, and I expect you to keep your word." She uncrosses her arms and rubs her hands together. "My job is done. I'm leaving."

I trace the tiny features of Noah's face with the pad of my thumb. "Give it a week. *Please.*"

"My flight leaves in three days."

"Heather—"

"If you hoped me seeing him would change my mind, you were wrong." She tips her head toward the little man in my arms. "Neither will holding him."

Revulsion seeps through me when she turns around and walks away without giving us another glance.

How did I ever love this woman?

That love splinters into disgust.

Trailing a finger over Noah's peach fuzz, I whisper, "Looks like it's just you and me against the world, buddy."

CHAPTER ONE

Jamie

Five Years Later

NINE HOURS DOWN.

Three to go.

Three hours until I can go home, finish that box of Thin Mints I shouldn't have bought, and binge-watch a show on Netflix.

Netflix and cookies.

Netflix and single.

Netflix and story of my life.

"Tell me he finally agreed?" Lauren, our charge nurse, asks—referring to the appendicitis patient who's been refusing an appendectomy all night.

I nod. "After his wife promised to buy him a new TV."

She scoffs. "I'd love to say someone being bribed to have life-saving surgery is a shocker, but after working in the ER for so long, I'm not easily shooketh."

"Tell me about it." I glance around the emergency room. "What's next for me?"

It's been a slow night at Anchor Ridge Memorial Hospital, and as much as that's a good thing, it can get boring.

She points down the hall. "Exam room three. Five-year-old with a fever." Her tone turns bubbly as she wiggles her shoulders. "Dad is *super hot*, by the way."

I shake my head and tap my knuckles against the triage desk. "I'll let you know if I need anything."

"Ask him for his number," she half-whispers with a thumbs-up.

I roll my eyes and dismissively wave my hand. "Absolutely not."

"All work and no play makes Jamie a grumpy doctor."

"Yeah, yeah, yeah." I spin on my heel and walk to the room.

The door is cracked, and I knock, snatching a pair of latex gloves on my way in.

"Hello, I'm Dr.—" I stop, stumble back two steps, and cover my mouth with my hand.

Holy crap.

My body tenses, and as soon as my gaze meets his, his jaw flexes.

I struggle for words as anger and disgust line his face.

Words I'd planned if this moment ever happened.

Unfortunately, those words become a scared bitch and run away.

"Cohen," is all I manage in a whisper.

He stands tall from his chair, his narrowed eyes pinned to me, and moves to the side of the bed, blocking my view of the patient.

Lauren's words hit me.

"Five-year-old ... "

My attention slides from Sir Pissed Off, and I shift to the left.

"Oh my God," I whisper, gaping at the little boy in the bed.

A little boy whose eyes are sleepy and nose is red and irritated.

Those sleepy eyes, a walnut-brown with a slight slant, match his father's.

The same with his thick ash-brown hair.

But the dimple in his chin and heart-shaped face match *hers*.

"Is this ...?" My hand shakes when I point at him.

It's a dumb question.

Even if he says no, he'll be a liar.

"What are you doing here?" he repeats, his tone harsh.

If I wasn't at a loss for words, my smart-ass self would throw out something along the lines of, *What do you think, dumbass? I'm sporting a doctor's jacket with my name embroidered on it.*

But I don't.

Because I can't.

It's a challenge, wrapping my head around them being here, let alone dragging out my sarcasm.

"I'm your doctor," I finally say before signaling to the boy. "I'm *his* doctor."

Sound cool. Confident.

You're the fucking professional here, Jamie.

"We want a different doctor," he hisses, his voice low enough so only I can hear.

"I'm the *only* doctor on shift tonight." I'm speaking to Cohen, but the boy holds my interest.

He's watching this exchange, his eyes pinging back and forth between his father and me with curiosity on his tired face.

"We'll go to another hospital then."

"Why, Dad?" the boy whines, sniffling. "I don't feel good, and what if I puke in the car?"

"I want another doctor." His broad shoulders draw back.

He raises a brow when I hold up a finger, turn, and scurry out of the room.

I rush over to Lauren. "Can you watch the boy in three for a minute? I need to talk to his father privately."

She peeks up at me from her computer and tilts her head to the side. "Yeah … sure."

Cohen is pacing the room when we walk in.

"A word," I say, jerking my head toward the doorway.

Cohen's attention darts to the boy, and he delivers a gentle smile. "I'll be right back, buddy." He gives him a quick peck on the head and swings his arm toward the door, his eyes cold. "After you, Your Highness."

Lauren throws me a curious glance when he walks past her, and I shrug as if this isn't about to be awkward city up in here.

As we leave, I hear Lauren asking the boy what his favorite cartoon is.

Cohen keeps his distance while I lead us into a private room, the one reserved for breaking bad news to families.

I speak as soon as I shut the door, "Cohen—"

Too bad he doesn't let me get more than his name out.

Rude.

His deep-set eyes level on me. "This is a conflict of interest, Jamie. The nurse can help us. We don't need you."

"We don't need you."

The memories of the last time he said those words to me smack into me like a headache.

It was the last time I saw him.

The last time he looked at me with the same resentment.

Either he doesn't realize how hard his insult hit me or he doesn't care.

I snort, anger biting at me. "What do you think I'm going to do, huh? Kidnap him?"

"Considering who you're related to, who knows?"

"Wow." I clench my fists to hold myself back from smacking him in the face since his words are like a slap in mine. "You have some nerve."

It'd make for some bad headlines if a doctor slapped a patient's father.

There's no apology on his face when he holds up his hands. "Just saying it how I see it."

"Then allow me to *say it how I see it.*" I thrust my finger toward the door. "You have a sick son in there, and it's *my job* to treat him. Don't like it? I don't give a shit." I shove past him, stalk out of the room, and don't check to see if he's following me.

"Everything okay?" Lauren asks, her eyes glancing over my shoulder, and I realize Cohen is behind me, still keeping his distance.

"Peachy," I chirp before approaching the bed and smiling down at the boy. "What's your name, honey?"

"Noah," he croaks.

Even though I was sure it was him, my head spins at his confirmation.

I tenderly squeeze his arm, and my tone turns cheerful. "Hi, Noah. I'm Dr. Gentry. Can I ask some questions about how you're feeling?"

He nods.

Cohen stalks to the other side of the bed, his eyes on me, and Lauren migrates to the corner, her nosy ass interested in this shitshow.

"He has a fever," Cohen tells me, his tone softer.

"For how long?"

He scratches his scruffy cheek. "Over twenty-four hours."

"Appetite?"

He shakes his head. "Not even sugar. I can hardly get him to drink, and he has no energy, which is *very* rare for him."

"Cough?"

"Yes."

His jerk attitude settles while we turn our attention to Noah. I ask question after question as I take his temperature and go through all the motions.

"Symptoms tell me it's the flu," I say, removing my gloves and tossing them into the trash. "We'll do a test, and I also want to run some blood work to make sure we're not missing anything."

Cohen nods. "Thank you."

I smile at Noah. "We'll get you back to feeling good in no time." I give Lauren, who's gathering supplies for the test, a head nod and leave the room.

I'll definitely be pairing wine with those Thin Mints tonight.

Lauren comes scurrying into the doctors' lounge ten minutes later. "Whoa, what was that about? Dude was super nice to me but acted as if you'd pissed in his Cheerios."

Here goes.

A chill sweeps up my neck. "That's my sister's ex … and her son … the ones she left."

"Oh, Jerry Springer."

CHAPTER TWO

Cohen

OUT OF ALL THE DOCTORS, it had to be her.

Jamie fucking Gentry.

Heather's younger sister.

A woman I demanded stay the fuck away from Noah and me.

I moved two towns over from Mayview to Anchor Ridge, Iowa, to prevent this shit from happening.

The last time I saw her was a few days after Noah was born. That was five years ago, and even though she's changed, there was no disputing it was her when she walked in. The moment our eyes met, I jumped to my feet, dread spilling over every rational thought in my head.

She can't see him.

She can't know him.

Anger shook through me as we stared at each other. Her eyes—so similar to the woman's I despised—only pissed me off more.

Noah is sleeping, and my back straightens in my chair at the sound of a tap on the door. I slump in relief when it's my younger sister, Georgia, coming into view and not Jamie.

Hopefully, Jamie listened and won't come back.

"I came as soon as I left work," Georgia says, collapsing in the chair next to me.

I shoot her a stressed smile. "Thanks."

She bites into her lower lip, her gaze sweeping from one side of the room to the other, and taps her foot. "This might sound super random, but did you know that Heather's sister is here?"

"Yep." I stretch out my legs. "She's Noah's doctor."

"Wow." She whistles. "Awkward."

"Tell me about it."

"I wish I had been here at that first exchange."

I drop my head back, hoping to release the tension in my neck. "I nearly had a heart attack when she walked in."

I'm positive she felt the same.

Jamie's face revealed every thought running through her head.

Shock, hurt, anger.

The same shit her sister made me feel.

"Did you ask for another doctor?"

"She's the only doctor here tonight."

She lowers her voice. "Does Noah know who she is?"

"No, and it'd better stay that way." I move my neck from side to side before standing. "Can you keep an eye on him while I grab a quick coffee from the waiting room?"

"No, there's no way I can handle him," she says with a roll of her eyes. "He's acting like an animal. Too much energy."

I ruffle my hand through her hair, and she smacks it away.

"Fucking smart-ass."

"Grab me a coffee too. Please and thank you."

I pour our coffees and almost make it back to Noah's room Jamie-free, but she steps in front of me before I do.

Determination is set on her too-pretty face, and she crosses her arms. As much as I'd love to tell her to fuck off, I can't. The nurse's eyes are glued to us like we're her favorite soap opera.

There sure is enough drama for us to be one.

"Cohen, we need to talk," Jamie says.

I match her stance, folding my arms across my chest, and grip the coffees tight in each hand while adding a scowl to one-up her. "If it's not about Noah, I have nothing to say to you."

She stretches out her hand and separates her fingers. "Five minutes. That's all I'm asking for, and it *is* about Noah."

"Three minutes." I'm not doing shit on her terms.

She throws her arms up before collapsing them to her sides. "Fine, three minutes."

I trail her when she starts walking, and the nurse smirks when we pass her. We're back in the room she dragged me into earlier, and she shuts the door behind us. I can't stop myself from chuckling when she stands in the doorway, crossing her arms again as if she's geared to stop me from leaving.

As if she makes the fucking rules.

Her thick honey-brown hair is longer than it was so many years ago and swept back into a ponytail, a few curly strands loose around her face. She's wearing blue scrubs—even though they shouldn't look hot, they do on her—and a white jacket, the words *Dr. Jamie Gentry, MD, Emergency Medicine* embroidered on it in red stitching.

She's gorgeous—even with the similarities between her and Heather. Prettier—because she doesn't have a black fucking heart. Long gone is her geeky phase. Now replaced with a beautiful, confident woman, and by the look on her face, she is about to be a pain in my fucking ass.

"I tried calling you for months, Cohen," she snaps before raising a finger. "No, wait. I tried calling you for *years*."

"What did I tell you?" I reply, setting the cups down on a table. "If it doesn't involve Noah, I have nothing to say to you."

"Seriously?" She grimaces. "Act like a grown man here."

"Trust me, I *am* plenty of a grown man."

"Really? Because your behavior screams more of a child's than a man's."

"This conversation is what's childish. What do you want me to tell you, Jamie?" I scrape a hand through my hair and blow out a stressed breath. "I changed my number."

"Thank you, Captain Fucking Obvious. *Why* did you change your number?"

"Put two and two together. You're smart."

She shoots me a cold look. "Asshole."

I shrug.

"He's so big, Cohen." Her features, along with her tone, relax. "And he has your eyes. Fatherhood suits you."

If this is her trying some reverse psychology shit, it won't work.

"Fuck your compliments, Jamie," I snarl. "Saying nice shit to me and being Noah's doctor won't change anything between your family and me... between *you and me.*"

"Why?" she questions with disdain, taking a step closer. "What did I do to you to take away the chance of knowing my nephew? To take away my parents' first and *only* grandchild? We never turned our backs on Noah when Heather said she was leaving. We opened our arms—"

"And asked to fucking adopt him!" Anger fires through me. Anger that's been embedded in me since Noah's birth and can finally be released. "You wanted to take him from my arms!"

"That isn't fair to say it like that," she states, repeatedly shaking her head while delivering a pained stare. "They were worried."

"They had nothing to worry about."

"With your job—"

"My job makes me incompetent of being a father?" I snort and scowl at the same time. "If anything, it's given me patience. I can easily clean up spills and vomit, and I have no issue dealing with a lack of sleep. My job has made me the *perfect fucking parent.*"

She stays quiet as worry covers her face. She's searching for her next words, wanting them to be perfect.

"I can expect you won't tell Noah who you are?" I ask.

She doesn't answer.

"Jamie"—I seethe—"you're his fucking doctor. That's it."

Her face turns stern. "I won't say anything."

I tip my head down and grab the coffees. "Thank you. Now, I need to get back to my son."

She jumps in front of me when I attempt to beeline around her. "If you change your mind—"

I hold up my hand and talk over her because I'm a jackass like that., "Not fucking happening, so don't bother finishing that sentence."

"Jesus, Cohen, will you stop interrupting me?"

"You can't see him, Jamie. It'll only confuse him."

"Why?"

"You're seriously asking me that fucking question?"

"Say I'm your friend." She edges closer, and I retreat. "Say I'm his aunt Jamie. Say whatever you want."

I lower my gaze on her. "I appreciate your help today, but that's all we need from you."

She glares at me, unblinking. "Oh, I get it. You're selfish … just like her."

My face burns, and I reply through gritted teeth, "Excuse me?"

"Withholding Noah from having grandparents," she says, my temper not scaring her off. "Withholding an aunt—"

"Georgia is a perfectly good aunt."

She digs in her pocket and pulls a card out between two fingers. "Noah has the flu. The nurse will go through the details for treatment with you. Here's my card if you need anything. Call me, day or night. If Noah is sick. If he isn't. If you change your mind."

I scoff., "Not happening."

She shoves the card in my shirt pocket, pats my chest, and turns to leave. I still, staring at her as she walks away.

Cursing under my breath, I stroll back to Noah's room. Jamie is gone, and the nurse delivers a hesitant smile before giving us the discharge information.

"What's that?" Georgia asks when the nurse leaves, referring to the card sticking out of my pocket.

"Jamie's card." I snatch the card and glare at it like it's ruined my night.

Georgia stops me when I start crumpling it in my hand. "Don't do that. She's a doctor. If you ever need help, you can call her."

"Noah has a doctor. There's no shortage of them around."

"Keep it." She pats my chest the same way Jamie did. "Don't be dumb."

CHAPTER THREE

Jamie

"YOU'RE A DOCTOR, huh? Does that mean you like blood and can stomach gory shit?"

I'm a firm believer in not wasting wine, but the longer my date speaks, the higher the chance he'll be wearing mine by the end of the night.

It wouldn't be completely wasted if it taught him a lesson, right?

Reason four hundred and fifty-three of why I hate blind dates: I'm set up with idiots who ask if I get pleasure from blood and gory shit as if I were Rob Zombie.

Hell, I'd rather be on a date with Mr. Zombie than this expensive-suit-wearing prick.

A suit that'd pair nicely with a soft red, if I do say so myself.

Normally, I'd roll my eyes and ignore his remark, but today is not my day. Thanks to a bolt of lightning striking my townhome's power line, I got ready for this joke of a date with no electricity—my iPhone flashlight and a sugar cookie-scented candle my only light sources.

All that trouble for this smug dick to smirk and ask me ridiculous questions.

On paper, he's perfect—wealthy, successful, handsome.

Realistically, he's a major tool bag.

"You're a criminal defense attorney, huh?" I relax in my chair and deliver a smirk more asshole-like than his. "Does that mean you like convicts and can stomach illegal shit?"

He lifts his chin with pride and waggles his manicured finger my way. "I see what you did there, beautiful."

Gag me.

He grabs his scotch from the table and casually leans back in his chair, and the glass dangles from his fingers. "Baby, there's no denying I love when the law is broken. The criminals, they flock to me. I'm damn good at my job, which means I make damn good money." His eyes brighten as if he's gearing to reveal a secret. "You know Freddy Louda?"

Who doesn't?

"The millionaire who trafficked drugs and murdered two women?"

"*Allegedly* trafficked drugs and murdered those women. I got him off with not one charge." He swipes invisible dirt from his shoulder. "I love it when the bigwigs with fat bank accounts need legal counsel. Hell, I bought a new Mercedes S550 from his case alone."

I grimace.

Lord, if I have to continue listening to his bullshit, I'll be joining the criminals he neglected to keep out of jail.

We can form a We Hate This Asshole gang, play poker, and share ramen noodles. Fun stuff.

I jerk my napkin off my lap, slap it onto the table, and snatch my purse. "Excuse me for a sec."

Forever actually.

"Sure." He licks his lips. "I'll cover the check. We can have dessert at my place."

Gag me again.

And not in the exciting, sexual sense.

Not that that's my thing, but still.

Gag me in a way that this is the worst date I've had—and there have been some terrible ones.

I roll my eyes, stand, and walk away without another word. A crowd surrounds the hostess stand, and I duck my head while passing them before rushing out of the restaurant.

I'm not dining and dashing.

I'll pay Asshole-at-Law back for my meal, but if I'd spent another second with him, my knee would have had a date with his balls.

I curse Ashley with every step while dragging my phone from my clutch.

"Listen, Ash," I screech when my best friend answers, "you're officially cut off from setting me up on dates. I should've ended it after the last disaster."

"Hey, he wasn't *that* awful," she argues around a laugh.

"He drew out a deck of cards at dinner and spent our meal showing the entire restaurant offensive magic tricks." I snort. "Oh, and after that lovely dinner, he was generous enough to suggest we go to his place to show me his best trick of them all. It wasn't pulling a rabbit out of a hat—"

"Which is unfortunate," she cuts in. "I've always wanted to learn how to do that."

"It was pulling his *magic snake* from his pants." I shudder, the memory of forcing back vomit hitting me, and my hatred toward the Houdini wannabe resurfaces. Asshole ruined chicken Bellagio for me, and damn it, pasta is my favorite carb.

"You are a Harry Potter fan."

"And you're clearly a fan of me being single for the rest of my life."

She sighs. "Look, Gregory works with Jared, and everybody says he's a nice guy. He's the best attorney at their firm. I even made Jared search his office for magic wands."

"A nice guy?" I scoff. "Have *you* had the pleasure of meeting my lovely dinner date, Gregory?"

"Well"—she pauses—"no."

"He's scum, and Jared should fire him."

"He's a partner. Jared can't fire him."

"Then tell Jared his partner sucks when he asks why I dipped out on our date."

"What?" she shrieks. "You can't *dip out* without saying good-bye."

"The dipping is done. My current situation is me standing outside, missing the glass of wine I deserted."

I should've chugged that shit before leaving.

Thou shall not waste wine unless it's throwing it at a bad date.

"He'll be insulted."

"Good. He deserves it for how many times he insulted me tonight. Consider us even. I'm ordering an Uber. Fingers crossed my driver has a better personality than my drug lord-loving date."

"Maybe you can ask him to show you his magic snake."

I groan and shiver, running a hand over my arm. "Tell Jared I'll Venmo the money back to Douchebag-at-Law for dinner. Love ya."

I hang up, and before I tap the Uber app, my phone rings with an unknown number calling.

"Hello?" I answer.

"Jamie, it's Cohen." His voice is low-toned, as smooth as my abandoned wine, and hasn't changed since high school. "Are you busy?"

I sway slightly, not from being drunk, but from the shock of this call. "No ... not at all."

"Noah was starting to feel better, and his fever went down. He returned to school, but earlier, they called, saying he had a fever again. I picked him up, but I'm unsure if we should make another hospital visit or ride it out as the flu again."

"Any vomiting?"

"A few times on my couch, yes."

"I can ..." My heart pounds, and I can hear my pulse in my ears. "I can come over and check on him if you want?"

A chilly silence consumes our call.

His answer could change everything.

Noah's life.

His life.

My life.

If Cohen opens this door, there's no going back.

"I'll text you my address."

———

COHEN LIVES fifteen minutes away from the restaurant.

Twenty away from my house.

I thank my Uber driver when we pull into the driveway of the
brick home with a bright yellow door, black shutters, and a beautifully
manicured landscape. A light shines over the front door, making it easy
for me to follow the path up to the porch, and I climb the concrete
steps.

I know where he lives.

His number.

I'm about to become a major pain in the ass for Cohen Fox.

A knot ties in my belly when I knock, and my stomach clenches
hard when he answers the door. Our eyes meet, a brief pause passing
before either of us says anything.

Exhaustion lines his perfect face. His eyes are heavy, his cheeks and
strong jaw unshaven, and his hair is messy. Even run-down, the man is
handsome—exactly my type. Although I'm not sure if Cohen is *exactly
my type* because I've crushed on him since I was sporting braces and
wearing training bras.

"Hey, Jamie," he greets around a stressed breath. "Thank you for
coming."

"Of course," I blurt out, the words coming out as one.

He retreats a step, straightening his back against the door as he
opens it wider, allowing me room to walk in. I follow him through
entry, a living room, and down a short hallway, the walls lined with
framed photos of Noah. Cohen's house is nothing like I expected—
nothing you'd see from a man who's spent years working in bars.

He stops in a bedroom where Noah is snuggled in his bed, sleeping
and facing us. A lamp—surrounded by a thermometer, bottle of water,
and a box of tissues—on the nightstand gives me decent light as I
glance around the room. It's clean. The walls and ceiling are covered
with glow-in-the-dark stars, and a chest overfilled with toys is in the
corner. A long shelf hanging on the wall is lined with action figures.

A light laugh leaves me when I hear Noah snoring, and he slightly
stirs when I settle on the edge of his bed, pressing the back of my hand
to his forehead. When I brush away strands of his hair, his eyes slowly
open.

"Hey there," I whisper with a smile, placing my clutch on the
nightstand.

"Hi," he rasps out around a yawn. "You're the doctor from the hospital."

I nod. "I sure am."

I peek over to see Cohen standing in the doorway.

Please tell him.

Tell him who I am.

That I'm not just the doctor from the hospital.

He stays quiet.

Just as fast as Noah's eyes opened, he's back to sleep. I check his temperature, return the thermometer to the nightstand, and grab my clutch, and as I'm about to stand, I spot Cohen at the foot of the bed. His hands are in the pockets of his sweats, and his gaze is leveled on me, his face indescribable. When our eyes meet, all the tension that filled his face when he opened the door softens.

Melts away.

I do a once-over of the room, stupidly making sure it's me he's looking at like this and not some random-ass ghost in the corner.

My cheeks turn as warm as Noah's forehead while the room falls quiet—an agonizing silence I'm unsure of how to break. Blame it on the lack of light, the slight darkness encompassing us, but in the still of this bedroom, in the faint light of glow-in-the-dark stars, we share a moment.

A moment that stalls my breathing.

One I'll never forget as I search his eyes for *something*.

Questions?

Answers?

What-ifs?

What if Heather had never left him?

How could someone leave this man ... this family?

The cord of this—*whatever it is*—snaps when Noah coughs. I tense, common sense smacking into me with a reminder to pull my shit together. Cohen steps forward, and our attention diverts to Noah. We wait as if his next move will be life-changing.

He doesn't wake up.

I cast a nervous glance at Cohen, and just as I do, he shakes his head and curses as he stalks out of the room. I place a gentle kiss on Noah's forehead before tiptoeing out.

Cohen is slumped on the couch when I walk into the living room, his hands clasped between his open thighs, his head bowed.

"No more fever," I say, proud of my voice for not wavering. "I think he'll be okay. Just keep him home for a few more days."

He lifts his head, the tension from earlier reappearing, now stronger than when he answered the door.

He rubs his eyes with the base of his palms as if trying to scrub away the connection we shared. "I'm sorry, Jamie."

"For ... for what?" My pride of not stumbling over my words has left the building, ladies and gentlemen.

"For taking you away from whatever you were doing." His gaze flicks down my body, and he signals to my short black dress and heels. "You obviously weren't home."

"What?" My next words come out in nearly a yelp as I force a casual smile and pull at the bottom of my dress. "This old thing? I hang out at home in it all the time. It's pretty much my pajamas."

He snorts while standing. "I took you away from a date, didn't I?"

I hold up a finger. "*Technically*, you took me away while I was *bailing* on a date."

"That bad, huh?" His lips flicker into a slight grin.

"Dating blows," I mutter, moving from one foot to the other. "They need an app that screens for douchebags."

He pulls out his wallet, plucks a fifty from it, and holds it out to me. "For your troubles."

I swat the money away. "I'm not taking that."

"It's cheaper than a hospital visit."

"Whether or not you want to acknowledge it, I'm Noah's aunt. Even if I just met him, if he needs anything, I come here as that. Not as a doctor you need to pay."

He hesitates before shoving the fifty back into his wallet. "Thank you."

Silence fills the room until I clear my throat.

"Let me, uh ... schedule my Uber, and then I'll be on my way." I open my clutch for my phone and unlock the screen.

"Whoa, you had to take an Uber here?" he asks as I focus on requesting a ride.

"It was no biggie," I answer with a dismissive wave.

I take Ubers all the time—to my waxing appointments, yoga, or when I've had too many glasses of wine after one of Ashley's terrible matchmaking dates.

I'm an *Uber out of desperation* kinda gal.

Thank goodness I snuck out of my date before I showed up as Jamie, Medicine of White Girl Wasted.

"Shit," Cohen hisses, scrubbing a hand over his strong jaw. "I'd give you a ride, but—"

"No way in hell am I letting you wake him up," I interrupt.

When I'm finished booking my ride, I smile. "Good night." I zip my finger toward the door. "I'll just wait outside."

He nods, and I feel him behind me as I walk to the door. I glance back, a quick glimpse, and nearly trip over my feet when he doesn't shut the door behind me.

No, he walks outside, a jacket in his hand, and plops down on the porch step. When I join him, he drags the jacket over my shoulders, and neither of us mutters a word as we wait for my ride.

It's strange.

It's uncomfortable but comfortable at the same time.

There's newness to this, but the familiarity still lingers at the edges.

We know each other but not the new parts, the hidden parts, the hurt parts.

I peek over at him, biting into my lower lip. "Will you tell me how Noah is doing in the morning?"

He nods. "I can do that."

There's no holding back my grin.

Our attention moves to the driveway when the Uber car pulls up, and Cohen gives my thigh a light squeeze before he lowers his voice, and says, "Good night, Jamie."

CHAPTER FOUR

Cohen

SLEEP IS LIKE A SCORNED EX.

It hates me.

Last night consisted of checking on Noah every few hours and thoughts of Jamie.

One of those I should've been doing.

The other I sure as fuck shouldn't have been doing.

For hours, I battled with myself on calling her, but finally, I broke down. For Noah. It was always a struggle to decide when to make hospital visits, and if I could get Noah checked out without dragging him to a hospital, I would.

Even when I'd crumpled up her card, I hadn't been sure if I'd actually toss it. It was more of a show for Georgia. An *I couldn't care less about Jamie* attempt. I'd shoved it into my back pocket and then slid it into my wallet when I got home—*just in case.*

Just in case I changed my mind, which was doubtful.

Or I needed her.

Or because I saw the love on her face as she looked at Noah that night.

That's Jamie's character—affectionate, caring, showing every ounce of her emotions on her face.

So I called.

I called, and she came.

Seeing her with Noah last night fucked with my head.

My chest ached, hurt squeezing my throat as I watched them.

It was what I'd wanted from Heather—what I've desired for Noah to have. Someone who cares about him as much as I do, a nurturer who comes running in the middle of the night when he's sick.

Even after I was a dick to Jamie, she was here.

Dressed in a sexy-as-fuck black dress and fuck-me heels.

When she walked in, I knew she'd been out, and jealousy consumed me. Whoever she'd been with, I hated the asshole. I gulped, holding back a shit-eating grin when she revealed she'd ditched the guy.

These feelings are wrong.

So damn wrong.

She's the sister of my son's mother, for fuck's sake.

If anyone's off-limits, it's her.

The attraction is mutual, no question about it. Years ago, Jamie drunkenly confessed her feelings for me, and considering I was dating her sister, I shot her down. Sometimes, when I'm tipsy ... or lonely ... feeling sorry for myself, I wonder what would've happened if I'd chosen her—the other sister.

What if I had taken a chance with her?

Then I tell myself it doesn't matter.

That it never could've happened.

It'd have been wrong on so many levels.

So why did I feel so drawn to her last night?

It has to be my dick.

That's a lie.

It was more than me thinking with my cock.

My heart tightened as I thought about someone like Jamie in Noah's life ... in *my* life.

I shake my head, calling myself stupid for even considering it.

My love life is nothing to brag about. After Heather left, I trusted no one, except Georgia. She, Noah, and my job are my life. As Noah grew older, I dated around, but nothing worked out. My job isn't the best place to meet women, but since I'm there so frequently, it's typically where I do meet them. Georgia has attempted to set me up with her friends, but not fucking happening.

Her friends are as big of a pain in the ass as she is.

After checking Noah's temperature again without waking him, I jump in the shower. My mind races as the water pours down my body.

Jamie asked me to tell her how Noah was doing today.

I can do one of two things: ignore her and act like last night never happened or be a man of my word and text her.

In the end, while drying off, I decide to be a man of my word.

One quick text.

A thank-you.

That's it.

It's the least I can do.

Grabbing my phone, I turn it in my hand as if it had the answer for everything.

I owe her this.

Me: Noah is doing better. Low-grade fever. Headache. No vomiting … thank God.

There.

I kept my word.

Not even a minute later, my phone beeps with her reply.

Jamie: Perfect! Just keep an eye on the fever, and I'm here if you need me.

"Here if you need me."

Why does she have to say shit like that?

I hesitate for a moment.

Me: I was thinking …

Don't do it. Don't do it, dumbass.

My heart convinces me to do something my head would never do.

Jamie: That's nice. You going to finish that sentence?

Fuck it.

Here goes.

Me: If you want to see Noah, you can come over when Georgia is babysitting. Spend some time together when he's feeling better.

Holding my breath until she answers, I wonder when I lost my damn mind.

Jamie: I'd love that! When is Georgia watching him next?
Me: Wednesday.
Jamie: I'll be there. Thank you.

I shove my phone into my pocket as Noah comes plodding into the kitchen.

Please don't break my son's heart.

Now, I need to figure out how I'll explain who Jamie is to him.

———

TWISTED FOX BAR is my dream come true.

I always wanted to be a business owner—be my own boss.

In high school, I'd been clueless on what I'd do, but I started bartending when I turned twenty-one. It was fast money and fast-paced. That job turned into several throughout the years, and eventually, I fell in love with it. I managed to snag promotions where I learned the business side of things and met friends along the way—some I kept, some I didn't, and I'm thankful for the ones who've stayed by my side.

My friend Archer and I combined our funds two years ago and opened the bar. Archer, being Archer, demanded he be a silent partner. No one but our friends knows how much he's involved. The only role he wanted outside of investing money was bartending and living a stress-free life away from the public eye. Our friends Finn and Silas came along for the ride.

We're the sole sports pub in the county, and our only competition is a run-down business that doesn't hold one TV. We purchased the large building for pennies on the dollar, gutted it, renovated it, and filled it with state-of-the-art shit. We created an environment for people to have good times with their friends. Dozens of TVs hang along the walls. Wood stools line the bar, and pub tables are scattered throughout the room—two-, four-, and six-tops. Sports memorabilia from the town and pieces I snagged at flea markets fill the empty spaces on the walls. There's a separate room with two pool tables and an area to play darts.

With the bar and Noah, I don't have time for much else—not that I'm complaining.

Being busy prevents me from overthinking shit.

It helps me forget my problems.

"How's the little guy feeling?" Archer asks when I stroll into the bar.

"You mean, after he went all *Exorcist* on the couch?" I joke, shaking my head at the gross-ass memory. "He's feeling better, but I'm still keeping him out of school."

He nods. "I'm sure he loves that."

Out of everyone, Archer is my right-hand man. This bar is our life, and without him, Twisted Fox would've never opened. Even though he put up most of the cash, he insisted we own the bar fifty-fifty. I argued that it wasn't fair, but he wouldn't budge.

Noah's babysitter, Sylvia, is hanging out with him today while I work. Paperwork isn't going to do itself. Archer manages the books, but I'm heavily involved in every aspect of the bar. It's my main source of income, my bread and butter, and I track every penny that comes in and goes out. Noah deserves the life I wanted growing up, and if I have to work my ass off to give it to him, then so be it. Maybe it's just me making up for his lack of a mother, but my world revolves around him and his happiness.

Plopping down on the chair behind my desk, I release a stressed breath. As funny as it sounds, work relaxes me. It derails my mind from the bullshit and makes me money. Win-win.

Single parenthood is a struggle. It was even harder when I didn't own the bar I worked in. Controlling my schedule wasn't an option then, and for the first three years of Noah's life, I was a bitter asshole. My tips lacked because I hated almost everyone.

And that was all thanks to Heather.

Never in my mind had I imagined her turning her back on us like she did.

Heather and I'd started dating in high school. Throughout the years, we'd broken up and gotten back together a few times, but we grew up. Three months after we moved in together, she became pregnant with Noah.

Everything was good.

Sure, the pregnancy was a shock, but we were excited about being parents.

Then, out of nowhere, she changed.

I should've known something was wrong when all baby-related interests stopped.

Hearing his heartbeat? No, thank you.

Making sure the car seat was properly installed in case she went into early labor? Not happening.

Like everyone else, I blamed it on the hormones. The baby books warned us about mood changes, bouts of depression, and lashing out. In my dumbass mind, those books knew everything. Too bad there were no chapters on the mother bailing.

Two months before Noah was due, while watching one of her stupid-ass reality shows, she turned to me and asked if we could put Noah up for adoption. I nearly fell off the couch when she said she'd discussed the idea with her parents. She explained, frustration slashing through her, that they'd offered to adopt him. She didn't want that because she'd have to see him, and she was scared they'd push her to have a relationship with him later. To stop that from happening, she asked me to sign over my rights. That way, another family, no one related to us, could adopt him.

As I absorbed what she'd said, my pulse sped while I waited for her to tell me she was kidding. Instead, she jumped up from the couch. With a smile on her face, she returned with papers—*the papers*—her name already signed on the line.

She already had the shit drawn up.

I told her she'd lost her fucking mind. We argued, and with anger firing through me, I stormed out and walked to the bar down the street—my attempt to drink away the bullshit.

Maybe walking out on her wasn't the smartest reaction, but she had been fucking smiling. *Skipping* out of the kitchen as if she wasn't asking me to sign my life over—a person I'd fallen in love with before he was even here.

I'd give up Heather before I'd ever give him up.

Every day for the next week, she begged me to sign. We'd argue, and I'd head to the bar. I became the bastard in the corner, drinking away his problems. Eventually, I ripped up the papers while Heather sobbed, begging for an out.

And I'd given it to her when I promised we'd stay out of her selfish life.

Noah didn't need to be around anyone who didn't want him.

Heather signed over her rights, and three days after his birth, she moved to Vegas. That was when I learned the reason she'd wanted out. She had fallen in love with a man she'd met online. A man who didn't like children—*what a fucking winner*—so fuck our child.

I cut off all communication, and we moved on with our lives as if she never existed. As much as I didn't want my son growing up without a mother, I knew we'd survive. I'd give Noah a happy life without her, and my family and friends have made up for that void pretty damn well.

Better to be without someone than to be with someone who doesn't love you.

I don't hate Heather for finding someone else.

I hate her for not standing up to that someone else for our son.

I haven't spoken to the mother of my child since the day we left the hospital, and I plan to keep it that way.

CHAPTER FIVE

Jamie

MY SHIRT IS CUTE.

The sweat rings underneath my armpits? Not so much.

Those sweat rings didn't exist twenty minutes ago when I left my house.

Hanging out with Noah and Georgia today has me more nervous than any blind date I've gone on.

I park next to a red VW Beetle in Cohen's driveway. The car has black polka dots on it, like a ladybug, and is hideous.

I'm also pretty sure it belongs to Georgia.

I make a mental note not to tell her it's hideous.

I can't mess this up.

No one in my family knows about my visit with them. I kept my mouth shut, scared that Cohen would back out. Hell, who even knows if today is a one-time thing he's giving me because I came over when Noah was sick?

I fan out my armpits before performing a quick smell check.

Don't judge me.

A girl doesn't want to be known as the smelly … doctor … friend … aunt?

Note to self: figure out who the hell Noah thinks I am.

I shake out my hands, as if I were preparing to run a 5K—tried it once and gave it a zero out of ten for fun—and hope Georgia has a better response to me than Cohen did.

My pace is slow as I walk up the steps, and when the front door swings open, Georgia appears in the doorway.

My shoulders relax at the sight of her bright pink lips tilting into a smile.

A smile is good.

"Hey, Jamie," she says.

"Hi." I give her a shy wave like the awkward person I am before gesturing to her. "Wow, you look so different … grown up."

Georgia is a few years younger than I am, and while she's always been pretty, she's drop-dead gorgeous now. Her eccentric style hasn't changed much. Even when she was younger, she was always doing something different—pink stripes in her hair, intense makeup, pigtails with tinsel in them. Today, her hair—what had once been a similar color to Cohen's—is dyed blond and pulled into two buns at the top of her head, and she's wearing a crop top with a kimono wrap over it and jeans with holes down the legs.

"Same to you." She whistles. "You're hot as fuck."

My eyes downcast as I blush.

"Come on." She waves me inside, and I find Noah in the living room, surrounded by a pile of Legos.

He eagerly jumps to his feet, a handful of Legos dropping from his hand. "Hi!" His attention snaps to Georgia, and he points at me. "This is your friend? She was my doctor when I was sick! She even came to our house too!"

His excitement settles my nerves and melts my heart. His T-shirt is black and says, *Snack so hard,* his pants are ripped in the knees—somewhat like Georgia's—and he's wearing checkered Vans. Noah is for sure a mini Cohen, definitely a future heartbreaker.

Georgia snags her black fringed purse from a leather recliner and swoops it over her body. "We're going on a sugar run. You game?"

I nod. "I'm game."

Who turns down a sugar run?

Especially in a stressful situation.

———

GEORGIA'S CAR is as uncomfortable as it looks.

I considered suggesting we ride in my car since it's not the size of a stroller, and the idea of being cramped in it with sweaty pits was nerve-racking. I kept my mouth shut so I wouldn't look like a pain in the ass already and loaded into her car, sweat pits and all.

Noah is in the back seat, rambling off his favorite snacks while counting them off on his fingers, "Cookies, cupcakes, cake, brownies, sprinkles."

I take in his every word. If Cohen allows me to see Noah again, I want to be the aunt who takes him out for sugar runs like Georgia.

When Georgia pulls into the parking lot of Sally's Sprinkles, my stomach twists, the urge to jump out of the car and run hitting me.

Out of all the places for a sugar run.

Georgia parks, kills the engine, and peeks back at Noah. "Remember our rule?"

Noah eagerly nods. "I get two cupcakes, but tell Dad I only had one."

He laughs, and Georgia high-fives him.

A wave of jealousy swims inside me.

If only Heather hadn't been so damn selfish, I could've had that with him.

Noah unbuckles his seat belt, and he holds Georgia's hand as we walk into the small cupcake shop. The bell above the door rings at our arrival, and small crowds are circled around tables, shoving their sugary goodness into their mouths.

The owner's eyes light up when she notices me.

I want to shrink and hide.

I was hoping it was Sally's day off.

"Jamie!" She beams, sporting the same blue eye shadow and pink lips she's had for years.

Noah darts to the counter, his feet stomping, and eyes the cupcakes lined up inside the glass counter. My stomach growls, and my mouth waters at the memory of how delicious Sally's cupcakes are when I stand next to him. The shop was once a weekly stop for me, but two years have passed since I've been here.

"Hi, Sally," I say.

Sally tells them hello, and her attention turns back to me. "I'm glad you came in. Just because you and my Seth broke up doesn't mean you can't stop in and enjoy your favorite dark chocolate, peanut butter cupcakes."

The mention of his name has my gaze darting from one side of the shop to the other.

So far, Seth-free.

The shop hasn't changed with its bubblegum-pink walls and bright red tables and chairs, and Sally is wearing her *Sprinkle Me Up, Baby* apron Seth bought her for Christmas a few years back.

Sally rubs her hands together. "What can I get for you guys?"

I peek over at Noah and tilt my head toward the counter. "Do you know what you want?"

"Hmm …" He taps his finger against his chin. "So many yummy choices." His attention flicks to Georgia. "How many am I allowed to have again?"

"Two," she answers.

He holds up four fingers. "*Please.* I won't eat them all today."

Georgia shakes her head while fighting back a smile. "Three, and that's final. We'll have to stash the third one somewhere in the house."

He jumps up and down and starts pointing at his cupcakes of choice for Sally—Funfetti, Oreo, and chocolate.

Just as I'm about to order the cupcakes I've missed so much—my ass, not so much—my name is called. I jump at the familiar voice, and my hand flies to my chest at the same time as Seth walks toward us from the back room. He stops next to Sally, wearing a stunned expression on his face.

It's not that we ended on bad terms. The shock is from not seeing him in so long, and I wasn't expecting it. I'm not rehearsed in the whole *running into your ex* thing since I haven't had many exes.

Sweat rings while running into your ex.

Good times.

I'll be taking six of those cupcakes to eat away my embarrassment later.

Noah peeks over at me with a raised brow. "How do you know him?"

As my mind is scrambling for the best lie, Seth laughs.

"I used to be Jamie's boyfriend," he answers for me.

"Well, shit," Georgia whispers, bumping her shoulder against mine. She lowers her voice. "You could've told me we were walking into your ex's lair."

"Boyfriend?" Noah says, sticking out his tongue. "Yucky yuck."

I give Seth a look, and he holds up his hands in innocence.

"What, babe? Just answering the kid's question."

Seth's face is unshaven, and his hair is shaggier. He looks good, mature, and the goofy smile on his face reminds me of why I was so attracted to him. We dated for almost two years, and this was where we met. I used to study here while eating my frustrations out on my homework. Sally had insisted on fixing me up with her son, but I'd declined. The next day, Seth had sat down at my table with my favorite cupcake in his hand and asked me out.

He was a good boyfriend, yet the day he asked me to move in with him, I broke things off. I was too busy with med school, and he wanted more than I could give.

He deserved more.

Medical school and a love life don't go hand in hand.

"Cupcakes are on the house!" Sally squeals, packing up a box of cupcakes, adding plenty of dark chocolate, peanut butter ones.

"In that case," Georgia says, "can you add two more red velvets?"

I elbow her side as Sally snatches another red velvet. "No, you don't have to do that." I grab my wallet from the bag and pull out my credit card.

Georgia stops me. "I was totally kidding. I invited you on this sugar-binge trip. It's only fair I pay for it. Plus, you ran into your ex. You can't make a girl pay for sugar after that happens."

"It was good to see you, Jamie," Seth says, winking at me before returning to the back room.

Sally refuses to take either of our cards, and five minutes later, I reluctantly accept the free cupcakes.

"You know, he's still single and ready to mingle," Sally adds, wiggling her brows.

Georgia cracks up while I cover my face in embarrassment.

———

OUR NEXT STOP is the park.

We sit at a picnic table, and Noah devours his cupcake in seconds. The frosting is smudged around his mouth when he asks Georgia for another. She shakes her head, and he frowns when she insists he let his stomach rest.

"I'm going to go play then," he says, grabbing his cupcake liner and crumpling it in his hand. "Johnny from school is over there." He tosses the liner in the trash and takes off toward the playground.

I swipe my finger through the frosting on my cupcake and glance at Georgia from across the table. "What did Cohen tell Noah? Who does he think I am?"

She shoves a bite into her mouth and slowly chews it before answering, "A friend of mine." There's a hint of apology on her face before her expression turns serious as if something hit her. "And to be clear, you *can* be *my friend*—as long as you make sure your skank-ass sister stays away from Noah."

The protective aunt bear is coming at me, claws slightly drawn in warning.

"Heather lives in Vegas," I rush out, the need to assure her that'll never happen powering through me. "She, uh … married the man she left Cohen for and has only been home a few times."

"Good. I hope she stays there forever."

I only nod.

I have never been close with Heather, and our relationship turned sour after she left Noah. It put a strain on our family, nearly broke us, and she didn't talk to my parents for a year. It was two for me until my parents begged me to reconcile with her.

I did it for them, not her.

Making up is my tolerating her the few times she comes around—those visits typically when she needs money because her piece-of-shit husband can't hold a job.

"It was a big deal to him, you know," Georgia adds, "Cohen letting you see Noah. For years, he's called you the sworn enemy."

I lick frosting off my finger. "I never did anything to him."

"Directly, no, but your family did."

"We were in a tough spot. Heather swore they were putting Noah up for adoption. It terrified my parents."

"Cohen assured them *plenty of times* that wouldn't happen."

"We had Heather in our other ear, swearing he'd change his mind after Noah was born because he wouldn't want to do it alone."

She scowls. "You should know my brother's character better than that."

"I know." I release a heavy sigh. "It was chaotic for us, and all we had was Heather's side. Cohen would be a single father, and he was always in bars—"

"Whoa. I'm going to stop you right there. Cohen isn't *always in bars* like he's out partying. He works in one."

"I know that—"

"And now, he owns one," she adds, talking over me.

I pause, biting into my cheek. "Really?"

She nods.

I wait for her to tell me which one, but she doesn't. Not surprising. They're only giving me a glimpse into their lives, but I'll take it.

Is that desperate?

Maybe.

But this is what my family has wanted forever.

Noah has been the topic of countless conversations.

Now, I know what a great kid he is ... and I want to know him more.

———

"HOW LATE DOES COHEN WORK?" I ask Georgia.

We're back at his house, high on sugar, and Noah and I just finished a Lego house.

A badass Lego house if I do say so myself.

"It depends." She checks her watch while sitting cross-legged on the couch. "My guess is, he'll be home around nine. Archer, his partner, is working the late shift tonight. I work there too, and if I'm not working, I'm hanging out with Noah or in class." She smiles in pride. "We have a group-effort thing."

I return the smile. "I'm glad Noah has a good support system."

Noah loudly yawns. "I'm sleepy."

"Sugar crash," Georgia says around a laugh. Her phone beeps, and she glances at the screen before looking at me. "Cohen is on his way home."

I push myself to my feet. "That's my cue to leave."

She scrunches up her nose. "Why?"

"I want to dodge any awkward convos the best I can."

"You're leaving?" Noah asks, peering up at me with a furrowed brow. "Will you come over again?"

My heart hurts at the sad look on his face, and I run my hand through his hair. "Of course I will."

"Can we get cupcakes again too?" He jumps to his feet, nearly knocking over the Lego house. "Your old boyfriend can give us some!"

"We can definitely get cupcakes," I answer with a chuckle.

"I think you've won his heart," Georgia comments.

"When will you come back?" Noah questions, the words quickly falling from his lips. "Tomorrow?"

"I don't know about tomorrow because I have to work," I answer. "Let me check with your dad. Does that sound good?"

His eyes are alert, the sleepiness vanishing. "My dad will say yes! He said you're a nice doctor! I asked if you were his girlfriend, but he said no. I'll tell him he can't be your boyfriend now because you like boys who give you cupcakes. Dad doesn't make cupcakes." He stops and takes a quick breath before going on, "Maybe he can learn because I think you'd be a good girlfriend. I'll ask him!"

My eyes grow wider, the more he rambles.

"If you haven't noticed," Georgia says when he finishes, "Noah is bold and idealistic."

I'd say so.

I give him a hug, promise to see him again, and say good-bye to Georgia. When I get in my car, I pull out my phone and grin at the selfie we took at the park.

Later that night, my grin returns when Cohen sends me a text, saying Noah wants to hang out again.

CHAPTER SIX

Cohen

"DRUNK DUDE, Mohawk, at the pool table," Georgia calls into my office, barging in. "He's asked at least three women to suck his dick, he spit in a guy's face, and … I'm not even going to describe what he's doing now."

I stand from the chair behind my desk and stalk over to the camera monitors across the room. Spotting the culprit doesn't take long. A lanky guy sporting a Mohawk with a face tattoo is dry-humping a pool stick between his legs and twirling his arm in the air as if he were riding a horse.

Jesus, fuck.

Owning a bar is all fun and games until shit like this happens.

Goofy drunks? I can handle.

Sad drunks? I pat them on the back and pour them another beer on me.

Drunks who repeat stories? I nod and pretend I've never heard it before.

What I fail to have patience for are idiots humping pool sticks.

"Shit," I hiss, storming out of my office with Georgia behind me.

I cut through customers and head straight to Mohawk, who's still sliding the stick against his junk while grinding against it.

Yeah, that thing is going right in the dumpster.

"You," I yell when I reach him, gesturing toward the door with my thumb, "Stick Humper. Time for you to go."

He snorts and ignores me, but thankfully, he removes the stick from his legs.

At least we're getting somewhere.

"Out," I demand.

Like the douchebag he's proven to be, he doesn't listen. Instead, he snatches a beer from a pub table and chugs it, a smirk playing at his lips when he finishes.

"Come on, man," I say. "Don't make this complicated. You're drunk. Have one of your buddies drive you home, so you can sleep off the booze. You can't stay here and harass my customers."

Years of working in the bar industry have taught me the best approach to these situations is keeping my cool and suggesting a plan for them to get the fuck out.

Finn, my friend/bouncer/part-time bartender, appears at my side. "I got this, Co."

I swing out my arm, stopping him, and shake my head. "Nah, I think he'll listen."

"I don't," Finn states, straightening his broad shoulders and clenching his fists.

Mohawk slams the empty beer bottle onto the table, shattering it, and the people around him jump back. Finn shoots forward before I can stop him and captures the back of Mohawk's shirt, causing the stick to drop from his hand. Mohawk grunts when Finn jerks him away from the table.

"Time to go, asshole," Finn snaps.

The crowd breaks, and all attention is on Finn as he drags Mohawk toward the exit.

A few chicks in the corner clap their hands, and another guy yells, "About damn time!"

Their cheering is interrupted by Polly, my newly hired bartender, scrambling in my direction and yelling my name.

"Cohen!" she shrieks, her attention bouncing between Finn and me. "That's my boyfriend! Tell Finn to let him go!"

"Your boyfriend is out of here," Finn yells over his shoulder, her demand not stopping his mission.

Polly throws her purple hair over her shoulder and kicks out her hip. "If he's out of here, *I'm* out of here."

I scrub my hand over my face while groaning.

I don't need this high school bullshit today.

"What'll it be?" Polly asks. "Kick him out or lose a bartender?"

"I'll mail your last paycheck," I reply with no hesitation.

No way am I allowing a twit dating a Post Malone wannabe to give me ultimatums. I should've known it wasn't a good idea to hire Polly when she said she drank Fireball for breakfast.

"Are … are you serious?" Polly's eyes widen at the response she didn't expect.

She picked the wrong bar to work in if she thinks her boyfriend can pull that shit.

I cross my arms. "Dead serious."

"Fine." She stomps her foot. "Good luck handling this crowd with one bartender."

My head throbs at the reminder.

It's a game day, and we're busy as fuck. Polly and Archer were my only available bartenders tonight. Finn is working the door, and I was finishing paperwork before leaving for the night. Noah's babysitter, Sylvia, is scheduled to leave in an hour, and I hate running late.

"Good luck with your scumbag boyfriend," Georgia retorts.

"Fuck you," Polly screams before shooting her glare to me. "And fuck you too, Cohen." She whips around and chases after her loser boyfriend.

I run my hands through my hair and suck in an irritated breath.

Georgia sighs, patting my arm. "Don't stress, big bro. I'll cover the bar."

I shake my head. "You're waiting tables, and you have class in the morning."

"And?" She flashes me an amused grin. "It won't be the first time I've pulled an all-nighter and then gone to class. I like to think that I'm a professional at it actually."

"I'll act like I didn't hear that," I say with a pointed look, and she follows me to the bar. "Not to mention, you and Archer will kill each other if I let you work with him. I can't be down two more bartenders."

"I got this, Co!" Archer shouts from behind the bar while two men argue over a game call in front of him. The way his eyes cut to Georgia in irritation confirms he overheard our conversation. "She's not working with me."

Georgia flips him off. "You're a dick."

Archer shrugs, pours a beer, and then slides it down the bar to a regular.

"Let me call Sylvia," I say, fishing my phone from my pocket and heading toward my office.

Five minutes later, I'm walking out of the office, my shoulders slumped.

"Is Sylvia staying?" Georgia asks.

I shake my head and scrub a hand over my face.

She pauses for a moment before saying, "What about Jamie?"

I move my hand to stare at her. "What?"

"Ask if she can watch him."

"Not a good idea."

"Oh, come on," she groans, tilting her head back. "She's been hanging out with him for weeks now."

"Not alone."

"It won't be that long, she's a doctor, and everything will be okay. Heather is still in Vegas."

I flinch. Not once since Jamie came into our lives have I asked about Heather. Just her name puts a bad taste in my mouth.

It's not that I doubt Archer can handle the crowd alone, but customers will bitch if it takes too long for their drinks. Bars aren't known for patient customers, and we can't afford to lose the business, especially on game nights. They bring in a shit-ton of money.

Archer shakes his head when I join him behind the bar. "Go home. I'll call Silas."

"Silas is at some convention," I reply, referring to our friend. Silas bartends, does all of Twisted Fox's marketing, and fills us in on the latest alcohol trends.

"*Or* I can do it since I'm *already here*," Georgia comments before cracking an arrogant smile Archer's way. "I promise to stay on my side of the bar, and I won't trip you this time—even though you deserved it last week … and will probably deserve another tripping … or a swift kick in the nuts."

There's no way the two of them can work together.

"Give me a minute."

I scroll through the Contacts in my phone and hit Jamie's name.

Here goes.

CHAPTER SEVEN

Jamie

IT'S six in the evening.

I'm living a very exciting social life by chilling in bed and watching Netflix.

Alone.

No Thin Mints this time.

They're all gone, and I'm all out of Girl Scout sources to get more.

Might have to search the black market later.

I'm licking Cheetos cheese off my fingers when my phone rings, and I nearly drop it when Cohen's name flashes across the screen.

He never calls.

We've texted a few times, but since I've started hanging out with Georgia and Noah, I communicate through her.

I'm unsure why I drag in a calming breath before answering, "Hello?"

"Jamie." My name sounds stressed, leaving his mouth. "Are you busy?"

"Nope." *Cleaning cheddar fingers doesn't count as busy, right?* "What's up?"

"An employee just walked out, leaving me stuck at the bar, and Noah's babysitter can't stay any later. Is there any way you can hang out at my house until I can get there? If not, I completely understand. Georgia suggested you might be—"

"That's no problem," I interrupt before he talks himself out of the idea.

"I wouldn't ask, but I'm in a bind."

"I can be there in about ten minutes." I jump out of bed and scramble for clothes that don't make me look homeless.

"Thank you. I'll let the babysitter know you're coming. If you need anything, call me. If I don't answer, call Georgia."

"Gotcha. I'll be there."

———

A GORGEOUS, college-aged blonde answers Cohen's door.

No wonder Noah says he wants his babysitter to be his girlfriend.

She stands up straight, and her words are chirpy. "Hi! I'm Sylvia. You must be Jamie."

I nod, and when I say hello, it's not nearly as chirpy as hers.

She retreats a step, allowing me space to come in. "It's nice to finally meet you. You're all Noah talks about." She peeks back at me with a frown. "I feel bad I can't stay later, but I'm going out of town."

"Totally understandable. I'm happy to help."

"Jamie!" Noah shouts when I come into view. He punches his hand through the air before dashing across the living room to give me a hug.

Bending down, I hug him back, squeezing him tight and savoring the moment. The more we hang out, the closer we get. This little boy has sent a wave of happiness through my life, and moments like this, even though they're joyous, still send a flash of fear through me.

That motherly instinct has hit me.

The love for him in my heart is there.

Whether that's good or bad, I'm not sure.

I'm playing by Cohen's rules, going at it minute by minute.

Cohen could have a bad day and decide no more Noah visits for me.

I could say the wrong thing, and he could pull away the happiness we've created.

The thought is terrifying.

Never did I think I'd get so attached in such a short amount of time, but Noah has won me over with his radiant and childish heart. He's funny, a ball of energy, and the sweetest little guy. Cohen raised him right, and a sense of guilt twists my heart that we'd ever doubted him.

Noah gives Sylvia a hug good-bye along with a kiss on the cheek, and we make ourselves comfortable in the living room when she leaves. Cartoons are playing on the crazy-large TV, and Noah has his action figures displayed on the floor, perched up as if they were watching the show with him.

Cohen's house is warm and comfortable, very homey. The walls are painted a light gray throughout the entire house with the exception of Noah's blue bedroom. The couch is cushy, which I love. Nothing's worse than a stiff couch. Two brown suede recliners sit on each side of the couch. Blankets are everywhere—thrown over those recliners, a Spider-Man one spilling over the arm of the couch—and brown suede pillows that match the recliners are scattered around. Just like in the hallway, pictures of Noah are everywhere. School pictures, pictures of him and his family, and ones of him with others.

Twenty minutes later, Noah looks back at me. "I'm hungry."

"You haven't eaten dinner?"

"Sylvia made me chicken nuggets and gross broccoli, but I'm hungry again." He pats his stomach.

"What would you like to eat?"

He provides a sly grin. "Pizza."

I snatch my phone from my bag. "Let me check with your dad."

"Dad won't care. I'll save him a slice and a half."

Yeah, not pushing my buttons with this one.

I could see Cohen banning me for giving Noah a pepperoni instead of a broccoli sprout.

Me: Is it cool if we order pizza?

He texts me back a few minutes later.

Cohen: Since I'm sure he won't let you say no, that's fine.

Me: He agreed to save you a slice and a half.
Cohen: Tell him I appreciate his generosity.

"Good news," I tell him, pulling up the pizza shop app to order. "Pizza it is!"

––––––

THIS IS my mom's third call.

Her seventh text comes through.

Mom: Are you alive? I thought you had the night off at the hospital?

Knowing my mom, she won't stop calling until I answer.

"I'll be right back," I tell Noah before walking to the kitchen and returning her call.

"Honey, why have you been ignoring my calls?" she answers. "I've been calling you all day."

"Sorry," I grumble. "I've been busy."

"Doing what?" Her voice is stern and worried. "Are you working too many hours at the hospital again?"

That is a regular question from her.

"No, Mom. I'm working regular ER doctor hours," I answer.

"Which is too many hours! I don't understand why you won't work in a practice. Your father does."

"I don't want to work in a practice."

"Hey, Jamie!"

My hand tightens around my phone at the sound of Noah yelling my name, and I turn around at the same time he comes barreling into the kitchen.

He jumps up and down, his voice rising. "Can I have a cookie?"

"Who's that?" my mom asks.

I gulp, unable to speak. Instead, I nod as I give Noah a thumbs-up, and he dashes to the pantry. A package of cookies is in his hand when he turns and scurries to the table.

"Jamie!" my mom yelps.

I hear the wrapper opening when I speed-walk to the bathroom and shut the door behind me. "I'm babysitting."

"Babysitting? Babysitting who?"

"A kid." My stomach sinks.

My mother won't stop at that answer.

"I'd assume so. Whose kid?"

She's also always been a nosy one.

To lie or not to lie.

My pizza threatens to come up while I fight with myself on how to answer.

"It's Noah, Mom," I reply, resting my back against the door. "I'm babysitting Noah."

The line goes silent, and I double-check that she didn't hang up on me.

"I'm sorry." She clears her throat. "Did you say you're babysitting Noah?"

I nod even though she can't see me. "Yes."

Another silence.

"Heather's Noah?"

"Yes."

"What?" Her voice lowers. "How?"

I hold the phone closer to my face and lower my voice. "I can't exactly go into the details at the moment."

Her shocked tone morphs into an angry one. "How long has this been happening behind our backs?"

I shut my eyes, hating the betrayal in her voice. "It's not behind your backs." When she doesn't reply, I release a heavy breath. "It hasn't been long. I wanted to make sure it stuck before I got anyone involved. I plan to ask Cohen if you can see Noah, but you can't tell Heather about this, okay?"

"Jamie, you know I don't like secrets."

"If you want Cohen to even consider letting you meet Noah, you should start liking them with this one."

Noah yells my name again.

"Look, I have to go," I rush out.

"Call me when you leave. I want to know what he's like." She sighs. "Snap a picture if you can."

CHAPTER EIGHT

Cohen

IT'S after three in the morning when I pull into my garage.

After Noah was born, I saved every penny I could and bought the three-bedroom brick ranch. For years, Noah, Georgia, and I lived here together. She only moved out a few years ago.

Now, it's just me and my mini-me.

I texted Jamie a few times throughout the night to check on Noah and make sure she was okay with staying so late. Around nine thirty, she told me Noah passed out on the couch, and she was putting him to bed.

Never in a million years would I have thought Jamie would be in my house, watching Noah while I worked.

I hear the TV when I walk into the house, but there's no sign of life in the living room. I circle the couch to find Jamie sleeping with a Spider-Man blanket wrapped around her.

Staring down at her in curiosity, not creepiness, I absorb her beauty. We haven't seen each other since the night she came over when Noah was sick.

It's better that way.

I kept my distance to avoid what I'm doing now—drinking her in as if she were the best drink I'd ever poured. Her golden-brown hair spills over the edge of the pillow and covers half of her tan face. Even in Jamie's dorky days, she was cute. Her lips are pouty, and I know she has two dimples that pop through her cheeks when she bursts into laughter. Her green eyes light up any room.

There's more to Jamie than her looks.

She has the warmest heart of anyone I've ever known.

I dip down and whisper her name, and her eyes slowly open, one at a time.

"Sorry." A deep yawn leaves her. "I dozed off."

I shove my hands into my pants pockets and chuckle. "He can be a handful."

She snorts, rubbing her sleepy eyes. "Oh, he's nothing."

I retreat a step when she rises and stretches out her arms. My eyes are on her when she stands, grabs the blanket, folds it into a neat square, and settles it on the end of the couch. Without a word and with another yawn, she snags a mug with the bar's logo from the table, and her fuzzy-socked feet pad through the living room to the kitchen.

My gaze is on her, my eyes taking in every inch of her ass, which makes me a rude bastard. Her black yoga pants hug her body, accentuating her plump ass, and I love how casual she looks tonight and how comfortable she seems in my home. Sure, seeing her in that black dress was nice, but this is so much more.

The kitchen is quiet as she rinses out her mug and places it in the dishwasher as if she owned the place.

My mouth turns dry as I rest my back against the cabinets and search for the right words. "How's life going?"

How's life?

Lamest fucking question.

When did I lose my game?

"Life is living at the hospital while playing Let's See How Many Coffees Jamie Can Drink Before She Has an Anxiety Attack."

My eyes return to her ass when she crouches down to shut the dishwasher.

"I get you on the coffee." I chuckle as I take the few steps to the kitchen table and collapse into a chair. I grab the pizza box, sliding it to me, and cringe when I open it. "What's this trash?"

She arches a brow. "Pizza."

"Did you torture my son with this *pizza?*"

"Uh … yeah."

"Listen, there's a lot of shit I'll take, but feeding my son this pineapple demon of a pizza is where I draw the line."

"He loved it, thank you very much." She smirks and surprisingly sits across from me. "Have you ever tried Hawaiian pizza?"

"Nope, nor do I care to."

"What is it Noah said you tell him?" She taps the side of her cheek, thinking. "You have to try foods before you decide you don't like them. Practice what you preach, Fox."

Nausea turns in my stomach when she slides the pizza box closer to me.

I push it back. "Nasty-ass pizza. Hard pass."

"Cohen, try the damn pizza."

"Look, I don't want to be a dick and make you clean up my vomit after I eat this garbage. Plus, I don't want my house to smell."

"For a guy, you're dramatic as fuck."

I chuckle. "Oh, really?"

"Really."

"It's weird, hearing you cuss."

The Jamie I knew was shy, timid, definitely not this outspoken.

This Jamie is confident, funny, and a fucking smart-ass.

She scrunches up that cute nose of hers. "Why?"

"You hardly muttered a curse word in high school."

"Well, I didn't think you were dramatic as fuck then." A smirk plays at her lips, her dimples slightly making an appearance. "Had I, I would've told you the same."

I can't help but chuckle. "There's always been a little rebel inside you."

She rolls a hairband off her wrist, smooths her hair into a ponytail, and ties it back, stray strands framing her face. "*Puh-lease.* The most rebellious thing I did in high school was go to that stupid party." Her cheeks redden before she buries her face in her hands, speaking through them, "Oh my God. I can't believe I brought that up."

Our conversation is about to grow more interesting than a damn pineapple pizza debate.

I straighten my shoulders, a cocky smile crossing my face. "I was your first kiss, wasn't I?"

When she uncovers her face, she's glaring at me. "You don't know that."

"I was," I state, matter-of-factly.

"Oh, piss off." Her hand waves through the air. "It sucked, by the way."

Leaning back in the chair, I'm already enjoying every word of this, knowing it'll just get better. "I don't doubt that. You cornered me in a bathroom and drunkenly stuck your tongue down my throat."

My breathing slows at the memory. Heather lost her shit when she spotted Jamie at that party, but I made her chill out. Jamie didn't have much of a social life, and I was happy that she was finally enjoying her teenage years. I plowed through the crowd and made it clear that she could only take drinks from me. Later, when I went to take a piss, Jamie shoved herself into the bathroom behind me and locked the door. Before I could stop her and ask when she'd lost her mind, she pushed me against the door and attempted to suck my face off.

It was bad.

She was so inexperienced.

I turned her down, she cried, and then I drove her home.

We never brought up that night ... until now.

"That's why I don't drink cheap vodka anymore," she says.

"Oh, really?" I lean back in my chair. "What's your drink of choice now? Pineapple juice to match your pineapple pizza?"

"Wine, thank you very much. It's never convinced me to stick my tongue down someone's throat where it doesn't belong." The blush on her cheeks hasn't disappeared.

"Does it make you stick your tongue down throats you should?"

She bites into the edge of her lip. "Can we stop talking about me, and you eat the damn pizza?"

I'd much rather talk about her sticking her tongue down throats.

And other places.

Well, not anyone's throat.

Maybe talk about her sticking her tongue down my throat.
Or vice versa.

I shake my head, mentally slapping my forehead. "If it's gross, you owe me fifteen mushroom pizzas."

"Ew." A fake gagging sound falls from her mouth. "I don't trust people who eat fungus on their pizza."

"Fruit on it is better?"

"Quit delaying and eat the damn pizza."

My stomach growls, but not because I'm hungry. It's tightening, gearing itself up to ingest something disgusting. Jamie's eyes are pinned to me, and she's nearly bouncing in her chair. My upper lip snarls when I pick up a slice, bite off the corner, and chew it as slow as Noah does his broccoli.

I'm making the same disgusted face.

"So?" she asks eagerly when I swallow it.

"Just as I suspected." I clasp my fingers together in a fist, hold it over my mouth, and make a choking noise. "Nasty as hell."

She rips off an edge of crust from a slice and tosses it at me. "You suck."

We're in need of a subject change. I can't have her asking me to try any more nasty shit.

"You know," I say, "I never told Heather about that night."

CHAPTER NINE

Jamie

I PULL IN A BREATH.

Whoa.

He said her name.

Not once in the six years they've been broken up has Heather said his name.

If it wasn't for Noah, you'd think their relationship never existed.

A few years ago, when Heather was in town, I asked if she regretted leaving them.

She answered with a friendly, "Fuck off," and stormed out of the room.

Her pig of a husband, the man she'd stupidly ditched Cohen for, grunted and muttered something along the lines of, "Fuck kids."

A real winner there, sis.

I told him to, "Fuck off," next, and the day was filled with everyone wanting the other to fuck themselves.

My eyes meet Cohen's, and a tingle sweeps up my spine. Even though this is an embarrassing moment, I have no compulsion to flee.

We're having a good time.

"I figured you hadn't tattled, given I wasn't strangled in my sleep,"

I say, cracking a smile. "Thank you for that. It's nice to be alive and breathing."

He shrugs. "We all do stupid shit the first time we're drunk."

"Fun fact: not everyone attempts to make out with their sister's boyfriend. Total slut move on my part, which I take full accountability for." I pause, holding up a finger. "To you, I take responsibility. With Heather, I'm taking that shit to the grave."

He's right about it being the first time I got drunk. For someone with a 4.0 GPA, I was clueless about how potent vodka was and how stupid it could make you. I chugged that shit down like it was Kool-Aid, trying to fit in, and then threw myself at a man who wasn't mine.

After our *incident*, I didn't drink for three years.

In college was when I realized that not all alcohol was cheap vodka that would have you puking up your guts and kissing guys.

"You were what"—Cohen scrunches his brows together— "sixteen?"

"Sixteen, stupid, and slutty."

I couldn't look at him for weeks. Anytime he came over, I left the room. I was ashamed and terrified he'd tell Heather. She would've tattled to my parents, and all hell would've broken loose. But Cohen pretended it never happened, and at times, I wondered if he even remembered.

Maybe I wasn't that memorable.

"What if I told you it was the best kiss of my life?" Cohen asks, grinning playfully before licking his lips.

I flip him off. "Shut your mouth before I shove that pizza in it."

"I know it was the best kiss of yours." His smile turns cocky.

"Please. It lasted five seconds before you shot me down."

"Yes, because you tasted like pineapple pizza."

"And you tasted like cheap beer and tacos. Not hot."

"I won't argue with that. I had some shitty taste in liquor back then."

And shitty taste in girlfriends.

He clasps his hands together, resting them on the table, and it reminds me of a dad about to give their child *the birds and the bees* talk. "Seriously, though, pineapple breath and all, thank you for coming tonight."

"Thank you for letting me in his life," I whisper. "I know it was hard for you."

His gaze darts to the other side of the kitchen.

Whenever I bring up Noah, Cohen changes.

Vulnerability flashes in his eyes.

He's unsure if me seeing Noah is the right thing to do.

Please don't doubt me.

I'll never hurt either of you.

I swear it.

I'm playing, and I will always play by your rules.

He knocks his knuckles against the table before sliding out of his chair. "Sorry for taking you away from whatever you were doing by asking you at the last minute. I'm sure you were busy."

"Nope, just in bed." I chew on the inside of my mouth.

He tilts his head back. "Now, I feel like shit for dragging you out of bed." His head lowers as if something quickly hit him. "Wait, why were you in bed that early?"

A strangled laugh leaves me. "I was awake … just chilling."

A low chuckle from him eases me a bit. "Just chilling, huh?"

"Yep."

His lips twitch into a relaxed smile. "What does one do while *just chilling* in bed?"

"Eat ice cream." I wrinkle my nose while rambling off my list, "Complain about insomnia." I snap my fingers, and my voice hitches. "Oh! And eat Cheetos—the puffy kind, of course. Sometimes, if I'm feeling crazy, I throw Netflix into the mix. My shifts have been chaotic lately, and it's been difficult to maintain a normal sleep schedule."

Last week, we were short a doctor and two nurses in the ER, so I picked up the slack.

He scratches his chin. "What does Jamie watch in bed while chilling?"

"*The Office* reruns usually or a serial killer documentary."

"You have no idea how much I'd pay to binge-watch a show that isn't cartoons or even eat in bed. If Noah catches me snacking in bed, he'll try to do the same. Kid's a messy eater. In all seriousness, though, I'm proud of you for going for your dream."

Rising from the chair, I clap him on the shoulder. "You sound like a proud dad at graduation."

He clasps his hand over mine, squeezing it. "Hey now, I heard you babble on about wanting to be a doctor for years. I'm glad it worked out."

As happy as his words hit me, my attention is pinned to his hand over mine.

To his touch.

The way his large hand perfectly blankets mine.

The warmth of his skin over mine.

I shut my eyes, telling myself to pull away but not having the strength to.

He blows out a long breath at the same time he releases my hand. "It's late."

I retreat a few steps, maintaining distance, and groan when he pulls out his wallet.

Not again.

"Nope," I say, pushing the wallet away. "If you even think of taking anything out of that, I'm kicking your ass."

He snags a bill and slides it between two fingers, holding it out to me. "For taking you away from your Cheetos and Netflix."

I narrow my eyes on him. "Put it away."

"Jamie—"

"You can pay me back by allowing me to see Noah more. How's that?"

He stiffens at my response, and his face changes into a look I've only seen once—when we were in Noah's bedroom. We lock eyes, and I feel my pulse in my throat.

"I'll give you that." His voice is gentle when he reaches forward, wraps a strand of my hair around his thick finger, and clips it behind my ear. "Good night, Jamie. Get back to your Cheetos and Netflix."

I suck in a breath.

Cheetos?

From the way he's looking at me, I'll be getting back to my vibrator.

His eyes are half-lidded and tired when I tell him good night, and he walks me to the door, standing on the porch until I drive away.

When I get home, I pour a glass of wine to pair nicely with my Cheetos and go to bed.

CHAPTER TEN

Cohen

"I UNDERSTAND you want to wear your Spider-Man light-up sandals, buddy, but it's cold outside. Your toes will freeze off."

I'm crouched on one knee and having a standoff with my five-year-old son about fucking light-up sandals at the ass crack of dawn.

Noah scowls at me. "I don't care. I don't need all my toes." He holds up his tiny hand and separates his fingers, wiggling them. "I got ten of 'em."

I scrub a hand over my cheek. I'm functioning on three hours of sleep, and I still need to make breakfast and drop Noah off at school on time. "How about this? I'll buy you Spider-Man boots if you put *those* boots on. Neither one of us is getting our way here, bud."

He tilts his head to the side, thinking. "If I listen, *you* are getting your way."

Schooled by a kindergartener.

I stare at him, searching for my next move, but he sighs as if annoyed with me.

"*Fine*," he groans. "I'll wear the boots *if* you put an extra pudding cup in my lunchbox."

"Sold!" I high-five him and stand. "Put on your boots, and let's get moving."

Noah pulls the bright red boots up each foot and stomps into the bathroom. I spike his hair with gel and spritz cologne on his wrist, and we head into the kitchen, the smell of his cologne filling the hallway when he sprints down it. I bought him the cheap shit last month in hopes that he'd stop stealing mine.

He dances in his seat at the kitchen table while I heat his oatmeal —the kind where the dinosaurs hatch from their eggs after it's warm— and I make his lunch while he eats. Normally, I have everything ready the night before, but the fiasco with Polly and Mohawk fucked up my schedule. I was exhausted and crashed into bed as soon as Jamie left.

After Noah scarfs down his oatmeal, he jumps from his chair, and we load into my Jeep. The drive to school isn't a quiet one while he talks about how pretty his babysitter is and then complains that I'm not bumping Kidz Bop.

After I drop him off, I head to the bar for another day of work.

———

"HEY, BIG BROTHER."

I glance up, drying off a glass, and set it to the side as Georgia skips over to me.

She plops down on a stool, sets her salad container on the bar, and opens it. "How'd last night go?"

I grab another glass. "You were with me last night. Remember?"

"How'd your night go with *Jamie*?" She stabs a piece of lettuce and shoves it in her mouth.

That's where she was going with that.

Not surprising.

"I went home. She went home. That's it," I lie with a shrug.

That's it.

That's definitely not it.

We talked. We laughed. We joked.

We brought up secrets.

Even though I had been tired as fuck, ready to collapse into my bed when I walked into the house, I could've sat at that table and talked to her all night.

Then we started talking about our kiss.

The kiss we'd shared years ago that was anything but hot.

My chest expanded, and my dick stirred at the thought of kissing her again—better this time.

Hotter this time.

Me not pulling away this time.

I prayed she didn't notice me staring at her plump lips as I wondered how it'd feel to brush mine against them.

"Lame," Georgia groans, breaking me out of my thoughts before dropping her fork and staring at me, a shit-eating grin on her face. "I have a great idea."

"Keep that idea to yourself," I grumble.

"Ask her out."

Georgia liking Jamie surprises me. When Noah was a baby, Georgia sided with me about Heather's family—including Jamie—not seeing Noah. Like me, she saw them as a threat.

"Mind your business."

"She doesn't know how to do that," Archer says, strolling behind me to grab a cocktail shaker.

"And just like that, my appetite is ruined," Georgia snaps, her cold glare pinned on Archer as she slams the lid back onto her salad.

I gear up, ready to block it because her face suggests she's about to throw it at him. As annoying as it is to hear them argue like fucking children, it at least takes the attention away from Jamie and me.

I signal back and forth between them. "You two need to quit acting like you're Noah's age and get along."

Archer walks away without replying and helps a customer.

Sadness crosses Georgia's face as she scoops up her hardly eaten salad. "I'm out of here. I'll finish my food somewhere that's asshole-free."

"You don't have to go." I set down the glass and then scrub a hand over my forehead.

She and Archer have been arguing for years, and no one knows why. Eventually, it has to end because it's giving me a goddamn headache.

Just as I'm about to lock them in a room to work on whatever the fuck their issue is, Silas's voice rings through the bar. "Hey, yo! We have that new vodka everyone is talking about!"

Silas comes into view with a heavy box in his hands. He groans as he drops it onto the bar next to Georgia.

"You mean, the vodka Lola told you to buy?" I ask.

"Obvi," Georgia replies for him with a snort. "He'd pierce his dick if Lola told him to."

Lola is one of Georgia's best friends who works for one of our liquor distributors. She tends to sucker Silas into purchasing whatever alcohol she's promoting.

"Bullshit," Silas says, shooting Georgia a glare before plucking the box cutter sticking out of his pocket and slicing the box open. He pulls out a bottle with a label I don't recognize and holds it up. "Now, who's up for testing this bad boy?"

"Hard pass. Lola already made me try it, and it's potent," Georgia says before wiggling her fingers in a wave, scooping up her things, and scurrying out of the bar.

"Over here!" a customer yells, swinging his arms in the air. "I'm up for taste testing anything!"

Silas hops over the bar and spins the bottle in his hand. "Any takers from someone who *works here*?"

The taste tester won't be Silas. He works in a bar yet doesn't drink.

Silas points at me with the bottle.

"Nope." I shake my head. "I'm about to head home."

He snags a shot glass and pours a shot. "Archer, my man! Looks like you're the winner!"

Archer grumbles curses under his breath, captures the glass, and swallows down the shot. "It's okay. Nothing to orgasm about." He hands the shot glass back to Silas with a shrug and walks away.

"That dude needs to get laid," Silas says, shaking his head.

"Lack of pussy isn't his problem," I comment.

Archer has his fair share of women. He comes from money, and even though he tries to hide it, women fawn over him as if it bleeds off him. The difference between Archer and other guys is that he doesn't broadcast his hookups. He's quiet and private, but given the shit that happened to his family, I don't blame him. He's rough around the edges, bulky, and broad-shouldered. He's a better fit for a bouncer than Finn, but Archer laughed in our faces and threatened to kick our asses when we suggested it.

Finn raises a brow.

"It's Archer being Archer," is my only explanation.

"Georgia probably put him in a bad mood. Anytime they're around each other, it's a negative-ass vibe. They need to bang and get it over with."

"Dude, what the fuck?" I seethe, shooting him a look of warning. "That's my sister."

He holds his hands up, palms facing me. "Oh shit, forgot about that."

I flip him off and smack him upside the head.

He jerks back. "Dude, what the fuck *to you?*"

"Oh shit, forgot it's painful when someone hits you." I signal to everyone behind the bar. "All of you assholes know my sister is off-limits."

That's been my rule since day one. Whenever a friend meets her, I make it clear he stays away from her. Georgia is grown and going to date, but I've worked with my friends long enough to know they're not the guys for her. They hook up with women, women throw themselves at them, and none of them can hold a relationship without fucking it up.

Not happening on my watch.

They all know that, and they respect that.

We've never had an issue.

If that changes, that person will no longer be my friend.

And I'll kick the bastard's ass.

CHAPTER ELEVEN

Jamie

"YOU STILL MAD AT ME?" Ashley asks, sliding into the booth across from me at our favorite smoothie joint.

I haven't talked to her in weeks. She and Jared went on an off-the-grid-to-find-myself vacation with no phones, no WiFi, and no Netflix. Not a good time, in my opinion. Since she's been gone, I haven't had a chance to tell her about the Cohen situation.

Ashley has been my best friend since third grade. We were the class nerds who spent our weekends doing homework and reading books while hanging out. We had a similar goal—to become doctors.

We were roommates in college and med school. She met Jared and moved out of our apartment and into his condo last year.

While I took a job in the ER, she took one as an OB/GYN. When she offered me a position at her practice, I declined. The ER holds my heart. It's stressful, but I love the unknown. People come to us at their most vulnerable times. I wanted to be a doctor to help people, and the ER is what makes me happy.

"Sure am," I answer, sipping on my açaí smoothie.

"Come on," she groans. "How was I supposed to know he was a D-bag who liked gangsters?"

"Jared knows what kind of guy he is."

She wrinkles her nose and rubs her bottom lip. "You see … Jared doesn't exactly speak to him."

"What the hell?" I shriek, tossing my straw wrapper at her. "You set me up with a guy *neither one of you* speaks to?"

Ashley takes a long drink before answering, "I know *about* him. Sometimes, I talk to his assistant when I visit Jared at the office. She said he was a winner, so I set you up." She throws her arm out before placing her hand over her heart. "What if someone gave me the opportunity to set you up with a Hemsworth brother? I wouldn't say no because I hadn't personally met him."

"Big difference," I mutter, shooting her a dirty look.

"Look, my goal is to find you love, and I'm doing the best I can over here. Not all of them can be winners. It's called a process of elimination."

"I'll find my own love, thank you very much." I sip on my drink. "No more blind dates from you."

"Where will you find dates then?" She pushes her fire-red hair away from her face and leans across the table. "Did you finally decide to take my advice and join Tinder?"

"Tinder sounds better than Ashley Finds Me a Date, so possibly," I lie.

"Look, give me another chance." She presses her hands together in a praying gesture. "I'll check attorneys off the list. Jared has plenty of frat brothers."

"Absolutely not. Frat boys are the worst."

I stupidly lost my virginity to a frat boy I was tutoring my sophomore year of college. He invited me to a party, and one thing led to another. A week later, he hired a new tutor, who I then caught giving him a blow job.

"Technically, they graduated and are no longer frat boys."

"Thank you, next," I sing out.

"No accountants, no former frat boys. Anyone else on your no-no list, you picky pain in the ass?"

"No one you suggest."

She pouts, and her response comes out in a whine, "You're no fun.

Get married, so I can deliver an amazing maid of honor speech. I demand to take credit for you finding the love of your life."

I roll my eyes.

She perks up in her seat. "How about this? You let me apologize with margaritas tomorrow. You have to forgive someone who offers margs—*top-shelf* margs."

"As great as that sounds, can I take a rain check?"

"Why?" Amusement crosses her freckled face as her lips curl into a smile. "You find a boyfriend? Is that why you're turning down my fabulous list of men?"

"First off, it's far from fabulous." I squirm in the booth. "Don't kill me for not telling you this, but you have been MIA."

She tips her drink toward me. "Don't you dare say you got married, and I missed my maid of honor speech."

I prepare myself for her impending freak-out. "Cohen came to the ER with Noah."

"What?" she shrieks, catching the attention of the people around us. "Off the grid or not, I'm pissed you didn't send a letter, a raven, a tele—whatever the fuck they did before phones were invented—to tell me this!"

"He blew me off at first, but I gave him my card. A few days later, he called, asking for help because Noah was still sick, and it has kind of"—I search for the right explanation—"progressed from there." I snatch my smoothie and suck it down.

"You're bailing on me to hang out with Noah and his *daddy*?" she squeals, shimmying her shoulders from side to side. "I like it. I like it *a lot*."

"Gross." I scrunch up my nose. "Don't say it like that."

"Fine, to hang out with Noah and the guy you've wanted for years."

"Guy I've wanted for years?" My cheeks burn. "I haven't seen him in *years*."

"And?"

"And he was a total ass to me. He's not the guy who dated my sister. He's different."

"Obviously. Your sister fucked him over. That kind of betrayal will change a man."

I nod in agreement.

"Ask him out."

My eyes widen, and it's my turn to shriek and gain people's attention, "Are you nuts?"

"What will it hurt?" There's not a hint of sarcasm on her face.

I flick my hand toward the door. "Go away and get back to giving Pap smears."

"What will it hurt?" she repeats. Placing her elbows on the table, she rests her chin in her hand and stares at me dreamily. "I think you two would be super hot."

"Did you bump your head when you were doing that eat, pray, love shit? Not only is he my sister's ex but he's also the father of her child."

"Heather lost any right to him and Noah when she left him for that scumbag." She leans back and shrugs.

I play with my straw, and it squeaks as I move it in and out of the cup. "Still doesn't make it right. Heather didn't do anything to *me*."

She snorts. "She cut off all your Barbies' hair after claiming you were too old to play with them. She made fun of you like it was her job. Remember when she broke your grandmother's antique clock and blamed it on you?"

Struggling to sound defensive, I say, "Payback isn't sleeping with her ex, and that was childish stuff she did to *me*."

She sighs. "It sucks when your bestie is in love with someone but won't make her move."

"I don't love him," I say harshly, looking away from her.

"Don't bullshit me. You told me *yourself* you loved him."

When I glance back at her, my narrowed eyes meet her entertained ones. "I told you that my freshman year of high school when I didn't date, no guy paid attention to me, and he was always around. It was a stupid crush."

She tips her head to the side. "Look on the plus side, bestie. You won't have to endure any more of my blind dates."

"Cohen or no Cohen, I'm still not enduring any more of your blind dates. I'd rather have my period for a year straight."

"Make sure you make an appointment if that ever happens, okay?"

"I'm still not hiring you as my gyno."

"Lame." She checks her watch, frowns, and slides out of the booth. "Find out when I can meet the little guy, and if anything happens between you and Cohen, don't wait a damn month to tell me, okay? I don't care where I am. I want all the deets."

————

MY THROAT TIGHTENS as my nerves go into overdrive.

I considered driving to Cohen's house to ask him this, but I don't have panties big enough to do that. So like the scaredy-cat I am, I call him.

"Hey," he answers.

Playing with my hand in front of me, I inspect my nails in an attempt to control my anxiety. "Do you have a minute to talk?"

"Sure," he drawls, curiosity in his tone. "What's up?"

"My parents want to meet Noah," I rush out before I lose my nerve.

My hold tightens around the phone, and I glance around the hospital cafeteria, wondering if I'll need Xanax by the time this call ends. This request can piss him off enough that he won't talk to me again.

"You told them?" he hisses, and my eyes slam shut at his tone.

It's a mixture of shock and anger.

As if I betrayed him.

My wish of him taking this lightly is not coming true.

"It was an accident." Tears prick at my eyes, regret sliding through me as my hands start to shake.

"An accident?" he slowly repeats, calling my bullshit.

"My mom called when I was babysitting Noah. I ignored her calls, but she kept calling. I was worried it was an emergency."

"Jamie," he warns.

"I didn't plan for her to find out. She heard Noah in the background and asked who he was."

"You couldn't tell her he was someone else?" The bullshit-calling is still evident in his voice.

"I suck at being put on the spot, and I suck even more at lying, which some would find a very honorable trait."

"You know what another honorable trait is?"

"Forgiveness?" I squeak out.

"Keeping your word that no one would find out."

"Cohen," I say his name like a statement.

"Jamie," he mocks in the same tone.

"I give you my word that they won't tell Noah who they are. Please give my parents this. Even if just for one day. My mom's birthday is this week, and it'd make her day."

"I don't care what'd make her day."

The call goes silent, and the anxiety feels so similar to when my mom called, asking who was in the background.

"I'll think about it," he finally states.

"That's all I'm asking for."

"No, you're asking for *a lot* more."

CHAPTER TWELVE

Cohen

JAMIE: **Bad news. I'm sick, and I can't pick up Noah. I'm so sorry.**

I drop my pen on my desk and grab my phone to answer her text.

Jamie was supposed to pick up Noah from school today. She's done it a few times this month, and he loves his time with her. They go to the park or the movies, and she takes him to get cupcakes.

Man, my kid is easily won over with sugar.

Me: It's cool. You need anything?

Do you need anything?

What the hell am I doing?

Nothing. This is normal. Not out of bounds.

Right?

I'd reply the same to my sister or one of my friends if they were sick.

Jamie: I'm okay. Thank you for the offer, though.

Me: Get some rest. I'll get Noah from school.

Jamie. Thank you, Cohen.

I slide my phone into my pocket and glance over at Archer. "I have to go. I'll have Georgia come in and cover my shift for a few hours when she gets out of class." I rub my temples, already anticipating the backlash of hearing him bitch.

"Why?" Anger radiates off him, and he throws the paperwork we were discussing on my desk.

"Jamie is sick and can't pick up Noah from school."

"Find someone else to cover," he snarls, scratching the scruff on his cheek. "I'm not working with her."

"Look, whatever beef you two have, it doesn't need to be brought up here. You work here. She works here. Get the hell over it."

He glares at me. "As part owner, shouldn't I have a say in our employees?"

"Not when she's my sister."

"I'll call Silas."

"He's out of town."

"Whatever, man," he grumbles.

I take that as his acquiescence, and thirty minutes later, I'm in the school pick-up lane. The back door flies open, and Noah jumps into the back seat.

A frown takes over his face as he looks around. "Where's Jamie? I thought she was picking me up today."

I stare back at him in excitement. "She's not feeling well, so you get to hang out with good ol' Dad today."

"Ah, man," he mutters with a frown.

"What am I, chopped liver?"

"She was going to take me to the cupcake place."

I frown back at the disappointment on his face. "How about I take you to the cupcake place?"

He thrusts his arm into the air. "I'd love that! Can we get Jamie one too? She loves cupcakes, like me. It'll make her feel better."

Just as I'm about to say no, I take in the elation on his face.

No way can I say no to that face.

It's probably why I've been a sucker for most of Noah's requests throughout his life.

"Sure."

He dances in the back seat. "Can I pick it out? I know her favorite."

"Of course."

I text Georgia, asking for Jamie's address, before putting the car in drive. She's brought Noah there a few times to hang out at Jamie's place. She called it a change of scenery, but I call it Georgia being nosy and wanting to know where Jamie lives.

———

SALLY'S SPRINKLES is a cupcake shop that sits on the corner of Main Street and Maple in our small town square.

I've been here a few times, but Noah and I tend to visit the frozen yogurt shop when we go out for dessert. When we walk in, my mouth waters at the sweet smell of baked goods wafting through the air. Noah wastes no time in skipping to the glass counter.

"Hi, Noah!" greets the woman wearing a frosting-stained apron.

"Hi, Sally!" He wiggles in place while debating his options.

My gaze pings back and forth between them. Other than giving her our cupcake choices, we've never talked to this woman before, let alone know her name.

I'm assuming she's the owner, hence Sally's Sprinkles.

It hits me that Noah has been here with Georgia and Jamie. That must be how they know each other.

"No Jamie or Aunt Georgia?" Sally asks.

Noah shakes his head. "Aunt Georgia is at school, and Jamie is sick. We're going to bring her cupcakes to make her feel better!"

Sally's hand flies to her chest, a grin taking over her wrinkled face. "You're so sweet. She'll love that."

I kneel to Noah's level. "What'll it be, buddy?"

"Hmm …" He puts his finger to the side of his mouth, deep in thought, before pointing at a dark chocolate one. "She'll love that one!"

"She most definitely will," the woman squeals. "Those are her favorite."

Noah tips his thumb toward me. "This is my dad."

"Oh, it's nice to meet you! I'm Sally." She wipes her hands on her apron and waves to me as I stand.

Noah peeks over to me. "Her son and Jamie used to be boyfriend and girlfriend," Noah explains as though he were the head of the gossip committee around here.

Raising a brow, I feel a surge of jealousy tightening around my throat. "Oh, really?"

What the ...?

I shouldn't care that Jamie had a boyfriend.

Sally nods repeatedly. "My Seth was heartbroken when they broke up, but med school was demanding." An exasperated breath leaves her. "If only they'd get back together now that she's out of school."

Fuck Seth.

He had something I want—something I can't have.

I'll never have.

I clap my hands and rub them together. "All right, Noah, have you decided which one you want?"

No more talk of Jamie's former boyfriend.

Noah nods, and we leave Sally's Sprinkles with a box of cupcakes.

CHAPTER THIRTEEN

Jamie

FUCK BEES.

No longer will I share any Save the Bees Facebook posts.

Sorry, Cheerios.

My bottom lip is the size of a toddler's fist.

All because one got into my can of LaCroix and stung me when I took a drink. The swelling has shrunk some, but it still appears I had a lip injection gone wrong.

I hated canceling on Noah, but there was no way I was going to go out in public looking like this. I'll buy him extra cupcakes and maybe an action figure the next time I see him.

Shuffling from my kitchen to the living room, I hold a bag of frozen strawberries to my mouth and plop down on the couch before snatching my phone. The bag drops on my lap when I see a text sent fifteen minutes ago.

Cohen: Mind if we stop by? Noah has something for you.

I'm struggling to come up with an excuse when the doorbell rings. I snatch the strawberry bag, set it on the table, and tiptoe to the door. When I peek through the peephole, Noah and Cohen are standing on my porch, and there's a familiar pink box in Noah's hands.

"I hope she's home," Noah says. "Everyone knows you have to stay home when you're sick unless you have to go to the doctor. Isn't that what you tell me, Dad?"

"It sure is." Cohen knocks again before peering down at Noah, who now appears heartbroken. "Maybe she's napping. We'll leave the cupcakes here, and I'll text her to grab them when she can."

"But what if someone steals them?" Noah whines.

My stomach burns with shame. I pull in a jagged breath, open the door, and cover my mouth.

"Hi, guys," I say, my voice muffled under my hand.

Noah holds up the box, a proud smile on his face. "We brought you cupcakes to make you feel better."

I return the smile at the heartwarming gesture and am unclear if they can make out my words. "That's so sweet. Thank you." Not wanting to be rude, I wave them in with my free hand.

They don't move.

Cohen scratches his head and nods toward my mouth. "Is everything okay, Jamie?"

He has the hot dad vibe going on with his sweatshirt layered under a jean jacket, holey jeans, and Chuck Taylors.

I nod. "Mm-hmm."

"Why don't you uncover your mouth then?"

I don't.

"Jamie," he says my name like a warning.

I slowly remove my hand, waiting for the gasps and questions.

"Oh."

"Yeah, oh." I gulp.

"What happened to your mouth?" Noah blurts.

Cohen shoots him a *don't be rude* look before his attention returns to me. "Are you allergic to something? I can run and grab you some Benadryl."

"I took some already." My words are still muttered, my lips not making it easy to speak.

Turning, I do a once-over of my house when they walk in. It's clean, but since I've been lying around, whining about my lip, I haven't exactly picked up today. An empty yogurt container is on the living room table next to the bag of strawberries and a bottle of water. A shag blanket is nestled in the corner of my couch, and a lavender candle is burning, the relaxing scent wafting through the air in an attempt to calm me.

My townhome has an open floor plan, allowing you to see the living room and the kitchen past the peninsula island separating the two rooms. Cohen carefully takes the cupcake box from Noah and sets it on the kitchen table. Noah doesn't waste a moment before opening the box and snagging one.

He jumps up and down and comes dashing toward me. "Here! I picked it out just for you."

The blue frosting lining his mouth tells me he's already devoured one cupcake.

I rest my hand over my heart and set the cupcake on the counter. "I'll eat this in a bit, okay?"

Noah nods.

Cohen shoves his hands into his jacket pockets and leans back on his heels. "Sorry if we're intruding, but Noah insisted on seeing you and bringing you the cupcakes since he thought you were sick."

I signal to my jumbo lip. "This qualifies as sick. No way am I going out looking like this."

"Why?" He smirks. "They look cute."

I smack his shoulder as I pass him. "Shut up."

He chuckles.

Noah is at the table, shoving another cupcake into his mouth, and I start straightening up my mess.

"How'd you know where I lived?" I ask Cohen.

"Georgia."

Noah hops up from his chair and barrels toward the living room. "Let's watch cartoons!"

"We can get out of your hair," Cohen says when Noah flies past him into the living room.

"You've already seen my face, so there's no hiding it. I could actually use the company."

"I figured you'd be eating Cheetos and watching Netflix." He winks at me.

"I save those for my wild nights, remember?"

"Ah, yes. I see it's frozen fruit and yogurt day instead."

Noah makes himself comfortable in the yellow paisley print chair with the remote in his hand and starts flipping through channels.

"Noah," Cohen says in his dad voice, "you can't turn people's channels without asking them."

Noah frowns. "You let me turn channels all the time."

"*At home*. We're at *Jamie's* home."

"It's totally fine," I say. "Flip away."

Noah shrugs and stops at a cartoon.

I fall on one end of the couch, and Cohen takes the other.

He looks around the room. "I like your place. It suits you."

I drive a hand through my hair, realizing it's a hot mess, but all I can do now is roll with it. "I mean, I do live here."

"You know what I mean. It matches your personality."

I shift to face him. "What exactly is my personality?"

"Sophisticated but fun. Stylish but not too overboard or tacky."

"Hmm …" I tap my chin. "Has someone been reading Martha Stewart magazines?"

"Smart-ass," he grumbles, cracking a smile.

My townhouse does scream me. The two-bedroom home isn't large, which was number one on my wish list because less cleaning. My father had all my appliances updated, and I changed the deep brown cabinets to a clean white, making the place brighter. An electric fireplace—another item on my wish list—is under the TV.

All my furniture is white, and I've scattered color throughout the room with my décor—bright pillows, large candles on my coffee table, and two bookshelves lining a wall, filled with medical textbooks, paranormal romances, and thrillers.

"Speaking of homes, your crib definitely doesn't suit you. I was expecting a man cave," I say.

"It's the Martha Stewart magazines. She knows her shit."

I cock my head to the side. "Family man design is all the rage."

He points at himself. "Funny, because that's what I am, minus the whole cheesy dad T-shirts and tacky jokes."

"Uh, that cheesy dad joke was plenty tacky."

"Dad! It's my favorite!" Noah shouts, turning back to look at us while pointing at the TV where *Toy Story* is playing.

Cohen scoots in closer to me, bows his head, and whispers, "To be honest, the sequel is nowhere near as good as the first one."

I raise a brow. "Look at you, Mr. Cartoon Critic."

"What can I say?" He shrugs. "I know my shit."

"Dad!" Noah yells. Briefly peeking back at us, he furrows his brows. "We're not allowed to say that word."

"Shit—shoot, sorry," Cohen replies with a chuckle.

I elbow him. "You're in trouble now."

"Who would've known the hardest part of raising a kid was not cursing around them?" He shakes his head. "It's not like I work in a school where I regularly have a PG-rated vocabulary."

"Speaking of work, do you have to go in tonight?"

"Nope. Georgia and my friend Archer are covering for me."

I glance away, fake focusing on Buzz Lightyear, when I ask, "Which bar do you own?"

"Twisted Fox Bar." There's no mistrust in his tone. No sign he doesn't want me to know.

Buzz loses my attention while Cohen reclaims it.

"Really? You were voted one of the top bars in the state."

"Heck yeah, we were." Pride shines on his face.

Noah's gaze whips back to us. "Dad! Bad word!"

"I said *heck*," Cohen argues.

"My teacher, Mrs. Jones, said we're not allowed to say heck either."

"Jesus," Cohen mutters. "Mrs. Jones is on my nerves."

Noah responds, "Shh … this is my favorite part of the movie. You guys watch, okay?"

I nod, feeling like a kid in time-out, and talking toys are the only sound in the living room.

Noah is engrossed in the movie.

Cohen? Not so much.

Me? I couldn't care less about Woody.

Sorry, not sorry.

I steal glances at Cohen, and there's no missing the way his eyes flash to me every few minutes. We're not snuggling, this isn't romantic, but I never imagined I'd be on my couch with him, watching —*ignoring*—a movie. With each peek, I take in the differences in him from the past and how maturity has changed him.

Dark stubble covers his cheeks and the angular curve of his jaw.

The old Cohen had smooth cheeks and was cleaner-cut.

His laid-back clothes are different than when he went to clubs.

The man who was once the life of the party now makes cartoon character-shaped pancakes.

Heather never deserved him, his love, and she definitely doesn't deserve the man he is now.

How could you turn your back on them?

If only I'd been older.

If only he'd seen me as more than just his girlfriend's geeky sister.

If only he hadn't dated my sister.

But then again, I would've never known him.

Is that a good thing?

Did fate bring Cohen and me together?

Did it bring Noah into my life?

Shaking my head, I mentally slap myself for my stupidity.

Cohen will never be anything more to me than my sister's ex-boyfriend.

I'll never be anything but the little sister of his ex-girlfriend— albeit less annoying and geeky.

What made me fall in love with Cohen was how he treated me. He'd give Heather shit when I wanted to watch a movie with them and she'd scream at me to leave a room. My parents were lenient with them and allowed Heather to have sleepovers at his house even though they knew his mom was always MIA. I'm shocked Noah was their first pregnancy. They screwed like teenagers who'd just discovered sex.

I adored her relationship with Cohen.

Everyone knew it.

Everyone teased me about it.

Noah's snoring breaks me out of my thoughts. I stand, grab a blanket, and wrap it around him.

"We should get going." Cohen lifts to his feet. "He has school in the morning, and I need to make dinner. He won't be happy when he finds out dinner doesn't consist of pizza or cupcakes."

"What's on the menu then, chef?"

"Cheese quesadillas."

"Oh, yum."

"I'll have to make you some when you come over sometime."

I scrunch up my face. "It's so weird."

"What is?" He turns to look at me.

"You cooking, being responsible, being a *dad*."

"Hey now, I knew how to cook before I was a dad. People seem to forget I took care of Georgia before Noah. We couldn't eat fast food all the time. It was too expensive and bad for our health."

"Good point. I don't know why I ever doubted you."

His face falls at my words.

My voice lowers and softens. "I'm sorry, Cohen. From my parents and me, we wish everything had happened differently."

"I appreciate that. I grew up with your family. You knew I was the parent for Georgia when I was a teenager. I could take care of a baby in my twenties. I'm not fucking selfish, and it hurt."

My parents and I went to the hospital when Noah was born, assuming Heather would change her mind, but nope. That was when they asked Cohen to allow them to adopt Noah.

It was wrong.

We saw how over the moon Cohen was about becoming a father.

"Trust me, we hate how things went down. My mom recently asked for your number to apologize, but given how private you are, I didn't want to cross any lines." I hesitate, my stomach twists, and my head hurts, in fear I'll piss him off. "She also asked for a photo of him, which I haven't sent either. I'm following your rules here."

A pained expression passes over his features. "Your parents really want to meet him, huh?"

"You have no idea."

His shoulders straighten. "All right then."

"What?"

"They can meet him."

I perk up. "Really?"

"On the condition they don't tell Noah who they are. You're Georgia's friend, they're your parents, and you're just babysitting for me."

"I understand. I promise." I clasp my hands together and hold myself back from squealing. "Thank you so much."

His voice hardens. "Heather had better not be there."

"She's in Vegas and very rarely comes home. It's been over a year."

"Good." He runs his tongue over his lips before gesturing to mine. "Ice that."

I touch my lips because I'd forgotten about the swelling then salute him.

He collects Noah in his arms and sends me a polite wave, and then they leave. I snag a cupcake and shove half of it in my mouth.

I love this new Cohen.

How he's coming around and letting me in.

No longer is he being as cold and callous as he was at the hospital.

What's changed in him?

And what does it change with me?

CHAPTER FOURTEEN

Cohen

MY NERVES HAVE BEEN on fire since Jamie picked up Noah today.

My stomach clenches when I ask myself why I agreed to let her parents meet Noah.

Sheila and Ted Gentry are good people and had been nothing but warm and welcoming since I met them. Even with their wealth and status, they weren't unhappy that their daughter brought home a boyfriend who came from a broken home and was living off the system. They helped my family and me, and even though it pissed me off, I knew their asking to adopt Noah came from a good place. They were willing to step up and parent Noah if no one else would.

I glance up at the sound of the front door opening and hear Noah blabbing about how long he held his breath underwater. I smile, knowing he must've gone swimming at her parents' house. Noah comes darting in, ready to tell me about his day, and just as I'm about to ask him a million questions, the sight of Jamie stops me.

Her face is blotchy, and she's struggling to hold back tears.

She's seconds away from a breakdown.

I stride to the fridge, pull out a pudding cup, snatch a spoon, and hold them out to Noah. "Go eat this in the living room, and we'll be in there in a minute."

"Really?" His eyes widen as if I grew another head. "I can eat it on the couch?"

"Just this once."

I pat him on the head, and he grabs the goods before dashing into the living room.

She's practically shaking when I step closer.

"Jamie," I say, "what's wrong?"

"Please, Cohen." A single tear slides down her cheek. "Don't hate me."

Those aren't good words to hear.

Especially after where they've been.

I stare at her, trying not to jump to conclusions, and wait for her to continue.

She doesn't, but the sobs come.

"Jamie," I say, "you're scaring me here."

She opens her mouth, shuts it, and then slowly opens it again. "I took Noah to my parents' house, like we agreed."

I nod and stay silent.

"I told him they were my parents, like we agreed."

"Good."

"Everything was going fine." Her voice, her jaw, her hands—they're all shaking. "We were swimming and then …"

"And then what?"

Her gaze drops to the wood floor. "Heather showed up."

A storm rolls through me, an anger I've never experienced, and the urge to throw something consumes me.

I don't.

I don't because Noah is in the next room.

"The fuck?" I hiss. "You promised me, Jamie."

It's done.

She's done.

It'll break Noah's heart but no more Jamie.

I stepped out of my comfort zone and did this for her.

And it was all a fucking lie.

"I know," she cries out, keeping her voice low. "No one knew she was coming. It was out of the blue—"

"Bull-fucking-shit," I snarl. "Maybe *you* didn't know, but your parents did." *Out of the blue, my ass.* "Heather lives in a different state, and you want me to believe she was just in the neighborhood?"

Her green eyes are pained, anguished, as she gapes at me. "My parents were as shocked as I was. She came to surprise my mother for her birthday. We tried to hide Noah. Trust me, we don't want to mess up seeing him, nor did we want her to say something that'd confuse him."

"Did she see him?"

She nods. "She did."

I grind my teeth. "Did she talk to him?"

The thought of her telling Noah who she is sends a bitter taste in my throat.

The thought of my son's head being fucked with is a stab to the heart.

"At first"—she stops to level her breathing—"I told her he was a kid I was babysitting, but then Noah introduced himself."

"Did she tell him anything?"

"No."

My anger falls a level.

"She stormed out of the house as soon as she found out who he was because she didn't want her husband to know Noah was there. You have nothing to worry about with Heather. I promise you. She was mad that he was there." Every muscle in her body is tense. "I'm sorry. I really am."

I pace in front of her. "This is what I was scared of."

"I'm sorry," she mutters again.

Jamie doesn't deserve this anger.

This hurt.

The respect and the compassion I have for her calm me.

I run my hands through my hair, taking the last of my anger out on the strands before blowing out a long breath. "It's not your fault."

She frantically rubs her arms up and down.

"That asshole wasn't around my son, was he?"

"No," she rushes out. "He was chain-smoking outside, and I hurried and got Noah out of there. They were driving to his family reunion." She steps forward and rests her hand on my chest. "I give you my word, Cohen. Nothing has changed for her. She's no threat to you … to Noah."

I rest my hand over hers, the warmth of her skin underneath mine settling me. "I trust you, Jamie." My hands move to her shoulders, and I squeeze them before slowly massaging them for a moment. "Relax."

Her eyes are watery when I finally step back, my arms falling to my sides before I raise one to cup her jaw in my hand.

"It's okay," I whisper. "I trust you."

She bows her head. "Thank you."

Time to make light of this situation.

My dad mind shoots straight to how I help Noah with his tears.

"Looks like someone might need a quesadilla," I say, my tone teasing.

She laughs, wiping her eyes. "You mean, looks like someone needs some tequila?"

Turning on my heel, I reach into the tallest cabinet above the fridge and extract a bottle of tequila I save for moments like this.

Moments when I need to clear my head.

I pluck two shot glasses from another cabinet, fill them to the rim with tequila, and hand one to her. "To us not giving a shit about Heather."

She picks it up without hesitation. "To us not giving a shit about Heather."

There's a *clink* as our glasses hit together, and the tequila burns as it seeps down my throat.

Fuck.

It's been a minute since I've drunk this shit.

Blowing out a breath, I wipe my lips with the back of my arm and groan. "Tell me that helped."

Instead of answering, she pours another and shoots it down. "Now, *that one* helped."

I chuckle and rub my hands together. "Now, how about the quesadilla?"

"A quesadilla sounds amazing."

Without thinking—because I'm an idiot—I kiss her forehead. "Everything is good. Don't worry about it."

Her mouth drops open, and Noah, with perfect timing, comes stomping into the kitchen.

"Pudding cup is gone!" He holds it up. "But my belly is still hungry."

I snatch the tequila and shove it back into the cabinet while Jamie places the shot glasses into the dishwasher. With how flustered we are, I'm shocked one of us didn't drop anything.

"How about a quesadilla?" I ask Noah, raising my voice and forcing it to be as playful as possible.

At least, I'm hoping it sounds that way.

"Woohoo!" Noah shouts. "I love quesadillas!"

I gesture for Jamie to sit down, and she does. Noah starts rambling about school and random shit while I get to work. Jamie listens to Noah, engaging in his conversation as if she were being told the world's secrets while I drag out the quesadilla essentials. My mind is on the kiss as I warm the flour tortillas in a skillet.

It was a friendly peck, I tell myself while topping one with cheese.

One I'd give Georgia or one of her friends if they were upset, I think while flipping it over.

I remove the quesadilla from the skillet, drop it on a plate, and start on another.

That's it.

Innocent.

I've convinced myself our relationship is nothing but platonic when I drop the plates in front of them and grab the salsa, and then we dig in.

I believe Jamie.

I saw the pain in her eyes, the honesty in her words, and the fear.

No way is she capable of faking that.

She never even had to tell me.

That's why, while we clean up, I invite her to Noah's basketball game.

"NOAH IS GOING to kick some ass today," Finn says, sliding down the bleachers in the YMCA gymnasium until he's sitting next to me.

"Hush," Grace, Georgia's friend, warns behind him, slapping his shoulder. "There are kids around. Use your PG voice."

Finn groans, throwing his head back. "Just because you use your PG voice at all times doesn't mean I have to."

Georgia, who's sitting next to Grace, smacks the back of his head. "She's an elementary school teacher, dimwit. She has to use her PG voice."

"And I'm a bouncer at a bar. I don't." He rubs the back of his head. "And you're brutal, Georgia."

Most of the gang is here for Noah's basketball game. We erupt in cheers when he runs onto the court with his team, wearing his red uniform and matching tennis shoes. I love the support we have.

Georgia will be at our side, no matter what. She calls us The Three Musketeers. After our father left and our mother fell victim to addiction, I was there to pick up the slack. I was her big brother, and if my parents weren't going to care for her, then I was. I fed her, made sure she was at school every day, helped her with her homework, and provided anything she needed.

Lola and Grace are always a help to us and love Noah to death.

Silas, Finn, and Archer are the same.

Maliki, one of my best friends, is here too. He owns Down Home Pub, a bar in the next county. It's nice we can visit each other's bars, and we've never felt a sense of competition.

We all have fun together.

During the summers, we regularly have cookouts at my house.

"Hi," Jamie whispers, squeezing into the spot on the other side of me. "I tried to get out of the hospital as fast as I could."

I glance over at her with a smile. "You're good. The game hasn't started yet."

The woman behind Jamie taps her shoulder, and we both peek back at her.

"Hi. You're Noah's mom, right?" She points at Jamie. "It's nice to finally meet you." She presses her hand to her chest. "I'm Mary, the teacher's assistant in Noah's class."

Jamie's face pales while I nearly fall off the bleachers.

"Oh, no," Jamie stutters, "I'm not his mom."

Mary blinks. "That's what he said when you picked him up from school last week." Her head tilts to the side. "You're a doctor, right?"

Jamie nods.

Thank fuck no one else is paying attention to us.

My heart batters against my chest. I wish it'd fall out, and I could give it to my son, so he'd have more. I believed I had it all figured out, playing the role of both parents.

I was wrong.

Just as they say a daughter needs her father, a son wants his mother.

Hell, I want that for him.

The memory of the first time he asked me why he didn't have a mom slams into me. He was four, and I hadn't been prepared for it. I froze, words not coming, and it took me a moment to get my shit together.

I knew whatever I said would break his heart.

She didn't want you, was what I wanted to say.

That way, Noah would never track her down.

It's what my mother had told me and Georgia about our father, and I gave no fucks about finding him.

He hadn't wanted me, so I didn't want him.

Sure, it'd crushed me when she told me, but it made me stronger. I never held out hope that he'd return one day, and I was thankful she'd fed me the truth.

Would my son feel the same way?

Would he appreciate the truth, or would it break him?

Those were my worries.

The truth had shattered Georgia. For years, she wondered where he was and why he didn't want her. Eventually, she tracked him down with the hope that he regretted leaving us.

He didn't.

He had two other children.

Two other children he was a dad to.

A real dad to them.

She'd left with a larger hole in her heart.

She finally had to come to terms with not being wanted.

Who will Noah be—me or Georgia?

Wanting the person or not giving a shit?

In the end, I told him the truth.

There were mixed reactions.

His therapist said I was wrong.

Georgia said she understood.

I'd prepared the little guy's heart, so it'd be stronger.

Maybe it was wrong.

Maybe we weren't so much alike, and the pain from the absence of a parent was harder for him than me. It could be different because he lost a mother, not a father. I had plenty of friends with fathers not in the picture. Mothers not in the picture were less common.

I have a feeling if Noah ever seeks out Heather, it'll be the same as what happened with Georgia.

"Maybe there was some confusion. I'm not—" Jamie stops and gives Mary a warm smile. "It's nice to meet you." She whips around, setting her eyes on the court, her shoulders tense.

Not as tense as mine, but pretty damn close.

These are the moments I feel like a failure.

I don't regret Noah, but I regret who his mother is.

Never in the time we'd been together—nearly a decade—did I think Heather would turn her back on us like she did.

Her actions have made me question any type of relationship.

I haven't been celibate, having my fair share of hookups, but that's it. I'm too weak to give them what they want. My heart is too untrusting after giving my all to someone for so long, only to get shit on.

My guard is up for both of us.

So I fuck a little here and there, but I always go home to Noah.

Noah sends us a wave from the court before they start the game.

"He looks adorable in his uniform," Jamie says, leaning into me.

"Grace tried to bedazzle it," Finn comments.

"It would've been cute," Grace argues.

"Sorry, babe, but no."

Finn gets smacked in the back of the head again, this time by Grace, and he chuckles.

Our circle is strange—a heap of sexual tension.

Grace and Finn flirt like no other, and they're opposites. She's the sweet schoolteacher while Finn is far from innocent. He's been through hell and back, and he refuses to ask Grace out, in fear he'll rub his tainted life on her pristine one.

Sexual tension bleeds off Lola and Silas. Everyone is waiting for the day they bang. They share the same personality—sarcastic assholes who date around and avoid commitment.

That leaves Archer, Georgia, and me as the odd ones out.

Archer isn't a dater.

Georgia is too busy enjoying life for a boyfriend—or so she says.

And I have my issues.

"Go, Noah!" Georgia cheers.

Pride punches me while I watch him play. It's entertaining since most of the kids don't know what the hell they're doing, but Noah is having a blast.

Since the kids are just learning the game, there isn't a winner.

"Jamie, you're going out for tacos with us," Georgia insists after the game.

Everyone's attention whips to her in expectation, and her eyes avert to the bleachers that are clearing out.

One thing I appreciate is how they're not acting strange around Jamie, as if it were normal that she's here even though they all know the situation.

"Come on," Noah says, moving to her side and jumping up and down.

She shoots me a questioning look.

"Yeah, come on," I say, throwing my arm back to gesture toward the doors.

———

"AT LEAST YOU have decent taste in tacos," I tell Jamie.

She's sitting next to me at the best taco joint in town.

Granted, La Mesa is the *only* taco place in town.

The food is to die for, and Noah loves their nachos and cinnamon churros. We eat here a few times a month with the gang since there's enough room for everyone and an arcade in the back for the kids to play games.

Jamie points at me with her fork. "At least, *you* have decent taste in tacos."

"How about we agree we *both* have decent taste in tacos?"

"Fine, but I ordered first, so you copied me."

I chuckle, turning in my chair, and rest my elbow on the table while focusing on her. "I order the same thing every time!"

"As do I."

"Mm-hmm."

"Ask Ashley."

"You two still best friends?"

She nods. "Yep, and she'll confirm I'm a creature of habit. Shredded chicken tacos have always been my go-to." She bites into her lower lip. "I do get their quesadillas sometimes too. They're delish."

I throw my head back. "Can we both agree my quesadillas are more *delish*?"

Everyone around us is having their own conversations, and Noah is in the arcade, playing with Georgia, while Jamie and I are wrapped in our own little world.

"You have a major hard-on about your quesadillas, huh?"

"They're my specialty." I wink at her.

"Dad!" Noah comes barreling toward us and snags a churro from his plate. "Can I hang out at Jamie's tonight?"

Like when Georgia asked Jamie to come to dinner, everyone's attention darts to her. The table falls silent.

And also like when Georgia asked her, she appears uncomfortable as she shifts in her chair.

Noah pouts out his lower lip. "Pretty, pretty please?"

Not only has he put Jamie on the spot, but he's put me on the spot too.

"Buddy," I chime in, "we don't know if Jamie has plans tonight."

"I mean, I have the night off," Jamie rushes out, her eyes directed at me. "I don't have any plans and would love the company."

"Yay!" Noah dances in place with the churro in his hand. "We can eat cupcakes and watch cartoons and play games."

"*You sure it's okay?*" I mouth to her.

She nods with a smile before mouthing, "*If it's okay with you?*"

I glance back at Noah, who's chomping on his churro. "All right, you can stay over there, but you have to promise to behave."

"I will!" Noah chirps.

Silas slaps the table. "Looks like we're having guys' night!"

"Are we doing Twisted Fox or Down Home?" Maliki asks.

We tend to have guys' night at one of our bars. When one of us needs a break from our workplace, we go to the other's.

"Twisted Fox," Finn says. "That way, we can try to talk Archer into joining us."

"Why does it only have to be guys' night?" Georgia asks. "I nominate it to be guys' and girls' night."

Georgia lives up to the little sister role through and through. Even as a grown-up, she crashes my parties and always has to be in the know. Not that I mind. I love that she enjoys spending time with us, and that way, I can also keep an eye on her.

"It can't be a guys' and girls' night because Archer will act like we have the plague if you're there," Finn says.

"Archer can kiss my ass," she fires back.

"It's okay. We'll have a girls' night," Lola says, a sly smile spreading along her bright red lips. "At Twisted Fox."

Georgia laughs, reaches across the table, and high-fives her.

"It'd be nice if you stopped stalking us, ladies," Silas comments, smirking.

Georgia turns her attention to Finn. "Prepare for men to hit on

Grace at our girls' night since you want nothing to do with us, and you can't cockblock her."

Grace's cheeks redden as she hisses Georgia's name.

"Nobody is hitting on any of you," Finn snaps.

Lola rolls her eyes. "Someone had better hit on me."

Silas flips her off.

I lean in to whisper in Jamie's ear, goose bumps crawling up her neck as I get closer. "Seriously, if you have plans, I can be the bad guy and tell Noah no."

She massages her hand over her neck, as if attempting to erase her reaction to me. "No plans, seriously. Go have fun."

———

I DON'T REMEMBER the last time I had a guys' night.

Sure, every so often, I have drinks with the guys before heading home, but nothing like this.

Whiskey—a rarity for me—is in my glass. I tend to stick to beer when I drink.

Noah is in good hands tonight, and I need to drink away my thoughts of the woman whose hands he's in.

My relationship with Jamie is changing. She's becoming like family to us.

Noah is falling in love with her.

And me?

When she's around, my heart clenches—and also battles with my brain.

It's right, my heart says.

It's wrong, my brain chimes in.

Finn, Silas, Maliki, and I are huddled around a table in the corner of the bar, shooting the shit. I called in our part-time bartender to cover for Archer tonight, and we've been trying to drag him away from the bar for an hour, but he's reluctant.

"How's the bar going?" I ask Maliki.

He shrugs, circling his hand around the neck of his beer bottle. "Same shit, different day."

At one time, Maliki and I had planned to open a bar together, but when his father nearly lost their family bar, he moved home and took over. Before opening Twisted Fox, I checked with him to make sure he was cool with it. We aren't direct competition, but I didn't want to step on anyone's toes.

He was fucking ecstatic for me.

And wanted to kick my ass for doubting if he would be.

"Oh, wow, fancy seeing you jerks here," Georgia says, coming into view.

Lola and Grace are behind her with drinks in their hands. They set their drinks down, then drag another table and stools next to our table, and join us.

"Isn't the little sister supposed to quit being annoying to the big brother when she gets older?" Finn asks.

Georgia narrows her eyes on him. "Shut up. Don't act like you don't love it when Grace is around."

Grace's cheeks redden, and she twirls a strawberry-blond strand of hair around her finger. "Are … you okay with us interrupting?"

"You know I don't care," I say, jerking my head toward the guys. "Neither do they. They just like giving you a hard time."

"*Almost* all of you don't care," Lola chimes in, her attention moving to Archer, who's talking to the bartender.

"Which is why Georgia needs to go sit in the corner by herself when Archer comes over," Finn states.

"Archer isn't a child, so you need to stop worrying about how he feels." Georgia shrugs. "I'm cooler than him anyway."

"That is true," Silas says. "She's nowhere near as grumpy as Archer."

"Archer is only grumpy when Georgia is around," Finn argues. "Cause and motherfucking effect."

Georgia rolls her eyes. "He'll get over it."

"Will either of you ever explain why you hate each other?" Silas asks.

Grace's and Lola's eyes nervously shoot to Georgia.

"Our personalities clash," Georgia answers before downing drink.

People stop at our table to say hi and offer to buy us drinks. We might have some pain-in-the-ass customers, but I love the majority of our clientele. Archer remains behind the bar, slinging drinks while also eyeing us, and I'm clueless whether he'll join us now since Georgia is here.

He can get the fuck over that.

"Have you decided what we're doing for Noah's birthday?" Georgia asks.

"He's narrowed it down to a snow resort, a water park, or Chuck E. Cheese," I answer.

"Dear Lord, please don't let it be Chuck E. Cheese," Silas says with a shudder.

"Why?" Lola asks. "Don't all your nineteen-year-old girlfriends love Chuck E. Cheese?"

"Piss off," he grumbles, and they both crack up in laughter.

Swear to God, they need to fuck and get it out of the way.

Same with Grace and Finn.

Scratch that. It'll only create more problems if my friends start fucking Georgia's friends.

Thank fuck none of them have a thing for Georgia.

We'd have problems.

I love my friends, but that's against bro code.

It's crossing the line.

Just like me thinking about touching Heather's sister is crossing the motherfucking line.

So why do I want to?

As I sit here drinking, why is she on my mind?

"Look who's finally joining us," Georgia says, wiping away my thoughts.

Archer is standing at the table, a Jack and Coke in his hand and a glare on his face. Seconds later, he turns around and storms away.

Georgia jumps up from her stool. "Oh, my God!"

She scurries behind Archer, grabbing his elbow, and he swings back to look at her. They exchange words, him tipping his head down as they talk to each other, until he runs his hand through his hair. He nods, and when they return, Archer slides a stool next to me and sits.

We drink.

We laugh.

We have a good-ass time.

Three hours later, I grab my phone to text Sylvia and inform her I'm on my way home. My hand freezes at the realization that she isn't babysitting.

It's the first night Noah has stayed somewhere other than my home or Georgia's.

I'm letting Jamie in.

And I hope to God she doesn't rupture our hearts.

CHAPTER FIFTEEN

Jamie

MY PHONE RINGS at the same time I crawl into bed.

To say the day has been exhausting is an understatement. I worked a double before Noah's game and went to dinner, and then Noah and I watched movies when we got home. Noah crashed on my couch a few hours later, and I carried him to my guest bedroom. He whined as I tucked him in the same way Cohen had the night Noah was sick.

When I grab my phone, I see Cohen is calling.

He called to check in on Noah a few hours ago and told him good night.

Is he that paranoid that he's calling again?

No way am I waking up Noah.

"Hello?" I answer, stuffing a pillow behind my head and making myself comfortable.

"Hey, Jamie," he says, his voice sounding off. "How's my guy doing?"

What's *off* about his voice is the slight slur with each word.

"The better question is how are *you* doing?" I reply with a laugh.

"What do you mean?"

"Come on. You're drunk as a skunk."

He chuckles. "You know, I've never understood what that saying means, and I hear it a lot at my job."

"Yeah, me neither." I stretch out my legs and fight back a yawn, not wanting him to end the call because he thinks I'm tired. "Did you have fun at your guys' night?"

"Actually, I did."

"That's good."

"It's been a while since I've detoured from my two-beer rule."

"Two-beer rule?"

"Georgia has been swamped with work and school, so Noah has been with Sylvia more. I get nervous he'll need something or that he'll get hurt. Not that Sylvia is a bad babysitter. I'm just a nervous-ass dad. So if I grab a drink, it's two beers."

"But tonight?" My heart races as I cross my ankles and then uncross them.

"Tonight, I know he's in good hands."

Biting away the urge to squeal, I grab the fluffy pillow next to me and place it against my smile.

"I'm sorry for being such a dick to you at first." An exasperated breath leaves him. "My trust in people is shit."

I drag the pillow away, still frazzled. "I get it. I'd be protective too."

"I love that you understand. That you get me." A light *hmm* leaves him. "It's hot."

I force a nervous laugh and wait for him to tell me he's kidding.

He doesn't.

All he does is wait for me to say something.

"Wow," I drawl. "You really are drunk as a skunk."

"Guilty as charged."

"Do you need a ride home?"

"I'm home. Silas was the DD. He's having issues with his girlfriend and crashing on the couch. She doesn't like when he has guys' nights."

"Lola? Did the girls not crash your party?"

I don't see Lola being that overprotective of Silas, but if I had a boyfriend that hot, I'd probably want to keep an eye on him too.

"Silas wishes Lola were his girlfriend. Hell, we all do."

"But he flirted with Lola all day."

"Lola won't date Silas, so he has Helena. None of us are exactly sure what Helena is to him—girlfriend, fuck buddy, definitely a pain in his ass, and she's a nightmare. His dumbass let her move into his place last month. So when they fight, he crashes at one of our places to avoid her."

"That sounds like a mess."

"Guys like us"—his voice turns strained—"we're not built for relationships anymore."

"You're not built for a relationship because of Heather?"

"Because of Heather," he whispers.

"One bad relationship, and you're done?"

"One bad relationship?" he scoffs. "Jamie, I got fucked over big time."

For a moment, I'm at a loss for words. I don't want to bad-mouth my sister, but no way am I sticking up for her actions. She did fuck him over big time.

"What about you?" he asks, snapping me away from my thoughts. "You dating anyone? Word is, the Sprinkles heir held your heart."

Oh, my God.

"The Sprinkles heir?" I bite back a laugh.

"Sally Sprinkles's son."

"How do you know about Seth?"

"Noah. My kid is quite the gossiper."

I'd say so.

How did this conversation go from him to me?

"I dated Seth when I was in med school," I explain, my heart roaring in my chest. "I was too busy for a relationship, so we didn't do much of the dating life. It was mostly us, you know, hanging out."

"You mean, fucking?"

My cheeks turn a bright red, and I'm happy he can't see me. "I'm so not answering that."

"Why not?" he groans. "You throw me any question, and I'll answer it."

"No, because you're ... you."

"Heather said you eavesdropped on her talking to her friends about us having sex when you were younger and even listened to us *you know* a few times."

"Gross. I *overheard* Heather talking about your sex life because the girl has a big mouth. Yes, I also heard you banging from her bedroom since we *shared a wall.*" I make a gagging noise. "Trust me, you and my sister never made sex sound hot. She sounded like a dying bird."

"And what did I sound like?"

I shut my eyes and remember the vomity memory.

He didn't sound like a dying bird.

He moaned Heather's name.

Vomit.

Told her she felt good.

Gag me.

Once.

That was the only time I heard them.

After that, I used my allowance and invested in some quality sound-canceling headphones.

"How long has it been since *you* had sex?"

My mouth falls open as my skin tingles. "I'm most definitely never, ever having that conversation with you." I pause and add another, "Never," for extra measure.

He laughs. "Oh, come on. Give a drunk man some entertainment."

"I'm sure you have someone in your Contacts you can call for entertainment."

"What if I don't want someone else's entertainment? What if I want *yours?*"

The hell?

What has suddenly changed with him?

"You're drunk," I say sternly. "You need to get some rest."

"Is that doctor's orders?"

"That is the doctor's orders."

"Dr. Jamie is no fun."

"Never said I was fun."

"Noah says you are."

"Noah says I'm fun because I play with him, give him candy, and buy him pizza."

"Sounds pretty damn fun to me. Let's be fun together."

"Okay, now, this is *really* when I say good night."

There's a brief silence, and when he speaks, all humor has ceased, "Why couldn't you have been older?" There's pain in his voice. "Why couldn't I have chosen the other sister?"

His pain causes me to release an anguished sigh. "Cohen—"

"Seriously, Jamie," he cuts me off. "The fact that I'm thinking about you is … I don't know … messed up? But I can't help it."

"You need to get some sleep." I release a drawn-out breath. "Good night, Cohen."

"Good night, Jamie," he whispers. "Sleep tight."

———

DOES COHEN REMEMBER LAST NIGHT?

That's my first thought when I wake up.

It's what runs through my mind as I make Noah French toast.

Cohen's words have consumed me.

"Why couldn't I have chosen the other sister?"

If only I'd been older.

The problem is, all we have are what-ifs.

It's like a never-ending story.

Crossing any lines between us would be some Jerry Springer shit.

And Jesus, it'd confuse the hell out of Noah.

He's already telling people I'm his mom.

My gaze moves to the rug rat as he drowns his French toast in syrup. My heart sinks. It has to be hard for him not to have a mother. Anger toward Heather plows through me.

How could she do that to him?

To both of the boys who deserve so much more than being abandoned.

I'm in the kitchen cleaning up when Cohen texts me.

Cohen: Is it cool if I pick up Noah around noon?

Nervousness and anticipation zip through my veins.

A shift is happening between us.

I shut the dishwasher, scurry to my bathroom, and fluff my hair out with my hands while staring in the mirror.

Why am I stressing?

Why am I trying to impress him?

With a groan, I pull my hair into a ponytail.

No looking cute for him.

Bad Jamie.

Hopefully, he sticks with that same rule and shows up, looking like a hungover mess.

My yoga pants stay on, and I pull a loose sweatshirt over my head.

I pour myself another cup of coffee and join Noah in the living room where he's watching cartoons. The urge to find out why he said I was his mom is on the tip of my tongue, but I don't have the courage to ask.

It's not my place.

Plus, I don't want to embarrass or confuse Noah.

I suck down the rest of my coffee at the knock on the door. When I open it, my wish that Cohen would look like a hungover mess isn't granted.

No, he looks hot—as per usual.

He leans against the doorframe, a smile on his lips. "Hey. How'd everything go?"

"Great," I say, my voice too chipper, too unlike me. *Until you drunk-dialed me and sent me for a tailspin.*

I scurry backward before walking to the kitchen. He shuts the door behind him and joins me. I look like I crawled out of the hole I'd wanted him to crawl from since I slept like shit after his little mindfuck phone call.

"How much sugar did he talk you into?"

I laugh. "Not much. The churro gave him enough of a sugar high."

We hear Noah's footsteps before he comes into view.

He runs to Cohen and hugs his legs, grinning up at him. "Hi, Dad! I missed you!"

Cohen returns the hug with a tight squeeze, happiness in his eyes. "Hey, buddy. I missed you way more."

"How was your night?" I ask after Noah runs back to the living room to finish his show.

If Cohen remembers our call, his face doesn't give it away.

"Good. I had the first relaxing night in my bar than I think I've ever had."

"Did the whole crew show up?"

He raises a brow. "The whole crew?"

"Yeah, your squad."

"Squad? Who am I, Taylor Swift?"

"Wow, you know Taylor Swift has a squad?"

"Noah digs her." He smirks. "He's a Swiftie, so it's hard for me not to be one too."

"Who would've thought that behind all that hard-ass persona, you get down to 'Shake It Off'?"

He holds his hands out, palms facing me. "Whoa, whoa. Settle down there. I don't get down to it. I *tolerate* it."

"My show is over now!" Noah says, running back into the kitchen. "I'm hungry."

"I was going to make some lunch," I tell Cohen. "Want some?"

He tilts his head to the side. "What's on the menu?"

"Your options are grilled cheese, pizza rolls, or turkey sandwiches."

"Ah, such delicacies."

I shrug. "Shush, or you'll starve."

"What are pizza rolls?" Noah cuts in.

"The best food ever." I whip my attention to Cohen, mustering the most serious look on my face I can manage. "He's never had pizza rolls? What kind of monster are you?"

"As a doctor, should *you* be eating pizza rolls?"

I playfully bite my lip before swatting at him. "Listen, pizza rolls and coffee are my main food groups."

Noah taps Cohen's leg, looking up at him. "What's the difference between pizza and pizza rolls?"

"Pizza rolls are like bite-sized pizza," I explain, preheating the toaster oven, opening the freezer, and pulling out the bag of pizza rolls.

"Ooh, sounds yummy!" Noah says, holding up both hands and separating his fingers. "Can I have this many of them?"

Cohen pats Noah on the back. "Sure. Go have a seat at the table."

Noah hops to the table while singing the theme song of the cartoon that was playing.

I cut the bag open and drop the pizza rolls on aluminum foil while waiting for the toaster oven to heat. "These will probably help with your hangover," I comment, patting Cohen's stomach when I pass him.

"Dad, what's a hangover?" Noah asks.

Cohen chuckles. "One lesson you'll learn is that he picks up on everything you say." His gaze pings to Noah. "It's what adults say when they aren't feeling well."

"Cool! I want to be an adult and have a hangover."

"You can't say that until you're an adult," Cohen scolds, his tone still gentle.

Cohen leans against the counter next to me. "Who says I have a hangover?"

I drop a pizza roll on the floor, and he picks it up.

"I mean, you were with your friends, so it was an assumption." I dramatically gesture to his face. "Your face also looks like it was run over by a car."

"Run over by a car?" He throws the pizza roll across the kitchen, and it lands in the trash can. *Show-off.* "Thank you for the nice compliment."

"Always happy to serve them." I slide away from him. "Do you want something to drink? Water to wash down the Advil?"

"I'll take a water, no Advil." He signals toward the pizza rolls. "And be sure to throw me some of those in there for the hungover dude."

"Nope, none for the haters." I still add more.

"Pizza rolls were my jam when I was twenty and ate like a kid in college with no priorities involving a healthy diet."

I elbow his stomach, and he lets out a, "Humph."

While the pizza rolls bake, Noah tells Cohen about all the fun he had here last night, and as they talk, I make our plates.

We sit at the table like one cute, dysfunctional, will-never-happen family.

"These are delicious," Noah says, licking sauce off his fingers. "I want to have them every single day, okay, Dad?"

"Yeah, not happening." Cohen pops the last one in his mouth.

Noah's attention shoots to me as a mischievous look comes across his face. "Jamie will let me come over and eat them whenever I want."

I laugh and poke his shoulder. "Not if I eat them all first."

He hugs his belly while cracking up in giggles.

Noah is munching on a cookie he bribed out of me when Cohen stands to help me clean the kitchen.

"Can we talk about what happened yesterday?" he asks, close into my space.

"Sure," I drawl, uncertain of which situation he's referring to.

"I don't know why Noah told people you're his mom, but I'll talk to him about it."

"Oh, right." I sigh. "My guess is, he doesn't want to be the odd one out."

"Mine too." His face falls. "It sucks because I can't do anything to fix it. Any other issues, I find a way." He runs his hands through his hair. "When he has school events, I'm the only one there for him—Georgia, too, sometimes—and I see the look in his eyes when he watches his friends with their mothers. He wants that, and fuck, I want that for him."

I work to keep my voice as soothing as possible. "I know it's hard, and I wish Heather would get her head out of her ass."

He recoils, stumbling back a step, and his stare turns cold. "Heather will never be Noah's mother. She has no place in our lives, period, Jamie."

I shuffle my feet on the floor. I opened the box, so I might as well explore some. "You've never wondered …?" I abruptly stop, questioning if I'm about to make the right move before asking, "What if she returns and wants to know Noah?"

"Nope." His voice is rough. "She signed over her rights and isn't shit to him. It'll stay that way." He shakes his head, torment on his face. "It's bad enough she saw him at your parents', and her behavior further proves my point. Hell, she didn't even want to see Noah. She was afraid her fucking boyfriend—"

"Husband," I interrupt.

"Husband," he grinds out. "She doesn't deserve any of that boy's love." He jerks his head toward Noah.

"I understand." I offer him a comforting smile—or at least, I hope it appears that way.

My question has changed the mood of the room.

No more pizza roll jokes.

Talk of Heather has ruined that.

His shoulders slump. "I wish I'd chosen a better mother for him."

"Why couldn't I have chosen the other sister?"

My head spins, and I step closer, rubbing his shoulders. "Hey, don't be too hard on yourself. He's lucky to have such a great father."

"That'll never fill the need for a mother's love. Obviously, look at what he told his teacher."

"Eventually, you'll find a woman who can be that figure for him." *And I'll hate her.*

"We have Georgia"—his eyes lower, sorrowful but with a hint of hope in them, and then they meet mine—"and you."

CHAPTER SIXTEEN

Cohen

SILAS CLAPS me on my back while passing me behind the bar. "Don't make any plans tomorrow night."

"Why?" I ask.

"We have a double date."

"No, we don't."

"Yes, we do." He throws his head back and groans. "Helena's cousin is in town."

"That's a big *hell no*."

"Why?"

"Helena's cousin is annoying as fuck, and Helena is crazy as fuck. Not people I want to spend my night with. No offense to you, man."

"Oh, come on. She liked you last time she was here."

"Hook her up with Archer."

He scoffs. "Archer doesn't have the patience for her. He said, 'Fuck no,' before I even finished my sentence."

"Neither do I, so fuck no. Ask Finn."

"He's working."

"I'm sure you have another friend."

"Come on," he pleads. "One night. All you have to do is sit at the table with us, drink, laugh a few times, *maybe* let her kiss your dick."

I shake my head, shuddering. "Nope."

"What about kiss your cheek?"

"Also a no."

"You didn't have a problem with her before."

"Oh, you mean, the first time I met her when she drunkenly tried to drop to her knees underneath the table here and blow me?"

He points at me with his lollipop. "See, she liked you!" He presses his hands together in a begging motion. "A few hours. That's all I'm asking. Hell, you don't even have to listen to her. Just nod and agree with whatever she says."

"I don't have a babysitter." That's always my get-out-of-jail card.

"Georgia and Lola already agreed to babysit." A shit-eating smirk covers his face. "I bought them tickets to one of those ice-skating shows."

"You already found a babysitter for me, you jackass?"

He releases a booming laugh. "I knew you'd use that excuse."

I narrow my eyes at him.

"Do it for me, man."

"Fine," I grumble. "But you're taking one of my shifts this weekend."

He snaps his fingers and points at me. "You're the best."

"I know; I know."

He turns to look at me and walks backward. "Who knows? Maybe you two will hit it off this time."

"The odds of my dick falling off are higher." I blow out a noisy breath. "I'm not staying out late, either."

"Okay, old man."

———

"YOU SURE ARE DRESSED like shit for a date," Georgia comments, falling onto the couch when she walks into the living room.

"You can't see how excited I am?" I give her a cold stare. "Thanks for throwing me under the bus."

"Pardon you. He asked Lola, and I'm only along for the ride." She grins. "Who's the lucky woman you're dressing homeless for?"

I look at the floor as I mutter the answer, "Helena's cousin."

"Silas's Helena?"

I nod.

"Ew, sorry." She perks up when I glance back at her. "Maybe you'll get laid."

I dramatically fake dry-heaving. "Don't ever talk about me getting laid again."

"Oh, come on." She props her feet on the coffee table. "We're adults here. You don't think I know how Noah was made?"

Noah comes rushing out of his bedroom, saving me from this dreaded conversation, wearing one of my hats, a T-shirt, and dinosaur socks over his jeans that hit the knees. "I'm ready!"

———

AT LEAST SILAS was smart enough to have us "double date" at the bar.

I slipped Archer twenty bucks to come over and say he needed me to do something in the office.

That was twenty minutes ago, and his ass still hasn't made his way over here.

The smart-ass grins he's shooting my way confirms he's fucking with me.

I'm giving him ten more minutes before I tell Becca to kiss his dick.

It's not that Becca isn't attractive.

She's gorgeous.

Thick blond hair, nice *fake* breasts, and a body fit for men's magazines.

She's smart.

The problem is, we don't click.

There's no spark.

Our lives are too different.

She's twenty-one and in the stage of her life wrapped around partying and having a good time. There's nothing wrong with that. That was my scene before I had Noah. My priorities have changed, and even though she insists she loves kids, dating a man with a child is harder than she thinks.

The woman is always second in line.

"And that's why I stopped drinking raspberry vodka," Becca says, cutting me away from my thoughts and stopping my glare pinned at Archer.

I tilt my head and phony smile. "I'm not a fan, either."

She laughs before releasing a sigh. "You weren't listening to a word I said."

"Sorry." I scrub a hand over my face. "My brain is scrambled right now. I've had a long day."

She takes a drink, her red lips wrapping around the straw. "I get it. This is your workplace. We should've gone somewhere else. Helena yelled at Silas when he came here, but I told her it was cool." She shrugs. "It's a fun place." She taps my shoulder. "But get out of work mode and into fun mode."

"I'm working on it." I grind my teeth while Archer acts like he hasn't noticed my signals to save me.

"Maybe tomorrow we can go to dinner?" Becca asks.

I frown. "I don't have a babysitter tomorrow."

She caresses my arm. "You can bring Noah. I'd love to meet him."

"I'd love to meet him."

I hate when chicks say that.

Noah isn't meeting anyone until we've had at least five dates. I refuse to bring new women in and out of his life.

Maggie, one of our waitresses, stops at the table. "Cohen, Archer said he needs you."

About damn time.

I slide off my stool and shoot Becca an apologetic glance. "I'll be back."

"Mmkay." She grabs her drink and takes a long draw, shimmying her shoulders from side to side.

I shove Archer when I make it behind the bar. "Took you long enough, asshole."

"What?" He smirks. "You looked like you were having a blast."

I narrow my eyes at him.

"Not to mention, Silas outbid you. He paid me fifty to wait longer to bail you out."

"You sneaky bastards."

He laughs. "I would've done it for thirty. Now, since I bailed you out, why don't you bring another keg up here, will ya? Might as well make yourself useful."

CHAPTER SEVENTEEN

Jamie

I FACETIME COHEN'S phone a few times a week and talk to Noah.

It's become the highlight of my day.

I get home, shower, throw my hair into a messy bun, and hit Cohen's name.

My face shows on my screen as it rings a few times before it's answered.

I nearly drop the phone, and my mouth goes slack when the woman comes into view.

A drop-dead gorgeous woman.

"Hello?" she answers.

A deep tinge of insecurity wracks through me as I notice how different we are. Her hair is down in loose waves, her eyeliner is winged with a precision I could never master, and her low-cut top shows more cleavage than any of my push-up bras can manage.

"Is, uh"—I play with my messy bun, an attempt to make it look not so sloppy—"Cohen there?"

"Why?" She puckers her lips. "Who are you?"

"A friend." I'm gripping the phone so tight that I'm waiting for it to crumble in my hand.

"What kind of friend?"

"Is Noah around? I called to talk to him."

"Why do you want to talk to his son?" Something hits her, and she lowers her voice, scooting in closer to the phone's camera. "Oh, my God. Are you the baby mama?"

"What? No. Can you just tell them Jamie called, please?"

"Not if *Jamie* doesn't tell me who she is."

"Who's that?" Another girl comes into view before a dirty look forms on her face, and a snarl leaves her.

Oh, this is the mean one. Definitely.

"Why are you calling Cohen?" the mean one asks.

"Whoa, whoa." Silas is the next person I see.

It's like they're passing me around in a game.

"Oh, hey, Jamie," he says with a smile.

"Um, who is Jamie?" Mean Barbie snaps.

"There it is," Cohen says in the distance. "I thought I'd lost my phone."

There's a moment of silence.

"Wait. Becca, what are you doing on my phone?"

"Um …" *Becca* bites into her lower lip. "It rang, and I didn't want you to miss a call."

"It's Jamie!" Silas informs him.

I still and hover my finger over the End button.

"Oh shit. Hey, Jamie," Cohen says, jerking his phone out of Becca's hand.

"I'm getting another call," I say before hanging up.

It's a slap in the face.

Another reminder.

I cannot fall for Cohen.

He'll never be mine.

CHAPTER EIGHTEEN

Cohen

"WHERE'S NOAH?" Maliki asks, standing next to me while I season the burgers on the grill in front of me.

We're in my backyard, having a barbeque. It's something I try to do a few times a month when the weather is nice. I invite everyone. We eat a shit-ton of food, play cornhole, and hang out. Our lives can be shitstorms sometimes, so it's nice to catch up.

There's nothing better than enjoying a beer with your friends and playing some yard games.

That sounds way more honky-tonk than it is, I swear.

"He's with Jamie," I say, flipping a burger.

Jamie and I have returned to our avoidance game since the Becca incident. I tried calling her on my way home to apologize, but she hit the *fuck you* button. She hasn't FaceTimed us since, and it's sucked. We started looking forward to her calls. She'd tell us hospital stories or embarrassing memories of me when I was a dumbass teenager, and Noah would burst into laughter. Sometimes, she'd even read him bedtime stories.

Shame hits me whenever I think about what happened.

I took that away from him.

"Oh, he's with Jamie, huh?" Maliki says, covering his smirk with the neck of his beer when he takes a drink.

"Don't give me that look."

He situates his hat, drawing it further down his forehead, hiding his eyes. "What look?"

"How about we talk about your little girlfriend instead?" I grab my beer and suck it down.

"Nice subject change, jackass."

I shrug. "I like her, and you seem happy."

"We're friends. She needed somewhere to stay. The end."

"It'll be a good story you tell your kids one day about how you met their mom because you were kicking her out of your bar."

"Funny," he grumbles, handing me a plate, and I start loading it with the cooked burgers.

Maliki brought his *roommate,* Sierra, with him. He and Sierra have been playing a cat-and-mouse game for years. It started when she kept sneaking into his bar, underage, and he kept kicking her out. When she turned twenty-one, they became friends, some shit happened in a relationship she was in, and now, she's living with him. The way they look at each other and how his arm was wrapped around her shoulders in ownership as they strolled through my backyard scream that they're more than friends.

Just as I'm about to tell him I'm offended that he's lying to me, Georgia yells, "Hey, Jamie!"

Even though I've been expecting her to drop off Noah, adrenaline speeds through my chest at the sound of her name. I turn around at the same time Noah slams into me, nearly knocking me over. My brow arches as he waves something in the air.

"Jamie bought me an iPod!" he announces.

An iPod?

The hell?

Noah doesn't need a damn iPod at his age.

Not wanting to rain on his parade, I shoot him a smile, and we head over to Jamie, who's talking to Grace, Lola, and Sierra.

"An iPod?" I ask when I reach her. "You spoil him too much."

Even though I know the true intentions of the iPod.

Jamie laughs; it is fake and fraudulent, and it pisses me off. "It's for selfish reasons, so we can FaceTime."

I frown—mine not fake. "You always FaceTime him on my phone. It's never been a problem."

She's gone back to communicating through Georgia again as though we're playing fucking telephone on the playground, which has resulted in dozens of questions from my nosy sister. I planned to bring up the FaceTime call Becca answered to Jamie today, but with all the attention on us, it isn't the time.

It'll have to wait until I can catch Jamie again when she's not avoiding me.

Her face is blank when she replies, "You're busy sometimes."

I wince before checking myself, deciding to go a different angle with this. Maybe I can get her to stay and corner her later, make her talk to me.

"We have plenty of food." I sweep my arm out to gesture to the table loaded with burgers, hot dogs, chips, and every other barbeque food you can think of. "Stay."

Hang out.

Let me explain myself.

Don't be pissed at me.

"Thanks for the offer, but I can't." She kneels and hugs Noah. "Make sure you call me, okay?"

Noah hugs her back and salutes her. "You got it!"

She kisses the top of his head and waves good-bye to everyone, not giving me one more glance.

"She is pissed at you," Georgia sings when Jamie is out of earshot.

"She's not pissed at me," I say, imitating her high-pitched voice.

"Why's she pissed at you?" Grace asks.

"She FaceTimed Cohen to talk to Noah the other day, and some chick answered, asking Jamie twenty-one questions about who she was." Georgia rolls her eyes and glares at me. "That's why she bought the iPod."

I'm well aware.

"I need to stop telling you stuff," I mutter before shaking my head, grabbing Noah, and throwing him over my shoulder.

Noah shrills in laughter, clasping his arms around my neck, and I take off, running across the yard.

I drop him to his feet when we reach Silas and Finn, who are playing cornhole. Noah shows off his iPod to Finn while I shove Silas's shoulder.

"I can't believe I was dumb enough to let you set me up on that date," I hiss to him. "Jamie hates me now."

"Oh, so that's my fault, huh?" he asks.

"Damn straight."

"Maybe it is my bad, but it's *your* bad for not talking to her about it. *Your* bad for not telling her about the hard-on you have for her."

I roll my eyes and shake my head before playing a round of cornhole with Noah and the guys, hoping it'll take my mind off Jamie.

CHAPTER NINETEEN

Jamie

"DON'T FORGET. We're going out for Kelsey's birthday," Ashley reminds me from across the table.

We're having lunch at the deli across from the street from the hospital. It's her lunch break, and my shift just ended. I can't wait to go home and take a nice long bath. As much as I love work taking my mind off my issues, I need to clear my head. The call with Cohen's date *Becca* has been on my mind since it happened, and I can't seem to shake the jealousy that consumes me anytime I think about it.

Cohen isn't mine.

He never will be.

I went to the Apple store and bought Noah an iPod to make sure an interrupted by a gorgeous girl phone call didn't happen again.

"Dinner, right?" I ask.

Kelsey is our friend from med school, and every year, we go out for our birthdays.

"Nope. She switched it up this year, and we're going where her boyfriend wants." She rolls her eyes and fakes enthusiasm. "Yay!"

"Where's she having it now?"

Ashley bites back a grin. "He likes sports."

"Okay …"

"He likes watching sports at *sports bars.*"

I glare at her, knowing where she's going with this. "A sports bar not around here, and where I don't know the owner, correct?"

She shakes her head, her grin now in full effect.

I've kept her updated on all things Noah and Cohen. She even met Noah once and had dinner with us.

"Oh, darn." I smack my knee. "I forgot I have plans."

"You do have plans." This time, she tries to hide her smile while biting into her straw. Doesn't work. "Going to Twisted Fox and hanging out with yours truly are your plans."

"I had a super-long shift today." I fake a yawn.

"You had a super-short shift today."

"How do you know?"

She grabs her phone, unlocks the screen, and shows it to me. "Remember when I texted you last week, asking if you had the night off, and you said this? Not to mention, you just got off work."

I glare at our text message thread where I told her I was most definitely open tonight.

Damn texts get you caught every time.

It makes it really hard to lie in today's day and age.

"I agreed to go to dinner, not a bar."

"You've never had a problem with going to a bar before, Miss Loves Her Wine."

"The problem isn't going to a bar. It's going to a bar owned by a man I have issues with." I shoot her a *so there* look.

"Since when and why do you have issues with Cute-Boy Cohen?"

"A.) Quit calling him that, creep, and B.) since I called his phone and some cranky chick answered, questioning me like I was the mistress calling *her* husband."

"You don't have to talk to him then. I'm asking …" She pauses and holds up a finger, her face turning serious. "No, I'm *telling* you that you're coming."

"Fine, only because I know you'll show up at my house and annoy me until I agree."

"Damn straight, I will."

"I seriously need to rethink this friendship."

"You love me. Make sure you dress cute."

FINN GIVES me a head nod when he notices me walking into Twisted Fox. "Yo, Jamie. I didn't know you were coming tonight."

Neither did I until a few hours ago.

"Hey." I wave. "It's my friend's birthday, and this is where she wanted to come."

Tell that to Cohen, so he doesn't think I'm randomly showing up and being all stalkerish.

Ashley snags my hand, and I follow her through the packed bar, looking around while also maneuvering through the crowd. The place is nice, and even though it has a hometown-bar vibe, it's updated, fun, and hipster-friendly. It for sure brings in plenty of business.

I've heard great things about Twisted Fox, and I'm happy for Cohen.

Kelsey stands on her stool, waving her hands in the air, and motions for us to come to the table where she and her boyfriend are sitting. She jumps off her stool and gives us each a hug, and I hand over her gift.

"This place is a madhouse," Ashley says as we sit down next to each other.

"Okay, bouncer dude is hot," Kelsey's friend Carrie says, falling down on the stool next to Kelsey, puckering her lips and focusing her attention on me. "He seemed to know you. Is he single?"

Ashley and I groan at the same time.

Carrie isn't my friend, and I dread when she goes out with us. She calls every damn guy we see hot. Waiters, bartenders, random guys walking down the street, women's husbands.

I've witnessed her get bitch-slapped for it once.

Fun times.

It's not that Finn isn't attractive with his light brown hair, muscles, and cocky smile. It's that he isn't Cohen—tall, his face handsomely rough. Even though they both sport scruff on their face, I love how dark Cohen's is. How well it matches his eyes.

After graduation, Kelsey took a job working for a plastic surgeon and is now dating said plastic surgeon. Carrie asked for a discount on a nose job—after calling him hot, of course.

Before I get the chance to answer her, Georgia comes skipping to our table, a bright smile aimed at me.

"Look who it is! What can I get you, babe?" she asks. "We have some amazing cocktail specials tonight, and to be honest, the one I named after myself is *delish*."

I laugh, grateful she's not making this awkward. "I'll take a Georgia then."

"Good choice." She winks at me and takes the table's orders.

Ashley and Kelsey order the Georgia too.

I hope it's not too strong. Wine and margaritas are the drinks to my heart, and I haven't wandered into territories of anything stronger. The last thing I want to do is get drunk and make a fool of myself in front of Cohen again.

Georgia shoves her pencil behind her ear and through her braided hair and tells us she'll be back in a snap. She takes the long route on her way to the bar, dodging Archer, and gives Silas her order.

"There's Cohen," Ashley shrieks, suggestively elbowing me.

"Who's Cohen?" Kelsey asks.

"He's the owner," Ashley answers.

Ashley points at him, and that's when I finally gain the nerve to look in his direction.

I lose my breath. He's behind the bar and in deep conversation with Archer. He's wearing a bright blue V-neck shirt with the bar's logo on the right side of the chest and jeans—a bottle opener sticking out of a pocket.

The sound of a woman yelling his name steals his attention, and he walks to the end of the bar to talk to her. I can't take my eyes off them as she leans across it, whispers something, and laughs. Cohen nods, retreats a few steps, then starts making a drink. When he hands it to her, she blows him a kiss.

"Cohen is good people," Heath, Kelsey's boyfriend, says.

"He's hot," Carrie says, licking her lips.

Just as I'm about to shove her off the stool and tell her to back off, Georgia returns with our drinks and does the job for me.

"He's off-limits," she says, handing the glasses and beers to us.

"Your boyfriend?" Carrie asks, raising a drawn-on brow.

"My brother."

"What about the other bartender?" Carrie signals to Archer.

Like with the other guys, I don't blame her attraction to him. Archer is built like a football player with broad shoulders and an expansive chest, and unlike the other guys who are clean-cut—shorter hair, light on the scruff—Archer's hair hits the base of his shoulders, and his facial hair is on the heavier side.

Apparently, Twisted Fox doesn't only deliver in drinks and bar food; it also always delivers in hot-as-hell eye candy. If they sold a yearly calendar, it'd have its fair share of sales.

Georgia throws Carrie a death glare. "He's also off-limits. Don't speak to him and don't look at him, or I'll break your fingers." She gives her a tight smile, and the table goes quiet. She perks up as if she didn't just go Cujo on Carrie. "Anything else I can get you guys?"

We do a mixture of shaking our heads and telling her no.

"That girl will scratch your eyes out if you talk to that bartender," Kelsey warns Carrie. "Find another guy to hit on because I don't want her to spit in my drink or have my birthday ruined by you getting beaten up. I love you, but I will not be stepping in."

Carrie rolls her eyes. "Whatever. There's more fresh meat around here."

I sip on my Georgia and engage in conversation as the TVs roar around us. People cheer, groan, and argue at game calls. My gaze flashes to Cohen every few seconds, and even though I've tried to stop it, no one is as intriguing as him.

He's in his zone.

Jealousy wraps around my heart anytime a woman talks to him.

Maybe this is what hurt Heather, what ruined their relationship—Cohen working in bars. She hated his job, and if there's anything I can understand about Heather, it's that. Seeing girls flirt with him sends a wave of insecurity through me as I compare myself to each one of them.

Heather did attempt to work at a bar with him but couldn't handle it. She got into a fistfight with another waitress. My sister isn't a fan of working, and I blame my parents for that. While I focused on studying, Heather focused on partying and Cohen. When she wasn't with Cohen, who worked, she was with her friends, talking about him.

There was a time my sister was obsessed with the gorgeous man behind the bar.

A time he was obsessed with her.

A time I had the biggest crush on him.

I know the moment Georgia tells Cohen I'm here when they turn in my direction. When his eyes hit mine, I glance away, acting as if he hasn't been my main focus of entertainment. I rest my hands in my lap, innocently looking around the place in an attempt not to appear to be the stalker that I apparently am.

After my third Georgia—two of them I hadn't ordered, but Georgia kept dropping them in front of me—I'm in need of a restroom break. I scope out the sign on the wall signaling toward them and head in that direction. Since there's only one way, no matter what I do, unless I climb the walls, I have to pass Cohen.

"Jamie," Cohen calls out, waving me over to the bar.

I halt, not wanting to be rude, and walk toward him. I force my best shocked expression while timidly waving at him. "Oh, hey."

An awkward silence passes between us.

We've briefly spoken since the barbeque, and hell, even that wasn't much of a conversation.

He gestures to the bottles of liquor lining the shelves behind him. "What can I get you?"

I play with my hands in front of me, a slight buzz zipping through my blood. "Your sister has already loaded me up on Georgias."

"Oh hell, be careful. Those babies will sneak up on you."

I nod in agreement. "Pretty sure I tasted the alcohol bleeding through my veins with every sip."

"Cohen!" a waitress yells, stalking our way. "I need your help."

"Archer or Georgia will take care of anything you need." He shoots me a sympathetic smile before walking around the bar and following the waitress.

Perfect timing.

No weird convos with him.

Just my luck.

I don't bother asking Archer for anything, but I pay a glance at him before continuing my journey to the restroom. That's when I see Carrie flirting with him.

So much for her looking for fresh meat.

Georgia leans over the bar, snags a piece of ice, and throws it at them. It hits Archer's cheek, and he whips around, glaring at her.

Whoa.

We're all definitely missing something there.

I need to ask Georgia what's up with her and Archer.

"I'm waiting on drinks, asshole!" Georgia shouts.

"Make them. You know how," he says dismissively.

Her hands park on her waist. "I thought you didn't want me behind the bar?"

Archer ignores her.

"All right then." She throws her pen down, jumps over the bar, and starts grabbing an alcohol bottle.

He swings around and storms toward Georgia before attempting to pull the bottle from her hand. "Chill out."

She jerks away from him. "Screw you."

I'm probably the only one paying enough attention to notice her voice breaking in the end and the defeat on her face.

Archer tips his head down and whispers in her ear, but no anger leaves her face. It only mixes with hurt, and she slams the bottle onto the bar before walking away from him. Archer's head hangs low for a moment before he gains control of himself. Carrie perks up but then frowns when he walks to the other side of the bar and yells for Silas to switch sides with him.

Maybe I should come here more.

This shit is better than Netflix.

I scurry to the restroom, check my appearance, noticing the flush in my cheeks, and on my way back to our table, a man steps in front of me.

"Hey, baby," he slurs, his breath smelling like stale beer and chicken wings. "Can I buy you a drink?"

I bite into my lip, reading his shirt, and cringe.

It says *Orgasm Donor*.

His black hair is gelled back, and *too much* is happening with his cologne.

"No, thank you," I say as politely as I can.

His shoulders square up. "Why?"

"I have a full drink at my table."

He leans in closer, causing me to stumble back and smack into someone. She gives me a dirty look and shrugs away from me.

"How about I join you?"

"Table is full, too, actually." My throat constricts, the bar swallowing me up and feeling ten times smaller than it did minutes ago.

When I move to step around him, he blocks me.

"I've been watching you all night. There's plenty of room for me to slide in and get to know you, darling."

I clench my fists, my nails biting into my palms. "I have a boyfriend."

He makes a show of eyeing the bar. "I don't see a boyfriend here."

Jesus Christ, dude, take a freaking hint.

Fed up, I decide to take the blunt route.

"Look, I'm not interested."

His stare turns icy. "Why the fuck not?"

I tense when an arm wraps around my waist, but as soon as I hear his voice, I settle against him.

"Hey, baby," he says loudly, nearly in jackass's face.

"Cohen," the man stutters, his gaze shooting back and forth between Cohen and me. "You're her boyfriend?"

Cohen drags me in closer to him, my backside hitting his thigh. "Yes, so leave her the fuck alone. Don't even look at her."

"Shit, sorry, man. No disrespect."

"You need to apologize to her, not me."

"Sorry," the guy says, wide-eyed, before scurrying away from us.

Cohen's arm doesn't drop from my waist when I turn to face him.

"Thank you," I whisper.

He gives my hip a gentle squeeze. "I got you."

When I turn around and head back to the table, I'm shocked that he stays behind me.

"I'm on break," he explains, taking Ashley's abandoned stool.

Her boyfriend showed up, and they've practically been sucking face all night.

"Are you having a good time?" Cohen asks, shifting to face me.

I nod. "It's been forever since I've gone out."

"And you decided to come here? I'm honored." He places his hand over his heart and bows his head.

I sweep my hand toward Kelsey, who's standing between her boyfriend's legs as they whisper sweet nothings to each other. "It's her birthday."

"Ah, so you didn't come here for me?"

I laugh. "She's my cover. I'm actually here because I'm obsessed with you. I've been peeking through your windows at night, but I'm taking my stalker-ship to the next level and creeping on you at work."

"Finally! The truth comes out." He rests his elbow on the table, placing his chin on his knuckles, and looks pleased as he stares at me. "Have you been here before?"

I shake my head. "Twisted Fox virgin over here."

"I'm happy I was here when you popped that cherry, but I am disappointed you haven't been here before."

"I didn't want it to look too weird, me showing up here after finding out you owned it."

"It wouldn't have been weird." He chews on his lower lip, and his gaze clings to mine. "I owe you an apology for what happened with Becca."

"What do you mean?" I reach across the table, steal Ashley's half-full Georgia, and suck it down. "I have no idea what you're talking about."

He lifts his head to level his eyes on me. "Don't bullshit me."

"There's honestly no need to apologize."

"I also want to apologize for whatever drunken shit I said the night I called when you had Noah."

I glance around the table in search of another drink to swipe. All the glasses are empty around me, leaving me with nothing to chug down to give me the liquid courage I suddenly need.

"Now, I *really* have no idea what you're talking about," I finally say, my eyes darting to the table next to us.

He chuckles. "I saw in my call log that I called you that night and *vaguely* remember what was said."

"New subject." I hold up my empty glass. "This was so good! I'm going to need another if you want to talk about awkward conversations that will only make this conversation as awkward as they were."

"You sure you don't want to talk about it?"

"I'm absolutely positive I would rather talk about anything else in the world but that."

"Amuse me." He leans back and crosses his arms. "Tell me how big of an idiot I made of myself."

"You didn't make an idiot of yourself."

"Does that mean I made myself sound cool?"

I slap his shoulder. "You definitely sound like a dad. *Made myself sound cool?* I can't believe I used to crush on you."

He cracks a smile. "You're not giving me much to work with here, babe."

Babe.

He called me babe.

Good thing there's a dim light in the bar, or he might notice the heat creeping up my cheeks.

"It was an"—I search for the right word—"entertaining conversation."

You asked why you couldn't have chosen the other sister.

There's no way I'm going the honesty route.

"You admitted to loving Hawaiian pizza," I say, a smile playing at my lips.

"I call bullshit on that." He smirks.

"I am going to kill your bartender," Georgia snaps, storming toward our table. "Like, legit kill him—or at least slice and dice his balls."

Saved by the little sister.

She halts when her eyes focus on us—our bodies facing each other, close enough that our shoulders slightly brush when we move, and we're in our own little world, half-whispering in the corner.

"I'm definitely interrupting something. You two get back to … whatever." She stops to snap her fingers. "And tomorrow, you can bail me out of jail for coworker homicide." She whips around and stomps away.

"Heather did always call Georgia a cockblocker," Cohen says with a shake of his head.

"Ah, I bet." I heard her complain about how much time Cohen spent taking care of Georgia all the time.

"Georgia didn't like Heather."

"Not too many people do around here."

"Georgia likes you, though."

"She hardly knows me."

He fixes his stare on me. "Georgia reads people well, and with that, she's guarded with who she lets in. Sure, she was concerned the first time you came over, but after that, she's had nothing but good things to say about you. According to her, she likes *your vibe.*"

Georgia saying she likes *my vibe* doesn't surprise me.

She talks and dresses like a nineties hippie.

"Too bad it took you so long to like *my vibe.*" I cringe after the words leave my lips. "That was so lame. I did not mean for it to come out that way." I point at the empty glass. "Blame it on the Georgias."

"It wasn't *your vibe* I didn't like. It was concern." He rubs the back of his neck, a hint of defensiveness in his tone. "Your sister, she fucked me up, and I saw her as the root of your family. The further away from her life, the better." His hand brushes mine. "No offense."

"None taken," I squeak out. "I understand."

"That's why you were always my favorite."

"Oh, cut the shit." My eyes harden as a spike of jealousy darts through me, and there's no stopping the change in my tone. Maybe it's the liquor or him saying *favorite* or that I want to return to the friendly, flirty conversation we were having before this. "I wasn't your favorite when you were screwing my sister. *She* was."

He dips his head down, his peppermint breath hitting my cheek at the same time his lips brush against my ear. "Did I love your sister, Jamie?" He pulls back, not fazed that he's nearly giving me a heart attack with his lips, his proximity, this conversation. "Absolutely. We had our issues, and at times, I knew she wasn't the best person. What I also knew was, she was by my side through everything when I was growing up. My mom issues, my fucked-up family life, all of it."

I set my attention on the straw in the empty cup and play with it. "She was."

Heather was once a decent person who was head over heels in love with Cohen.

I stay quiet, unsure of how to reply.

"What about you?" he asks. "I remember you had a terrible date and had a thing with Sprinkles boy, but anyone else in the picture?"

"Nope," I quip, biting into the straw.

"Really? Come on."

"My job is my orgasm." *Oh God, my response is too similar to Orgasm Donor dude's shirt.* I shudder.

"Kinky." He grins. "Mine too."

I hold up my hand. "Can we stop talking about orgasms? I have a big mouth when I drink, and I tend to make an idiot out of myself." I throw my head back and laugh. "At least I'm not trying to make out with you this time."

"Unfortunately."

"Please, you were a terrible kisser."

He chuckles. "I like Tipsy Jamie."

That only makes one of us.

"Tipsy Jamie makes a fool of herself."

"Tipsy Jamie is more open."

I cross my legs. "Drunk Cohen is also more open when he calls me."

He clicks his tongue and points to me. "Tipsy Jamie won't tell me what Drunk Cohen said."

"Tipsy Jamie is officially going to stop referring to herself in the third person. Drunk Cohen should follow her lead."

"All right, you crazy kids," Ashley says, hopping off her stool and pulling the bottom of her dress down as Jared stands behind her. "Time for me to go." Her attention whips to me, a smirk playing at her lips. "Are you going to hang out here and call an Uber later, or do you want a ride home?"

I peek a glance at Cohen, whose eyes are crestfallen while he waits for me to answer her. He doesn't want this night to end as much as I don't.

"I'll call an Uber," leaves my mouth at the same time, "I can give you a ride home," comes from Cohen.

Ashley grins. "You heard the man." She kisses my cheek. "Smoothies tomorrow, okay?"

"If you aren't hungover."

She laughs and uses the same tone as she did before. "Hungover smoothies tomorrow, okay?"

I point at the bar after she scurries away, my attention on Cohen. "Do you need to get back to work?"

He shakes his head. "I'm off for the rest of the night. I was about to head out, but then I saw you and thought I'd stop and chat."

"You're not on break?"

"It was an excuse to sit down and talk to you since you'd been avoiding me."

"As I've said many a time, I was not avoiding you."

"You bought Noah an iPod."

I throw my arms up. "What kid doesn't want an iPod?"

"You bought it to *avoid* calling me."

"I didn't want what had happened with Blondie to happen again. It wouldn't look good if one of your girls caught me calling."

His face contorts in disgust. "Whoa, Becca is not my girl."

I flick my hand through the air. "You know what I mean."

His voice turns serious. "I forgot my phone on the table while hanging out with her and some friends. I hadn't wanted to go out with her, but Silas begged me."

I can't stop myself from snorting. "I'm so sure he had to beg you to go out with a hot girl."

"I have nothing to hide. She shouldn't have answered my phone, and for that, I'm sorry." He bumps his shoulder against mine. "You can start calling us again whenever."

"I actually FaceTimed Noah earlier." After getting the heads-up from Georgia that Cohen was at work.

He frowns. "Don't you miss seeing this face too?"

I pout out my lower lip. "Are you feeling left out, Mr. Fox?"

"A little bit, yes. Here I thought, I was a good time."

"I'll think about calling your phone next time."

"Oh, you'll *think* about it? That's so kind of you."

I playfully flip my hair over my shoulder. "I'm super nice."

"And gorgeous."

I wince, and he catches me before I stumble off the stool.

My response comes out in a stutter, "What?"

How dare he pull that out on me.

When I'm sitting on a stool and tipsy nonetheless.

He draws in a long breath before scrubbing a hand over his face. "Shit, sorry."

"Uh …" I do another once-over, searching for a drink, wishing Georgia would randomly drop one in front of me like she has been doing all night.

Of course she stops now.

"Not sorry that I said that because you do look amazing. I'm sorry I shocked the shit out of you." His hand cups his chin before he caresses it, staring at me, waiting for my response.

"Thank you," is all I can muster out.

It's not that I don't believe Cohen, that I doubt he's attracted to me. It's that I hate that he is. I hate that I'm attracted to him.

It'd make our relationship much easier if he weren't.

Cohen's phone ringing interrupts this super-awkward, weird talk.

He fishes his phone from his pocket, and a smile fills his face when he shows me the screen. "It's Noah." He answers the call, moving the screen back to face him, "Hey, buddy!"

"Hi, Dad," Noah replies on FaceTime.

Cohen's stool squeaks as he drags himself closer to me. "Look who's here with me." He tilts the screen, so we're both in front of it.

Noah's face is so close to the camera that I can see up his nostrils, and a few seconds later, he drags it away, his eyes wide.

"Hi, Jamie!" He looks back and forth between Cohen and me in suspicion. "Where are you guys? On a date?"

"We're just hanging out," Cohen answers while I chew on my cheek uneasily. "I'm about to come home, okay? I'll be there before bedtime to tuck you in."

"Is Jamie coming over too?"

Cohen shakes his head, and apparently, I no longer know how to speak. "No, Jamie is going home to her house."

"Ah, man," he groans. "I think she should come over too."

Cohen's voice lowers. "Maybe another time."

"All right." He grins. "Will you ask her what I asked you to?" Noah looks all secretive while Cohen looks nervous.

"I'll ask her tonight," Cohen says with a head nod.

"I'll see you when you get home." He waves at us. "Bye, Jamie!"

I return the wave and find my voice. "Good night, honey."

Cohen hangs up, and I grab my purse from the back of the stool.

"Looks like it's our curfew," I say, laughing as I stand.

"The kid does make the rules." He taps his knuckles against the table. "Let me tell Archer and Georgia I'm heading out. Be right back."

I play with the strap of my bag. "Are you sure you don't want me to take an Uber?"

"You're not getting an Uber." His tone is flat, and he walks away.

I grab my phone when it beeps with a text.

Ashley: OMG! I'm obsessed with you two being all snuggly in the corner.

Me: Stop.

Ashley: It was cute!

"You ready?" Cohen asks, returning a few minutes later.

I slide my phone into my bag. "Whenever you are."

CHAPTER TWENTY

Cohen

JAMIE LOOKS GORGEOUS.

Breathtaking.

As soon as she walked in, she had my full attention. I did my best to hold back from staring at her the entire night and *finally* acted like I noticed her when Georgia pointed at her table, telling me my future girlfriend was there.

I didn't plan to venture to her table before leaving, but when I saw that jackass hitting on her, there was no stopping me.

My hand rests on the arch of her back as I lead her through the bar to the employee entrance. She's quiet as we make our way toward the Jeep, and I open the door for her before slipping into the driver's side.

She tucks her bag into her lap. "Thank you for the ride home."

"I got you," I answer, looking over at her before reversing out of my spot. "Anytime, and come back to the bar *anytime*."

"I'll remember that."

I drum my fingers against the steering wheel. "Are you busy next weekend?"

"Not that I'm aware of."

"It's Noah's birthday."

"Oh, yes. He's told me all the things he wants."

"That's my son." I hesitate, the question I'm supposed to ask Jamie at the tip of my tongue. *Is this a bad idea?* "We're going to Ski North. It's a few hours from here."

"Ah, Ski North. The place where they have fake snow and forced us to go on field trips."

"He asked me to invite you."

There. I did it.

What Noah had asked.

Granted, it'll be more difficult than just asking.

She's quiet for a moment. "I mean, sure. That'd be fun."

Here comes the problem.

"I checked the cabin availability since we made reservations already, and unfortunately, there isn't anything open."

She frowns, and when we stop at a stoplight, there's a *why are you telling me this then* expression on her face. "Oh."

"We have a two-bedroom. If you're up for it, you can stay with us. I'll crash on the couch, and you can have my bedroom."

"No, I don't want you to do that."

"I thought you knew I'm a fucking gentleman. Come on. Noah wants you to come, and it's his birthday. Georgia and her friends will be there too."

Does it sound like I'm begging too much?

"Let me check that I won't be on call."

"And if you aren't, you're game?"

"I'm game."

I grin.

"I do want to make it clear that I am *not* skiing or doing anything of any physical sort. My workouts are yoga, work, and Pilates. Not extreme sports."

"Skiing isn't an extreme sport."

"It is in my book. You can break your bones."

"You won't have to ski. You can watch us."

I pull up in front of her townhouse and put the Jeep in park.

She unbuckles her seat belt. "Thank you for the ride."

"Thank you for the company tonight."

She lets out a long breath. "Can I tell you something?"

"Shoot."

"The night you called me drunk, you asked why you couldn't have chosen the other sister."

My eyes widen as I stare at her underneath the streetlight.

Shit. That's what I remember saying, but I didn't want to bring it up in case I'd imagined it.

That thought has hit me too many times, and I wasn't sure if it'd left my mouth.

"That doesn't surprise me," I say, my mouth turning dry. "I was drunk, and my drunk ass likes to be honest."

"You can't." She frantically shakes her head. "You can't say things like that, Cohen."

"I can't be honest?"

There's sadness in her eyes. "Because you did choose her."

"It was a lot more complicated than that. You were so much younger than I was, and I met you while I was *dating her.*"

"I also wasn't pretty then."

"Excuse me?"

"Not tooting my own horn here, but I'm not the geeky kid I used to be."

"Are you shitting me? Why do you keep thinking you were geeky? Because you were smart?" I snort before releasing a harsh breath. *Will she quit with the* I'm not good enough *attitude?* "You had goals, which I love about you." Another harsh breath leaves me. "My feelings, our situation, are complex. It crosses lines even though we technically haven't *crossed any lines.* I'm trying my hardest not to ruin this ... to ruin your relationship with my son because of our ... feelings."

"So am I."

"We're teetering very close to that line."

"What are you saying? Where are you going with this?" She laughs, and there's an edge in her voice. "Forget it. I should've never brought it up. Stupid Georgia drinks. Tell her I'm never drinking those things again."

I turn, facing her, and move a strand of hair away from her face.

She shuts her eyes. "Can we act like I never brought it up?"

Hell no.

We shouldn't throw it under the bus, but I don't know what else to do.

"Sure," I say, "we can."

I never knew I was such a good liar.

CHAPTER TWENTY-ONE

Jamie

I ZIP MY SUITCASE SHUT.

Cohen offered for me to ride with him and Noah.

Since I didn't want to drive by myself, I took it.

Here we go again.

Crossing another line.

Cohen said he'd take the couch, so it's not like we're sharing a bed.

Ski North is a ski resort a few hours away from town that offers skiing, tubing, and other activities I know nothing about. They're open year-round, and they use artificial snow when there isn't any. I'm not an outdoorsy person, and when we traveled here for school field trips, I would hang out in the ski lodge—which will also happen on this trip.

Noah rambles nonstop the first two hours of the ride, telling us how excited he is to play in the snow.

Eventually, exhausted from his excitement, he passes out.

"I love my son to death," Cohen says, stealing a glance at Noah, "but damn, silence can be a great thing sometimes."

"Silence can be boring," I reply.

"That why you work in the ER? You like chaos all the time?"

I shrug. "I like staying busy. It keeps me out of my head."

"Same, but it's so much better when it's quiet, so your head can rest a moment." He clicks his tongue against the roof of his mouth. "You like chaos. What else is different about Jamie Gentry now?"

"I thought you liked silence? Let's try that the rest of the ride."

He laughs. "Consider this our road game. We can make it chaotic if you want?"

I shift in my seat to glare at him.

"All right, you dated the Sprinkles heir—"

"Stop calling him that," I cut in, playfully shoving him.

"Have you dated anyone else? Doughnut Doug's son?"

"I am so strangling you in your sleep tonight."

"Don't make me scared to sleep on the couch." He peeks back at Noah. "We have an hour. You entertain me. I'll entertain you."

"That sounds way more suggestive than it should."

He lifts his chin. "Okay, Dr. Mind in the Gutter."

I decide to give in. If he asks questions, then I get to ask questions. Although I'm not sure if I want to know anything pertaining to his dating life. Maybe I'll get deeper, ask him his darkest secrets, what he thinks about when he jacks off at night, stuff that will make him squirm, as he enjoys doing to me.

"Fine, I've dated some, but it was hard in med school. I thought I'd make up for it after graduating, but dating seems to be at the bottom of my to-do list." I jokingly punch his arm and decide against asking him make-him-squirm questions. It'd open a door, but he'd do the same—or worse. "What about you?"

"I've dated some, not much." There's no squirming on his part.

I suck.

"Dated women who like answering your phone." As much as I hate talking about the call, I'm also mean, as I love hearing him say she means nothing to him.

"I have not dated, am not dating, nor will I ever date Becca," he grinds out, the subject irritating him.

"She sure made it seem like you were."

"She was jealous."

"Jealous?" I poke my chest and squint at him. "Jealous of what?"

"Of the gorgeous woman who called my phone."

His answer should make me smile, giddy, but it does the opposite.

"Don't say that," I mutter.

"What?"

"A gorgeous woman?" I roll my eyes, possibly seeming bitchy, but from what I've witnessed, Cohen has his fair share of *gorgeous* women who don't sport scrubs and Cheeto cheese on their lips instead of pink lipstick.

"I'm confused about how Becca looked makes you any less gorgeous."

I snort.

"Wait." He lowers his voice. "Do you seriously not believe I'm attracted to you?"

Just as I'm about to answer—well, just as I'm *thinking* of an answer—Noah saves me.

"I have to potty," he whines. "Really, really bad."

Cohen sends me one last puzzled look. "Looks like a pit stop is in order."

————

"NOPE, NOT HAPPENING," I say. "Over my dead body, which will happen. My body will be dead if I do this."

As soon as we arrived at Ski North, nobody wanted to go along with my brilliant plan of getting *settled* before hitting the slopes—or not hitting the slopes and grabbing some hot chocolate from the ski lodge.

Everyone *but* me wanted to be outdoorsy.

Ew.

We loaded our bags into the cabin, and we're now in the store thingy place where you rent shit to go down hills and break limbs.

"I promise, it's super easy," Grace says, patting my shoulder.

"Yeah, kids do it all the time," Georgia pipes in.

"It'll be fun," Cohen says, joining the peer-pressure party.

"Breaking bones is not fun," I grumble.

He chuckles. "You won't break any bones."

"I told you that I don't do extreme sports. I do yoga. It's safe and calming. Snow and velocity are not calming."

He gestures to Noah and then Grace's niece, Raven, suiting up. "The *kids* are doing it."

"*All the kids are doing it*," I mock. "You're like the cute kid in class, asking me to do PCP."

He leans in, his lips going to my ear, and he's chuckling again through his words. "And you said I'm dramatic as fuck."

I groan when he pulls away. "Being a doctor has taught me to take extra precautions. I've witnessed too many accidents from people with better coordination than me, a girl who never picked up the skill of jumping rope."

Cohen holds out his hand. "I'll bet you fifty bucks you won't fall— or at least, you won't break something."

"Why would you make that bet? I can easily fall right now and win that fifty."

"Because I know you won't, and you like to play fair."

I frown. "Fifty bucks isn't worth a broken bone."

He throws his head back. "We'll put you on the beginner hill with the kids."

"No thanks on seeing elementary students ski better than me." I glance around. "Maybe I'll try the snow-tubing thing. The chances of me not smacking into a tree in a tube might be better odds."

"Actually, it's not."

I groan.

"What if I hold your hand?"

"That sounds more dangerous."

"Come on, Jamie!" Noah says.

"You got this!" Georgia adds.

I feel like such a fun-sucking loser.

"All right"—I throw my arms out and then allow them to slump to my sides—"I'll do it."

———

"I TOLD you it was a bad idea," I grumble, shooting Cohen a death glare.

I should've never gone down that hill—beginner or not.

Just like I said, skiing is not a good time. You slide down a snowy hill with no helmet—or if you're like me, you *tumble* down a snowy hill with no helmet. I'm not sure what went wrong, but I lost my footing and tripped.

It went downhill from there—literally.

"Wrong. You said you'd break something," Cohen argues, handing me a Ziploc bag filled with ice and wrapped in a paper towel. "All your bones are in place."

"But my ankle is as swollen as the tree I hit."

Not swollen or painful enough to go to the hospital.

It just sucks.

Not to mention, it was embarrassing.

More humiliating than me trying to drunkenly make out with Cohen forever ago.

Kids—yes, kids—were staring at me, a few of them stopping gracefully on their skis to help me after my fall. I was tempted to go home, but Noah came running over to me, giving me a big hug, so I decided to stay.

"The swelling will go down," he says. "We'll try again tomorrow. I wonder if they make ski training wheels."

I roll my eyes and place the ice on my ankle. "You're smoking crack if you think I'm hanging out on Murder Hill again."

"What will you do then? Become a snow-lodge bunny?"

"Damn straight."

We're in the cabin, and thankfully, I dropped my bag into the bedroom upstairs before my accident. It's a decent-sized cabin with a large kitchen and a living room, and it's decorated how you'd expect a ski cabin to be—an antler chandelier, pillows, blankets, beds, curtains with bears on them, and a comfy plaid couch.

He jerks his head toward the staircase. "Do you need a piggyback ride to your room?"

I shoot him a dirty look.

He turns around and bends down, showing me his back. "Come on. Hop on."

Noah is sleeping. He exhausted themselves skiing today. Tomorrow, they're going out again

"Ugh, fine." I slide the ice bag into the pocket of my pants, and he assists me onto his back.

"Piggyback might not be the best idea." He snaps his fingers before placing me back to my feet. "Stand."

"What?" I stare at him, unblinking.

He waits for me to do as he said.

I sit, clasp my hand around his shoulder, and lift myself, using his body as leverage. As soon as my feet graze the floor, he picks me up in his arms, wedding-style, and I gasp.

"This is going to be much easier."

I clasp my arms around his neck, tucking myself into his body, and the aroma of his aftershave relaxes me. I love it. It's masculine with a hint of menthol and officially my favorite smell. I'd love to wake up with my sheets smelling like him.

Just as soon as it seems he's lifted me into his arms, he's up the stairs and carefully depositing me on the bed.

"I'll be in the living room if you need me," he says, walking backward and stopping in the doorway. "Yell before your uncoordinated ass comes down in the morning. I can't have you falling down the stairs." He taps his knuckles against the door. "Open or shut?"

"Shut, please," I croak out.

"Good night, Jamie."

I love the way he says that to me.

There's always a burn of gentleness in his tone.

"Good night, Cohen." I shut my eyes, inhaling a deep breath, and just as I'm opening them, he's closing the door.

After my skiing tragedy, I asked Georgia to grab my pajamas and toothbrush from my suitcase. We went into the restroom, where she helped me change, rolling the bottom of my flannel pants up to give my ankle room to be its new swollen self, and I brushed my teeth.

I fluff my pillow a few times before snuggling into bed, whiffing

Cohen's aftershave that somehow rubbed onto my skin while wishing he were lying next to me.

————

I SET my iPad to the side when Cohen sits next to me on the couch in the ski lodge.

I've been hanging out here all day in my snow-bunny outfit to match the feel of the place. If I'm not skiing, I might as well look cute in my chunky white sweater and black velvet leggings.

I brought snow boots, too, but swollen ankle.

We had a birthday lunch for Noah, and then everyone, except me, went skiing.

"What are you doing?" I ask.

Just as I came prepared to look hot on this trip, Cohen did too. Although I'm not sure if that was his reasoning behind his puffy black vest bunched over a gray sweatshirt.

"Figured you could use the company." He hands me a mug. "Hot chocolate?"

I take a sip before pushing my arm out, holding the mug away from me and scrunching up my face. "Jesus." My voice lowers. "Did you spike the hot chocolate?"

A sly smile passes over his lips. "I might have added a few drops of Fireball in there."

"This'd better not be an attempt to get me drunk and back on that hill."

"Negative. You can't even ski sober, let alone drunk."

"Rude."

I wrap both hands around the mug and take a slow sip. Good thing my grasp is tight because my body goes into freak-out mode when he sets his mug down and grabs my foot to examine my ankle.

"The swelling has gone down."

I stare down at it. "Thank God."

I shiver, my blood tingling, when he starts massaging my ankle, his abrasive fingers gently stroking my skin.

"At least you can say you've skied before."

It takes me a minute to gain control of my voice, and his touch is soothing, relaxing my body. "I'm never telling anyone about that ski nightmare."

"Jamie has never skied—got it."

"You don't have to hang out with me," I say. "You can hang out with Noah."

"I got ditched for a hot tub and air hockey at the girls' cabin. Noah is loving hanging out with Grace's niece." He rests my ankle in his lap, his hand not leaving it, and relaxes. "Thank you for coming."

"Thank you for inviting me."

"And I'm sorry you got hurt."

I laugh. "I'm blaming you for that one, Mr. You Won't Get Hurt. Next time, we're doing something safer that doesn't involve coordination."

He gestures to my ankle. "You want to head back to the cabin and put some more ice on this?"

I nod, biting into my lip.

Thankfully, I packed a pair of Birkenstocks and have been wearing them since last night. He grabs them from the floor and slips one onto my hurt foot, and I slide my other foot into the shoe after he helps me up.

Our arms are looped together so he can help stabilize me while we walk to the cabin. He settles me onto the couch when we make it inside, lifts my body so I'm lying down across it, and asks if I need anything.

I shake my head. "Look at you. You'd make a pretty good doctor yourself."

He straightens his vest collar. "Yeah, I know."

I roll my eyes. "Dr. Cocky."

I chew on my nails when he lifts my feet, plops down on the couch, and situates my foot onto his lap just as he did in the lodge.

This feels so personal, especially since we're alone. The only other times we've not had Noah around are the night at the bar and when he took me home.

When he turns on the TV, it's on a channel with an image of a burning fireplace.

A cheaper way to give it that cozy, warm cabin feeling.

He holds up the remote. "Anything you prefer to watch?"

I gesture to the TV. "This is my favorite show, actually."

"Finally, I meet someone who shares the same taste as I do." He releases a heavy breath. "If you ask me, I'd say this fireplace channel gives this place a romantic feel."

I stiffen against the couch, hoping he doesn't notice how tense my leg is, and snort. "Romance is the last type of *feel* we need at the moment."

His fingers move up my ankle, casually making small circles along my skin. "Good point."

My heart rages against my chest as the air in the room grows thinner, and though the fireplace isn't real, it suddenly seems warmer. My mouth opens and then shuts as a somber silence happens.

"Fuck it," he grumbles, shifting to face me. "Jamie, what the hell are we doing?"

The question sends a throb through my head ... and my heart. It's not a simple *what are we doing* question.

The answer isn't a simple, *Why, Cohen, we're sitting on the couch in front of a faux fireplace.*

Nor is it, *We're waiting for Noah to return, so we can act like we were never alone together.*

The answer he's looking for, the one I'm so terrified of giving, is something along the lines of, *I have no idea, but the way my heart grows wild when you're around or as you touch just my feet, I want more. We both want more, but we have to stop it. Shut it the hell down.*

It's a disaster waiting to happen.

A disaster, from the heated look and the need in his eyes, that will happen.

Unless I pull away.

Unless one of us comes to our senses.

And as much as I crave his touch, I'm terrified.

Fucking terrified.

Do I need to stay away from Cohen to stay away from heartbreak?

If something happens with Cohen, it's not only our hearts that would be shredded.

It'd also gash so many others'—Noah's and my parents'. They'd never look at me the same.

"Quit overthinking it," Cohen grinds out. "Tell me what you want."

His eyes are on mine as if he's begging for an answer, a confirmation that what's riding through him is also riding through me.

He grumbles, "Fuck it again," and my breath hitches when he moves.

I shut my eyes, expecting him to drop my foot and leave. They fly open when I feel a weight over my body. Cohen has one hand resting on the back of the couch while the other moves to cup my face as he settles above me.

His eyes meet mine.

No bullshitting him allowed.

This is when I turn stupid.

When I decide not to answer him with words but with my lips.

I wet them before tilting my head forward and brushing them against his.

He hesitates, shocked, but then crashes his onto mine.

Our kiss turns deeper, and I moan when his tongue slides along the crease of my lips. I open, allowing him entry, and he tastes like Fireball and chocolate as our tongues meet.

Cinnamon has never tasted so delicious.

He groans into my mouth, raw and rough, and I part my thighs in invitation, and he slides between them. I groan, soft and shuddering, when he jerks his hips forward, and the buckle of his jeans brushes against my core over my leggings. They're thin, as are my lace panties, and the friction ignites a fire through me.

"Oh my God," I whimper, bucking my hips, silently begging for more.

What he gives is better.

My pulse races when he pulls away, our breathing ragged, and his gaze captures mine while he levels himself on his knees before unzipping his vest.

It's not the hot chocolate intoxicating me.

It's him.

The vest drops off his shoulders and lands on the floor. I bend forward to drag off his sweatshirt next. Waves of lust coil through me as my hand lands on his six-pack and then drifts up his muscular chest. My eyes drop to his waist, eyeing his hard-as-a-rock erection through his pants.

"I want you, Jamie," he says, his voice thick.

Desire runs through my veins as we frantically start moving. It's not easy—with my hurt ankle, the narrow couch, and through the thick layers of clothes.

Damn ski-lodge clothes.

Why do you need to be so layered, heavy, and complicated?

Our breathing is heavy, and when he pulls away, his pants are unbuckled, his shirt is gone, and my bra strap is hanging loose over my shoulder. My tongue darts out, and I lick my lips again while waiting for his next move. His strong hand slides up my leg, between my thighs, and he cups me through my leggings. Skillfully, he rubs the base of his thumb against my clit. I gyrate my hips, grinding against his touch, and frown when he stops. That frown turns upside down when he moves his hand and shoves it inside my leggings.

"Open wider for me, baby," he groans. "Give me more room to play with you."

I do as I was told, my body shaking, and one of my legs falls off the couch. He draws back as he starts jerking my leggings and panties down my body, careful of my ankle, and tosses them onto the floor.

My heart rate skyrockets at the realization that I'm bare in front of Cohen—in only a bra, no panties—and he sweeps his gaze up and down my body, drinking me in.

"I'll keep saying it until you believe me," he whispers. "You're goddamn beautiful." He slides a single finger along my slit, skimming it up and down. "You're soaked for me."

Back and forth, he moves.

Like a torturous asshole.

A gorgeous, torturous asshole.

"Cohen," I hiss, "I need more."

My back arches, coming off the couch, when he shoves two thick fingers inside me. I squeal, squirming underneath him, while he strokes me, his eyes on his fingers.

"Take off your pants," I croak, meeting his thrusts. "Fuck me, Cohen."

His gaze flicks up to meet mine. "You want me to fuck you, Jamie?"

Just as soon as the words leave his mouth, Noah's voice screams through the cabin, "Dad! I want a hot tub for my birthday!"

Cohen's fingers are out of me in seconds, and he jumps off the couch, scrambling for our clothes. I sit there, my hand on my chest, and my head is spinning. He slings my leggings to me, and there's no way I'm getting them on.

"The blanket," I yelp, pointing at a throw on a chair.

He tosses it along with my sweater to me at the same time he slips his shirt over his head.

Noah comes crashing into the room. "I want a hot tub for my birthday!"

Even though we're covered and most likely in the clear, my heart hasn't calmed. Cohen slides a hand down his shirt, smoothing it out, as I tighten the blanket around my waist.

How am I going to get these leggings back on without Noah seeing?

As if he can read my mind, Cohen tells Noah it's time to brush his teeth.

My ankle throbs when I stand, and while keeping the blanket tight around me, I dash up the stairs, ignoring my ankle pain.

Cohen peeks his head into the doorway of my bedroom at the same time I pull my sweats up my waist, his eyes refusing to meet mine. "Can you watch him for a minute?"

"Yeah." I rub my arms. "Sure."

He nods in thanks, and I see his back as he rushes out of the cabin.

CHAPTER TWENTY-TWO

Cohen

WHAT THE FUCK *was I thinking?*

I scrub a hand over my face and instantly regret it when the scent of Jamie hits my nostrils.

The scent of her pussy.

My fingers were inside her.

She was wet for me, and hell, I wanted to fuck her more than I'd wanted anything.

I storm toward the bar in the ski lodge. As I trek in, I see Archer sitting alone at the bar.

As much as I love my friends and that they came along with me, I'm happy no one else is here.

Archer glances at me, raising his brow when I slump down on the chair next to him. "Damn, dude, you definitely look like you need a drink. A motherfucking strong one."

Stupidly, I rub my hand over my face again. I slide Archer's glass over, grab the napkin that was underneath it, and wipe my hands. "I need a few of them."

He signals to the bartender and orders us a round of Jack and Cokes before giving me his full attention. "What happened? You and Jamie finally fuck?"

I flinch. *Am I that easy to read?*

"Is that a yes?"

I don't answer him.

I need the booze before I can give him story time.

The bartender drops my drink in front of me, and I mutter a quick, "Thanks."

"How was it?" Archer pushes.

"We didn't fuck."

"Something happened, though." It's not a question. It's a statement. "How was it?"

"Fucking wrong. That's what it was."

"Wrong because there was no connection or wrong because of who she is to you?"

I knock back my drink in seconds, slam the glass onto the bar like the assholes do at my bar—the ones I want to kick out—and order another.

"Wrong because of who she is to you, I take it."

"She's my son's aunt. Hell, he doesn't even know she's his aunt. She's my ex's sister. Her family attempted to take my son away from me, and now, I'm fucked. If Noah loses her, it'll break his goddamn heart. All because of my stupidity."

Archer doesn't ask *what* happened.

He isn't like that.

He won't make snide remarks or jokes.

"What are the reasons it could be right between you two?"

"Nothing."

"Yet you still hooked up."

I give him a hard stare.

He shrugs, grabbing his drink and taking a sip. "You're attracted to her. There's something there. Go for it."

"Attraction doesn't always mean it's a good idea."

He tips his glass my way. "True."

His phone rings, and my attention hits it before he has a chance to silence the call.

"Why's my sister calling you?"

He shoves the phone into his pocket. "Who knows? Probably to yell at me or ask me about work."

"I didn't know you had each other's numbers."

"We work together." It's his turn to finish his drink off in one swig. "Look, you're my friend. The situation you're in is weird, and I don't blame you for not crossing a line. I can't tell you what to do." He pokes my shoulder. "Only you know how far you want to take it, how much you want her, how fucking broken you'll be if you lose her. Whatever your choice, just remember, it's on you. Either way, I'll support you, but in the end, I hope whatever you choose makes you happy."

His phone rings in his pocket again, and he ignores me, his face stressed.

The bartender serves our next round, and this time, we knock them back at the same time, as if my stress has rubbed off on him.

That, or he was already that way, and like me, that's why he escaped to the bar.

Archer stays at the bar, not looking at his phone, not watching TV, just thinking, when I decide to head back to the cabin.

He mutters a, "Good-bye," along with a, "Good luck."

———

"THE END," I hear as I walk up the stairs.

I peek into the door of Noah's room to find Jamie parked on the edge of the bed with a book in her hand.

Noah's eyes are sleepy and his smile lopsided when he notices me. "Hi, Dad! Jamie read me my bedtime story tonight. She said I should wait for you, but I told her I was tired and that you could do it tomorrow."

Guilt floods me.

I should've been here.

Not drinking away the regret of finger-fucking Jamie.

I nod to the book when Jamie timidly looks back at me. "It's his favorite."

She bows her head, her cheeks blushing. "That's what he said."

"Bedtime," I say as the room grows silent.

Noah nods. "Night, Daddy! Night, Jamie!"

Jamie scrambles off the bed, cringing when her foot with the hurt ankle hits the floor, and pain or not, she manages to get as far away from me as possible. I walk farther into the room to kiss Noah's forehead and tuck him in tight.

We leave the room, and when I shut the door, she presses her back against it, catching her breath.

"Jamie," I whisper, turning to face her.

She shakes her head. "Nope. I'm not having this conversation."

"We need to—"

"My ankle is swollen, and my mind is confused." She looks up at me with fear and confusion swimming in her eyes. "And I need a shot of whatever the hell you were drinking."

I massage the area between my brows with my thumb. "I fucked things up."

She sighs. "It was bound to happen."

I nod in agreement.

"I need to get some sleep."

When she goes to hobble around me, I capture her elbow. "Jamie—"

"What happened, happened. We were drinking spiked hot chocolate. We can blame it on that."

I tip my head down and lower my voice in case Noah turns nosy. "We had, like, two sips."

"Two sips too many, obviously."

"Why can't I get you out of my head?"

Her lip trembles, and she slumps against the wall behind her. "Why can't I get you out of mine?" She rakes her hand through her hair before pulling it. "I wish our situation were different."

I solemnly nod. "Me, too, but do you think it's that wrong?"

"I honestly don't know what to think anymore. When this started, when you walked into that hospital room, my entire world changed. Even when I pleaded to see Noah, I never thought this"—she signals back and forth between us—"would happen. I didn't foresee that storm, and now, I don't know what the fuck to do with it."

"You think I did?" I grind out.

"Neither one of us did." She blows out a tired breath. "This is the wrong time, the wrong place, to have this conversation."

I nod. "Agreed."

I assist her to her bedroom, stopping at her doorway this time—as if we are worried that, if I go any further, we'll end up in her bed.

"Good night, Jamie."

"Night, Cohen."

I trek down the stairs and make my pallet on the couch.

I don't sleep.

All I do is lie there and think.

I'm so fucked.

———

"DON'T FORGET," Noah shouts from the back seat, rocking from side to side. Kid had too much root beer at lunch. "I'm spending the night with Aunt Georgia tonight!"

Every year for his birthday, Georgia and he have a sleepover where she spoils him rotten with sugar and fun before he passes out in exhaustion.

They go to the movies and dinner, and he always looks forward to it.

"I didn't forget, buddy," I reply.

To say this morning was awkward is an understatement. Good thing my child loves to talk because it's what saved me from engaging in too much conversation with Jamie. We woke up, packed our shit, said good-bye to everyone, and left. We stopped for a quick lunch through the drive-through, and I let Noah listen to his Kidz Bop shit, knowing damn well I'd have a headache from it later.

Since Jamie's car is at my house, I go straight to mine.

She doesn't utter a word as I do.

Jamie sits in the living room while I pack Noah's overnight back—vetoing him wearing his swim trunks with cowboy boots and a sweatband around his head.

Where the hell did he even get a sweatband?

When we're done, Georgia and Jamie are in the living room, talking about Georgia's classes. As soon as Georgia and Noah are out the door, I decide to jump right in before either I chicken out or Jamie leaves.

If I hesitate, it might never happen.

The question has been on the tip of my tongue since it slid into her mouth last night.

"Jamie," I say, sprawling out on the couch with my legs spread, "why'd you kiss me?"

She stares at me with reluctance in her eyes. "I wanted to show you my skills have improved since high school." The smirk fighting at her lips tells me she's damn proud of her answer.

Those were probably the words on her mind since we pulled away last night.

"Definitely have improved," I reply, and my dick stirs at the memory of how soft her lips were and how responsive she was to my touch. "Now, tell me the *real* reason you kissed me."

She hesitates, opening her mouth and then closing it before shutting her eyes and blowing out a long breath. "I kissed you because I've never felt this way about anyone, and out of all people, it has to be you."

I spread my palm over my chest. "That sure makes a man feel good."

"You know what I mean," she says with a sigh. "The guy who's definitely, one hundred percent, without a doubt off-limits to me is you—the one I definitely, one hundred percent wish weren't."

"Why am I one hundred percent, all the rest of the shit you said off-limits to you?"

She winces. "You need me to answer that question? I never thought you were one hundred percent clueless."

"There are a million reasons it could be. What's the *main* reason you don't want me to touch you again? You don't want my mouth back on yours?"

Is it because of Noah?

Heather?

Because you think I'll break your heart?

All of the above?

"You chose her." Her response is merely a whisper, and I'm surprised I made out the words.

My chest squeezes tight. "Why do you keep saying that? I didn't choose her over you. You were younger than me—*much* younger—and I met you because I was dating Heather." I throw my arms out. "There was never a lineup, an ultimatum, that said, *Choose Heather or choose Jamie*. At that time, you were my girlfriend's little sister—too young, and no offense, but too immature. And I'm not going to lie to your face; yes, I was in love with another woman. I *believed* I was in love with another woman."

Her face twists in pain.

My heart does the same.

My words have struck a nerve.

Hell, they have with me, and I was the one saying them.

I continue before she smacks me in the face and leaves, "Did my thoughts sometimes change as you got older? Was there ever a doubt in my mind after you shoved me into that bathroom and kissed me? Yes. That night, the urge to pin you against the wall, to teach you how to kiss so I could keep kissing you, burned through me, but I didn't. I couldn't. You weren't mine—"

"And you weren't mine," she shrieks, unshackling the hurt and anger my words created.

"I wasn't yours," I repeat with a bowed head before tilting it up, my eyes set on her, hoping she can read the honesty in them. "I was a different man then. And I'm not spouting this bullshit because Heather is no longer around, and I see you as a second choice." I slap my hand over my heart. "I let you in, Jamie, even when I'd sworn the door would never open again. I did that, not with the intention or the *thought* of the feelings emerging, because you're the kindest fucking soul I know. I opened myself up because you're beautiful, inside and out. I tried to keep my distance by not being around when you saw Noah, but that didn't work." My heart hammers against my chest. "I fucking crave you, Jamie. As much as I want to stop it, I can't."

Her jaw drops as she gawks at me, and I stand in front of her.

"This is it. Me handing my heart to you, giving you the decision to stay here, kiss me again, or tell me to go fuck myself. It's your call, and if you leave, I'll never bring this up again. I won't take Noah away from you. We can speak in passing and remain friends."

I kneel on one knee, our eyes on the same level, and hers are glossy as they stare at me.

"It's time we set this straight, and by setting it straight, I'm letting you make the decision. You have more to lose than I do. Me? I'm one hundred percent in. There's no question that the feelings I have for you are much more than platonic. You make the call."

CHAPTER TWENTY-THREE

Jamie

"I FUCKING CRAVE YOU."

"One hundred percent in."

"You make the call."

Like the night I came over when Noah was sick, this moment will change everything.

Our lives.

Our relationship.

Our hearts.

What makes you a stronger person?

To hold your happiness, so others won't lose theirs?

To break your own heart?

If I say yes, I'd be choosing him over Heather.

He stares at me in expectation, waiting for an answer—if I'll break our hearts or dive into something I've wanted for years.

My brain scrambles with indecision.

I'm not someone who makes rash decisions.

If my feelings weren't this strong for Cohen, if being with him didn't set my heart on fire and it was only sexual attraction, I'd already be out the door.

I'm not out the door because I don't want to lose him.

To lose what's happening between us.

"Cohen ..." I search his face for any apprehension. There's none. "Will you break my heart if I do this?"

"No," he replies with no hesitation, and his hands stretch over my thighs. "I know the pain of your heart being shattered, and I'd never put you through that. Never." He gently squeezes my thighs. "That's why I'm stopping myself from kissing you, from pinning you onto the couch and touching you. Don't think there isn't fear on my end. You can break my heart just as much as I can break yours. And to be honest, while doing my best not to sound like a pussy, I'm not sure how I'll recover from yours with how deep I'm starting to care for you."

Honesty is in his eyes.

I reach out, splaying my hand over his chest, feeling his heart beating madly.

As my answer, as I make a decision that will spin my world on its axis, I lean forward and press my lips to his.

"Thank God," he breathes against my mouth, tasting like fresh mint, and he cups his hand around my neck, deepening our kiss.

His hand moves from my thigh to circle my waist, and he pulls us up. As he gets to his feet, I wrap my legs around his waist, a struggle at first with my swollen ankle. He cups my ass, keeping a tight hold on me. We devour each other, and no questions are asked when he walks us to his bedroom and kicks the door shut behind us. With me in his arms, he flips on the light before gently laying me down on his bed.

It's my first time in his bedroom.

Black bedding. Black furniture. Deep gray walls.

More masculine than the rest of the house. Definitely Cohen.

Chills run down my spine. The weight of his body over mine is perfection. Our movements are slow, our touches soft, unfaltering.

Unlike last night, there's no uncertainty with us.

I want this.

He wants this.

We need this.

My legs tremble, and his hands are chilly as they strip me of my shirt. He tosses my shoes over his shoulder and slides my pants down, goose bumps following his every touch. His breathing is labored when he draws back and levels himself by pressing his palm against the mattress. My breathing matches his as he drinks in my half-naked body.

"Perfection," he whispers, reaching out with his free hand and skimming the base of his knuckles against my cheek. "So damn beautiful."

He gently squeezes my chin, and the air becomes heavy as he moves down my body. With each inch he drops, the harder my breathing drags. I'm close to a heart attack when his head aligns with my black hipster panties—not exactly the sexiest panties, but he shows no complaints while dragging them down my legs. As soon as they're flung to the side, he pushes my thighs apart, situates himself between them, and starts torturing me.

His facial hair is rough around my thighs, and his tongue teasingly strokes my slit once.

"Holy shit," I gasp, hearing a light chuckle from him.

"You like that?" he questions, peeking up at me, his brows raised.

"Definitely like that," I whisper.

He nods, delivers a smirk on his lips, and mercilessly drives his tongue inside me. I lose count of how many moans escape me when he dips his fingers inside me, moving his tongue to gently suck on my clit, and I moan, losing myself.

My eyes shut, and I'm close.

Close to Cohen giving me the best orgasm I've ever had.

Sure, I've done this before but never like this, never with a man who seems to already know what sets me off.

And he does know because as soon as I'm on the brink, he shoves another finger inside me.

"Mmm, you're about to come for me," is all I hear before I let go.

I arch my back.

Lose a breath.

The need for more sets me on fire.

His mouth meets mine, his kiss hard and deep, and I taste myself on his tongue. My head spins as I lift forward, clutch the bottom of his shirt, and drag it over his head, flinging it across the room.

"I want to see your cock," I say, boldness taking over me.

He pulls back, allowing me room to rise, and his hips are aligned with my eyes. His erection strains against his jeans, and my mouth waters.

That's from me.

I did that.

I'm aching for him.

Soaked for him.

With shaking hands, I unbuckle him. The slow movements are long gone. We're back to our frantic touching as I shove his pants and boxer briefs down his waist. His cock springs free, so hard and inches away from my mouth, and his head falls back when I suck on the tip of him.

"Fuck, Jamie," he groans.

I shift, angling myself to take the full length of him inside my mouth. His hand reaches down, cupping my head, and he pushes more of his dick inside.

I might have a big mouth for shit-talking, but a mouth for taking in a cock as large as Cohen's isn't one of my traits apparently.

I gag for a moment, and he pulls back, his cock falling off my lips.

"Shit, sorry," he whispers. "I didn't mean to get carried away."

"It's fine," I say, my eyes watering. "It's been a while, and you're huge. I'll probably need to practice that a few times before I become a skilled head-giver—"

I'm cut off by him pushing me down on the bed and hovering over me.

"We can practice that skill later. I'm sure your pussy can handle my cock just fine."

My eyes widen.

That might take some adjusting as well.

He kicks off his shoes and starts undressing while I focus on his hard cock—its size and how amazing it'll feel inside me. My attention moves from his dick at the sound of a drawer opening. He withdraws a condom, tears it open with his teeth, and slides it on.

I hold in a breath, hoping my vagina won't be as difficult as my mouth in the whole Taking in Cohen's Cock game, and he positions himself at my entrance.

He levels his hand on my stomach. "Breathe, baby."

I nod, biting into my lip, and do as I was told.

"You good?"

"I'm good."

His hands grip my thighs as he pushes himself inside me. My lip twinges as I bite into it, Cohen's size stretching me, and I relish in how perfectly he fills me.

"Fuck, Jamie, you're tight," he hisses, and when his eyes meet mine, they're intense—a look I've never seen before.

"You good, baby?" he asks, his hips raised but not moving.

I nod. "I'm perfect. This is perfect."

With my words, his hands move from my thighs to my ass, and he tilts my hips up before giving me one hard starting thrust.

Then another.

And another.

He grips my waist in ownership as he pumps in and out of me. "How do you want me to fuck you, Jamie?"

"Oh my God, just like that," I whimper, rocking my hips in sync with his.

I'm drunk on him—his touch, the filthy words flying from his mouth, and his cock.

Our hips slap together.

Our moans are loud.

The sound and smell of sex are in the air.

My arm reaches back, and I clench the sheets when he drops my waist, his sweaty chest hitting mine. He pumps his hips forward, the headboard now beating against the wall as he fucks me.

"Tell me you're close," he says, reaching up and squeezing my breast.

"I'm close."

His mouth crashes onto mine.

I come apart first and nearly break a nail as I take my orgasm out on his sheets.

My eyes fly open when his pace quickens, and his face squeezes before he groans my name.

Damn, he's hot when he comes.

———

"HOW ARE we going to explain this to Noah?" I ask Cohen.

After another round of sex, we raided the kitchen for snacks.

Who knew screwing could work up such an appetite?

After I scolded him for buying sugar-free fruit snacks, he lifted me onto the counter, fucked me, and told me to shut my mouth. I then proceeded to tell him his pudding selections were trash, to which he then ate me out on the kitchen table.

We're back in his bed, and I pop a pathetic excuse for a fruit snack into my mouth while waiting for his answer.

Beggars can't be choosers.

I'm going to need to up Cohen's snack game if he wants another sleepover with me.

"Whatever we tell him, guarantee he'll be one happy-ass kid. He loves you."

Do you love me?

My stomach clenches.

I should've asked more questions before I allowed him to screw me senseless and nearly choke me to death with his cock.

He squeezes my thigh. "What's going on in that complicated mind of yours, babe?"

Deciding honesty is best, I turn to face him. "Do you love me?"

He gags on his fruit snack, his hand groping his throat, before clearing it as the snack goes down. "Do I love you?"

I nod. "Yes."

"Did I not make myself clear in the living room?"

"You said you *craved* me." I pull the sheet up my naked chest. This talk feels more intimate than us actually being intimate.

"That, I definitely do."

He leans forward to brush his lips against mine. I taste the fruit snacks, minus the sugar, and he gives me one last simple peck before drawing back.

I lick my lips, savoring the taste of him. "But you didn't say that exactly. Didn't say those three words."

"Neither did you," he deadpans.

Are we ready for that yet?

How is it easier for us to have sex than to say I love you?

Why is it harder to give yourself away emotionally than physically?

He clears his throat. "Should we save that conversation for another day?"

I nod.

He rolls on top of me, using his legs to separate mine, and laces our fingers together, holding them over my head. "I don't want to scare you away." He licks a line up my neck before trailing his mouth back down with soft kisses.

I tilt my head, giving him better access to do with me what he pleases, and wiggle my hips at the feel of his erection sliding against my leg.

"What I feel for you, I've never felt for anyone else," he whispers into my ear before shifting.

I grab his chin, no longer caring about the words, and press my mouth against his.

Sex now.

Anxiety-inducing talks later.

CHAPTER TWENTY-FOUR

Cohen

I'VE NEVER HEARD a ringtone more annoying.

It's loud.

Some classical music-sounding shit.

And it's ringing over and over again.

Jamie slides out of bed and starts hopping around the room on her good foot, scrambling through the clothes tossed around the bedroom.

"Where the hell is it?" she mutters, tossing a shirt behind her, and she finds the phone underneath it. "Hello?" Her eyes widen as she listens to whoever is on the other line, and she shrieks, "What?" seconds later.

I sit up at the shock in her voice.

"Let me call you back, and I'll be there."

She hangs up the phone, and her search turns frantic as she finds her clothes. Her hands shake as she slips her panties up her legs.

"Jamie," I drawl, panic pulling up my throat. "Are you going to tell me what's going on?"

Her shoulders droop. "Heather is in the hospital."

I freeze, my eyes wide.

"She's in the ICU in Vegas. My parents are booking me a flight now. I'm sorry, Cohen, but I have to go."

I run a hand over my face, taking in her words. "What happened?"

"I have no idea. My mom is a hot mess. I could barely make out her words. She didn't provide much info, except that I needed to meet them at the airport."

"Keep me updated, okay?"

She nods.

I rise, ready to slip out of bed and kiss her good-bye, but she rushes out of the bedroom before I can stop her.

CHAPTER TWENTY-FIVE

Jamie

I'M A SHIT PERSON.

A pathetic excuse for a sister.

While Heather was being rushed to the hospital, I was having sex with her ex-boyfriend.

Not that I knew it was happening, but still.

The Most Terrible Person in the World award goes to yours truly.

I couldn't look at Cohen when I ended the phone call in his bedroom. I have no idea what his face looked like when I broke the news about Heather. I was scared to see it, so I stormed out, not giving him another word.

I drive home and start packing a bag, and thirty minutes later, my mom texts me with flight information. Luckily, she managed to snag us direct flights to Vegas with our flight departing in only two hours. My father is the psychologist of one of their hotshot pilots, so that has its perks.

"Is everything okay, honey?" my mom asks when I find them in the airport terminal. "You look exhausted. Did you not get enough sleep last night?"

I am exhausted. I was fucking my sister's ex all night.

"I slept fine, Mom," I answer. It's not a lie. I did sleep perfectly in Cohen's arms.

She gestures to my leg in concern. "Why are you limping? Did something happen to your ankle?"

"I think I sprained it." I shrug. "It's no big deal."

The issue—why I look like a raggedy bitch—was the wake-up call I received.

My beautiful mother, whose chestnut-colored hair is usually pulled back into the perfect bun, resembles a different person. Her eyes are red and puffy, tears linger around her eyes, and she's close to another breakdown.

I wrap my arms around her, squeezing her tight, hoping to soak away some of her pain. I hug my father next, worry laced on his face, but he's handling it better than my mother.

We sit down, and I hold my mom's hand until our flight is called. While we load into our first-class seats, I still feel Cohen's hands on me.

I still smell him on me.

The words he whispered in my ear as he thrust inside me ring through my mind.

He's texted a few times, but out of guilt, I shut off my phone.

I slap my eye mask over my face and fall asleep.

Guilt and shame make you one tired bitch.

———

AS SOON AS our flight lands, we throw our bags into a cab and go straight to the hospital. Dragging our luggage through the waiting area, my mother charges toward the nurses' station, crying as she repeats my sister's name until a doctor comes out.

"She's in bad shape," the trauma surgeon explained after introducing himself.

As a doctor, I know the severity of those words.

Whatever this bad shape is, it'll break my parents.

"What happened?" my father asks.

The doctor lowers his tone and jerks his head toward a corner in the waiting room. "It seems to be a domestic dispute that ended violently."

"Domestic dispute?" my mother shrieks. "Are you saying that Joey hurt her?"

Before the doctor can answer, a woman approaches us. "Are you Heather's parents?"

"Yes," my father answers, stern-like.

"He beat her up. He beat her up really bad," the woman says. "And then he shot her."

Either she's clueless to how terrible her delivery is, or she doesn't care.

A sob escapes my mother. "What?"

"Your daughter suffered a gunshot wound," the doctor says, shooting the stranger an irritated look. "The bullet hit her thigh, and luckily, it didn't rupture any veins or arteries. It went straight through, leaving no dangerous shrapnel. Your daughter is very lucky the bullet hit where it did."

"So … she's …" My mom's voice shakes before she continues, "She's not going to die?"

"She's not going to die," the doctor confirms. "She'll just need time to heal."

"Can we see her?" my father asks.

The doctor nods. "Of course."

With our luggage in tow, we—including the random chick—follow the doctor through the emergency room and up an elevator, and we land in the ICU wing of the hospital. The door to Heather's room is open, and my mother wastes no time in dashing into it, rushing to Heather's side.

I gasp as I circle the bed, and she comes into view.

Her eyes are black and blue, IVs are pumping fluid into her, a breathing tube is in her mouth, and she's hooked up to beeping monitors.

My stomach churns with guilt.

I really am a shitty fucking person.

"Sweetie," my mom sobs, grabbing her hand. Then she brushes her other hand along Heather's forehead. "My sweet daughter."

My father joins her, wrapping my mother into a hug as she lets loose into his shoulder. I'm frozen in place, the need to comfort my mother barreling through me, but I let my father do the job. As a doctor, I'm used to seeing grief, tears, family members breaking down, but it's different when it's your family.

"We treated the injury, and the surgery was successful," the surgeon explains. "We're keeping an eye on her, but recovery is very promising."

"Thank you," my father says, giving him an appreciative smile.

The surgeon leaves, and the stranger steps to my side.

"I'm Pat," she says, "Heather's neighbor and the one who called your parents."

"Thank you," my father says. "We don't know what we would've done had you not called us. We might not have found out about this."

"You're welcome."

They introduce themselves—my mother, Regina, and my father, Jack—and then I do the same.

Pat explains that her apartment is next to Joey and Heather's, and hearing them argue wasn't anything new. She also says that him putting his hands on her wasn't new either, but it was the first time she heard a gunshot. She immediately called the police, and they were there in minutes. They arrested Joey and rushed Heather to the hospital.

"You have my phone number if you need anything," Pat says when she's finished. "Can I come check on her tomorrow?"

My father tells her, "Yes," and thanks her again before she leaves.

I pull a chair up for my mother, softly asking her to sit down, and then do the same with my father. Taking the one in the corner of the room, I sit and stare at my sister. The room is quiet, the beeps of the machines the only sounds, and I don't bother turning my phone on.

I sit there.

I think.

I question my actions.

And I hate myself.

———

FOUR HOURS LATER, the breathing tube has been removed.

Her recovery is quickly improving.

"Gentry girls are strong," my father claims.

We stare at Heather and wait for her eyes to open.

When they do, my mother jumps for joy and calls out for the doctors, and they rush into the room.

"Sweetie," my mother says, tears swelling in her eyes—tears that haven't stopped since we entered the room. "I'm so happy you're okay. We're here, honey."

"What happened?" my father asks. He's a man who gets straight to the point, no matter what.

"Joey beat the shit out of me," Heather snaps.

I wince, my mother flinches, and my father tilts his head to the side at her harsh tone.

Whoa.

I was not expecting that.

She definitely woke up on the wrong side of the hospital bed.

Why's she so angry?

Her eyes cut to me. "I don't want to hear any shit either. None of that *I told you so* bullshit."

What the hell?

"Never!" my mother says. "We're here for you, honey. No one, even you, knew Joey would do something like this."

I did.

Dude's a fucking psycho.

"Good." Heather's eyes cut to me in disdain. "I don't want to hear anyone's judgmental bullshit. I'm stressed, and I don't know what to do."

I look around the room.

I've never had a patient wake up this angry, especially after surviving a gunshot wound.

"Don't know what to do?" my father asks. "You're coming home. That's what you're going to do."

"I need to talk to Joey first before I do anything drastic."

I shut my eyes, inhaling a deep breath, and wait for my mother's freak-out.

"Talk to him?" she screeches. "You need to stay away from him."

"Pat said they arrested him. The jerk is in jail," my father says.

"He'll bond out," Heather says. "He always does."

"What do you mean, *always does*?" my dad asks, pushing his glasses up his chubby nose. "How many times has he been arrested for this?"

"I need to talk to him," Heather says, ignoring my father's question.

"He could've killed you!" my father yells, gesturing to her in the bed. "He did this to you, and you want to *talk to him*?"

"Jack," my mom whispers.

"No, don't *Jack* me," he seethes. "This has gone on for too long, Heather. It's time to dump the trash and come home."

"He's my husband."

"Leave him," I finally say from my corner. "Divorce him."

Heather rolls her eyes. "Of course that's your almighty input, Jamie."

I look away, choosing to ignore her.

"Honey, you need to close this chapter of your life and come home," my mother says.

Heather shakes her head, her voice cracking. "I've burned too many bridges there. That's why I've stayed here for so long."

My mother grabs her hand. "You haven't burned any bridges. We all love you."

"I hurt Cohen … I gave away my son. I can't go back there and see him. What if I run into him with another woman? I'll die, Mom. I'll die!" She glances at me. "Does he have another woman?"

I shrug. "I don't know."

Her eyes narrow. "Don't you see him all the time since you see Noah?"

I cringe when she says his name.

She's never said it before.

Never acknowledged him.

Now, she wants to know about his life?

I shrug again. "We talk sometimes."

"Move home. Maybe you can reconcile with him," my mother says in an attempt to give Heather hope. "Apologize. It's been years."

She sighs. "I don't know."

"You were perfect together. You're older now. Maybe you can mend what you broke."

"Excuse me." I stand. "I need to make a few calls and get some fresh air."

I inhale deep breaths when I step out of the hospital, take a seat on a bench, and pull out my phone. Hesitation runs through me as I power it on and stare at his name.

I have to do this.

I'm a grown-up.

I've never been one to run from my problems.

"Hey," Cohen answers after one ring as if he's been waiting by his phone. There's an edge of relief in his voice. "How's everything going? What happened?"

My head throbs. "Her husband shot her."

"Holy shit. Are you serious?"

"I am."

"Is she …?"

"She's going to be okay."

"Good, good." He blows out a long breath. "Are you staying there? When are you coming home?"

"We're going to stay in a nearby hotel for the next few days while she recovers."

"Will you call me when you can talk?"

"Yes."

"Thank you."

"Tell Noah I miss him."

We say good-bye, and I sit on the bench, contemplating my life choices for thirty minutes before going back inside.

———

"LET'S hope your sister finally leaves that jerk," my mom says, throwing down a fry and scraping her hands together, removing the salt.

Visiting hours ended twenty minutes ago, and we stopped for a quick burger before going to the hotel. My mother offered to stay the night with Heather in her room, but Heather declined, claiming she wanted to rest in peace.

"She'd better," my dad says, dipping his fry in ketchup. "She might be a thirty-year-old woman, but I'm going to put my foot down on this."

My father, an award-winning psychologist, is used to people taking his advice. Well, everyone except my sister. He's smart, a great father, a straight shooter, but he doesn't take any bullshit. I grew up proud that my father was a doctor, and there were tears in his eyes when I graduated from medical school.

My mother taught high school English for years before retiring last month. She and my father have the perfect marriage, the perfect balance of sweet and strict. They've made it thirty-five years, and I only anticipate they'll make it another thirty, happily married.

My mother pats his arm. "She's scared, honey. She knows life won't be the same as it once was when she was home, and Anchor Ridge is only twenty minutes out of town. She'll see Cohen, and if he doesn't accept her apology, it'll break her every time."

Not as much as she broke him.

"Will it?" I chime in. "She made it clear she didn't give two damns about Noah when he was at your house."

If my parents think Cohen will take her back, they're setting her up for failure.

A surge of panic hits me.

What if she does come home and begs for Cohen back?

What if she wants them to become one big, happy family?

I can't see Cohen reconciling with her, but I also couldn't see her leaving them years ago.

You never know what's going through people's minds.

"Jamie," my mom says, breaking me away from my thoughts.

"Huh?" I blink at her.

"I asked if you thought Cohen would be open to talking to her."

"Do you want the truth?"

She nods.

"No."

Her face falls. "Cohen doesn't seem like a man who holds grudges."

I give them a *really* look.

"It took him *years* to allow us to see Noah. Do you think he'll let Heather walk back into their lives? And we don't even know if that's what she'll do. She's flaky—"

"Your sister was shot. Have some compassion," my mother says. "You're a doctor. You know the pain people suffer through these situations."

"I'm not trying to be mean. All I'm saying is, let's see what happens, and when the time comes, I'll talk to Cohen."

We have more to talk about than just that.

On the way to our hotel, I call my work and explain Heather's situation, apologizing and swearing to make sure my shifts will be covered. The hospital is understanding, telling me not to worry, but I still do. I tell my parents good night, kiss my mother on the cheek, and am exhausted by the time I walk into my room.

I collapse onto the bed face-first, yell into my pillow, and breathe when lifting myself up.

I needed that.

I get ready for bed and wait until after Noah's bedtime before calling Cohen.

"Hey," he answers, his voice sleepy.

"So ..." I drawl, searching for words.

"This feels a little off," he says for me.

"Just a little."

"Do you regret it?"

My heart quickens at his question. "I don't know," I whisper around a tight throat.

"How do you not know?"

I give him honesty because it's what I'd want from him. "I'm scared, Cohen."

"Why?"

I rub my temples, hoping to release some tension, but it doesn't help. "This seems like a slap in the face, Karma, for what we did."

"What happened to Heather was not your fault," he grinds out.

All my frustrations, my lack of sleep, my exhaustion rise. "You dated her for years. Years!"

"What the hell? We're back to that?" he seethes. "I told you not to take that step with me unless you were certain it was what you wanted, unless you were certain that I didn't give a shit about my past with Heather."

Hurt clenches my heart as memories hit me.

Memories of him and her.

Of their love.

Why is this happening?

"You had a baby with her," I say, sobs approaching. "Even if that love isn't there any longer, it once was, and I slept with you." I lower my voice as if I'm telling a secret. *Hell, everything we're saying is practically a secret.* "If my family finds out, especially after this, they'll hate me."

"Heather moved on and found someone else. I moved on and found you. That's how breakups work. The moment she turned her back on us was the moment any love I'd had for her was gone."

"How would you feel if the man she moved on with was your brother?"

"I don't have a brother."

"Hypothetically!"

"Fuck hypotheticals."

"You'd be pissed."

"Different circumstances, Jamie. Different fucking circumstances."

My heart breaks as I gather the strength to do what I don't want to but what needs to be done. "Last night was a bad idea. Can we act like it never happened and go back to normal?"

I hate myself for this.

For throwing away last night.

For making it seem like it was nothing to me.

A ragged breath leaves him. "Wow, be just like her."

"What ... what do you mean?"

"Turn your back on us because shit gets a little complicated."

"This is different." I sniffle, pulling in a few breaths to stop myself from breaking down. "I'm not turning my back on anyone."

"You want to go back to us avoiding each other? Done."

He ends the call.

CHAPTER TWENTY-SIX

Cohen

I SLEPT on the couch last night.

As soon as I got into bed, my sheets smelled like Jamie.

I ripped them off, stomped to the laundry room like Noah does during his tantrums, and threw them in the washer.

My mind is dead.

My heart is dead.

This isn't a situation you can easily ask advice on.

It's different. Unconventional. Confusing.

I'm not a heartless bastard. I feel bad for Heather, but that doesn't mean I'll forgive her.

That I'll give her a pass for her absence and let her hop back into our lives.

She was the heartless one when she walked out.

Noah bounces in his seat after finishing his oatmeal. "Can I FaceTime Jamie?"

I stop rinsing out his orange juice glass. "I don't know if that's a good idea right now. She's out of town."

I haven't talked to Jamie since I hung up on her.

Noah slides off his seat and disappears from the kitchen. I snatch his bowl and am on my way to the sink when I hear the FaceTime ringtone blasting through the living room. I peek around the corner to find Noah with his iPod in his hand, smiling as he stares into the screen.

He waves into the camera when the call is answered. "Hi! I called to see Jamie."

"Jamie ran to the restroom, but I can talk to you for a moment. Do you remember me?"

I throw the bowl into the sink, hearing it shatter, and I rush into the living room. I snatch the iPod from him as if he'd been watching porn and end the call.

Noah frowns, reaching out to take the iPod from me, but I pull away. "Why'd you hang up?"

"That wasn't Jamie," I answer, nearly out of breath.

"I know," he chirps. "It was her sister. I met her when I went swimming."

The iPod rings, and a selfie of Jamie and Noah pops up on the screen.

I decline the call.

"We'll call Jamie later, okay?" I say.

"But why?"

"How about I take you to get some frozen yogurt?"

That changes his mind, and ten minutes later, we're in the car.

———

"YOU LOOK LIKE HELL," Archer says. "What happened?"

"I'm fucked." I swipe my beer from the bar and take a long swig.

It's after hours, and I typically don't stay late, but I need a beer, time to clear my head. Georgia is watching Noah, and I instructed her not to let him talk to Jamie. I hid his iPod in the glove compartment of the Jeep. I'm not taking any chances of him seeing Heather again.

"Fucked in a good way or a bad way?"

"Jamie and I hooked up—*again.* Only this time, we actually fucked."

He only nods, giving me his full attention, and waits for me to continue.

"The next morning, she got a call that her sister—*my ex*—was admitted into the hospital."

"Oh shit, what happened?"

"Her husband had shot her."

"Damn. Wasn't expecting you to say that." He pours himself a whiskey straight and carries the bottle with him as he sits down next to me. "Have you talked to Jamie?"

"She and her parents went to Vegas, where Heather is." I drag my hand through my hair. "I should've kept my hands to myself. I messed this up for Noah. If Jamie disappears from his life, it'll kill him."

"Jamie doesn't seem like the type to run away from Noah because shit didn't work out between you two."

I pull at the wrapper on my beer. "Never say never. Heather didn't seem like the type to walk out on her family, but she did, leaving my son without a mother. I don't put anything past anyone anymore."

I sound like a whiny asshole, but I'm lost.

Lost with no one to talk to.

Sure, Georgia is always there for me, but this goes beyond a chat with my little sister.

Archer claps me on the shoulder. "I'm here for you, man. If you need time off, I got you. I'd say I'm good for advice, but you know I'm shit at this. Silas, Finn, hell, even Georgia are better options for a heart-to-heart than I am."

I grab the bottle and drink straight from it. "Bullshit. You say that to scare people off. There's a heart buried in that cold chest of yours."

"Words of wisdom or not, I have your back."

———

"WHEN WILL I SEE JAMIE AGAIN?" Noah asks, his lower lip sticking out while I tuck him into bed.

It's the fifth time he's asked that tonight. That's not counting the times he's asked to FaceTime her.

"I told you, she's out of town," I answer for the fifth time.

We haven't spoken since I ended our call her first night in Vegas. I've debated on calling her back, but I decide against it every time.

She hasn't reached out either.

Maybe it's for the best.

Maybe Noah will forget about her.

Doubt it.

I can't forget about her.

"When she gets back, can we go on another trip together?"

I tap his forehead. "Hey now, you know that was your birthday trip. You have to wait until your next one, silly goose."

He giggles as I tickle him, hoping it'll take his mind off Jamie. It doesn't.

"Can Jamie come too?"

"We'll see."

"Can we turn Jamie into my mom?"

I freeze, my hand covering my mouth, and my heart breaks for my son. "No, we can't."

Just like I was straight-up with him about Heather, I need to do the same with Jamie.

No false promises for my son.

"Why not?" he whines.

"Jamie is our friend." I pat his bed. "That's it."

"Can't she be my friend *and* my mom? Ricky's mom isn't his real mom. His real mom died, and then his daddy married another woman. Ricky calls her mom now. He says kids get new moms and dads all the time. Can I do that too?" He sighs. "Let me ask Jamie. She'll say yes. I'll FaceTime her tomorrow."

The iPod is going in the trash.

It's getting burned.

No way is Noah going near it again.

I squeeze his side. "You can't ask her that. Jamie is just our friend. I'm not marrying her."

"Will I have another mommy like Ricky someday?" His voice breaks at the end, and the hurt on his face kills me.

I smile gently. "Yes. Someday."

I'll give him hope on that.

I can't stay a single man forever.

He perks back up. "It'd be so cool. Ricky's new mom makes him peanut butter and jelly sandwiches in the shape of dinosaurs! Dinosaurs, Dad!"

I'm going to kick Ricky's dad's ass if his kid doesn't stop telling mine stories.

I've never been a crier, but goddamn it, I'm close to losing my shit.

That can't happen in front of him.

My stomach twists at the same time as my eyes water.

"You need to get some sleep."

He nods. "Night, night. Love you, Dad."

"I love you too."

I cover my face when I reach my bedroom and gain control of myself.

Then I get on Amazon and search for fucking dinosaur cutouts for sandwiches.

CHAPTER TWENTY-SEVEN

Jamie

"YOUR SISTER IS COMING HOME and moving in with you."

We're in the hotel's restaurant having dinner, and I wince and stare at my mom, waiting for her to tell me she's kidding.

She doesn't, and I take that as my cue to chug my wine.

"I'm sorry, what?" I ask, setting the empty glass down.

"Heather agreed to divorce Joey and move home."

My mother's face lights up in happiness, and I feel bad that I'm about to burst that bubble.

"Mom, that's not a good idea."

"Heather doesn't want to be thirty, living with her parents—"

"Thirty and living with her sister is better?"

"Jesus, have some compassion. She was shot!"

That's all I'm going to hear about for years.

Anytime Heather wants something from me, they'll throw that in my face.

She recovered quickly, and we found out the bullet had barely grazed her. She's in pain but walking with the assistance of crutches.

We've been here for a week, and I'm going home tomorrow.

Apparently, Heather is coming home with me.

I'm not trying to be a bitch, but my parents have more patience with her than I do, and the old Heather—the heartless Heather—is returning with each day we visit.

"I have plenty of compassion for her, but you know we don't get along," I say. "She'd do much better with you and Dad helping her get her life in order."

A wrinkle forms on my mother's forehead as she scrunches up her face. "I already told her yes. She's not asking for much, Jamie. Give her this. Give *your father and me* this."

"Mom—"

"We already told her yes."

"You can't approve someone to move into *my home* without asking me."

My mom delivers a skeptic look. "We didn't think it'd be an issue." She sighs. "Heather also plans to reach out to Cohen about Noah. She thought staying with you would be a great way to ease him into it, make him feel more comfortable."

"That's not a good idea." *I refuse to be used as a stepping stool for Heather.*

My mom pats my hand. "Heather is finally growing up, sweetie."

I pick at my chicken. "That's nice, given she's in her thirties."

"Not everyone is as responsible as you," my dad inputs, staring down at me over his newspaper. It's not an insult; it's a compliment.

"You need to quit bailing her out," I argue. "Let her move home —*move in with you*. She doesn't always have to get her way."

"No one is bailing her out, honey," my mom continues. "She's moving home and needs a helping hand."

"Will she get a job? Sit around my place all day? What's the plan here?"

"She plans to work, yes."

I stay quiet.

"This isn't a yes or no thing," my father finally chimes in. "Do this for your sister. Give it a month, and we'll find her an apartment."

"Fine." I stand from the table. "I need to pack my bags."

I leave the restaurant and take the elevator to my room. I fish my phone from my pocket, curses flying in the process, and go to my call log. That's when I notice a FaceTime call from Noah from a few days ago.

It's not a missed call, and I haven't talked to them since Cohen hung up on me.

I FaceTime Noah first.

No answer.

With a nervous breath, I FaceTime Cohen next.

Declined.

Seconds later, he calls through with a normal voice call.

"You want to tell me why Heather answered a FaceTime call with Noah the other day?" is what he says after I answer.

Whoa.

It's a smack in the face.

Heather never told me that.

Sure, I left my phone in her room a few times when I ran to the restroom or the vending machines, and I let her borrow it to make calls.

I grab my suitcase and start packing. "I had no idea that happened. I'm sorry, Cohen."

"Not to be a dick, but I don't want you FaceTiming Noah until you're home and she's not around."

Oh no.

Cohen will take this worse than I did.

I bite into my lip. "I need to tell you something."

"What's up?"

"Heather is moving home."

"Goddammit," he hisses. "Tell her to stay away from us. We live in a different town, so it shouldn't be an issue."

Wait, there's more.

"She's moving in with me." I hold my breath, waiting for a reaction I know won't be pretty.

"Oh, is she?"

"I had no choice in the matter. I tried to say no, but my parents insisted and put me on a guilt trip."

"I get it. Heather has a way of always getting what she wants," he scoffs. "I'm not trying to sound like an asshole, but I'm frustrated."

I plop down on my bed next to my suitcase. "I don't want this to stop me from seeing Noah."

"No way am I letting him around her."

"What if he comes over when she's gone?" *It's not like the three of us can hang out now without it being weird anyway.* I chew on my nails while waiting for his answer.

"She can pop up at any time."

I chomp into one extra hard and spit it out, taking my Heather anger out on my manicure. "Looks like I'll go back to doing visits at your house with Georgia."

"We've really fucked this up, haven't we? You were right. We shouldn't have crossed that line. It was a mistake."

A mistake.

God, it hurts when he says that.

Did it stab a knife through his heart the same way when I said them to him?

"Is that Jamie?" I hear Noah ask in the background.

"Yes," Cohen answers. "Would you like to talk to her?"

Seconds later, Noah speaks through the speaker, "Hi, Jamie!"

"Hi, honey," I say, his voice relaxing me.

"Can I come over and hang out? Can we get cupcakes?"

I laugh. "I'm actually out of town right now, but what about when I get back?"

"Yes! Can Dad come too?" The call goes quiet for a moment, and I can hear low whispers. "Dad said I need to get ready for bed. Good night!"

"Good night," I whisper with a twinge of loneliness.

I miss them.

I wait for Cohen to take over the call, but he hangs up.

———

"HONEY, I'M HOME!"

A stiffness forms in my jaw.

My head aches, and I roll my eyes before anyone comes into view.

Heather crutches herself into my house like she already owns it with my parents behind her. She does a once-over of the place. "Kinda small." Her eyes flash to me. "Tell me my bedroom is a decent size."

My attention snaps to my mother, and she mouths, "*Be patient*," to me.

"Mom will show you your bedroom," I reply flatly from the couch.

Her hand flicks in the air as she follows my mom to the guest bedroom. I washed all the bedding, set up the features on the smart TV, and added a few candles, hoping to at least make it homey for her.

Also hoping she'll find her bedroom comfortable enough to spend all her time in there.

"Are you sure Jamie won't let me have the master?" I hear Heather ask.

My father sits down in a chair, concern etched into his forehead when he looks at me. "Thank you, Jamie. I know this will be hard, and I'll try to get her out of here as soon as I can, but this is for your mother."

I nod. "The faster, the better." I groan when I hear Heather complaining about the size of her TV next. I lean forward and lower my voice. "Her apartment was a hellhole compared to my house. What's her deal?"

My father lifts his arms and then drops them back onto the armrests in frustration. "I know just as much as you do."

"Can I have some money to get clothes until Pat mails mine?" Heather asks when they return to the living room.

"What about borrowing some from your sister?" my dad asks, shooting me an apologetic look.

Heather pays a glance at me before scrunching up her nose. "Jamie and I don't exactly have the same style."

I glance from the scrubs I'm wearing to her tight jeans, low-cut top, and crutches. While she was in the hospital, she complained that her crutches would ruin her outfits.

Definitely a different style.

Not that I'm judging her style, but I don't like the way she's judging mine.

Heather sits on the arm of a chair—an expensive chair that doesn't carry a sturdy arm—and I grit my teeth to stop myself from yelling at her.

"I'll also need toiletries and a phone. Joey paid all our bills and shut mine off."

My dad pulls himself up from the chair with a groan. "I need to run to my office. Your mother will take you out for things tomorrow, and until then, you can borrow Jamie's phone when needed."

Another apologetic look from him is shot my way.

The look I shoot his way is annoyed.

I hug them good-bye and kiss their cheeks before they leave.

Heather doesn't.

She mutters a good-bye, heads to the kitchen, and rummages through my fridge. "A little help in here please."

When I walk into the kitchen, she has a Coke in her hand, and there's a bag of chips and a bottle of wine on the counter.

My favorite wine.

"Pour that into a glass and carry those for me, will ya?" she asks, heading back into the living room without waiting for my response.

I roll my eyes, release a breath, and open the wine bottle. When I return with the glass of wine and chips, she's on the couch. I take a seat in a chair and cringe as she loudly starts chomping on the chips while double-fisting her drinks as if the Coke is the chaser to the wine.

I sit up straight and focus on the news playing on the TV.

"Can I use your phone?"

I peek at Heather, taking in her expectant expression. "Sure. Do you need to make a call?"

Since the FaceTime call with Noah, I'm reluctant to let her use my phone.

Crumbs fall onto her shirt and the chair as she talks with chips in her mouth, "I want to check Facebook."

I stand. "You can use my laptop."

She shakes her head, more chomping. "I also want to call Pat. I heard asshole Joey already has a new girlfriend."

How tragic.

"Should you care about that?" I ask, grabbing my laptop that's charging on an end table.

"He was my husband," she snaps. "Obviously, I should. You'd know that if you had a husband."

I roll my eyes, fighting back the urge to fling the phone at her head.

She wiggles her fingers. "I also need to call Mom to ask when she's picking me up tomorrow."

I hesitate a moment before handing her my phone. As she takes it, my eyes stay on her hand, and I feel like a cheating spouse as she uses her greasy chip fingers to scroll down the screen.

Please, Cohen, don't call or text.

It might be wrong, being all secretive, but what else am I supposed to do?

Heather calls Pat and spends thirty minutes interrogating her about Joey's every move.

"Can you do me a favor?" she asks me, my phone in her hand after she ends her Joey drama.

"Depends on what it is," I answer, not catering to her like my parents do.

"Talk to Cohen for me."

"For what?" I play dumb.

"I want to see Noah."

"That isn't going to happen."

"Why not?" she snarls.

"Cohen hates you, for one."

"We can talk and work things out. He always loved our make-up sex." She shimmies her shoulders. "I'm sure I could still do a good job. He loved it when I did this thing with my tongue—"

I cut her off, "I'd rather not hear about that."

She sighs. "We had our ups and downs—"

I interrupt her again, "Downs? You left your family."

She narrows her green eyes at me and swipes her straight brown hair off her shoulder. "Whose side are you on? I'm your sister. He's nothing to you."

"That's enough." I hold out my hand. "Give me my phone back. I have shit to do."

"Am I right? Is he nothing to you?" She eyes me skeptically. "You don't seem very open to the idea of me seeing Cohen. Is it because you want to be the only woman in their lives? You want to be Noah's mother. You want *my* life?"

I clench my fist, holding myself back from pouring that wine over her head. "That's not your life. Never was. Never will be."

She sets all her kitchen shit on the floor, relaxes in her chair, and plays with my phone, bouncing it from one hand to the other. "Wow, your little high school crush hasn't stopped, has it? You know you're not Cohen's type, right?"

"I'm not doing this with you," I grind out.

"Why? Have you slept with him?" She scoffs when my eyes widen. "You have, haven't you?"

"You don't know what you're talking about." I jump to my feet. "Give me my phone."

She smiles when it beeps with a text. "Oh, looky here. A message from Cohen." She reads it out loud. "*Let me know when you want to come over, and we can talk.*" She taps one finger against her mouth while she starts to scroll through something on my phone. "Hmm … look at all these text messages."

I stand in front of her and hold out my hand. "Give me my phone." When she goes to stuff it under her armpit, I'm faster from her and snatch it from her hold. "You need to go to Mom and Dad's. I don't want you staying here."

"Why? Do you want me gone so you can keep fucking the father of my child?" A giggle leaves her. "How do you like my sloppy seconds? You probably couldn't wait to have him, could you?" She thrusts her finger into her chest. "Remember, he was mine first. He chose me first."

The string to my patience snaps. "I was too young for him then."

"You think that's it. Your age? You've always wanted my life, my looks." She peeks over her shoulder in a suggestive, smug way. "My friends, my boyfriends, my *sex life*. You think because you're a doctor, because the braces are gone, because you're *somewhat* attractive that Cohen will want anything to do with you?" She snorts. "You're pathetic. Out of all the guys out there, you ho yourself out to him."

I grab my keys and purse. "I'm leaving."

"Run away from facing the facts that Cohen will never want anything to do with you beyond sex."

I lean down and get in her face. "I'm running away from slapping you in the face. After what you've gone through, I want to be a decent person and not do that."

Her face is still, her eyes buggy, and she doesn't talk shit again until I pull away to leave. "Now, you have morals? You can't hit me but have no problem fucking my man?"

"He's not your man!" I scream. "He stopped being *your man* when you left him for *another* man. He's not yours. He doesn't want you. Get over it and move on—like you did when you left him and his newborn."

"*Our* newborn."

"Says the woman who signed over her rights."

With that, I turn around and leave, slamming the door behind me.

———

"MOM, I WANT HER OUT," I cry into the phone.

I managed to hold the tears in until I got to my car. I broke down and cried, slamming my hand against the steering wheel while fighting to forget Heather's insults.

"What?" my mother asks.

"Heather," I burst out. "I want her out of my house before I put her belongings on the curb."

"Honey, I asked you to be patient with her. She went through something traumatic."

I clench my jaw and fist at the same time, inhaling the scream I want to release.

If I have to hear my mother use that as her excuse one more time, I'll lose it.

I don't blame my mother. It's not her being mean. She has a heart, one that's too big at times, and has missed my sister. She cried for months after she left.

"I understand and hate what happened to her, but we didn't even last one night before our first fight. We can't live together."

She clears her throat. "Does this have anything to do with you and Cohen having a romantic relationship?"

"What?" I croak out.

"Heather called a few minutes ago—"

"She called? How did *she call*? She doesn't have a phone."

"I'm not one for technology, but she said she was calling me on her iPad."

I grind my teeth.

She only wanted my phone to look through my shit.

To play games with me.

"She said you admitted to sleeping with Cohen?" She drags out a low breath. "Jamie, how could you do that to her? To our family?"

"I never admitted *anything* to her!" I scream.

"Is she lying?"

"I have to go. I love you."

"Jamie—"

"I have to go, Mom!"

I hang up and start my car, and with tears in my eyes, I go to him.

Not Ashley.

Not my parents.

Cohen.

CHAPTER TWENTY-EIGHT

Cohen

JAMIE IS STANDING in my doorway with tears running down her cheeks.

She runs into my arms, and I slam the door shut behind us.

"Baby," I whisper, "what happened?"

She sobs into my shoulder. "They know."

My stomach falls. "Know what?"

"That we slept together."

I freeze before gaining control of myself and rub her back. "How?"

"Heather had my phone when you texted, and she looked through our messages. I don't know. I guess she put two and two together," she says into my shoulder, some of the words muffled. "I didn't admit it, but she called my parents and told them what I did."

She breaks down harder, and I pull her away, holding her at arm's length, wiping away her tears with my thumb.

"My mom believed her! She believed her before even asking me."

My throat is tight, and I cup her face in my hands. "I'm so sorry. This is all my fault."

She sniffles, gaining some control of herself, and glances around. "Where's Noah?" She shakes her head. "I can't believe I came over like this."

"He's with Georgia. He's missed you, and we're trying to take his mind off it."

Her lower lip trembles. "Trying to replace me, I see."

Never. No one can replace you.

"This is complicated. I don't know what the hell to do."

"I know." She breaks down again, and I drag her closer.

I run my hand down her hair, kissing her forehead, and whisper, "We'll figure everything out."

"Will we?"

She peeks up at me, and my gut clenches at the sadness in the eyes I've fallen in love with, and when our gazes meet, it sets us on fire.

Eye contact has always been a dangerous game with us.

Always leads to trouble.

And feelings.

And touching.

To us hoping we can be more than what we're allowed to be.

"I wish this weren't so complicated," she whispers.

"Me too, baby. Me too."

She relaxes against my body, and even though they're not supposed to, our lips meet. I hesitate, waiting for her reaction, and she doesn't think twice before deepening our kiss.

It feels like home.

Like where we've always belonged.

We kiss hard.

As if we don't know when it'll happen again.

Or if it *will* ever happen again.

I cup her jaw as we kiss, using it as my way to tell her how much I care about her. I kiss her, using my mouth to show her how much I'm fucking falling in love with her.

She falls to her knees and starts unbuckling my jeans, my cock standing at full attention, waiting for her warm mouth.

I fail him when I pull her back to her feet. "I need to be inside you."

She nods, biting into her lip.

I retreat a few steps. "Take off your shirt."

My cock twitches when she does.

"Lose the bra."

She does.

"Your pants."

She starts tearing her pants down her legs.

"And your panties. I want to see every inch of you, every inch of you that belongs to me, whether you like it or not. That's why you came here, right?" I cup my aching cock against my jeans. "You came here because you belong to me."

"Yes," she whispers. "I belong to you and only you, Cohen."

"Damn fucking straight."

When she's fully naked, I charge toward her, wrap my hand around the back of her neck, and kiss her hard. She moans into my mouth, saying my name, and I walk her back to the couch and bend her over the arm of it. She glances back at me as I pull my shirt over my head, smack her ass, and drop my pants.

Our eye contact makes another appearance when I slam inside her.

She whimpers underneath me, arching her back, and I slide one hand down her spine while using the other to grip her waist.

"Fuck, baby," I groan, slapping her ass again as our bodies rub against each other's.

"Yes, Cohen," she moans. "I love you inside me."

"Yeah, you do." I change course, grind my hips, and move in circles, hitting every spot inside her that I can.

She bucks against me, her face pushed against the cushion, and when I know she's about to come, I pull out of her.

"What the—"

I twist her around, pull her legs around my waist, and hustle to the bedroom. Dropping her onto the bed, I waste no time before pushing back inside her.

"You feel so good," I say between breaths, grabbing her legs and tossing them over my shoulders.

"I'm coming," she moans.

"Yes, come on my dick, baby."

She does, and I curse with each rough thrust I give her until I find my own release.

I'm staring down at my cock still inside her pussy when another, "Fuck," hisses through my lips.

She glances up at me as I slowly pull out of her while dropping her legs at the same time.

"We didn't use a condom." I stare at her pussy, taking in the evidence that I was there. I love it, but I also know it was irresponsible as fuck. "Shit, this is on me. I'm sorry."

It got too heated.

We wanted each other too much.

"It's okay." She offers an easy smile.

"Are you on the pill?"

"No," she answers before glancing away. "But there's not much we can do about it now. I'll get a Plan B tomorrow."

Her response eases me, and I reach forward to run two fingers over her slit, pushing more of my juices inside her.

It's a bad move on my part, but her underneath me, with my come inside her, is a big fucking turn-on. She doesn't turn away, doesn't stop me, and I lean down to kiss her before falling on my back.

"Why does your cock feel so good?" she asks, her body still shaking, and she sounds almost annoyed.

"Why does your pussy feel so good?" I counter before shifting so I'm halfway on top of her, my semi rubbing against her thigh.

"We have to stop this," she says, widening her legs so my cock falls between them.

I run my hand up her stomach, cupping her breast, and thrust my hips forward, groaning while sliding my cock over her clit. "I like this."

Her nipple tightens as I play with it between my fingers, and she squirms beneath me. "I hate how much I love this."

"I love how much you love it."

"Heather wants to make things right with you."

I halt at the mention of her name.

There goes that mood.

I collapse onto my back and scrub a hand over my face—my cock not nearly as excited as it was. "Heather can fuck herself."

She turns onto her stomach and slides in closer to me. "My parents want her to make things right with you."

"No disrespect, but your parents can fuck themselves too."

Not trying to sound like an ass, but Heather isn't making shit right with us.

There's no making it right.

She'd better stay away from Noah and me.

Jamie thrums her fingers over my chest. "They're going to make me end things with you."

My chest caves in at the thought of losing her—*again.*

If she's still planning on leaving us, why is she here?

Her leaving isn't what's driving the anger through me.

It's *why* she's leaving.

She's walking away because someone else is telling her to— stomping on my heart, on her own, and on my son's heart because of *their* opinions.

Fuck their opinions.

Fuck them.

"With her situation—" she starts.

I cut her off, "Her situation doesn't have jack shit to do with us. Her being here won't change the fact that I'm falling in love with you or that I want to be with you. I don't care about her."

Her body goes still, her legs straightening, and her eyes widen in shock. "What?"

I blink. "What?"

"You said it … those three words." A smile tilts at her lips.

Here goes.

I grab her knuckles and brush them against my lips before kissing the front of them. "I was an idiot not to say it then, but the timing felt forced, too expected, even though the moment I slid inside you, there was no uncertainty in my mind that I was falling in love with you. I wouldn't risk my heart, your heart, my son's heart for a quick fuck if mine didn't bleed for you. I love you, and I will fight for you. She can't tear us apart."

"Cohen," she breathes out, "I—"

She stops when my phone rings. I'd ignore it, given this is a critical moment in our relationship, but it's Georgia's ringtone. Since she has

Noah, I give Jamie's knuckles a squeeze before sliding out of bed, my cock in full view, and step into my sweats.

"Hello?" I answer when I grab my phone from the living room.

"I'm in the driveway," Georgia says in a whisper, most likely not wanting Noah to hear her.

"All right?" I pay a glance at the front door before heading back to the bedroom.

"Jamie's car is here, so before we come in, I wanted to make sure everything is good."

Apparently, my sister can read me like a book because she knew something had happened between us at the realization that Jamie wasn't coming around anymore. I attempted to explain she was out of town, but with Noah complaining about his lack of FaceTiming with Jamie, my sister knew. We grew up and are too close for her not to know that Jamie and I slept together.

She claimed it was written all over my face—the love I had for Jamie and the loss over when she left us.

Understanding dawns on me. "Give us five."

"Gotcha."

I hang up the phone, toss it onto the dresser, and start collecting our clothes. "Georgia is outside with Noah."

"Shit," she hisses, getting up, and we start pulling our clothes on.

When we make it into the kitchen, Jamie's hair is a tangled mess, and my shirt is on backward. There's no question we look awkward as fuck. Jamie's face is puffy, her eyes red from her crying and our halfway there heart-to-heart. We're sipping on water when Georgia and Noah barge into the house.

"Hey, kids," Georgia chirps, her eyes pinging between Jamie and me.

"Jamie!" Noah shouts, bouncing from one foot to the other before exploding toward her. He hugs her legs. "I've missed you so much!"

My head spins when I notice the tears in Jamie's eyes.

She kneels to hug Noah. "And I've missed you so much."

He peeks up at her, excitement on every inch of his face. "Are you hanging out with us tonight?"

Georgia walks over to me, leans in, and whispers, "I can take him back out if you want to talk—or maybe light a candle to drown out the smell of sex in the air. I stashed a cinnamon candle in the guest room for when I stay the night. It smells like Fireball. I actually might have one in my car." She pauses. "A candle, not Fireball, unfortunately, because it appears you two could really use a shot of some strong shit right now."

Noah is blabbing about how he's been playing with the toys he got for his birthday.

I massage my throat before answering, "I think that's a good idea."

Jamie is on the verge of losing it the longer she hears Noah talk about everything she's been missing.

"Noah, my man," Georgia calls out, and Noah turns to look at her. "Let's go get some cupcakes!"

Jamie kisses the top of his head, tears hitting her cheeks, and scurries to the bathroom.

"Can I wait for Jamie to get back?" Noah asks. "She can come too!"

"No, I don't think Jamie is feeling well," Georgia says.

He frowns. "We'll bring her one back then. I know her favorite-favorite-ist."

Georgia squeezes his shoulders. "She'll love that. Let's get going before they're all gone." She glances at me. "I'll call before we come back."

"*Thanks,*" I mouth to her.

Noah hugs me good-bye, and they're out the door a minute later.

"They're gone," I shout, an edge to my voice, and I meet Jamie in the living room.

"I need to go," she rushes out before holding up her phone. "Everyone in my family is blowing me up."

"And?" I hiss. "It's your life."

"My family is also my life! You and I both know what we have is sex—"

The fuck?

"Is that how *you* feel? Can you clarify what you're thinking? Unless you forgot, fifteen minutes ago, I said I was *falling in love with you.* And correct me if I'm wrong, but you lit up like a fucking lamp when you heard me say it. That sure as hell doesn't scream it's only sex."

She throws her arms up. "Yes! I'm in love with you! Yes! Hearing those words was everything I've ever wanted to hear, but do you honestly think we can make this work? You've had sex with both me and *my sister!*"

"This is different," I grind out. "And you know it."

"My family won't see it that way." She repeatedly shakes her head. "Other people won't see it that way."

A knot forms in my stomach, twisting in defeat, and I sit down on the edge of the couch. "Heather fucking ruins shit again."

"I'm sorry," she whispers, her face just as broken as my heart.

"What was that then? A good-bye fuck?" Anger knots in my stomach next, overtaking the defeat. "Do you do that to all the guys you fuck over?"

She cringes at my harsh words. "Screw you! I didn't come over here with the intention of us having sex."

"What was your intention then?"

"I don't know." Her chin quivers. "I was sad. I needed someone."

"Needed someone or needed *me?*"

"You!" she screams. "Goddammit, you!"

Her answer ignites a fire inside me.

I stand when she starts pacing, wrap my arms around her waist to stop her, and spin her to face me. "Why are you walking away from us? Why are you breaking your own heart?"

She peers up at me, her face puffier, her body quaking. "I can't love you because I can't keep you."

I take a step back. "All right, I get it."

She winces. "What?"

"Run away like your sister. I already know how to handle it." I stalk across the room, open the door, and gesture for her to leave.

"Cohen," she whispers, her eyes wide.

Anger pivots through me.

Fuck this.

Just as I never tracked down my father, just as I haven't reached out to Heather, I'll never beg for someone to love me.

For someone to stay with me.

If you don't want me, you don't fucking want me.

I'll take it.

Sure, it'll kill me to move on, but I'll handle it.

I'm a strong man.

I can lock that cage back around my heart.

"You're right," I say, my throat tight. "We can't keep each other. I already let one woman fuck with my head, one woman who made me doubt our love, and I refuse to do it again."

"Cohen," she repeats.

"Get out!" I scream. "I'm not playing these bullshit heart games—not with my feelings and damn sure not with my son's on the line. We'll act like you and I never happened and go back to how it was. I won't take Noah away from you—*for him, not you*—but I won't be giving you one more goddamn piece of me."

She bows her head, the sobs back. "Okay."

We don't look at each other when she passes me.

When she lets us go.

I slam the door behind her.

———

FINN CHARGES INTO MY OFFICE.

I glance up from my paperwork and raise a brow.

He scratches his head. "You have a, uh … visitor."

"Okay?"

"Heather is here."

I flex my fingers around the pen in my hand. "Are you shitting me?"

He shakes his head. "You want me to tell her to kick rocks?"

Finn is my only friend who knows what Heather looks like. He went to school with us.

"Nah, I'll handle it," I answer, blood rushing to my ears. "Can you bring her back here?"

I can't make a scene in my bar, and knowing Heather, there will be a scene.

Minutes later, Finn returns with Heather on crutches behind him. He doesn't say a word before turning and walking out, shutting the door behind us.

Heather stands in front of me and doesn't utter a word.

She's waiting for me to take the lead, like the coward she is.

She's different, she's aged, yet she is still attractive. Honey-blonde hair similar to Jamie's but thinner, no dimples like the woman I love, but she's dressed sexy enough that men will be hitting on her here.

Not me, though.

There isn't one cell in my body that wants her.

That will ever want her again.

She's not my type. She's not the one my heart beats for, who my body craves.

It's her sister who does that.

Her sister, who has gripped my heart and owns it.

Her sister, who is a goddamn pain in my ass.

Her sister, who I haven't spoken to in over a week.

I stand. "How dare you show up here? At my motherfucking *business*."

She winces, shocked at my anger. "Jamie won't tell me where you live, so I asked around, and this is where I was told to find you. When can we sit down and talk?"

The name of the woman I love sends a knife through my chest.

"I'd prefer fucking never."

She releases a huff. "It's going to happen. I won't leave you alone until we talk this out."

"What do you want?" I hiss. "We have nothing to talk out."

"Hear me out."

"Nope. Leave."

"Please!"

Her begging sends a rush of memories through me.

Her begging reminds me of how I sounded when I was down on my knees, asking her not to leave us, pleading for her to at least stay for Noah.

"Fuck you," I snarl. "Did you hear me out when I begged you? You don't deserve one second of my time."

Her eyes lower, and she gestures toward the crutches. "I was shot."

"I'm sorry that happened to you, but it doesn't change our relationship. I wish you the best, but stay away from us."

"Why are you punishing our son from having a mother?"

"*My son*," I seethe, hating that she referred to him as hers. "Not yours."

"You can think that all you want, but I'm still his mother. I gave birth to him."

"News flash, Heather: you signed over your rights. According to the state, you are nothing to him." The pressure from how hard my jaw is clamped down will give me a migraine by the end of this conversation.

"What about Jamie?" she snaps, jutting her chin out. "What is she to him? If I signed over my rights, she's *nothing* too."

I grip the edge of my desk, my nails biting into the wood. "This has nothing to do with Jamie."

Her voice rises. "Yes, it does. Out of all the people to sleep with, *my sister?*"

"Leave before I have you escorted out." The wood from my desk is chipping.

"Are you going to lie and say you aren't fucking her?"

"Nope."

We're not fucking at this moment, so I'm not lying.

"Bullshit," she spits. "I'm sure she didn't wait long before jumping on your dick."

Disgust sweeps up my throat that she's talking about Jamie like that. "You need to leave."

She scoffs. "God, what a whore. Sleeping with her sister's ex."

I slam my hand onto my desk, causing her to jump, and scream, "Don't you dare talk about her like that. Jamie has nothing to do with what you did or why I don't want you anywhere near *my son*."

My voice is loud.

Booming.

Harsh enough that the entire bar can hear us.

At this point, when it comes to defending Jamie, I don't care who hears.

She curls her upper lip. "Do you want to be selfish and make Noah grow up without a mother?"

"You're the reason for that. Not me."

Her shoulders slump, her voice turning whiny as she takes this conversation another route. "Cohen. *Please.* I made a mistake."

Fuck, why does it seem like we're talking in circles?

"You did, and I won't make the mistake of letting you hurt my child again. Now, leave before I call someone to make you leave."

The tears start, the vulnerability she tries to hide creeping through. Heather isn't heartless. There's something inside her but not much. Selfishness is her main trait.

"I'm sorry, okay! I want my life back!" she cries out.

"How convenient. You want it now that the Vegas life didn't work out for you."

"Do you want to know why he shot me?"

I stay quiet.

No.

Because I don't want to feel sorry for her.

I want to keep hating her.

She doesn't care that I don't want to know. "He shot me because I didn't get my period, and he was scared I was pregnant."

I feel like an ass for rolling my eyes. "Considering he told you to leave your child, that isn't a shocker to me."

"I had a good man—*you*—and I messed it up." Her eyes are vacant, her words low, and it's almost as if she's reading this from a script. "I'll admit my wrongdoings. We weren't perfect, but we were good. We loved each other."

"That was the past."

"Is this because of my sister? You think you two will create this happy-go-lucky family? How in the world do you think that won't screw up Noah's head more than allowing me in his life?"

Circles.

That's all that's happening.

How do I kick her out of here?

The office door flies open.

"Sorry we're late," Georgia says, glancing back at Noah while they walk into the office. "This little guy talked me into stopping for ice cream."

She comes to a halt and shoves Noah behind her when she looks up and sees Heather. Disbelief and disgust cover her face, and I hold my breath, praying Heather doesn't utter a word to him.

The look on Georgia's face is terrifying to me.

I hope Heather feels the same way and doesn't want the wrath of my sister.

Georgia turns around, being sure she blocks Noah from seeing Heather, and kneels in front of him. "Why don't you go into Archer's office? He's in there." She playfully pokes him in the shoulder, but I notice her hand is shaking as she does it. "Let him know I told you where his candy stash is and to share with you."

Noah's eyes light up, and I'm happy Heather can't see them.

Can't see how great of a kid he is.

How his heart is so much different than hers.

"Really?" Noah says excitedly.

"Really," Georgia answers, whipping around and shutting the door as soon as he runs out of the room. A sneer is pointed in my direction. "What the fuck is she doing here?"

"I—" Heather starts.

Georgia raises her hand, cutting her off, and finally pays Heather a glance. "I didn't ask you. I asked my brother."

Heather glares at Georgia.

"If you're here to right your mistake, it's too late." Georgia's eyes, filled with fury, return to me. "I hope you agree with me."

I nod. "I've explained that a good hundred times."

Does it seem like we're ganging up on Heather?

Probably, but she can leave whenever she wants.

"If you need me to make her leave, I will," Georgia spits.

Heather rolls her eyes but doesn't move.

I tilt my head toward the door and rest my eyes on my sister. "Give us a minute. I don't want you getting in any trouble."

Curses fly from her mouth, and she gives Heather one last glare before leaving my office.

"He's so big." Heather releases a heavy sigh. "He looks like you, but he has my hair. He has my face."

He does, and I fucking hate it.

"Leave, Heather." I stalk to the door and jerk it open. "This is the last time I'll tell you. Leave. No one wants you here."

Her face falls, a single tear slipping down her cheek, and she slowly leaves the room, shooting me glances over her shoulder as if she's waiting for me to stop her.

I don't.

Call me a heartless bastard. I don't give a shit.

My heart beats for my son, and I'll stop anyone from hurting his.

CHAPTER TWENTY-NINE

Jamie

I'M WALKING out of the hospital, tired from a long shift, when my phone rings.

I pull it out of my bag to see Cohen's calling.

We haven't spoken since I left his house with tears in my eyes and regret in my heart.

I unlock my car with the remote in one hand and answer his call with the other, "Hello?"

"Tell your sister to stay the fuck away from us," he says, raw anger in his voice.

I stop before sliding into my car. "What?"

"She came to the bar, asking to see Noah, begging for her family back."

"What?" Apparently, that's the only word I can manage at the moment. I open the car door, toss my bag into the passenger seat, and get in.

"Make it clear that if she does it again, I'll have her arrested for trespassing."

"I told her it was a bad idea. I'm sorry." *I've told her multiple times, yet here I am, apologizing for Heather's bad behavior.*

"Tell her again. It should be easy since you're roommates."

"Not by choice and hopefully not much longer since I've told her to move out a few dozen times."

He stays quiet.

"I'll talk to my parents, ask them to make it clear she stay away from you. I'm sorry."

"I'm sorry too," he grumbles. "For being a dick." He releases a harsh breath. "I'm pissed, exhausted, and fed up with the bullshit."

I shut my eyes while taking in his miserable-sounding tone. "I understand."

"Noah wants to see you."

My eyes flash open, but before I can say anything, he continues, "Georgia is cool with you coming over and hanging out. She's watching him tonight if you want to stop by."

It's my turn to sound miserable. "We're back to that now? Back to having restrictions to hanging out with him? I thought you said you wouldn't do this, that you'd never take Noah away from me."

"This isn't me giving you *restrictions*. This is me making sure shit doesn't turn complicated."

My head aches. "What time?"

"Six."

"I'll be there."

"Cool. I'll give Georgia a heads-up."

We share a quick good-bye, nothing like the soft good-night tones he once gave me, and I hang up to call my mom.

Our relationship has taken a turn, and we've become distant since she questioned me about Cohen. When we do speak, he isn't brought up. Our conversations need to be centered around me asking when the hell Heather will be out of my house. If it wasn't for my mother's pleas not to kick her to the curb, it'd already be done. I tell her Cohen's threat about having Heather arrested for trespassing, and she swears to have a word with her.

———

"I SAID I WANTED YOU OUT," I say when I walk into my house to find Heather on the couch, munching on my Cheetos.

It's become almost a daily game between us.

Like with my mother, our conversations are limited to me asking her to leave and her asking if it's because I'm sleeping with Cohen.

Heather tosses her head back. "Look, Jamie, I'm sorry for how everything went down and how shitty I've treated you since moving in. You're right. I should be grateful you're letting me into your home. I've been anything but that. I don't understand why you're so angry with me, though."

I drop my bag onto a chair but snatch it back up, not wanting to risk Heather rifling through it. I've already caught her in my bedroom a few times and lied about setting up a camera, so she'd stay out of it. Not that I have Cohen shoved into my closet or anything, but that's my private space.

"I'm angry because you called Mom and told her I was sleeping with Cohen," I reply with a straight face. "You damaged my relationship with Mom by spouting out shit you know nothing about."

"I was angry, which I have every right to be," she spews out, placing the Cheetos to the side. She delivers a forced smile. "We all make mistakes. I'm sure you regret sleeping with my son's father, and I forgive you."

I roll my eyes at her half-assed *forgiveness* and don't bother correcting the *my son* part.

She pats the space next to her with a smile as half-assed as her forgive-me speech. "Come on. Let's watch a movie. We've never had the chance to really hang out and have sister time. Maybe it's time we got to know each other."

We've never had sister time because you always kicked me out of the room and told me to go read a book.

"Sorry, but I have plans," I say.

"Can I come?" She raises a brow.

"Nope. There's no plus-one."

"You're going to see him, aren't you?"

"Nope." *Technically, I'm going to see Noah.*

She crosses her arms and scowls. "Why can't I come then?"

"I'm hanging out with Georgia, and word is, you're not her favorite person."

She curls up her lips before pinching them together. "Wow, you seem to really be cozying up to them, huh?"

I ignore her comment, go to my bedroom to change out of my scrubs, and leave.

———

I ALMOST SAID no to going to La Mesa.

It'd only give me memories of coming here with Cohen.

Noah loves it, though, so I agreed.

I order something different than my usual.

Something different than what Cohen said he always ordered.

It's back to old times where I'm hanging out with Georgia and avoiding Cohen.

I hate it.

We devour our food, and then Noah goes to play in the arcade. I laugh as I watch him play some basketball game.

"You and Cohen need to talk about things," Georgia says from across the booth.

I glance at her as she sips on her margarita. "I take it, Cohen told you about us?"

I've been waiting for her to bring this up all night, and I'm surprised it took her this long. She knows something happened when she came over the day after my fight ... and random sex with her brother. With how nosy Georgia can be, she probably had a list of questions for him.

"Told me?" she replies. "Cohen doesn't tell me anything, but I can read my brother." Concern etches on her tan face. "He's heartbroken, and I've only seen him this broken a few times. He cares about you, Jamie. He was ready to take that step with you. He's falling in love with you."

"He's falling in love with you."

I'm half-tempted to snatch that margarita and suck it down.

"It's too messy," I croak out. "Ending it is for the best." I dip a chip in salsa and shove it in my mouth to stop from crying.

"How so? The only *messy* part of your relationship is Heather." Her nose turns into a snarl when she says my sister's name.

"She's my sister. It's too weird."

"Life's weird. Embrace that strange bitch and roll with it."

My shoulders slump as the truth pours out of me. "I want a boyfriend I can take home for the holidays. That'll never happen with Cohen. Sure, there was sexual tension. We hooked up, eased that tension, and now, it's over."

"Is that *tension* over because there was nothing there after you banged, or are you ending it because of Heather?"

Why does it seem like all I do is talk about Heather anymore?

"Either way," I say, "it can't happen. Better to end it now before we hate each other."

"I'll take, *Jamie, answer my question and stop bullshitting me* for two hundred dollars, please."

"I don't know." I throw my head back, wishing I'd ordered a shot of tequila. "Why do we always want the people we can't have?"

"Tell me about it," she grumbles. "Love can never be easy. What's that saying? *Love is patient, love is kind.* Bullshit. It's not that way with me. More along the lines of, *Love is painful, love is hell.*"

"And you're over here, telling me to throw myself *into* love?"

"The man you love loves you back. He wants to be with you. There's a difference."

"Is there a man you love, but he doesn't love you back?"

She shrugs. "Yep."

"Who is this man?" I'm almost positive I already know the answer.

"No one." She tightens one of her pigtails and looks away from me. "No one who matters anymore."

I drum my fingers along the table. "We've done enough talking about my love life tonight. Let's take a break for a moment and move to yours."

"That's not nearly as much fun." She frowns.

"Oh, come on. I have to live with Heather. Feel sorry for me and give me the scoop."

"Fine," she groans, her face going slack. "There's a guy, and things didn't work out between us. I kept holding on, hoping things would change, but I've come to the realization that I'm wasting my time. I told him I was done, and I'm at the point where I'm working through getting over it."

I hesitate before asking, "Does that guy happen to be Archer?"

Her eyes widen, and I've never seen her lost for words. "What?"

"Babe, I was secretly in love with your brother for years." My smile is compassionate. "I know what it looks like—the pain and longing for someone you can't have."

"Yet you can have that guy now." She leans closer to me, her voice lowering. "Archer and I have history, but when he found out Cohen was my brother, he pretty much told me to fuck myself. Now, I hate him."

"What do you mean, *have history*? Did you—"

"Aunt Georgia! Jamie," Noah yelps, appearing at the table with a stuffed frog in his hand. "Look what I won, you guys!"

————

GEORGIA STANDS up from the couch and looks down at me with a smile. "Cohen will be home soon, and I have a thing I need to get to."

"A thing?" I question, scrunching up my nose while in the kitchen with Georgia. "You can't have *a thing*. You're my babysitter, remember?"

And the person who helps me avoid Cohen.

I don't mind her leaving me with Noah.

"You're coming back after this thing *before* Cohen returns, right?" I ask.

"I trust you won't kidnap Noah," she answers.

Her words remind me of that night at the hospital when I asked Cohen if he thought I'd kidnap Noah.

"My brother was hurt and pissed about Heather's little visit when he enforced the whole *babysitter* rule," she says. "Everything will be peachy. I promise."

"Why do I feel like I'm being set up?"

Her hand moves to her chest. "I'm innocent, and I would never do anything like that." She laughs while I follow her into the living room where Noah is playing with Legos. "All right, big guy. Time for me to go. Jamie is going to stay with you until your dad gets home."

"Cool!" Noah jumps to his feet to deliver a kiss on her cheek, and she leaves me with the anxiety of having to face Cohen.

I help Noah with his homework, we build a pillow fort, and an hour later, he's asleep in it. Being with them tonight has helped ease my anxiousness from talking to Heather, but when Cohen gets home, it'll rebound in full force.

I bite at my nails when I hear the door open and footsteps approaching. This isn't a fear that it's a serial killer coming; it's fear of the impending conversation.

Be chill.

Act normal.

"Hey."

I turn back to see him from over the back of the couch. "Hi. I told Georgia you wouldn't be happy if she left me alone, but she ditched us."

"I told her it was fine," he answers. "She made it clear I was being a dick with the whole supervised-visit rule anyway, which I was. I'm sorry, Jamie."

There's nothing hotter than a man who apologizes.

Who owns his bullshit.

"I'm sorry too," I reply. "For everything."

My eyes follow him as he circles around the couch. He's wearing a shirt with the bar's logo on it, and he smirks at me as he takes in the pillow fort.

"Impressive."

I flip my hair over my shoulder. "They call me the Fort-Building Master."

He bends down to pick up Noah in his arms, and his son snuggles into his shoulder. I watch his back while he carries Noah down the hallway, and they disappear into his bedroom.

I chew at my nails again, then play with my hair, and then count my fingers while waiting for Cohen to return.

How will this go?

I'm not sure how much time has passed when he treks into the living room and collapses onto the chair next to the couch.

"You look exhausted," I can't stop myself from saying.

Good job, Jamie.

Start the convo with an insult.

Jamie Gentry, MD, Idiot of Relationships.

There's a distant look in his eyes before he rubs them. "I've had a lot going on these past weeks."

Guilt sweeps through me as I stare at him, speechless.

He sprawls out in the chair. "How have you been?"

I bite into my lip as I answer, "Do you want the truth or the fluffy answer?"

"The truth. I always want the truth from you."

I sag against the cushions. "I've been sucky."

His eyes, no longer as distant, meet mine in understanding. "We miss you, Jamie. *I* miss you."

Same.

So damn much.

I'm afraid to say those words, though. It'll only make things complicated, but I miss them so much that it physically hurts my heart. I cry in the shower, in my car while on my way home from work, and when I think about how much I miss being in Cohen's arms.

"I wish our situation were different," I whisper.

He scoots to the edge of the chair, spreads his legs, and rests his elbows on his knees, leaning in closer. "Our situation is what makes us, what brought us together. It's not fair to you, your heart, or me to break things off because of Heather's mistakes."

"You said you were falling in love with me," I blurt, moving toward a conversation I need to stay far, far away from. "Did you mean it?"

His words run through my mind day and night.

The look in his eyes, the emotion that was on his face, showed me the truth.

He meant it, but I want to hear him say them again.

I'm selfish.

"Do you think I throw those words around foolishly?"

"No." I shut my eyes.

He waits until I open my eyes before saying another word. "We can figure this out. Quit giving a shit what Heather thinks."

"It's not only Heather; it's also my parents. My entire damn family, Cohen. They're hardly speaking to me now."

I want to go back to the I love you *conversation.*

Those words from his mouth.

That's what I want to talk about.

Not Heather. Not my parents. Not the reasons we can't be together.

Tonight will be the last time I hear him say them to me.

"Explain the situation to them. Your parents are rational," he argues.

"It's hard not to look like an asshole when your sister was shot, and now, you're screwing her ex-boyfriend and the father of her child."

"Noah isn't her child."

"You know what I mean." Tears fill my eyes. "I'm sorry, Cohen. I really am. If things were different, had it been before Heather came home, it would've been easier for us to be together. But with her here, with what happened, it's changed everything." I wipe tears off my cheek, and my hands start shaking. "I hate losing you; trust me, it's the last thing I want. My heart is bleeding because of it, but I want to do the right thing, be a good person, and I don't want to let anyone down."

"You're letting me down."

My chin trembles. "I am."

"You're letting yourself down."

"I am."

"For other people."

"For other people," I repeat, covering my mouth in an attempt to stop the impending sobs.

It's the moment when I see it flash in his eyes.

Not anger.

Hurt, yes, but also understanding.

As if, in the pit of his heart, he knew this would backfire as much as I did.

That, no matter how badly we want it, it won't happen.

He grips the arms of the chair and pulls himself to his feet. "Guess it wasn't meant to be then."

I'm inhaling deep breaths when he stands in front of me and holds out his hand. I grab it, and he cups it tight as I stand, my body brushing against his.

He catches my chin between his thumb and forefinger with sadness in his eyes.

"Can we still be friends?" I whisper.

"Sure, fine, whatever."

I'm not sure who makes the first move, but our lips meet, and just like that, we fall into the same pattern we've had.

He groans my name into my mouth, grabbing my ass, pulling my front into his growing erection.

I pull away, my breathing ragged. "We can't."

His forehead rests against mine. "Gotcha."

———

IT'S after one when I get home.

"Where have you been?"

If there is any moment for Heather not to fuck with me, it's now.

I ignore her and start walking toward my bedroom.

"Were you with Cohen all night?" she shouts to my back. "Did you have sex with him?"

I whip around, and her eyes widen when I charge toward her. "You want the truth? Yes, I was with him."

Her mouth flies open. "You lied about hanging out with Georgia."

"I was with Georgia and Noah, and when Cohen got home, I was with him." I raise my voice. "And you want to know what we did, Heather? Do you really want to know?"

"I do."

"We didn't have sex."

We broke each other's hearts.

Which is worse than sex.

At least in just-sex situations, you don't feel broken after walking away.

She stutters for words.

"We broke things off." I inhale a deep breath to hold back tears. Unlike Cohen, she doesn't deserve them. "We broke things off *because of you*. Because, like the good sister I am, I don't want to hurt *you*. Like the good fucking person I am, I'm sacrificing my happiness for my family's—to do what everyone else thinks is right."

She wraps her arms around her, hugging her body. "I never asked you to do that."

I scoff, "Not directly, no, you didn't."

"You and he are wrong," she grinds out. "I've said it. Mom's said it. Anyone I've talked to has said it."

I can only imagine how many people she's told.

How many times she's played the victim.

I raise my arms before dropping them to my sides. "It doesn't matter who was right or who was wrong. It's done. To thank me, you can get the hell out of my house."

I turn around, ignoring her calling my name, and slam my bedroom door shut.

CHAPTER THIRTY

Cohen

THE GENTRY GIRLS.

They've been nothing but trouble in my life.

I'm on alert at all times now.

Nervous that Heather will pop up somewhere or that we'll run into her.

I've had nightmares where she tells Noah who she really is.

It's been two weeks since I've talked to Jamie.

She has been regularly hanging out with Georgia and Noah.

I won't take that away from my son.

No matter how hard she stomped on my heart.

I'm a big boy. I'll deal with it.

I pull my phone from my pocket when it rings, and I see the number of Noah's school flash onto the screen.

"Mr. Fox, Noah fell off the monkey bars at recess."

———

THERE'S no freak-out this time.

No animosity.

Awkwardness, some.

Sadness, a little.

Jamie isn't shocked when she walks into the exam room to find Noah and me. The nurse, the same one who was with us before, must've given her a heads-up we were here. We share a quick smile before she moves to Noah, her forehead scrunched in concern.

Even in pain, Noah perks up when he sees her. "Hey, Jamie!"

"Hi, sweetie," she says. "I heard you had a little fall on the playground."

"It hurts," he whines, limply holding up his arm to show her the damage.

While on the monkey bars, he tried to jump from one bar to another. He fell, and while using his hand to break the fall, he ended up hurting his arm.

She carefully inspects his arm, telling him how good he's doing, before glancing back at me. "It seems like a broken arm, so let's get an X-ray and see what we're working with."

I nod. "He was bound to break something by the time he hit his teens."

"Young kids and broken bones are definitely not a rarity here." She lightly pats Noah's leg. "Someone will come in shortly, take you upstairs, and give you an X-ray of your arm."

"Will it hurt?" he asks with a trembling lip.

"It won't hurt. And when you get back, I'll get you a sucker. How's that sound?"

"That sounds awesome."

"I'll check on him when I can," Jamie says.

I nod again.

Ten minutes later, the X-ray tech comes in and wheels Noah out of the room in his bed. I sit back in my chair and text everyone an update on Noah's condition. I place the phone on my lap at the sound of a knock, expecting it to be Noah returning, but Jamie steps in the room with a handful of suckers.

She holds them up. "For when he gets back."

"Mind if I get one?" I say.

She tosses me a sucker before setting the rest down in the empty chair next to me.

"How have you been, babe?"

We both wince when I say *babe*.

It fell out naturally. I hadn't meant for it to.

She shoves her hands into the pockets of her jacket. "Busy. Working."

"Heather still crashing with you?"

"Unfortunately," she grumbles. "Which is probably why I'm working like crazy. Avoidance seems like my life at the moment."

"Avoiding your sister and me." I pull out my best teasing tone. "I don't blame you for dodging Heather."

As much as I've tried not to, I fucking miss Jamie.

"If you ever need time away from her, my places are open," I stupidly offer. "You can hang out with Noah at my place or grab a drink at the bar."

She sends me a wavering smile. "Thank you. I'll remember that."

This conversation seems so forced.

The friendliness such a fraud.

"I don't want shit to be weird with us, Jamie," I say, blowing out a long breath. "What we had happened. I don't regret it, and even though it's made shit complicated, I would hate myself if I wasn't up-front with you about my feelings. I respect you, and if you think a relationship with me will hurt your relationship with your family, which, in turn, will hurt you, I understand."

"Cohen"—her face falls—"it's not that I don't want a relationship with you. If there's anyone I want, it's you. It was you years ago, and it's you now."

"But it's not me."

"I'm sorry," she whispers, her voice choked with emotion. "Please don't hate me."

I stand, not wanting her to be upset at work, and wrap her into a tight hug. "I get it," I say into her hair. "I don't hate you."

This is me being a responsible adult.

Being respectful.

Putting my feelings aside for my son.

CHAPTER THIRTY-ONE

Jamie

"YOU TWO TOTALLY BANGED," Lauren says, stopping at the vending machine next to me and swiping her credit card.

"What are you talking about?" I ask, avoiding eye contact and pretending to focus on my cheese crackers.

"Your sister's abandoned baby daddy. Something happened between you two." She bends down to grab her candy bar and then bumps her hip against mine. "I'd say sex—or at least oral."

"Please never call him her abandoned baby daddy again."

"Look, I'm not one to throw out lectures because I hate hearing them myself."

"Cool. Then, don't."

"But I'll make an exception this time."

"No, you don't have to do that."

I turn around, strolling toward the doctors' lounge, and she scurries behind me like a lost duckling.

"I've told you about Gage and me, right?"

I nod. "Broke up, didn't speak for years, and he hated you?"

She snaps her fingers. "Correcto. When he came back into town, he didn't want anything to do with me, but then we realized we were being idiots and wasting valuable time." She perks up. "Now, we're happier than ever, married, and we have the cutest kids in the damn world. All because we got our heads out of our asses and took a chance, not knowing what'd happen after."

"Sorry, babe, but there's a big difference between you reconciling with your high school sweetheart and me banging my sister's ex."

Her face lights up. "Ah, so you did bang?"

I narrow my eyes at her.

"Have I ever told you about my brother Dallas?"

"Nope, but if it's another *take a chance on love* story, hard pass. Give me a murder mystery."

"Dallas was married with a daughter—perfect, award-winning life. Then his wife died. He was broken, but one night, he drunkenly hooked up with *and knocked up* a woman who he'd once worked with. Willow, the knocked-up character in this story, had known his wife. She was afraid of being hurt, of being second in line, of what people would think about her. They played a similar game as you and Hot Dad are." She taps my nose between her last words. "Quit playing games and at least try to make it work. What will it hurt?"

"My heart. His heart. His son's heart."

"Don't break them then." She shrugs. "It's as simple as that."

I sit down, and she collapses next to me.

"Oh! Tomorrow is my birthday, and I'm sure you haven't gotten me a present yet, *but* what you can get me is for you to give it a try." She pokes my shoulder. "Ask him to dinner."

I give her a death glare.

"Whatever. Just wait until he finds another woman to give him a chance. You'll regret it then, Dr. Chickenshit." She pats my thigh. "Noah wants you to sign his cast too, by the way. Make your move."

I stand, wiping my hands down my scrubs.

"And his father wants you to sign up for a date with him. Possibly another round in the sack."

I shake my head, leave my snack on the table, and head toward Noah's room.

Cohen is standing next to Noah, signing his bright green cast. He holds the pen out to me with a friendly smile. "Your turn."

Our hands graze each other's when I take the pen from him, and his hips brush against my mine when he steps back to give me room. Noah sucks on his sucker while I sign my name along with a giant heart and a smiley face.

When Cohen glances at me, I jerk my head toward the corner of the room, and he takes the hint, following me. I blow out a series of breaths.

Here goes.

My hand rests on his shoulder. "Do you want to have coffee or go to dinner or something this week?"

Shock fills his eyes as he scratches his cheek, confused by my sudden change of heart. "Are you asking me out on a date?"

My chest lightens at his humor. "I'm not sure what I'm asking, so work with me here."

He tips his head down, and he nuzzles my neck as he whispers his answer, "I'll work with you however you want, Doctor."

I hold my hand to his chest and push him away before I drag him out of this room and straddle his cock. "All right, Mr. Suggestive, we're in a hospital."

He grins, his lips on the edge of mine this time. "I'll pick you up tomorrow."

"Cool!" Noah says. "Are we going to get cupcakes?"

Oh, shit.

How do we explain he's not invited to this hangout?

"You need to let your arm heal, buddy," Cohen says. "How about I get you cupcakes, and you can eat them while Aunt Georgia babysits you?"

Noah perks up at Cohen's suggestion. "Okay! That'd be so cool! Sylvia can sign my cast too!"

"Saved by cupcakes," Cohen whispers to me.

"Always saved by cupcakes," I reply with a laugh.

———

I INSISTED on taking an Uber to the restaurant.

The last thing I need is Heather from Hell making a big deal if she sees Cohen picking me up. I shudder at the thought and the situation I'd have had to deal with.

"Where are you going?" Heather asks. She's sitting on my couch, which seems to be her favorite place, while watching some stupid TV show.

"Out," I answer.

She pauses her show. "You look pretty dressed up. Can I come?"

"Nope."

She crosses her arms, her nose wrinkling. "Is it a date?"

I whip around, snatch my clutch, and leave without answering. She texts me a few times on my ride to dinner, asking why I'm such a heartless sister, to which I send her a line full of middle-finger emojis.

What great sister bonding we have.

Cohen beat me to the restaurant and is waiting outside when my Uber pulls up. As soon as he sees me, he rushes to my side.

"Jesus, you look fucking gorgeous," he says, circling his arm around my hips and kissing my neck.

My cheeks warm. "Thank you."

I lick my lips.

He looks gorgeous himself. Since we've always been in more casual situations, I've never seen Cohen dressed up before. Tonight, he has on black pants and a fitted blue blazer with a long-sleeve button-down shirt underneath it—the top three buttons undone.

He grabs my hand, walks us to the entrance, and opens the door for me. The hostess smiles when we walk in and leads us to a table in the corner. Cohen scoots my chair out for me before taking his, and I smooth out my dress while the waitress pours our waters.

Cohen orders a draft beer, and I stay with my water.

He raises his brow. "No wine?"

"Water is fine for now," I answer, playing with the napkin in my hand while changing the subject. "Did you know this is my favorite restaurant?"

He stares at me with pride. "I'd love to say yes, but I'm not a liar. I don't exactly date, but Georgia said this was the place to go if you're trying to impress a woman and get her to date you."

"I have to give it to the girl. Georgia knows her shit."

"She wants us to ride off in the sunset together, so she made sure to steer me well."

"She did seem adamant on us talking about our relationship."

"She likes to see me happy."

I wiggle in my seat. "Is that what you are?"

"Happy?"

I nod.

"Can't say I've been having a blast since you dumped my ass." He stops and cocks his head to the side. "Or not dumped my ass but told me *fuck you* since I don't think we made it to the dating part yet."

I offer an apologetic smile. "We kind of went backward on that one, huh?"

"Just a little bit," he says with a hint of a smile. "We can start over and do it the right way? I'll wine and dine you." He gestures toward the room. "We can share flirty texts, maybe even sext a few times, and then we can progress back to sex from there. All I want from you is to get closer, to try this out, to see how we'd be together."

His words put me at ease, confirming I made the right decision in asking him out and that I'd been stupid to turn my back on him without us trying.

Who knows? Maybe, in the end, we'll hate each other.

Not likely, though.

Even in the short time we've spent together, my heart belongs to him.

I stare at him, affection in my eyes. "I want that too."

"What made you change your mind?"

I bite into my lip. "Lauren, the nurse, had a heart-to-heart with me."

Maybe it was Lauren's not very helpful and very random family history stories that hit me with the reality of what I'd be losing if I stepped away from Cohen for good. A relationship that seems wrong to other people is the one that makes me the happiest. It might be one stirred-up mess, but deep down, I'd regret turning my back on Cohen if I did.

If other people don't like it, who cares?

Opinions aren't worth breaking my heart.

Eventually, my parents will have to forgive me. They forgave Heather.

Seeing Noah and Cohen in the hospital room and realizing I could lose them made me view things with a different perspective.

Cohen reaches across the table and takes my hand. "We got this. Neither one of us would be taking this chance if we didn't think it'd work out in the end. I don't want anyone but you, and quite frankly, I sure as hell don't want there to be any other douchebag for you."

———

"NO WAY in hell are you taking an Uber home," Cohen says, dragging me into his side as we walk out of the restaurant.

I laugh into his chest. "No way in hell are you taking me home, where Sisterzilla will see you."

He comes to a halt. "You don't have to go home. Want to come over and hang out?"

"I'm definitely game for that."

Cohen holds my hand on the car ride back to his house, and Georgia is on the couch watching TV when we walk in.

"Hey, you cute kids, you," she says in a squeaky voice while poking the air toward us. "The monster is in bed, knocked out, and I'm going home. Have fun. Practice safe sex, or don't practice safe sex. I'm down for being an aunt again."

Cohen gives her a stern look. "Good night. Be careful going home."

She gives each of us a hug good night—I love that she's more like a sister to me more than my own—and Cohen turns to look at me when she leaves.

"Food? TV? Bedroom?" he asks.

"TV in the bedroom?"

He jerks his head toward the bedroom and leads us there, his hand on the small of my back. "Let me give you some clothes to sleep in."

"Clothes to sleep in, huh?" I give him a flirty smile. "Being a bit optimistic that I'm staying the night, are we?"

"I'd be optimistic if I told you I wasn't giving you clothes to sleep in." He opens a drawer and pulls out a pair of sweatpants.

"What if I like the no-clothes idea better?"

His hand opens, dropping the pants onto the floor, and he takes three long strides in my direction before cupping my head and crushing his lips to mine. His tongue slides in my mouth without hesitation, his mouth tasting like beer and cinnamon, and I moan into it. I suck on the tip of his tongue, remembering how skilled it is and anticipating when it'll be pleasuring me again.

Soon, hopefully.

I drop my hand between our bodies, and he hisses when I squeeze his already-hard cock.

I love how hard he gets for me.

How much he wants me.

I unbuckle his pants and slide them to his feet at the same time I fall to my knees. His cock is in front of my face as I kneel before him, and I toss my hair over my shoulder. Another hiss leaves him when I fist his cock, pumping it a few times before taking it into my mouth. His head falls back, my name slipping from his lips like a curse, and I lightly tickle his balls. A hint of satisfaction runs through me when I take his entire cock in my mouth without gagging, deep-throating him the best that I can, and his knees buckle.

I suck him fast, and he's holding back, gripping my hair like he did last time.

"Yeah," he bites out. "Suck me just like that, Jamie." He groans, his words falling in rhythm with my sucking. "Just like that."

It's the reaction I craved.

He peeks down at me when I pull my mouth away and replace it with my hand, slowly stroking him.

"Pull my hair. Show me how fast and hard you want it."

His eyes shut, his hips jerking forward to match my hand. "You sure?"

I bite into my lip, nod, and then start sucking him again.

He, doing as I said, and plows his hand through my hair. I suck him harder, and he roughly pulls my mouth to his dick.

He warns me he's about to blow—a warning to pull away.

I don't.

I want to taste him.

Cohen's hand drops from my hair to my cheek, massaging it as I swallow his come. "My turn."

I yelp when I'm picked up from under my armpits and tossed onto the bed. I quickly cover my mouth.

"We have to be quiet," he says, leaning forward to pull my hand from my mouth and kiss me before drawing back.

He kicks off his pants as he walks to the door to lock it, and his shirt is next to go while he returns to the bed. I rub my thighs together to feed the arousal, anticipating what his turn will consist of, hoping it's something with his tongue.

Then his cock.

The determination and lust on his face as he comes back assure me that I won't be disappointed.

He kneels at the end of the bed, the same way I did at his feet, and slides my heels off.

"Where do you want my mouth first?" he asks, climbing up the bed and dragging his hand up my dress. He slips my panties to the side and pushes a finger inside me. "Here?"

I moan at the loss of his hand as he slips it higher, inching underneath my bra and cupping my breast.

"Or here?"

I gulp. "Between my legs. Most definitely between my legs."

He slides off my panties and rests my legs over his shoulders. "I've missed the taste of your pussy."

I shiver as he makes one long lick down my slit.

"Have you missed my mouth here?"

I nod, pushing my hips closer to him. "Every single day."

"Did you touch yourself, thinking about my mouth here?" He cups me before sliding three fingers inside me, causing me to yelp. "Shh …"

I throw my arm over my mouth, biting into it, hoping he doesn't attempt to get an answer out of me as he thrusts into me. If he does, it'll come out a lot louder than intended, and Noah might be a cockblock to us tonight.

He fingers me. He devours me with his tongue and his mouth. He doesn't stop until I'm writhing underneath him, biting my lip while saying his name and moaning.

One time.

Two times.

Three times.

He's torturing me, but it feels so good.

Cohen knows my body better than I do.

I push at his shoulder. "On your back."

The bed dips when he falls onto his back, and I straddle him, smashing our lips together.

Our kiss is hungry and passionate.

He smooths his hands over the backs of my thighs as we slowly make out, and I grind against him.

"Put it in, baby."

I suck on the tip of his tongue before pulling away, lifting, and falling down on his cock.

We both gasp as he fills me.

"So good," Cohen grumbles. Reaching up, he squeezes my breast, teasing my nipple. "So damn good." One of his hands falls, and he uses his thumb to play with my clit, moving it in circles with his hand.

I buck against him, biting into my lip so hard that I wouldn't be surprised if I drew blood. As I grow closer, I give him my weight, and my clit rubs against his groin as I rock into him.

It's coming. I'm coming. As soon as I hit my peak, I shove my face into his shoulder, sinking my teeth into his sweaty skin, and moan. He lets out a deep groan from the back of his throat, holding me in place, and thrusts underneath me until it's his turn to shove his face into my neck as he comes.

CHAPTER THIRTY-TWO

Jamie

HOLY SHIT.

Oh my God.

Is this really happening?

I stare at the stick in my shaking hand and set it alongside the others lined on my bathroom vanity.

"Jamie!"

I jump at Heather shouting my name on the other side of the door and banging on it.

"Are you alive in there?"

"Yes!" I shriek, fighting to control my breathing.

"What are you doing? You've been in there for over an hour!"

"I'm taking a shower." I dig my nails into the vanity. *Go the fuck away!*

"I haven't heard the shower running."

"I mean, I'm taking a bath."

"All right," she says, making it known that she doesn't believe me. "Have fun, taking your fake bath."

I flip off the door in frustration.

How will I explain this?

CHAPTER THIRTY-THREE

Cohen

"YOU'VE GOT to be shitting me," I mutter when Heather takes a seat at the end of the bar, and I stalk to her. "I told you not to come here again."

"I'm a paying customer," Heather fires back with a smirk.

I dip my head down and lower my voice. "Go be a paying customer somewhere else."

She snarls, "What if I'm here to deliver good news?"

"I don't care."

The only good news she can deliver to me is that she's leaving town again and never coming back.

She settles her elbow on the bar. "Did Jamie tell you she's having a baby?"

My heart nearly stops. "Excuse me?"

A hint of a smile plays at her lips. She knows she's caught me off guard, and she's loving it. "Did my sister tell you she's knocked up?"

I grind my teeth, refusing to answer.

She snorts. "She didn't."

"Leave."

Heather flips her finger back and forth. "The question is, is she having *your* baby or another guy's baby?"

"Don't come in here, trying to start shit," I hiss. "It won't work."

She settles her duffel-sized purse onto the bar, pulls out a baggie, and pushes it toward me. "Don't believe me?"

"What the fuck?" I say around a gag before sliding it back to her. "What is wrong with you? Who walks around with a bag of pregnancy tests?"

"I found these tests in Jamie's bathroom."

"And?"

I won't grant her the satisfaction of reacting to her games. She knew she'd have me on the *bag of pregnancy tests* surprise.

"They're not my tests, and we don't have another roommate, so they have to be hers."

I stay quiet, clenching my jaw, and wait for her to get the hell out.

"Since you two were … or are banging each other, I thought it might be something you'd like to know."

She needs to get out before my heart jumps out of my chest and lands in front of her.

"Appreciate the concern, but you can leave."

"Do you think the baby is yours?"

"Leave, Heather."

She stares at me, unblinking and unmoving.

Fuck it.

Jamie.

I need to talk to Jamie.

I turn, walk away from the bar, and charge toward my office. I slam the door shut behind me, tug my phone from the charger on my desk, and find a text from Jamie.

Perfect fucking timing.

Jamie: Is the offer to get some space at one of your places still open?

Do I ask her?

No way Jamie is sleeping around, and we've had sex a few times without protection.

That can mean only one thing: the baby is mine.

If those tests are even hers.

My hands shaking, I nearly drop my phone when I reply.

Me: Sure is.

Are you pregnant with my baby?

Is that why you're coming here?

Jamie: Are you at the bar?

Me: Yes. You want to have drinks?

If she's pregnant, she can't drink. She'll decline. I flinch, remembering her not ordering wine at dinner. Jamie has made it clear that, in stressful situations, a glass of wine and Cheetos settle her nerves.

Jamie: No. Maybe just some company, someone to talk to, vent to.

Me: I'll be here.

Here waiting for you to break the news.

To ease the crazy-ass thoughts spiraling through my head.

I slump down in my chair and cover my face with my hands.

A baby?

So many mixed emotions pour through me, and the memory of when I found out Heather was pregnant with Noah surges through me. I was shocked but ecstatic, and damn it, my stomach flutters at the thought of having a baby with Jamie.

Fuck. It'd be awesome.

She'd be the best fucking mom in the world.

I fidget with my phone, then a pen on my desk, and then a fucking paper clip while waiting for her. No way can I wait out in the bar. People will think I'm on speed, considering how pumped I am. I freeze, the paper clip falling through my fingers when there's a knock on the door.

I stand straight, expecting Jamie, but Archer walks in with the bag of pregnancy tests in his hand.

"Uh … whoever that chick was, she left a present for you." He cringes, flicks the bag onto my desk, and grabs the hand sanitizer next to my computer. "I didn't want to throw them out, and it'd look pretty damn gross if I left them on the bar. I'm pissed I had to pick up those things that most likely have piss on them."

I silently stare at the bag of tests.

"Did you get someone pregnant? That chick? What about Jamie?"

"That chick is Jamie's sister."

His jaw drops. "What the fuck? You're banging her sister now too? Dude, from what you've told me about her, that's dumb as hell."

I recoil at the thought of being with Heather again. "No, Heather has been trying to get back with me, but I told her to piss off. She's living with Jamie, and she claims she found the tests in Jamie's bathroom."

"Have you asked Jamie about it?"

I shake my head. "When I got back to the office to call her, with perfect timing, she texted, asking if she could stop by the bar."

"That sounds like a pregnancy announcement to me."

I groan and rub my eyes. "Heather is known to be a liar, so I can't take her word on shit."

"If Heather wanted you back, why would she tell you Jamie was pregnant with your baby? Wouldn't you want Jamie?"

"She insinuated that Jamie is pregnant with someone else's baby. Heather knows something happened between Jamie and me, but I'm not sure how much she knows."

"Gotcha." He taps a loose fist to his chest. "Thank fuck I don't do relationships. Sounds like a major pain in the ass."

"If Jamie doesn't give me a heads-up she's here and comes into the bar, will you send her back here?"

"I got you."

When he leaves, I shove the bag of tests into a drawer. I pace in front of my desk, gripping my phone, and wait for her.

What if she doesn't tell me?

Do I bring it up?

Confront her?

I tense when there's another knock on the door, and Jamie walks in, a shy smile on her face.

"Hey, babe," I say, dropping my phone onto my desk.

"Hi." She glances around the room, running her hands up and down her arms. "Are you busy? I didn't mean to bombard you. I just needed to clear my head. Heather has been driving me nuts, and there are only so many hours I can work before they tell me I have to go home."

I sit on the edge of my desk to keep from falling flat on my face.
"I'm never too busy for you." I stand, rush across the room to grab a
chair, and pull it toward her. "Sit down."

Don't shake.

Stay cool.

Calm.

Collected.

She raises a brow and straightens out her dress before sitting. "Are
you okay, Cohen? I can go—"

"No," I interrupt. "Stay."

She nods, hugging herself.

I lean against the desk and cross my ankles. "You look well."

Are you pregnant?

"I'm glad you think I look … *well*." She laughs. "Even though you
only saw me two days ago, and not much has changed."

"Do you *feel well*?"

"Do I *feel well*? Yes …"

"Anything big happen in those two days?"

"I mean, stuff has happened, yes. I've been working and—"

"Are you pregnant?" I blurt out.

Her eyes widen. "What?"

"Are you pregnant?"

"How did—" Her gaze moves from one side of the room to the
other. "What the …?"

"Is it true?"

She nods. "I was planning on telling you, just working up the
nerve, but apparently, you're the baby whisperer."

I scrub my hand over my face.

"Are you mad?" she whispers.

"Is the baby mine?"

She winces. "Are you kidding me?"

I hold up my arms. "I'm a dick for asking, and never would I
doubt you, but Heather was spitting out some bullshit about it being
someone else's."

"Heather?" Her brows scrunch together. "When did you talk to
Heather?"

"She came to the bar about an hour ago."

"She came to the bar," she slowly repeats.

I circle my desk, pull out the bag of tests, and hold it up. "She dropped these off and said she found them in your bathroom."

Her face turns bright red. "I don't know what's more mortifying. My sister going through my trash and packing up something so personal to me or that she brought them here or that you're holding them in front of me." She blows out a forceful breath. "Now, I'm really done with her."

I toss the bag on my desk, lock the door, and fall to my knees in front of her. "Come stay with me then. If you don't want to be near her and she won't leave, come to me."

She peers down at me, biting into her lip. "You'd be okay with me staying with you?"

"Absolutely."

I groan when she pinches my shoulder.

"And by the way, of course the baby is yours. Before you, I hadn't had sex in a year. You're lucky you only got a pinch and not a smack to the face."

I'm sporting a shit-eating smirk while running my hands up and down her thighs underneath the loose yellow dress she's wearing. "Are you really having my baby?"

She nods, flashing me a flirtatious grin. "I'm really having your baby."

"Wow." I kiss her knee. "This makes my fucking day."

"You're not worried that this happened too fast?"

I shake my head. "Sure, our relationship is new, but my feelings for you are strong enough that I'm ready for this—ready to jump headfirst and be with you, for us to be a family."

I groan deep in my throat as her eyes water, and I move my hand between her legs.

She laughs. "You're in a mood."

"Hell yes, I'm in a mood." I flip her dress up. "In the mood to show the woman who's having my baby how damn excited I am, how appreciative I am for her, and you deserve a reward for it."

She squeals when I move an arm to slip it around her waist,

dragging her to the edge of the chair, and I part her thighs. Ducking my head, I drag her panties down her legs and yank her closer to my face. I savor the sound of her moan as I softly suck on her clit before thrusting two fingers inside her.

"Look at that. My baby mama is soaked for me."

Her eyes are shut, and she's licking her lips. "You're really going to play out this baby mama thing, aren't you?"

"Damn straight." My tongue joins my fingers, and I start devouring her—sucking and praising her pussy.

I love how sensitive she is to my touch—how goose bumps cover her soft skin and how she shivers with my every thrust.

She comes on my tongue, tasting delicious, and I suck on my finger before smearing her juices on my bottom lip.

CHAPTER THIRTY-FOUR

Jamie

HEAT SWEEPS up my neck when Cohen walks me out of his office and through the bar. Archer raises a brow, taking in my wrinkled dress and the orgasmed-out expression on my face. When we reach my car, Cohen kisses me and asks me to come over later.

"That sounds nice."

I have some business to attend to real quick.

"See you later, baby mama."

"I'm so kicking your ass."

He winks and gives me one final kiss on my forehead.

When I arrive at my house, all the sweetness I had with Cohen evaporates, and my nails are drawn. I stomp up the porch steps, my hands itching to snatch Heather's shit and throw them out the window.

"Have you lost your fucking mind?" I screech before coming to a stop.

My parents, along with Heather, are sitting on the couch in my living room.

Heather's face is red with fake tears, my dad seems confused, and my mom looks hurt.

I zip my finger toward Heather. "I want her out of my house now.

I've been nice long enough. Put her in your house, get her an apartment—I don't care what you do, but if you don't make her leave, I'll do it myself."

"She wants me out, so she can hang out here, pregnant with Cohen's baby," Heather screeches.

"I want you out because you went all Oscar the Grouch and plucked pregnancy tests out of my trash can, bagged them up like you worked at a grocery store, and thought, *Gee, I think it'll be a good idea to take these to Cohen at his job.* You even insinuated that another man might be the father, like I sleep around!"

"Heather," my mother gasps, shooting her a concerned look, "did you do that?"

Heather stumbles for words. "She's having sex with Cohen, Mom! I think that gives me every right to be furious."

"Enough," my father yells.

Thank God.

"Heather, pack your shit," he demands.

Her eyes widen. "Wh-what?"

"Listen to your father," my mother says with an anger in her voice I've never heard before.

"Now," my father pushes, and she scrambles to her feet.

My mother jumps up to help her with her crutches, but Heather swats her away.

She points at me. "I can't believe you're taking *her* side. The woman who's having sex with the father of her sister's child. Your daughter is having his baby, and I'm the bad person?"

No one says a word, and when she realizes she's not getting the reaction she wants, she storms down the hallway to my guest bedroom, not even bothering with the crutches.

Heather is bitching as she throws her belongings into her suitcase.

I play with my hands in front of me to calm myself and dodge eye contact with my parents.

"Jamie," my mom says, causing me to look at her. "Is that true?" Her eyes drop to my stomach. "Are you pregnant?"

I nod. "Yes."

Not only did I take a million of the at-home pregnancy tests, but I also took a blood test at work to confirm.

Positive.

"That's your sister's …" She stops as if she can't finish the sentence.

I nod. "He is."

My father scrubs a hand over his face. "Jamie, this puts all of us in a stressful situation."

I fall on the chair across from them. "You guys know my heart." I place my hand to my chest. "You know I don't make stupid decisions. I love him."

My father rises from the couch. "It's not fair for us to have this conversation while your sister is in the other room, throwing a tantrum. We'll take her home and discuss this later."

I nod. "Thank you."

He kisses the top of my head, and tears are in my mother's eyes as she hugs me.

I go to my bedroom to avoid any Heather drama and wait until she leaves before coming out.

———

MY PARENTS RETURN AN HOUR LATER, Heather-free, and we sit down in the living room.

"How did this happen?" my mother asks.

"I've been spending a lot of time with Cohen and Noah, and I don't know … as we did, I developed feelings for Cohen. *Strong* feelings." A tear runs down my cheek. "This is complicated and puts you in a weird situation, and I get that. All I'm asking is for you to trust me, to believe in me, and to know that I've gone back and forth with Cohen. I've broken his heart, broken my own heart, by saying no to a relationship with him, but it's not fair to us."

"You're in love with him?" my father asks.

"I am."

He slaps his hands on his legs. "That's all that matters to me."

My mouth falls open. "What?"

"You were right about making responsible decisions. If this

relationship wasn't that serious, if it wasn't *love*, then you wouldn't risk it."

I glance at my mother, tears also on her face.

"You're having a baby, honey," she says with excitement. "It's a shock, yes, and it'll create some issues, but nothing will ever cause us to turn our backs on you. We love you."

I'm full-on crying.

My fears dissolve.

They don't hate me.

They aren't disappointed in me.

They still love me.

———

"A BIG BROTHER?" Noah shouts. "I'm going to be a big brother?"

Cohen nods, sitting next to me on the couch, and grabs my hand in his. "You're going to be a big brother, buddy."

Nothing will ever erase the memory of the beaming smile on his face.

He grabs my arm and jumps up and down. "I have a mom, and now, I'm going to be a big brother! This is so cool!"

Cohen and I shared countless talks on how to explain our relationship to Noah. Coming to a decision wasn't easy, and we hoped we were making the right one. We didn't ask for anyone's opinion, and in the end, we decided we wouldn't tell Noah I was his real mother's sister. Maybe, in the future, that will change, but he's too young to understand it now.

The risk of running into Heather is low. She started another online relationship, this one with Pat's cousin, and moved back to Vegas. My parents said when she left, she didn't utter a word of apology, a word about mending things with Noah and Cohen, and definitely nothing about me—not surprising. What she did ask for was money.

Cohen mentioned that she told him Joey shot her because she thought she was pregnant, but she took a test in the hospital, and it was negative.

A month ago, Cohen and I sat Noah down and told him that we were dating.

He didn't say, *Yucky yuck*, like he had when Seth told him he used to be my boyfriend.

It was the opposite reaction. He was as excited as he is now, bouncing on his tiptoes and then hugging me. The next day, he asked if I could become his new mom. I said I'd be there for him as much as any mom would.

We waited until now to break the big brother news. Other than Archer—given he had seen the pregnancy tests, which is mortifying— and my parents, we haven't broken the news to anyone else. As a doctor, I know things can happen early on in pregnancy, and I don't want to get anyone's hopes up. I also don't want to deal with questions if anything does happen.

"Do I get to pick the name?" he asks. "I bet I can come up with the best name ever."

Cohen laughs. "We'll have to see about that."

My hand breaks away from Cohen's hold when Noah plops down in the small space separating us and relaxes his head against my shoulder.

"This is the best day ever," he chirps.

I smooth my hand over his hair before kissing the top of his head.

Cohen asks Noah not to tell anyone yet and adds a bribe of three cupcakes if he doesn't.

Well, four cupcakes after negotiation.

CHAPTER THIRTY-FIVE

Cohen

"GENDER REVEAL PARTY TIME," Georgia sings, strolling through my backyard with a giant-ass baby bottle—shaped piñata in her arms. "Someone find out how and where I can hang this thing up, please and thank you." She turns in a circle and points at Finn before shoving it into his arms. "You have been nominated as the official piñata boy!"

"What the—?" Finn stops before dropping the F-bomb.

Grace has been growing on him.

I'd never heard of a gender reveal party until Georgia announced she was throwing us one. I still don't get the concept of it, but Jamie was excited, so that's all that matters. Georgia and Ashley planned the party, and my backyard is packed with our friends and family. My mother is here, sitting in the corner, and I've barely spoken a word to her. Georgia insisted I invite her and wants us to work on our relationship. According to my sister, my mom is clean and has been trying to right her wrongs.

Jamie's parents are here, both of them excited as fuck, which is awesome. Jamie loves them so much, and it would've crushed her if they hadn't accepted our relationship,. At the moment, Noah is sitting on Regina's lap as he shows off his iPad.

Yes, iPad.

Somehow, he talked Jamie into upgrading the iPod.

"Lincoln, Lincoln, Lincoln," Georgia says, walking over to the tall, dark-haired guy, plopping down on his lap and wrapping her arms around his neck. "When are you going to take me out on a date?"

Lincoln is Archer's brother who recently started working at the bar. His employment caused a few arguments between Archer and me. Lincoln is fresh out of prison, and the thought of a felon working in the bar put a bad taste in my mouth. What bothers me more is how often Georgia flirts with him.

How he ended up at our gender reveal party is beyond me, but I'm sure it was Georgia's doing.

Lincoln wraps his arms around Georgia's waist, glancing down at her. "Whenever you're available, babe."

"Why did I agree to this shit?" Archer grumbles, his eyes cold. "I don't do baby shower shit."

"First, it's a gender reveal party," Jamie corrects. "And second, you're here because you love us." She pats his chest while walking past us.

I keep my eyes on Jamie, watching her practically waddle to her parents and talk to them. She looks breathtaking. Her hair is curled into loose waves, and my cock stirs as I eye her dress, her belly sticking out in the front. As soon as I saw her in it this morning, I tossed her onto the bed, peeled it off her body, and then made love to her.

She put it back on to torture me.

"What crawled up your ass?" I ask, turning back to Archer. "You were fine fifteen minutes ago."

He shrugs and scrubs a hand over his face. "Not trying to be a dick. I'm just stressed."

"Stressed about what? The bar?"

"Nah, some personal shit."

"You know you can talk to me about whatever, right?"

He nods.

"You ready, guys?" Ashley yells, skipping into the yard with a black balloon in her hand. "Cohen! Jamie! It's time!"

I was as frustrated as Archer is now when Jamie informed me that the sex of our baby would be kept secret until this party.

Until we popped a damn balloon.

I wanted to know right then and there at our ultrasound appointment, and the anticipation has been killing me. Every day, I changed my mind on whether I thought we were having a boy or a girl. I backed off on my frustrations and agreed to wait because my pregnant girlfriend has me wrapped around her fingers.

Jamie snags my hand in hers and leads us to where our guests are crowded around tables, all eyes on us. She's nearly bursting at the seams when Ashley hands us both a pin and the balloon.

This is it.

Our hands wrap around the thin string of the balloon, and the crowd counts down. My hand tightens around hers, excitement pouring through me, and we stab our pins into the balloon as soon as they yell, "One!"

Pink confetti rains down on us.

"A girl!" Jamie yelps.

"A girl," I repeat, holding pieces of confetti and staring at them in my hand, still comprehending what it means. And then it dawns on me. "We're having a baby girl!"

The crowd erupts in cheers, some crying, others ready to run to us with congratulations.

I can't let that happen.

Not yet.

I turn around, skimming the yard for Georgia, and relief hits me when I see she's running our way with another black balloon. She hands it to me and retreats back, and Jamie tilts her head to the side.

Her hand covers her mouth, her eyes meeting Georgia's. "Oh my God!" Her hand leaves her mouth to grab mine. "Are we … having twins?"

Oh hell, this isn't how I thought she'd react to this.

I grip the balloon in one hand and give her a pin with the other. "Pop it."

There's a hesitation before she does, and a frown covers her face at the lack of confetti.

"Wait, what?" The sound of her whimpering tells me when she's spotted it—the ring box falling to the ground at the same time I drop to one knee. "Holy shit," she hisses.

"Cuss word!" Noah yells at her.

She laughs. Her face is splotchy from the tears of finding out we're having a baby girl, and they're streaming down her face now.

"That ... that isn't confetti," she whispers, staring down at me.

I peer up at her, playing with the box in my hand before popping it open. "It's definitely not confetti."

"Is it a *thank you for having my baby* ring?" she asks with an unsteady breath.

I snatch the ring. "It's more along the lines of a *will you be my wife* ring?"

"Holy shit," she gasps, her voice so low only I hear her. "Holy shit."

"Does *holy shit* mean yes or no?" Fear settles through me that she's not ready for this yet.

That I jumped the gun.

She waves her hand next to her mouth as if she's struggling to produce words, and they come out between breaths. "Holy shit definitely means yes."

I grab the ring from the box, and both our hands shake as I slide it onto her finger.

"See how good I was at keeping a secret, Dad?" Noah says, running to us. "I didn't tell anyone!"

"You sure didn't," I say, rising to my feet. "I'm proud of you."

Noah, like the nosy kid he is, went through my drawers—looking for a pair of my underwear to wear over his jeans with the outfit Georgia demanded she wasn't going anywhere with him in—and found the ring.

Thank fuck Jamie wasn't there.

That meant that not only did Noah learn my secret, but with the way he came into the living room, waving it, Georgia found out too. I learned my son is great at hiding secrets—not once did he let the cat out of the bag when we told him about the pregnancy, and Jamie seemed to have no idea about my proposing.

The Georgia thing worked out because she helped me plan the perfect proposal.

Jamie's eyes meet mine, and she reaches out, running her hand along my cheek. "Are you going to cry, Cohen Fox?"

I repeatedly shake my head, fighting back my emotions. "Nope. I got this."

"Let me go grab the cake," Georgia says.

She's been hiding it from us. She wouldn't let us open the fridge all day, in fear we'd peek.

I'm pulling Jamie in for a kiss as Georgia disappears inside of the house. A crowd gathers around us, people inspecting the ring and offering their congratulations.

"Is Georgia in there, eating all the cake by herself?" Ashley asks.

I glance around the yard, now realizing she's been gone for a hot minute. "Let me see if she needs help."

She's not in the kitchen when I walk through the back door. I open the fridge, thinking she's probably in the bathroom, and snatch the cake box from it.

I set down the cake onto the counter and peel back the corner of the box at the same time I hear the sound of people arguing in Noah's bedroom. I follow the noise and stand on the other side of the shut door.

"Don't bullshit me," Archer says. "You're flirting with him to fuck with my head."

"Screw you, Archer. Maybe I like your brother. Maybe I'll go on a date with him, and I'll kiss him. And you know what? I might even fuck him too!"

I stiffen at my sister's voice.

"Don't say that shit," Archer grinds out.

"Why? Do you think that because you fucked me, you can tell me what to do now? You lost that right a long damn time ago."

I swing the door open and take in the scene in front of me. "What the fuck?"

CHAPTER THIRTY-SIX

Jamie

I HEAR, "WHAT THE FUCK?" as soon as I hit the back door.

Oh no.

I was too slow.

Blame it on the pregnancy waddle.

Lola rushed over to me when she saw Cohen going inside to check on Georgia. She'd spotted Archer following her into the house with a pissed-off and determined look on his face, and she was positive they were about to argue.

Arguing that, knowing them, would lead to screaming.

I didn't say anything to Cohen because fistfights at your gender reveal party were so 2019, but Archer's anger had been pinned to Georgia, his nostrils flaring as she flirted with Lincoln earlier.

Georgia's secretive self still won't tell me what happened between them.

I turn down the hall to find Cohen standing in the doorway of Noah's bedroom with clenched fists. I peek around him into the room. Archer looks as if he's geared to block a punch to the face, and Georgia's eyes are as big as her mouth.

"She's my fucking sister," Cohen screams.

I grab his arm. "Nuh-uh. This isn't happening right now."

Make him think it'll hurt my feelings.

My pregnant, emotional feelings.

"Oh, it's happening," Cohen snaps.

Archer holds up his hands. "I'm out of here. You can rip me a new asshole tomorrow."

I take this opportunity to pull Cohen away. "Your *very* pregnant *fiancée* does not need the added stress of her *fiancé* fighting his best friend at their party."

Cohen's jaw works, and Archer's eyes stay on him as he leaves Noah's bedroom.

When I glance at Georgia, tears are in her eyes.

"Nope." She sniffles. "Today is about you two. Any dramatic conversations about my life will wait until later."

I snort.

Georgia isn't going to tell us shit.

———

"YOU KNOW what the hardest part of having a baby is?" I ask Cohen while sitting at the kitchen table, exhausted from the party.

He scratches his head. "Uh … having it?"

"Choosing a name."

He levels his eyes on me. "That's harder than pushing a tiny human out of your vagina?"

"You know what I mean. My list is fifty-seven names long. Be prepared for our child to have one long-ass name." I gesture to my list in frustration but smile when my diamond ring glistens underneath the light.

I love it.

The halo diamond has a vintage look to it, and the pavé diamonds along the band add more sparkle to it. I can't stop staring at it.

"If all else fails, we'll use Noah's idea," he suggests.

"We are not naming her Pizza Roll Spider-Man Diva."

"I think it's catchy." He massages my shoulders. "Put the list down. We have plenty of time before we need to choose a name. It'll come when we least expect it."

I frown. "Fine, but you're on *keep Jamie's mind occupied* duty then."

"Oh, I know how to keep you very occupied." He takes the seat next to me, and his tone turns serious. "Thank you for this."

"For the list of names?"

"No, for changing my life and sticking through the troubles with me even when I was an asshole. I never expected someone to come into our lives, and even though you were shoved into a messy-as-fuck situation, you stayed. You accept my son as much as you accept me. You love him as much as you love me. You stirred out emotions inside my heart that I never thought I was capable of having. Hell, you've stirred yourself perfectly into this family and made us whole." He clears his throat. "My engagement speech was something along those lines, but I didn't exactly get the chance to spit my game."

I rub my hand over his jaw before yawning. "I loved how it went down." I crack a cocky smile. "Admit it, you knew our lives were going to change after Noah's hospital visit."

He nods. "I was scared as hell and kept telling myself to stay away from you."

"Then you realized how amazing I am."

"I did."

"How sexy I am." I scrape my finger along the slice of half-eaten cake in front of me, collecting frosting, and lick it off, swirling my tongue along the tip. "How good I am in bed."

"Jesus," Cohen groans and grabs his dick before shutting my notebook and putting it to the side. "You need to get some rest."

I eye the erection forming underneath his jeans. "I actually need to get some dick."

"Dear God, pregnancy has made you extremely addicted to sex with me."

"Are you complaining?"

"Can't say that I am." He rubs my stomach. "We'll have this one, and then we can keep practicing for another."

"Wow, how many kids do you want running around here?"

"As many as *my wife* will have."

"Can we wait on the wife thing until after I have the baby? Homegirl doesn't want to miss out on champagne at her wedding."

"We can wait for whenever you're ready."

He helps me up and guides me to our bedroom.

Yes, our bedroom.

Georgia and Grace are renting my townhouse, and I moved in with Cohen and Noah.

I grin when he shuts the door behind us and wrap my arms around his neck, my eyes meeting his. "I can't believe we're having a baby." I hold out my left hand in the air, admiring the ring again. "And we're engaged. How did we get here?"

He sits me down on the edge of the bed, and my arms rise. He pulls my dress over my head and tosses it to the side. This has become a regular thing for us—him helping me undress since it's become harder for me to do with my belly.

"Well," he says, brushing his lips against mine before helping me up the bed, "you became a pain in my ass while also making me a happier man." He separates my thighs and splays his hand over my stomach, massaging my sensitive skin while staring at it in awe. "You made me fall in love with you, and now, I'm about to make you—my baby mama, the woman I love—my wife."

I smirk, running my finger along the seam of his lips. "I am pretty talented, huh?"

"Gotta give credit where credit is due, though, babe. I made you fall in love with me too." He dips his hand into my panties. "I also helped make this baby."

I roll my eyes. "The guy always loves to take the credit for shooting his sperm inside the woman."

He chuckles, and I raise my ass to help him drag my panties off.

"You did not make that sound romantic whatsoever."

"I wasn't trying to."

He laughs, and instead of him slipping his finger inside me, I ask for his cock.

He gives it to me, and with each thrust, he lists the reasons he can't wait for me to be his wife.

I'm amazing.

Beautiful.

Will look beautiful in a wedding dress.

Take cock so well.

He loves me.

I come, him doing the same minutes later.

As we catch our breaths, I glance over at him. "You know what one of my favorite things you do is?"

He raises a brow.

"It's weird, but the first night I came here, when Noah was sick, you told me good night in this sexy, heart-swooning voice. I almost fell for you right then. As I came around more, you kept doing it—even when we were nothing, fighting sexual tension, or hell, even breaking each other's hearts. Very rarely did you not give me a, '*Good night, Jamie.*'"

"Good night, Jamie," he says in that rough, deep, but soft voice I love, and his lips meet mine. "I love you."

"*Swoon*," I sing out before snuggling into his side.

"I have no idea what that means, but I'll take it." He kisses the top of my head. "I love you."

Cohen has stirred his way into my heart.

No drink is stronger than our love.

I can't wait for us to mix marriage and children into the cocktail that is our life.

Shaken

Archer

"YOU SELFISH BASTARD!" He charges toward me, his face darkened with fury.

The commotion around us—people crying, asking questions, breaking down—fades away.

I stay in place, unmoving, while waiting for the assault I deserve. The crack of my jaw is all I hear before the pain strikes, and I stumble back, wiping the blood from my lip with the side of my clenched fist.

Straightening myself, I prepare for the next blow.

It connects with my nose.

I don't fight back.

I deserve this.

I am a selfish bastard.

The old proverb, *One night can change your life*, is on the mark.

My life has changed.

Fuck the lifestyles of the rich.

I'm out.

CHAPTER ONE

Georgia

CALL me the queen of embarrassing moments.

Tripping up the stairs and face-planting at my high school graduation.

Side-swiping a car during my driver's test.

Today's embarrassment winner of the week is …

Drumroll, please.

Getting stood up for a date.

Even worse, while waiting on my date, the guy I'd dumped six months ago arrived with his. Lucky asshole's date actually showed, and I provided them with free entertainment as they witnessed my disaster.

It's what you deserve for swiping right on a dude with a mirror selfie as his profile pic, Georgia.

In my defense, it was margarita night, and I was third-wheeling it when said swiping ensued.

To recover from the mortification, I drive to my happy place—the coffee shop. Iced coffee never fails to pull me out of the *I'll be single for the rest of my life* funk.

"Jackpot." I smile when I spot an empty space before abruptly stopping. "You've got to be kidding me."

Parked next to the only available spot is a car—foreign, expensive, one of those you see in the movies with rich-people problems.

Parked is an understatement.

I pull into the sliver of a space, and like the mature and not-at-all-annoyed woman I am, I give the foreign-car-driving asshole no room to open their door. With a shrug, I step out of my car—American, cheap, one of those that always breaks down in the movies—and stroll into the coffee shop.

Fifteen minutes later, I'm walking back through the parking lot and fueling myself with cold-brew deliciousness. My sipping stops when I notice a man standing behind my car. Shoving my sunglasses down my nose, I take a better look.

"Siri, find me a tow company in the area."

The hell?

I scramble toward him, waving my arm in the air, and shriek, "Whoa! Don't call a tow truck!"

Is that even legal?

Lord knows I can't afford it if he does. I can barely afford my iced-coffee dependency.

When he turns, my breathing stalls, and I freeze. Momentarily, my car being towed becomes an afterthought.

The man is gorgeous.

GQ cover-worthy.

Looking every shade of pissed off.

The sight of him is stronger than any caffeine shot.

His sexy ruggedness—tall and built like a linebacker, broad shoulders, and muscle-bound biceps—is such a contrast to my small frame. Stubbled hair and scruff, trimmed to the jawline, scatters along the slope of his cheeks and down his neck. His hair, a shade matching the drink in my cup, is thick and hits the nape of his neck.

He's clean-cut *but not* clean-cut.

Fighting not to fit the profile of a wealthy man.

A man who gives no fucks … which unfortunately also applies to his parking.

He glowers as I make my way to him, and I keep a short distance between us.

"This your car?" His voice matches his appearance—cold and sharp, like a knife slicing through ice.

"Yes," I answer.

He stares, waiting for me to elaborate.

I take a loud slurp of my coffee before saying, "Please, put your phone away. No need to call a tow company."

"Did you just get your driver's license?" Authority fills his tone, as if he were scolding a child, when he signals to my park job. "Who parks like that? Do you need a booster seat to see over the steering wheel?"

Rude.

Short jokes are so grade school.

"The better question is who parks *like that*?" I scowl and gesture to his car. "You took a spot and a half. Not cool."

The collar of his simple white V-neck tee stretches out when he tugs on it. "That was the only available spot when I got here—"

"That means you can park however you want?"

"If you'd let me finish. When I got here, the car on the opposite side of me was parked like shit. A motorcycle was in your spot, so the way I parked provided plenty of room for the both of us." He holds up the coffee cup in his hand. "I planned to run in and out, but when I *ran out*, your car was in my way."

"I planned to run in and out, too, but when I *ran out*, I had to deal with you."

"Move it or get towed." He impatiently waves his phone in the air. "I have shit to do."

"You can't tow my car. It's not even legal."

"Call it a citizen's tow."

"Call it *you're an asshole*."

The frustration on his face grows. "Move your car. Nothing gets towed. Easy fix."

"You're an ass."

"Never said I was nice."

"Fine, whatever." I narrow my eyes while stalking toward him.

The faster I'm away from this asshole, the better. As I circle him, his slate-gray eyes meet mine, and I trip.

"Holy shit!" I yelp, pushing out my hands to save myself from face-planting. That save results in me losing my coffee.

"What the hell?"

I gulp and peek up at him while on my hands and knees. Coffee drips down his shirt, shaping into a forever stain. My cup is empty and upside down at his feet.

Scratch my earlier statement.

This is the embarrassment winner of my week.

Hell, the embarrassment winner of my year.

"I'm so sorry," I rush out.

He doesn't offer a helping hand as I lift myself and dust off my scraped-up knees.

When I go to pick up the cup, he retreats a step, worried I'll bring him more damage, and stops me. "Just go."

"I'm *sorry*," I repeat, stressing the last word.

He pulls at his shirt, inspecting the stain, and shakes his head. "Make it up to me by getting in your car and leaving."

My remorse spills into anger. "You know what? I take my apology back. I'm not sorry, you jerk."

"Cool," he deadpans, my insult bouncing off him like rubber. "Now, move."

"Asshole." I walk around him, sans tripping this time, and get into my car.

Curses fly from my mouth when I slam the door, crank up the radio, and flip him off as I pull out of my spot. I drive around the building and wait for him to leave before taking his old spot.

"Here we go. Coffee, round two," I mutter.

My phone rings when I kill the ignition, and Lola's name flashes across the screen over a selfie of us.

"You won't believe this," I say, answering my best friend's call before retelling her the coffee nightmare.

"Swear to God, this stuff only happens to you." She laughs. "And what a dick."

"Tell me about it." My head throbs from the lack of caffeine and the mess of today.

"You know, I have a hunch you'll run into each other again."

I snort. "Okay, Miss Cleo. That'd better not happen, or you'll be bailing me out of jail for purposely spilling coffee on him next time."

Queen of Intuition is Lola's nickname. I swear, the girl was a fortune-teller in her past life.

The hairs on the back of my neck stand at her remark.

Do I want to see him again?

My heart races at the thought.

CHAPTER TWO

Archer

Two Weeks Later

"TELL the attorney to score a better deal," I demand. "It's a bullshit plea."

"Archer." My mother's voice carries through my car's Bluetooth speakers. "Katherine works for the finest firm in the state. Trust me, she's doing her best."

"She can do better." *She has to do better.* "We're paying her a shit-ton of money to get him out of this."

"To get *them* out of this."

I snarl and tighten my grip on the steering wheel. "No, to get *him* out. I don't care about anyone else."

At the same time as my gaze returns to the road, the driver in front of me slams on their brakes. I ram my foot onto my brake pedal, hard enough that I'm waiting for my foot to hit the concrete, but I'm too slow.

"Motherfucker," I hiss when I jerk forward and rear-end the car. "Let me call you back."

I end the call and glance in my rearview mirror. When I see the car behind me is pulled to the side of the road, damage-free, a rush of relief hits me. Moments later, they pull back onto the street and drive past me. One less collision for me to deal with.

I swerve to the side of the road, my jaw clenching, and shift my car into park. The car I hit does the same.

An accident isn't what I need today.

Or any damn day.

I'm already dealing with enough wreckage.

I snatch my Italian leather wallet from the cupholder, stretch out of my car, and straighten myself. As much as I love my Aston Martin, they make them for tiny fuckers, not dudes hitting the six-six mark.

I glimpse at my newly purchased and shipped-from-England DBS Superleggera, and I grit my teeth. It'll cost a pretty penny to repair. My gaze flicks to the car I hit. There isn't much damage. It's at least a decade old and worth a few grand at most. I'll throw cash at the problem for a simple fix.

"You've got to be kidding me," I hiss when the driver steps out of the car.

The sour look coming from her confirms she remembers me. I slip my hands into my pockets and stroll toward the brat who blocked me in at the coffee shop a few weeks ago. If this encounter is like our last, it won't be as easy as I hoped. No doubt this chick is about to add more stress to my day.

"Just perfect," she yells, throwing up her arms. "It's the Prick Parker. Not only do you suck at parking but you're also a terrible driver."

She straightens her shoulders when I reach her. The woman might grate on my nerves, but she's drop-dead gorgeous. Every physical feature of hers matches her spitfire personality. Random pieces of her caramel-colored hair are braided, tumbling across her sun-kissed shoulders, and she's wearing short-shorts that show off her toned legs.

She has the face of trouble, of fun, of happiness.

She's a shot of serotonin in a crop top.

The opposite of me.

The type of person I steer clear of.

While she's a dose of pleasure, I'm a cocktail of misery.

My attention falls to her plump lips, and I lick my own, curious how she tastes.

Probably sweet.

Like a sugary doughnut or a juicy strawberry.

I shake my head to murder those thoughts. "Don't you know you're not supposed to slam on your brakes out of nowhere?"

"Don't you know there's a three-second distance rule?" She smirks, pleased with her comeback.

That smart-ass mouth.

Had this been years ago, I would've loved it.

Would've wanted to fuck it.

But I'm not that man anymore.

"I didn't expect you to stop for no damn reason."

"There was a reason."

"Which was?"

"A chipmunk ran in front of me."

"A chipmunk?"

"Yes!" she shrieks. "A chipmunk! Furry little thing." She lowers her hand until it's nearly touching the ground. "About yea high."

I stare at her, working my jaw.

"Oh!" she scoffs. "You'd rather me murder Alvin the Chipmunk? You truly are a heartless, shitty parker of a man."

"No, I don't want you to murder a damn whatever chipmunk." I scrub a hand over my face as cars pass us, surveying my situation with their nosy eyes. "Look, I'm in a rush. There's hardly any damage to your car—"

"Whoa." She gestures to her bumper, now renovated with a minor dent and scratches. "That *is more* than hardly any damage."

I rub my hands together. "I'll tell you what. We'll call it even."

"Excuse me? What do you mean, *call it even?*"

"You ruined my shirt during our last little run-in, and I didn't make you pay for it." I shrug. "Tit for tat."

Her jaw drops. "You think a ruined shirt is equivalent to car damage?"

"When the shirt most likely cost more than the car, yes."

"Wow," she calls out as if she were in front of an audience, and her mouth forms an *O*. "Alexa, show me the definition of a rich, arrogant prick."

It was a low blow.

Cunning.

Bragging about my wealth isn't a hobby of mine, but if it makes someone hate me, I'll boast away. Throughout the years, I've learned the easiest approach for convincing people to leave you alone is for them to dread your presence. No one wants to hang out with the brooding bastard.

She holds her chin high, awaiting my next move, for me to solve the problem for us. I have no issues with paying for the damages. Hell, I'll buy her a new car if she wants. The issue is compensating her while also maintaining a low profile.

"How about this?" I say, and her gaze meets mine in expectation. "Let's exchange information and not worry about a police report."

Another police report with my family's name added to the stack is the last thing we need.

She skeptically stares at me, and her words come out slow. "You're admitting it's your fault, correct?"

A rumble shoots through my skull. "Sure, it can be my fault."

"But it was your fault."

"That's what I said, sure."

"*Sure* isn't you accepting responsibility."

"Jesus, fuck." I rub the back of my starting-to-sweat neck. "It was my fault. You happy? You want me to get it tattooed on me?"

"That'd actually be kind of hot." She smiles in amusement. "Will you put my name next to it … or possibly my face? I once dated this frat boy—" She pauses, holding up a finger. "Correction: not *dated*. We talked, went to a few parties together, you know—"

"No, I don't know," I talk over her. "Nor do I care or understand how the fuck that pertains to our situation."

"My point is, he said I have a face made for art." She uses her full palm and circles her face through the air.

"Again, I have no idea how this pertains to me hitting your car." I shake my head. "I'll pay for the damages. Don't worry about mine."

"I'm not worried about paying for yours since it was *your fault*."

I cock my head to the side when I catch a hint of her perfume. Never in my thirty years have I met someone who smelled like cotton candy, like a damn carnival snack. Not even when I was the age of a kid who was excited to attend a carnival.

Like everything else, it suits her.

Gives way to her personality.

Has me wanting to get to know her more than I should.

To kill that, I open my wallet and riffle through the business cards until finding the one I need.

"Here's my info." I offer her the card. "Call this number. My assistant will get you taken care of."

She snatches the card from my hand and holds it in the air, reading it as if it were toxic. "A card? How do I even know this is you?" She points at my wallet. "Can I see your driver's license? Proof of insurance? You could run off, and I'd never see you again."

"Trust me, your damages will be paid." I grab the card, pull a pen from my pocket, and write my license plate number on the back. "I won't run off."

I turn around without giving her a chance to ask more questions.

"What the hell is happening?" she mutters.

I get into my car, and this time, I'm the one leaving her.

CHAPTER THREE

Georgia

I FOCUS on his license plate number when he pulls away.

Homeboy isn't leaving me high and dry with a banged-up car.

It matches.

Who knows their license plate number by heart?

Hell, half the time, I forget my birthday.

I sigh and lean back against my car.

Why do I always need a moment to refresh, to regain my thoughts, when he's around?

I play with the card in my hand. Expensive card stock. The name *Chase Smith* written in gold.

He didn't look like a Chase Smith.

Didn't put off a Chase Smith vibe.

The name is too simple.

Generic.

No offense to any Chase Smiths out there.

He was right about the damages being minimal, but I don't have the cash for even minimal repairs. When I get back into my car, I crank up the air-conditioning and make myself comfortable for some stalking.

I Google Chase Smith.

The results pop up with a list of generic Chase Smiths.

Frat boys.

Guys with fishing poles thrown over their shoulders.

Family men.

None of them the grumpy, handsome, *has a stick up his ass* man who keeps ruining my days.

I bet he doesn't use social media.

He doesn't seem like the type to post selfies or double-tap memes.

Not that he'd have many followers or likes with that stank attitude of his.

Damn you, Lola.

Jinxing me with the you'll run into each other again *shit.*

I call the number on the card to make sure I don't need to call the cops and report a hit-and-run accident. Rather, a *hit, stop, hand card, and run* situation.

"Hello, this is Kiki," a woman answers in a chirpy voice. "How may I help you?"

"Hi, this is Georgia Fox. Your boss, Chase Smith, hit my car and said to call this number."

"Ah, yes, he told me to expect your call." She proceeds to give me all the information I need.

———

TWO DAYS LATER, Kiki—a woman close to my mother's age with bright red hair and dark sunglasses—shows up at my door.

"From Chase," she says, handing over a thick white envelope and leaving.

It keeps getting weirder with this guy.

When I open it, I nearly faint.

It's cash.

I count the bills.

Fifteen thousand dollars.

Way more money than the damages would cost.

Way more than my car is worth.

Who is this man?

Is he into illegal shit?

A Mafia dude?

I pull out my phone to do the thousandth search of this mystery man.

Chase Smith, Mafia.

Nothing.

Chase Smith …

I want to know more about you.

CHAPTER FOUR

Archer

3 Weeks Later

FUCK THIS DAY.

And fuck tomorrow too.

I signal to the bartender for another shot.

He delivers.

This one's to failure.

I knock it back.

Ask for another.

This one's for defeat.

Another.

This one's for Lincoln.

Tonight, I've chosen to test my alcohol tolerance at Bailey's, a hole-in-the-wall dive bar. Over the past few months, I've become a regular here, spending more time in the run-down bar than my home, even though my penthouse holds a superior liquor collection.

You don't come to places like Bailey's for the liquor selection.

Or the customer service.

Or the decor.

You come when you've stopped caring.

Sometimes, you're so down on life that you want to pop a squat on a broken stool and drink cheap booze.

Bailey's provides privacy from my life without complete isolation.

The only person I had left in this shithole life is in prison now.

No matter how big of a dick I was to my brother, Lincoln, he never let me push him away. Now, it's me, the outcast of the family, drinking alone in a bar that reeks of mold and desperation.

As if the bartender, Ted, can read my mind, he slides another drink to me. My gaze lifts as I grab the glass, and my attention drifts to the opposite end of the bar. Every hair on my body stands when I see her. She drapes her purse over the ripped barstool and runs her hands down her patterned dress, smoothing out the wrinkles. When she slumps onto the stool, her posture mimics mine.

Why is she here?

Reasons swirl through my mind so fast that it's hard to keep up.

It's not her.

She doesn't belong in a place like this.

Man, this cheap shit knocks you on your ass.

I wipe my eyes with the heels of my hands, expecting to find an empty stool when I drag them away, but disbelief clouds my drunken brain.

It's her.

Ted approaches her with a smile—one too friendly for my liking —and she delivers a forced one in return while speaking to him. I edge closer, hoping to eavesdrop on their conversation, but there's too much chaos—people yelling over the loud music and glasses being moved around. He taps the bar, pulls away, and starts on her drink.

It's a struggle to make out her features underneath the faint, sorry excuse for a light shining above her. Even though I've consumed enough booze to stock a small distillery, my throat turns dry as I observe her. The distance separating us doesn't conceal her pain.

She's hunched over in defeat and flicking at the chipped wood on the bar.

The glow she carried before has faded.

Vulnerability owning its place.

The feisty, spot-blocking, chipmunk-saving, pain-in-the-ass woman is heartbroken.

She roughly snatches her phone sitting next to her, powers it off, and shoves it into her bag.

Georgia.

Kiki gave me her name.

Weeks have passed since I rear-ended her, but she's loitered my thoughts, surfacing when I grab a coffee or take the road where I hit her. There was a powerful urge to learn more about her during our encounters. Every time, *Want to grab a coffee to replace the one you spilled,* was at the tip of my tongue, but I bit into it, puncturing the idea.

It would've been selfish.

A woman like her doesn't belong with a man like me. She doesn't deserve to have her time wasted.

I'd never be what she wanted.

What she needed.

I'd siphon any bliss from her life.

To avoid that, I stepped aside and had Kiki handle the situation. I instructed her to pay Georgia more than what the car was worth, more than what the repairs would cost, and in cash, so not a penny could be traced back to me.

The Feds like manipulating shit.

I drink her in, swallowing a view that hits me harder than any drink behind the bar.

Someone did what I'd refused to.

Broke her.

I want to kick his ass.

I slug down my shot, killing it at the same time Ted drops hers off, and revel in the slow burn slipping down my throat. When I stand, my heart punches my chest in warning.

If you carry out this plan, it will change your night.

I make a beeline toward her, the alcohol controlling my every move and coaxing my drunken mind into thinking this is a good idea. Thankfully, there are open seats around her. The stool's legs scrape as I yank it out and sit next to her.

That sweet cotton-candy scent assaults me, adding to my intoxication, and I can almost taste the spun sugar.

She peeks over at me and downs her drink, and her tone is harsh when she speaks, "Are you serious right now?"

Not the response I was hoping for.

The response I should've expected, though.

Instead of answering, I lift two fingers in the air—a signal for Ted —and he comes over.

Gesturing to her, I say, "This one's on me."

She draws in a breath, contemplating whether to play this game, and focuses on Ted. "I'll have a Manhattan, please."

"Hennessy good?" he asks.

She nods.

Hennessy?

I took her for more of a margarita or lemon-drop drinker, sure as hell not cognac.

Ted's attention slides to me. "You?"

"I'll also have Hennessy." I rub my hands together. "Straight. On the rocks."

He tips his head down. "On it."

As soon as Ted's out of earshot, she turns and glowers at me. "Are you stalking me?"

"I was here first," I reply, fixing my stare on her. "The better question is, are *you* stalking me?"

She rolls her eyes. "You wish."

There's that attitude.

It isn't as snarky or as hateful as before but still lurks inside. The pain in her eyes confirms the woman I dealt with before isn't coming out tonight. Like me, tonight's drinks aren't for entertainment. They're to evade our reality.

I clear my throat, my eyes not leaving her. "First, let's start with what my stalker's name is."

Her jaw falls slack. "I'm *not* your stalker."

"Okay, what's my *not*-stalker's name?"

She can't know I asked Kiki about her.

She glares at me in suspicion. "Georgia."

"Okay, Georgia. Want to tell me why it looks like someone told you Taylor Swift quit making music?"

"It's personal." She clips a curly tendril of her long hair behind her ear. "Want to tell me why you look like a depressed dick?"

"It's personal." I pay a quick glance to Ted when he drops off our drinks.

She flips her hair over her shoulder, exposing the curve of her neck, before grabbing her drink and taking a sip.

What I'd do to run my lips over her soft skin, up the side of her neck, while whispering every way I wanted to pleasure her.

"You came to me, so you wanted conversation." When she plucks the cherry from the glass and plays with the stem in her mouth, my cock stirs. "What do you want to talk about? Chipmunks? Spilled coffee?"

"I figured you could use some company."

I should've thought this through before approaching her. Per my grandfather's advice, you always have a plan before undertaking a task. Going in blind only leads you into walls.

She signals to her face. "This face screams, *Give me company?*"

"Yes, it's interesting."

The crowd, the TVs, the hustle and bustle fade as I fixate on her. A sense of unworthiness hits me at seeing her so up close, so vulnerable, as if it's something I don't deserve. Even with her swollen eyes—my guess, a result from crying—and the mascara caked along the bottoms, she's gorgeous. Her effort of wiping off the makeup shows, but she didn't catch every inch.

I pinch the bridge of my nose to stop myself from reaching out and running a hand over her cheek, rubbing away the spots she missed and erasing the evidence of her pain.

"Interesting?" she fires back.

"It interested me enough to come over and be your company tonight." I grab my glass and take a slow draw of the cognac.

"There are plenty of other options for company." She does a circling motion around the room. "Other women. Go give them company because, forewarning, I won't be a good time."

And I look like I will?

"I'd rather have a drink with someone who's had as shitty of a day as I have, who isn't here for a good time, and who can sit with me in silence yet throw out a few comments here and there."

"And I seem like that someone?"

Gripping my glass, I raise it to my lips, but instead of taking a drink, I tip it in her direction. "I don't know. Are you?"

"So …" She taps her nails—colored designs on each one—against her glass before placing it on the bar. "You want to sit here in silence?"

"Silence. Small talk. Whatever."

"All right then. I guess we'll sit here and *whatever*."

I take a sip of my drink, the rich, spicy liquid coating my tongue, and stare while attempting not to make it obvious. She shifts her attention forward, and when her lower lip trembles, it crushes my soul.

She doesn't deserve sadness.

Pain.

People like me? We do.

I hardly know her, but I'd gladly rip away her pain and attach it to mine.

"You sure you don't want to talk about it?" I ask.

Let me fix this for you.

She shakes her head, releasing a sharp laugh. "Not interested in becoming the *crying drunk in the corner* cliché."

"I won't let you cry. Promise."

She scoffs.

I scoot closer, erasing the distance between us, and press my hand to my chest. "I'm an asshole, remember? You're too cool to cry in front of an asshole."

She releases a heavy sigh and hesitates. A wave of silence passes, and I nurse my drink while waiting. As badly as I want to beg her to spill her guts, I stop myself from asking.

It's her story. If she needs to take all night, so be it.

It's not like I have anywhere to be.

"It's daddy issues," she finally whispers. "No one wants to hear about a woman's daddy issues."

She's right. Generally, people don't.

But tonight, for some weird-ass reason, I want to hear hers.

"Daddy issues away." I slide my glass over, and it bumps against hers. "Look at it this way. I'm the best person to talk to. You'll never see me again. Unleash your bullshit on me, and I'll scrape an inch of the pain off your heart. It'll be our little secret—a secret no one in your life will know."

She downs her drink, and without thinking, I reach down to relax her bouncing knee, my hand resting along the bare skin underneath the hem of her dress. My head spins as I realize what I did, and I peek up at her. There's no reaction to my touch—no flinch, no side-eye—as if it were where it belonged.

"I'll need another drink for this." She holds up the glass. "An extra shot of truth serum."

Following her lead, I finish my drink, call Ted over, and order us another round. Not a word is muttered while we wait for the delivery of our *truth serum*. She doesn't give Ted the chance to set her drink down before she grabs it straight from his hand and knocks it back like a pro.

Ted shrugs, hands over my drink, and wanders off to take an order.

She points at me with the empty glass. "Don't say I didn't warn you."

"Lay it on me." I squeeze her knee, giving her the green light to start.

Her gaze drops to her lap, to my hand, and I wait for her to shove it away. Instead, she relaxes.

"My father left us when I was a baby," she begins. "Six months ago, I tracked him down, and today, I mustered the courage to visit him." She grimaces. "It was stupid to think he'd want to meet me, but he seemed like a decent man on social media. Married, tagged in pictures with his children."

A sniffle leaves her before she inhales a deep breath, and I give her knee another reassuring squeeze.

"I felt like a lost puppy who had found its way home when I showed up on his doorstep, but as soon as I introduced myself, the excitement, the hope, it died. That's when I realized I was the puppy no one wanted in their home. I was sent on my way, shown I wasn't welcome. He'd changed into the family man he needed to be but for another family."

My stomach knots at the thought of humiliation and rejection that raw.

The horror of being turned away as if you were nothing.

"I'm sorry." Before I can stop it, I rip myself open as deep as she did. "My father went to prison today." My tone is lower than hers. "And he took my brother down with him."

Her mouth drops open, shock flashing in her eyes.

I relax in the chair. "It appears we both have daddy issues."

"Your father ..." She clears her throat, searching for the right words. "He's in prison? For what?"

"Embezzlement." I pull my hand away from her leg and scratch my cheek. "Money laundering."

"I'm, uh ... sorry about that."

"I'm sorry about your shit."

I hold out my empty glass. She does the same, and we clink them together.

"To fucked-up fathers."

"Hear, hear."

Silence makes a reappearance.

"Can we talk about something else?" she asks. "I could use the distraction."

"We can talk about anything you want." The liquor is changing me into a different man—one open to speaking about his problems and hearing another's. "You decide."

Who is this guy?

Maybe it's the Hennessy.

The day.

The woman next to me.

She peeks over at me. "I don't know. Puppies, sports—which I know jack shit about, FYI—the Pope. Anything but my problems."

All those subjects sound like a damn bore. I fix my gaze on her, drinking in the view, and can't stop myself from saying, "Can we talk about how beautiful you are?"

Fuck!

Douchebag alert.

I'm *that* guy now.

The one who uses a cheesy-ass pickup line.

Not that I'm trying to pick her up.

"What?" she stutters, gawking at me.

"Just needed to get that out there." I shrug—an attempt to put off a give-no-fucks attitude.

When my gaze drops to her lips, she licks them.

"Thank you." She displays a hint of a smile, and I pride myself on providing some light in her darkness. "Tell me more about you, Chase Smith. Are you married? Dating anyone?"

I cringe when she says Chase. "Nope and nope."

She turns, settles her elbow on the bar, and leans against it, granting me her full attention. "Why not?"

"Shit doesn't always work out." *That's an understatement.*

She nods in agreement.

"What about you?"

"Single as a dollar bill. No hubby. No kids. I do, however, have a pet rock."

"Why single?"

"Shit doesn't always work out." She smirks.

"I like this game."

"What game?"

"Using each other's answers against one another."

"I must say, it's better than confessing daddy issues."

I smile.

She smiles back.

We order another round.

Drink and make small talk.

I find my hand back on her thigh.

As the night grows later, she leans into me.

When a laugh escapes her, I mentally pat myself on the back.

It's not much, but it's something.

Something other than sadness.

"You want to get out of here?" she asks all of a sudden.

I still, my hand tightening around the neck of my beer bottle.

I moved on to beer to save myself from getting too shit-faced.

Somehow, my goal tonight has shifted.

Because of her.

"Never mind." Her voice is unsteady as she flicks her hand through the air. "I swear, that isn't something I ask on the regular. I've never even had a one-night stand. I can count the men I've slept with on one hand—"

Unable to stop myself—and rougher than I should—I grip the curve of her neck and bring my lips to her ear. "How drunk are you?"

She shivers, goose bumps spreading over her soft skin, when I loosen my hold and trail my fingers along her neck. She lifts her chin, heat creeping up it, and allows me easier access. I tip my head down and replace my fingers with my lips.

My tongue brushes her neck when she says, "Tipsy, not drunk."

Her voice is clear.

No slur.

My cock stirs as I croak out, "Your place or mine?"

"Yours."

This is where I usually say I don't do sleepovers at my house.

I don't.

Instead, I press one last kiss to her neck before drawing back.

I pay our tab, and her hand finds mine as I lead us outside. The destination: my place. The short drive to my penthouse seems ten times longer, and unable to restrain myself, I slip my hand under her dress. She gasps, parting her legs, and I skim a single finger along the lace of her panties.

Back and forth, not going any further.

She whimpers, "More."

My thumb moves to her clit.

She's soaked.

So wet that I can feel it through the lace.

It's a struggle to hold back from plunging a finger inside her. The Uber driver eyes us suspiciously, as if he knows we're up to something. As soon as we arrive at my building, I grab her hand and lead her into the elevator.

When we walk into my penthouse, I briefly hear her say, "Nice place," before I slam my mouth onto hers.

I kiss her hard, tasting the alcohol on her lips, hitting me stronger than the Hennessy.

Fuck.

Fucking her will be the best antidote to my hell.

No alcohol will beat this.

No drug.

She's the one thing I never knew I needed.

Her kiss sets me on fire.

It's passionate.

Hot.

Our tongues meet, as if drawing the pain out of each other. Our mouths don't separate as I lead her to my bedroom. As soon as the light flicks on, I strip her, fling her dress across the room, and pull down the duvet on my bed. Grabbing her hips, I toss her onto the bed, and she lands on her back.

She holds herself up on her elbows.

I stand at the foot, stroking my chin, and admire her naked body.

The way her breasts bounce as her breathing turns heavier.

Her hard pink nipples.

Her smooth legs slightly parted as she waits for me.

My bed has never looked so damn tempting.

She gasps as I climb between her legs.

She moans when I take the first taste of her.

Licking my way up her slit before sucking on her clit.

So damn delicious.

I lick, slip my tongue in, add fingers until she's writhing underneath me.

As soon as she gets off, I frantically unbuckle my pants. She moves just as hurriedly, pushing them down, and I pull my shirt over my head. Seconds after, I slide the condom on and thrust inside her.

"Chase," she moans.

I freeze, squeezing my eyes shut, and she stares up at me in question.

Don't call me that.

Moan another name.

To stop myself from admitting my truth, I shove my face into her neck, tasting her sweet skin, and fuck her gently.

We're strangers in the missionary position, but it's like she fits me.

Gets me.

She begs for more.

I fuck her harder.

I savor her.

Her name leaves my lips as I explode into the condom.

Then round two starts.

When we're sweaty and all orgasmed out, I pull her into my side, drape my arm along her waist, and mold her body into mine.

I don't ask her to leave.

Don't kick her out of my bed.

What a damn mistake that is.

CHAPTER FIVE

Georgia

I'VE NEVER WOKEN up in a stranger's bed before.

Although is he considered a stranger if I let him bang my brains out last night?

The bright sunlight streaming through the wall of windows assaults my eyes, and I throw my arm over my face to block the rays. Giving myself a moment to adjust to the light, I move my arm, stretch out my body, and yawn.

My thighs ache.

My legs are sore.

My mouth is dry.

I shift in the crisp sheets.

Sheets that don't belong to me.

In a bed that doesn't belong to me.

It's *his* bed.

In *his* room.

My heart pounds at the memories of what happened in this bed last night.

I'd stopped at the bar yesterday to avoid going home and sulking in an empty apartment. My plan was to have a drink to settle my nerves, leave, and watch murder mysteries until passing out.

When Chase sat next to me, like a broken knight in shining armor, my night changed for the better. My view of him before—the arrogant ass—had dissolved, making me see him in a better light.

He made me feel wanted.

Needed.

Gave me more orgasms last night than I could count.

Blame it on my daddy issues, but on the day I felt the most discarded, he was there to collect the pieces and put me back together.

My stomach sinks when I glance around the empty room, and I shift my attention to the adjoined bathroom. The light is off, and I gulp at the silence hanging in the air.

"Hello?" I call out, my voice raspy and timid as if I were in a horror movie, heard a bump in the night, and Jason was coming to slaughter me.

Silence.

I clutch my arms against my chest as my heart batters against it.

Did he leave?

Reasons for the stillness rush through my mind.

He's waiting for me to leave.

He grabbed breakfast.

He bailed.

He's already been slaughtered by Jason.

Hell, at this point, I'd rather hear a chain saw than this silence.

Bring out the killer, please and thank you.

Let him murder my humiliation if this guy hit it and quit it.

Chase hadn't exactly been open to conversation during our first two run-ins. As I relaxed in his arms last night, I convinced myself what we'd shared—the drinks, secrets, and sex—made up for his previous asshole behavior.

"Hello?" I call out again.

No response.

My naivety strikes again.

I drop my hands to my stomach as the urge to vomit last night's drinks and this morning's embarrassment seep up my throat. I do another once-over of the room and form the sign of a cross when I spot my phone on the nightstand. The chill of the room hits me when

I reach out and grab the phone. Unlocking it, I hit Lola's name. My best friend is a pro in these situations.

"Lola," I hiss when she answers, gripping the phone tight against my cheek.

"Oh my God, Georgia," she groans. "It's eight in the morning. This'd better be an emergency and not you asking me to yoga again. Spoiler alert: not happening. Call Grace."

"I'm stuck at a guy's house," I rush out before she hangs up.

"What?" Her sleepy tone becomes alert.

"I'm stuck at a guy's house."

"How'd you get stuck at his house? Are you being held hostage? Do I need to call 911 … or send ransom money?"

"No," I groan. "I had sex with him last night."

"Good girl." She whistles. "It's about time you got laid."

"Not good, considering he's gone." It's a struggle to keep my voice low.

"Gone? Like, gone from the house or just the bedroom?"

"The bedroom."

"You haven't looked anywhere else?"

"I don't hear any noise."

"Hmm …"

"Tell me what to do."

"Have you slept with him before?"

"Nope. It was the first and *only* time." I rub at the throbbing temples. "He bought me a drink, and next thing I knew, we were having sex." More memories of that night hurl through my brain, intensifying my headache.

She laughs. "I hate when that happens."

"Enough small talk. *What do I do?*"

"Are you naked?"

Stupidly, I pull down the white sheet and check. "Yes."

"Get up and find your clothes."

I jump out of bed, the sheet still in tow to cover myself, and start gathering my clothes scattered throughout the room. I'm light-headed as I slide on my wrinkled dress, slip my panties up my legs, and shove my feet into my sandals.

"Done," I say.

"Step one, complete." Humor fills her voice. "Now, go look for any signs of life—outside, in the kitchen, in an office. Just because he's not in the bedroom doesn't mean he bailed."

Her words don't give me hope. When I pad out of the bedroom, I grab my bag that was drunkenly dropped to the floor when he dragged me to his bedroom. My sandals squeak against the marble floor as I move through the home, eyeing the wall of windows and modern furniture. As I hit the kitchen, I spot a box of doughnuts and two coffee cups on the counter.

"Breakfast is on the counter," I say.

"That's a nice turn of events," she replies. "Maybe he isn't a runner."

As I grow closer, I notice a note and cash next to the food. As I read it, I cover my mouth and gag.

Here's money for a cab or Uber.
You can see yourself out.
Don't worry about locking up.

What the actual fuck?

As if yesterday's rejection hadn't shred my heart enough, this guy tattered what I'd had left.

I pull in a breath to stop myself from crying. "He left a note."

"A note?" Lola asks. "Like a love note?"

My hands are shaking when I read it to her.

"Code red. Time to run. Take the coffee, snag a doughnut, and fuck him—differently than you did last night."

For a moment, I debate on staying—lounging around his lavish home until he returns, so I can call him out. I can take a bath in the massive whirlpool, drink the overpriced alcohol on the bar cart ... or pour it all down the drain in spite.

Or rob him. I'm sure I could find a pretty Rolex or piggy bank around this place. He deserves some good thievery. Unfortunately, unlike the man I slept with last night, I'm a decent person with morals.

Those morals could be somewhat questionable after last night.

I went home with a man who I'd previously Googled to see if he was in the Mafia.

With a doughnut in my mouth, I rummage through my purse for a pen. I fail but find something better. A rush of satisfaction shoots through me when I march to his bathroom and write, *Your dick is small*, in red lipstick across his mirror.

———

A LOUD YAWN escapes me when I fall in a creaky chair at my brother, Cohen's, kitchen table.

After leaving Chase's this morning, I took an Uber, the driver judging me for my walk-of-shame outfit, and picked up my car from Bailey's.

A bar I'll never return to.

I held my chin high during the drive to my apartment, showered, popped a few painkillers, and napped before coming to Cohen's.

Cohen isn't just my older brother; he's my entire family, bunched into one person. He stepped into the role of parenthood, playing the mother and the father, when ours wouldn't. He was my parent, big brother, provider, friend, babysitter, and also authoritarian. Had he not stepped up, my childhood years would've most likely been spent in the system, jumping from foster home to foster home.

"I need to tell you something." I pop one of Noah's fruit snacks in my mouth before gagging. "I'm also requesting you don't buy sugar-free fruit snacks again. Gross."

He peers over at me while washing a Ninja Turtle cup in the sink. "What's up?"

"I found Dad." My attention slides from him to the wall as guilt surfaces over hiding this from him.

The cup slips from his hand, falling into the sink, and the water sprays his shirt.

He quickly turns off the faucet, grabs a towel, and dries his hands. "Okay?"

"And I might've gone to see him yesterday."

"Jesus Christ, Georgia. Why didn't you tell me?"

"You would've said it was a stupid idea."

"From how you look, it was."

"Rude," I grumble, failing to meet his eyes.

Crossing his arms, he rests his back against the counter. "What happened?"

"He has a new family." I rub at my eyes—an attempt to stop the tears from surfacing. "A woman answered the door, looking like she wanted to kill me. My guess is, she thought I was his mistress. He knew who I was as soon as he saw me. When I blurted out that I was his daughter, the woman nearly fainted. She had no idea he'd had a family before her. He showed me the door and demanded I never come back."

He blows out a ragged breath. "I'm sorry, sis."

I shrug, and my voice cracks. "That chapter is closed now. No more what-ifs, you know? I wish I'd been like you and not cared about him."

As he stares at me, I take in the similarities he has to our father—tall, brown hair, sharp jaw. "Dad left when you were a baby. You never knew him, so no one can blame you for being curious. I never cared because I was seven when he bailed and knew what kind of person he was." He motions for me to stand. "Come here."

There's a sense of comfort, of security, when he wraps me into a tight hug. I cry into the shoulder of the only man who's never broken my heart.

"Screw anyone who doesn't want us in their lives," I mutter.

He squeezes me tighter. "Yeah, fuck them."

Fuck POS fathers.

Fuck men who ditch you.

Fuck Chase Smith.

———

I'M my heart's worst enemy.

No doubt if it could choose a different chest of residence, it'd pack up and haul ass.

My brain, on the other hand, is *my* worst enemy.

When I return home from Cohen's, I come up with the brilliant idea to call Chase. The problem is, I don't know *his* number.

What I do know is *his assistant's* number.

She answers on the second ring, "Hello, this is Kiki."

No going back now.

"Hey, Kiki," I say. "It's Georgia. I'm the woman—"

"I know who you are, honey," she interrupts. It's not a rude interruption yet also not friendly. More of a *why are you calling* tone. "What can I help you with?"

Here goes.

"Can you give me Chase's number?"

"Why?"

"I need to ask him a question."

"I'm sure I can answer that question."

"Not exactly."

"Let me put you on hold for a moment."

The line turns quiet, and I pull my phone away, checking to see she didn't hang up on me.

A few minutes later, she's back. "I'm sorry, Georgia. He's busy at the moment."

I need to talk to him, to know why he did what he did. Even if it's an answer I don't want to hear, one that'd break my heart, it's what I want.

"I can wait."

"Honey, you'll be waiting forever then."

"What?"

She sighs. "Listen, don't pursue him. Nothing will come of it. Arch —I mean, Chase will not take or return any of your calls."

Short, simple, no bullshit in her tone.

"All right," I say softly.

We end the call.

Briefly, I debate on driving to his house but stop myself.

For someone who doesn't want to talk to a hookup, why did he take me to his house?

I need to listen to her. To my gut. To Lola when she told me never to speak to him again. I need to remember every time he showed me his true colors—from threatening to tow my car to leaving me.

He's someone I never want to have a conversation with again.

CHAPTER SIX

Archer

One Month Later

"A BAR?" The question falls from my mother's lips in disdain.

I nod. "A bar."

"Archer, darling," she says slowly, "why don't you wait until Lincoln is released before doing anything drastic?"

"This isn't drastic."

"Starting a business out of the blue is drastic."

"Out of the blue?" I shake my head, clearing my throat to create the perfect sternness in my voice. "After grandfather's death, I wanted out but stayed for the family. It's not happening again."

She can push and plead all she wants, but this time, there's no changing my mind. No more arguing, no more working at a job I hate, no more stomach sinking in guilt when I take the elevator to the top floor at Callahan Holdings.

No. Fucking. More.

"You'll ruin the family's legacy," she argues.

"Blame that on Dad. Not me."

That *legacy* was trashed by Warren Callahan II when he pleaded guilty for breaking the law.

Since childbirth, my life plan has been to work for my family's empire. Callahan Holdings was founded by my grandfather decades ago. He purchased real estate—predominately farmland—dirt cheap and cashed out when it was commercialized. Callahan Holdings owns shopping centers, office buildings, and businesses out the ass. After my grandfather's passing, my dad promoted himself to president. I declined the VP position, and my younger brother, Lincoln, took the job. I became the chief operations officer—the smallest role I could take—but I quit when I discovered my father's fraudulence.

Knowing this would be her reaction, I waited to break the news to her until I was certain of the decision. For years, I've been questioned why I bartend. I don't need the money, but it's not what bartending is about for me. It's a therapy, slinging drinks and being in the zone. When I'm there, I'm not in my head, tormenting myself with regrets of my actions. Which is why, the day after Lincoln was sentenced, I decided I was not just returning to bartending; I was going to open a bar.

It's for my sanity, not the money. Even after quitting my job, I have enough in savings and from my inheritance to never have to work another day in my life.

"You're doing this because of him," she says.

We both flinch at her statement … at the mention of my grandfather.

It's harsh and terrible timing, yet it's true.

I shut my eyes, her remark a verbal punch to my gut.

"Sorry," she whispers, backing up and sitting on a barstool behind my twelve-foot kitchen island. "If this makes you happy, that's all I care about, but—"

"How'd I know there'd be a but?"

Josephine Callahan isn't one who loses easily. "As your mother, I believe you'll regret this decision." When she places her hand to her chest over her heart, her sparkling ten-carat wedding ring is on display. "Everyone knows your grandfather expected you to take over the company when he retired."

I grit my teeth, the headache resurfacing—the same one that

always comes when he's brought up. "Had he been able to see into the future, he wouldn't have."

"Honey, it was an accident," she stresses, her face softening. "Stop punishing yourself."

"Accident or not, it's on me."

My penthouse falls silent, and I sigh at the deep sadness on my mother's face. She's had a rough year, losing my brother and my father to correctional facilities. She's been left with the negative son who wants nothing to do with the lifestyle she lives.

She perks up on her stool, always one to mask her emotions. "Don't forget your grandparents' party is tonight."

Party.

My mouth turns sour at the word. "You know I don't go to parties." Those days are over.

"It's not *any* party, Archer. It's a small social gathering to celebrate their fiftieth anniversary. They'll be delighted if you show."

Small social gathering, my ass.

My grandmother doesn't do *small*. She's the queen of over-the-top parties. For my fifth birthday, she rented out an entire amusement park. My mother wasn't born a Callahan; she married into the name, but she was born into wealth by her parents.

My phone ringing stops this dreadful conversation, and I swipe it off the counter. My friend Cohen's name flashes across the screen.

"I need to take this." I hold up the phone and walk toward my office while answering, "Hey."

"Hey, man," he replies. "Barbecue tonight at my place. Come through."

I met Cohen when we bartended together. A few weeks ago, I called and asked if he'd be interested in starting a bar together.

"Nah, I'll have to pass."

"Come on," he groans around a chuckle. "For years, you've passed on all my invites. You're coming. We can talk business."

I rack my brain, searching for an excuse.

Excuses are a part-time gig for me.

I'm a fucking pro at making them.

Although a barbecue sounds better than my grandparents' party.

Looks like I'm choosing the lesser of the two evils.

"Sure, I'll be there."

I end the call, return to the kitchen, and tell my mother I can't attend *her* party because I have a business dinner.

CHAPTER SEVEN

Georgia

"THE HUNGOVER GEORGIA LOOK IS SERVING," Lola says, snapping her fingers from side to side in front of my face.

We're in Cohen's backyard for one of his barbecues. It's something he regularly throws together to catch up with his friends. Being a single father of a four-year-old boy, his schedule is hectic, and it's not like he can barhop to have drinks with the guys. His friends, Finn and Silas, are here and so are Lola and Grace, my besties.

I'm sitting at the table with the girls, Cohen is manning the grill a few feet away while talking to Silas, and Finn is pushing Noah, my nephew, on the tire swing Cohen recently hung from one of the massive trees.

Shuddering, I scrunch up my nose, remembering why I look like hell. "The hungover Georgia is tired and dehydrated—the aftermath of her dullsville date last night."

Lola waggles her finger toward me. "I told you an accountant named Bill would be a snooze fest, but *no one* listens to Lola unless it's advice on what liquors mix well together or if they need guidance on escaping a one-night-stand morning gone wrong." She shoots me a pointed look, and I flip her off.

I gesture to Grace next to me. "Blame it on her! She set me up."

"We all know Grace is …" Lola pauses and gives Grace an apologetic smile. "No offense, babe, but you're a terrible matchmaker. Your ex was *a priest*."

"Wrong," Grace argues. "He was *in line* to become a priest but relinquished the idea when he discovered sex was better than celibacy." She rolls her eyes. "Unfortunately, that sex wasn't *with me*, his girlfriend."

"Rat bastard," Lola mutters, dragging a hand through her straight jet-black hair.

Five minutes into my date last night, I realized it was a bad idea.

What did I think was a good idea?

Ordering one too many cocktails.

If the guy isn't providing decent conversation, it's time booze tapped in.

It's not Grace's fault.

While I like nice guys, I don't do *puppy nice*.

I need a man who challenges me, and that wasn't Bill.

Boring Bill talked about his mother and went into full-blown details about his lactose intolerance after I ordered cheesecake, and the way he fumbled with his fork while eating convinced me he'd be fumbling to find my clit.

Typically, I'm not so hard on men.

Maybe it's me still being caught up on Chase.

He didn't struggle with finding my clit.

I grab my water bottle and take a long drink—an attempt to wash away thoughts of him.

I swore off men after the Chase incident, and even though it wasn't a *breakup*, I did the whole *change your hair* thing. I'm now a blonde.

New hair.

Not new me because I can't get that *rat bastard* out of my head. I was stupid enough to believe a man who parked like a selfish idiot wouldn't smash and dash. My dumbass should've asked more questions, delved deeper into his asshole of a soul before taking a trip to his bed.

"You're thinking of him, aren't you?" Lola asks, interrupting my thoughts.

That damn intuition of hers.

Grace glances at me. "Thinking of who?"

Lola smirks. "Her one-night-stand runner."

"Oh," Grace says, her green eyes widening. "The coffee jerk."

"The guy who rear-ended her twice," Lola confirms with a nod.

I flip her off again.

They know about my Chase nightmare—how I stupidly went home with him without even questioning if he was a serial killer.

Lola laughs. "We do need to give homeboy some credit for the coffee and doughnuts. He provided ... what do they call it? A continental breakfast?"

"Funny," I grumble.

"Have you tried reaching out again?" Grace asks.

I shake my head. Kiki made it clear it'd be a waste of my time.

"I'm officially swearing off men," I say, slumping in my chair.

"What about the guy coming tonight?" Grace smiles. "The one Cohen is opening a bar with. Maybe he's single."

"I'm swearing off *all men*," I clarify.

A smile tugs at my lips. Not because of the man possibly being single but for my brother. Owning a bar is his dream, and it's finally coming true. The other day during Taco Tuesday, Cohen mentioned he was in talks of starting a bar with a guy he used to work with. Said guy is coming to today's barbecue.

"Archer Callahan will make a great business partner," Lola states matter-of-factly. "A great man to date? Definitely not."

"What do you know about him?" Grace asks.

"He's cool and wealthy as fuck, and he has bar experience," Lola replies. "Hell, he has straight-up business experience, given his family. The Callahans own half the commercial real estate in Iowa."

"The Callahans?" I cut in. "My brother is going into business with a Callahan?"

Lola nods. "You didn't know that?"

I shake my head. "At least I know Cohen will be in good hands."

Like nearly everyone else, I've heard of the Callahan family, but I don't know much about them.

Grace tilts her head to the side. "If he's so wealthy, why doesn't he work for his family?"

"Do you guys not watch the news?" Lola replies.

"Too busy," I say while Grace mutters, "I have homework to grade instead."

Lola leans in, ready to spill the tea. "His family was busted for doing shady shit. Archer's father was laundering money through the company, hiding funds overseas—all those white-collar crimes you see in the movies. The word is, Archer knew something sketchy was happening and quit—probably not wanting to star in the male reality show version of *Orange Is the New Black*. Feds went to town on his family's assets, and everything came crashing down. Archer and his mother were the only ones left unscathed."

I suck in a long breath—hyper-focusing on her words. The story, it's so familiar to what happened to Chase's family.

Surely, it couldn't be him, right?

People go to prison all the time.

I'm sure shit like that happens on the regular.

I gulp. "How do you know all this?"

"His father collects ... well, *collected* expensive liquor and was a regular customer at the distribution company I work for. They tend to send me to their high-profile clients since I'm a kick-ass saleswoman." She winks, swiping fake dirt off her shoulder. "Dude was nice, enjoyed flaunting his riches ... and hiding it apparently."

As if with perfect timing, Cohen yells, "Archer, my man! You came."

"Speak of the devil," Lola says, pointing over my shoulder.

My heart races when I turn in my chair to find Chase strolling through the backyard. I hold in a breath and wait in anticipation for another man to come into view.

For *Archer* to come into view.

Maybe he and Chase are friends.

"Archer finally shows his fucking face," I hear Silas call out behind me. *This motherfucker.*

Asshole gave me the wrong name.

Archer the asshole.

Seems fitting.

I turn to face my friends and lower my voice, "That's Archer Callahan?"

Say no. Please say no.

Lola nods. "Sure is."

I grip Grace's arm in panic. "That's *him*."

Grace blinks at me. "Who's him?"

"The guy I slept with," I hiss. "That's him!"

"What?" Lola shrieks. "You fucked Archer Callahan?"

CHAPTER EIGHT

Archer

THIS IS A FUCKING SHITSHOW.

When I scan Cohen's backyard and see *her*, a deep chill climbs up my spine, and I contemplate leaving.

She might've dyed her hair blond, but there's no doubt it's her.

Georgia.

The woman I should've never sat next to at the bar.

The woman I should've never touched.

The woman whose face still haunts my thoughts.

Why is she here?

Who is she to Cohen?

Jesus, fuck, please don't be his girlfriend ... or someone related to him.

Our eyes meet, and hers are darkened with resentment as she glowers at me. I wait on her next move before making my own.

Will she rat me out?

Smack me in the face?

She tightens her hand around the armrest of the chair but doesn't stand or make a move in my direction. After a good thirty seconds, I realize me standing there, staring at her, will only draw questions. I smash our eye contact, shove my hands into my pockets, and walk toward Cohen. With each step, I pray she's some random person to him.

Cohen turns down the grill's temperature when I reach him and circles it, and we share a one-armed bro hug.

"You fucker," Silas says, shaking his head. "I had twenty bucks on you not showing."

Cohen holds out his hand, and Silas pulls out his wallet before slapping a twenty into it.

I can't believe those fuckers bet on whether I'd come.

Actually, I can.

"You know the guys," Cohen says, and I spot Finn and Noah playing in the background.

Finn and Silas worked with us at a club a few years ago, and Noah tagged along with Cohen when he stopped by to pick up checks, drop off paperwork, do manager shit.

Cohen shifts and points at the table I'm avoiding. "This is my sister, Georgia."

His sister.

Of course it's his goddamn sister.

It couldn't have been his sister's *friend* or a neighbor.

No, it had to be my future business partner's sister.

Sure, he's mentioned having a sister a few times, but I never knew her name or what she looked like.

"Georgia, this is Archer," Cohen continues, clueless that his introduction is mentally knocking me on my ass.

No need for the intro, bro.

We're already acquainted.

I've touched her, kissed her, been inside her.

Knowing it'd look suspicious as fuck if I ignored his greeting, I slowly drag my attention back to Georgia. The phoniest smile I've ever seen is plastered on her face. I have to give her props; she's doing a kick-ass job at hiding her dislike for me. I swallow rapidly, waiting for her to rat my ass out.

Instead, she clears her throat before saying, "Hi," in a flat voice.

Her eyes refuse to meet mine.

She's looking straight through me.

I'm curious if Cohen is picking up on the tension, but he's smiling without one concern on his face. Her friends are a different story. Their attention bounces back and forth between Georgia and me, as if we're tonight's entertainment.

"Grace," the strawberry-blonde says with a polite smile.

"Lola," says the other—no polite smile from her. More of a scowl.

I recognize Lola. She's shown up at my father's office countless times to sell him overpriced liquor. I was convinced he was buying it because he liked to look at her, not for the product.

I tip my head in their direction. "Hey."

"I like your name," Georgia says. "It's *so* original. I would've pegged you for a Chase." She glances at Lola. "Doesn't he look like a Chase?"

Lola nods. "Come to think of it, you're absolutely right. You have Chase written all over you."

Cohen, finally realizing this isn't happy-go-lucky, shoots Georgia a *what the fuck* look.

"Beer?" he asks, changing the subject.

I nod. "Sure."

How about something stronger?

Something potent enough to wipe out the memory of how I spent a night fucking your little sister.

I spare another glance to Georgia as Cohen opens a red Coleman cooler.

Her glare is cold, and she mouths the words, *"I hate you."*

A Corona is shoved in my hand, stealing my attention from her, and I don't reply. I pop open the cap and take a long draw, and on my next peek at her, she looks as if she wants to chop off my dick and fry it on the grill.

Not that I blame her.

Sleeping with her was destructive.

It proved I was who I'd been labeled.

Selfish. Heartless. Asshole.

When I led Georgia into my bedroom, when I tasted her, when I thrust inside her, I didn't plan on bailing. The alcohol had swayed me into believing I was a better person that night, but then the reality of the next morning proved I had been wrong. Ditching her was a dick move, but it was the only choice I had.

I'd never let her in.

Never let *anyone in*.

It was better to end it that morning than to lead her on further.

Cohen returns to the grill, and when he opens it, my stomach growls at the sight of grilled chicken and steaks. I make small talk with Silas and Cohen—mostly them speaking and me inputting random comments every few minutes. Crossing my arms, I attempt to listen to the women, who are now huddled around the table, whispering. Randomly, one of them throws a dirty look in my direction, and I catch Lola subtly flipping me off.

"Food is ready!" Cohen yells. "Let's eat!"

"About damn time," Silas says, rubbing his stomach.

Noah and Finn come barreling toward us.

"Dad! Don't forget I want my burger cut into tiny little pieces," Noah shouts.

Cohen ruffles his hand through his son's hair. "I got you, buddy."

Georgia and Grace run into the house while Lola starts ripping open bags of chips. She pours them into brightly colored bowls.

Finn rubs his hands together. "I'm starving."

We make our plates and take our seats around the table. I wait until Georgia plops down in the chair she sat in earlier and take the one farthest from her. Sipping on my beer and eating chicken, I listen to them make small talk.

I blankly stare ahead as the group chats around me.

Act like I give no fucks.

It's who I am—a master of pretending and concealing my true self.

I'm a complex man—a once-heavily-sought-after book whose pages are torn, now shoved into the back shelf of the library.

Georgia, on the other hand?

She's so damn transparent—as easily read as a children's book not thrown in the back corner.

They've invited me to their infamous barbecues for years, but I always decline—until now that is. Sure, on a few occasions, they've managed to drag me to a sports bar, where I could input a few words while watching a game, but it's where I usually draw the line. Something personal like this—where it can lead to one-on-one talks and deep conversations—I steer clear of.

Then the shit with my family happened, and my life became consumed with attorney meetings and court dates. I couldn't go out because people would ask me endless questions:

Did you know they were breaking the law?

Where's the money?

Are you going to prison?

Will you be poor?

It's why I gave Georgia a fake name—something I do frequently. I know when someone recognizes me, and Georgia definitely didn't. After people find out who you are, they try to take advantage of the situation—ask for more money, sue, sell it to the papers.

Georgia is as quiet as I am. She picks at her food, hardly eating it, and forces a few laughs here and there.

My presence here has ruined her day, making me feel like an even bigger asshole.

———

COHEN SMACKS his palm on the table. "All right, let's talk business."

We're seated by ourselves while everyone else is playing cornhole.

On our slow nights, he talked about his life, how he'd raised his little sister after their father bailed and their mother was in a constant state of fucked up. We threw around the idea of starting our own bars, but doing it together was never a conversation. Our situations were different. Cohen had to work to start a bar, had to acquire the funds. That's not an easy feat for a single father.

When my family's fraud hit the news, I quit bartending because of the questions from drunken patrons who knew about my family. I wasn't sure what Cohen's response would be when I called him. Lucky for me, he was thrilled with the idea.

We've yet to talk specifics, but I want to open as soon as possible.

Hell, specifics might never be discussed if my sleeping with Georgia comes to light.

"You been doing okay?" Cohen asks.

"Happy the headache is over, not happy with the results," I answer.

He nods and sips on his beer.

His response is why I like Cohen. After that statement, people would normally give me advice on what to do—whether it be their opinions, questions, or what I might want to hear to get on my good side.

Cohen is cool, quiet, and not in people's business. He can be the face of the bar, *the boss*, and I'll sit in the corner, silently playing the bartender role.

I trust him, and that's one of the biggest things that matters to me.

"Are they filing an appeal?"

"That's the plan."

He claps my shoulder. "You know we got your back if you need anything."

"We got your back."

I've had friends for years, friends I've grown up with, cousins from my mother's side, and none of them have reached out to me. None of them have made it clear that no matter what happened, they were there.

"The bar will help take my mind off the bullshit," I reply.

"You sure you're ready for this ride?" Cohen asks. "I know you're feeling some type of way because of the sentencing, but I'm in this for the long haul, man. I don't want this to be a gig to temporarily take your mind off your problems, and then in a few years, when the dust has settled with your family's legal issues, you decide you want out. This is my dream, man, and I won't lose it."

"I'm one hundred percent in," I reply. "It's what I need to keep my sanity."

He's unhappy with my answer.

"I'll put it in our contract if that'll make you feel better. No backing out for seven years, and if I want to leave, you can buy me out for cheap. This is more for my sanity than for money."

"Sounds good, man. I talked to my bank about getting a loan, and I have money saved, but—"

"Whatever else you need, I'll cover."

He shakes his head. "Nah, you don't need to do that."

"I know, and that's why I am."

He holds out his knuckles. "Let's do it then."

Guilt surfaces for not telling him about Georgia and me.

I brush it off and fist-bump him, like the dick that I am. "Let's do this."

———

AFTER THE BEER, I opt for water.

I'll be leaving soon and dipping into something stronger when I get home. Until then, I need to find out where Georgia's head is. The last thing I want is to start the process with Cohen and then him bail as the ball starts rolling because he found out I'd slept with his sister. If Georgia tells him about my actions the morning after, he'll be done with my ass.

When Georgia walks inside the empty house, I follow her—thankful to finally get her alone while also hoping no one notices me on her trail. She's stayed with her friends the entire time I've been here, so this is my first open opportunity.

She whips around when the back door slams shut behind me, and we land in the kitchen. "Why are you following me?"

I scratch my cheek, searching for the right words. "This is a fucked-up situation."

She tilts her head to the side and pouts her lips. "Agreed."

"What do you want to do? Tell him? Act like what we did never happened?"

Her expression turns flat. "What did we do?" She coldly laughs and opens the fridge, turning around with a bottle of water in her hand. "You're a fucking asshole."

"We slept together. It was a one-time thing. It happens all the time."

You would've thought my response was a slap to her face because she retreats a step.

"Happens all the time? Maybe for you but not for me." Horror is on her face when she slams her water on the table. "Oh my God. How much *all the time* do you do it?"

"That's not what I meant." I backtrack. "I'm saying that people have sex and never talk again or act like it never happened all the time."

"If only we could be in the category of never talking again. You might as well have thrown my clothes out and told me to kick rocks." She grimaces, staring at me, wide-eyed. "Who treats someone like that?"

"You're right. It was a bad call on my part." *That's an understatement.*

"You think?"

"At least I provided complimentary doughnuts."

"*Again,* you're an asshole."

"So you keep saying." I scrub a hand over my face. "Are you going to tell your brother?"

She shakes her head. "If I do, he won't go into business with you." She signals between us. "This never happened. You never saw me naked. My brother will never hear a word of it. Got it?"

"What about your little gossip girl club?" I jerk my head toward the door. "From the looks on their faces, they know about us."

"Trust me, they won't say anything." She sucks in a breath before casting me a curious glance. "Who gives people fake names and has business cards with that fake name?"

I shrug, like it's not unusual. "Someone who likes to keep a low profile."

"That's not weird or anything." She scrunches up her nose. "You didn't look shocked when my brother introduced us. Did you know who I was?"

I shake my head. "I don't display my emotions like you. I can handle them maturely without making a scene."

"A scene?" She scowls. "I hardly made a scene. You would've been terrified if I had *made a scene.*"

With that, she walks away, bumping into my shoulder as she leaves.

———

THE COOKOUT WAS A BUST.

Good thing I'm not known for my great entertainment and sparkling personality. I chatted for a while before making up some bullshit excuse about needing to leave for my grandparents' anniversary party.

I'm a lying bastard.

Sue me.

I slump down on my couch, open the Dom Pérignon, and drink it straight from the bottle.

My little brother and father are sitting in a jail cell, and I'm left to pick up the pieces of a family that was already fucking broken.

I do a once-over of my penthouse when I take my next drink. One of the traits I inherited from my family is enjoying the finer things in life, so I'm grateful my shit didn't get seized. The Feds had been watching my family, had fine-combed our finances, but I kept my nose clean. I didn't take a dime of the dirty money, but that didn't mean I wasn't dragged into their mess. At first, the Feds threatened I'd join my father and brother, even when they had nothing on me, and then they switched tactics, begging me to snitch.

My father was embezzling money. It's wrong, yes, but he wasn't fucking murdering people. Even though my loyalty to him isn't as strong as Lincoln's, I stayed silent.

Lucky for me, the bulk of my money is from my inheritance and didn't come from committing crimes and shady shit. The bastards couldn't touch my accounts.

My brother's? They froze all his shit.

Although he was smart enough to sign a chunk of it over to my mother before he got caught up. I'm sure there's money for him in some offshore business account too. My dad is a businessman and was prepared in case this happened.

My head falls back.

Georgia Fox.

When I go to bed, flashbacks of our night together keep me awake.

How good she felt and how it killed me to hear her moan out another man's name when it should've been mine.

The reminder that I walked out on her floats through, overshadowing the good, and as I drift asleep, I hate myself.

CHAPTER NINE

Georgia

"DO you remember the diner where Mom used to work?" Cohen asks, walking into his living room and plopping down on the other side of the couch.

I toss my phone down next to me. "Mom worked at several diners."

Fast-food joints, factories, cleaning jobs—none of them lasted long. She was more of a fan of getting high than working.

"You know …" He snaps his fingers, struggling to remember the name. "The one on North Street, close to the park here in Anchor Ridge."

"Dawn's Delicious Café?"

He snaps one more time. "That's it."

"What about it? It shut down forever ago." I grab the bag of Cheetos I brought from home because Cohen doesn't buy junk food—*annoying*—and pop a cheese puff into my mouth.

Dawn, a woman in her late fifties and a recovering addict, owned the café. She took a chance on our mother and gave her a job. The problem was, our mom didn't like being on time or working, nor did she find it wrong to make drug deals in the parking lot.

After she was fired, she moved us a few towns over to Mayview, Iowa. It's where I grew up, but Cohen moved us back to Anchor Ridge when Noah was born to keep their distance from Noah's mother's family.

"The building is for sale."

"Cool." I pop another Cheetos.

"You think it'd be a good location for a bar?"

I'm quiet while considering my answer.

"The building has great bones," he continues. "Plenty of space, and it's a great location for traffic to maneuver in and out of. It needs work, not going to lie, but I think we can turn it into a kick-ass bar."

I nod in agreement. "I think it'd be cool … but it might drag up old memories."

The excitement on Cohen's face dissolves, and I wish I could take back my words.

"I don't give a shit about memories," he snarls.

Like with our nonexistent father, we don't have a healthy relationship with our mother. I know who she is. I just don't know where she is. She tends to bounce among rehab, jail, and crack houses. When I was seventeen, Cohen forbade her to come around me until she was clean. Unlike him, I don't hate her. I'm more disappointed that she chooses dope over her children. Cohen isn't as forgiving as I am. Once you screw him over, he's done with you. Maybe I'd be different if I were the one picking up all the responsibilities as a result of their neglect.

He shelters me from the struggles he's faced, so at times, I can be naïve. His goal was for me to grow up happy, to feel loved, and it's the same for Noah. Cohen puts up a hard front, but he's all about family. Once you're in his good graces, he's there for you, no matter what.

He stands, nearly a foot taller than I am, from the couch. "I'm meeting with the realtor today. Want to tag along?"

"Sure." I stop myself when a knot forms in my throat. "Will Archer be there?"

He nods, not sensing the change in my mood.

"Is it a good idea for me to come?" I bite into the edge of my lip, already anxious to possibly see the morning-after ditcher. "Maybe it should just be you two. I don't want to intrude."

"Intrude?" He chuckles. "You're my sister. You never have to worry about that ever happening. Archer won't care. He's a laid-back dude."

Laid-back dude, my ass.

———

"DAD, THIS PLACE IS SUPER SCARY," Noah whines from the back seat when we pull into the parking lot of the dilapidated building. "It looks dirty and gross. I don't want to go inside. There are probably ninety million bajillion ghosts in there. We'd better call Scooby-Doo so he can get rid of them before we do."

I laugh, unbuckle my seat belt, and turn to look back at him. "Scooby-Doo is on vacation, so you'd better stay close to me if you want to avoid ghosts."

Cohen throws me a *really* look.

"What?" I shrug.

He peeks back at Noah. "Little buddy, don't listen to anything your aunt Georgia tells you. There are no ghosts here. There are no ghosts *anywhere.*"

Noah scrunches up his nose, his gaze pinging back and forth between his father and me. "You tell me to listen to her when she babysits me."

"Listen to her then, but when it pertains to ghosts, she's lying," Cohen stresses.

"Aunt Georgia doesn't lie. That's bad."

"Exactly." I hold out my hand for a high five, and he smacks his small palm against it. "I don't do bad things."

My laughter cracks before dying out completely when I twist in my seat and see Archer's car—the same one from the accident. Meanwhile, I traded my car in for a shiny, *used* VW bug with the money he'd given me.

When his car door opens, my throat clenches, and I give myself a mental pep talk. He steps out, one long leg and then the other, and when his entire body comes into view, my breathing quickens. As soon as we're out of the car, I grab Noah's hand, declaring him my Archer-blocker for the day. I'll keep all my attention on him and act very invested in Scooby and Legos.

He slips his hands into his pockets on his walk toward us.

"Hi, Archer!" Noah calls out, jumping up and down.

My sweet nephew sees the good in everyone, even an asshole like Archer.

"Yo, Noah," Archer replies, failing to glance in my direction. "Hey, Cohen … Georgia."

My name comes out like an afterthought to him, and I narrow my eyes, restraining myself from flipping him off.

As he moves closer, my mouth waters.

Jesus.

Why does he have to look so damn hot?

I wish I'd had a case of drunk goggles that night—that alcohol had altered my hot-guy meter, and in real life, he was hideous.

But the universe is always against me, and he's just as hot when I'm drunk as he is when I'm sober.

"Hey there!" a woman—her age most likely around my brother's—shouts, walking toward us, her kitten heels crunching against the gravel. "You must be Cohen and Archer." She holds out her hand. "I'm Mariah."

She shakes Cohen's hand and then Archer's. I roll my eyes at the appreciative once-over she gives my brother. When she turns to Archer and does the same, a wave of jealousy hits me that shouldn't exist. Her gaze swoops down his body, taking considerably longer than she did with Cohen, as if she's imagining him naked.

Not that I blame her.

I smile, knowing I've one-upped her.

I *have* seen him naked.

Felt him thrust inside me.

Had his lips on mine.

Archer answers with a head nod, not giving two shits about her presence. Dude does not like conversation. At least it's not just me. He's a dick to almost everyone—with the exception of Noah because the kid is too cute to be a dick to.

If Cohen and Archer go into business together, I'll need to learn how to set aside the hurt he caused and reel in my hatred toward him. I'm not a bitchy person. People refer to me as fun, quirky, a smart-ass with a nosy side.

I'll never be able to fully stomp away the array of emotions I feel for the man. So, as much as I'll hate it, my time at their bar will be limited. Until I get my emotions in check at least. I'll blame it on school, which won't be a complete lie because classes have been kicking my ass lately.

Scratch that.

I won't let him win.

It'll be my brother's business too.

Let Archer deal with me *every single day*, like I'm a thorn in his side he can't pluck away.

I give her a slight wave as I introduce myself and Noah.

"As you can tell, the building needs some care," Mariah says, starting her tour of the old restaurant. "A bar would do well here, and you'd hardly have any competition. The owners are moving to Florida and want to sell ASAP, so they're open for negotiation."

The building is large with plenty of space to create a bar front and outdoor seating, and there's room in the back for the kitchen and office space.

It reeks of mold.

Loose floorboards creak with our steps.

The roof slightly sags.

Old kitchen appliances are shoved around the back.

Needs some care is an understatement.

Ugly but restorable.

When my brother wants something, he works his ass off for it. I have no doubt he'll do the same with this.

"Daddy, I need to potty," Noah says, grabbing his elbow and glancing up at him.

"Buddy, there's not a restroom in here," Cohen replies. "Can you hold it?"

Noah shakes his head, jumping up and down, and presses his hand against his pants. "I really, really, really need to go."

"My mom owns the alterations shop across the street," Mariah says, pointing toward the entrance of the building. "He can use the restroom there."

"Thank you," Cohen says with a sigh of relief. He grabs Noah's hand before glancing at Archer and me. "Keep looking around and tell me what you think."

The building turns silent as they leave, wood creaking in their wake. I should've faked needing to use the restroom and gone with them.

Archer fishes his phone from the pocket of his jeans and focuses on it without a peek in my direction, as if I were not even here.

"Wow," I say. "I see you're still a rude asshole."

"Still a rude asshole," he answers, his tone flat. "It seems it's your favorite thing to call me, so I won't try to change your mind."

"Why'd you do it then?"

"Do what?"

"Sleep with me. Why would you sleep with someone you can't stand the sight of?"

"Never said I couldn't stand the sight of you. The sight of you is very nice actually."

I snort. "Says the guy who won't even look at me."

He tilts his chin up, and his eyes meet mine with disdain. "Is this better?"

"No," I answer, waving my hand in the air. "Go back to focusing on your phone, or sit in your car, or leave. Any of those would be better."

"You were just mad I wouldn't look at you, and now that I am, you don't want me to?"

"Yes."

He shakes his head, and his attention returns to his phone. "I think this will be a good location for us. Tell your brother that."

"Are you sure? I'm worried if a restaurant didn't survive here, will a bar?"

"From what I researched, the restaurant was run-down, and the food was shit. Our bar won't be any of those things."

"Okay, Sir Know-It-All."

"Why'd you come?" he asks, the question falling from his lips so casually, like it's not rude. "Had you not, we could've avoided speaking to each other."

"My brother asked me to."

"You could've said no."

"Trust me, I tried to. If I'd refused, it would've sounded sketchy." I tap the side of my lips even though he's not looking at me. "Would you rather me tell him you fucked me, so then he'll understand why my new goal in life is to dodge any conversation with you?"

"We decided to keep it to ourselves."

"And that's exactly what I'm doing. That includes not making him wonder why I'm so against being in the same room with you. Cohen and I are close. He knows I'd never miss something like this with him."

"Gotcha. So I should expect to see you around?" He peers up at me.

"You should."

"Noted. Let's try to keep it to a minimum."

His words are a kick through my heart. I hold my head high when I pass him on my way back outside and stand next to Cohen's car with my arms crossed. As I wait, I'm haunted by flashbacks of the night with Archer—how he said the sweetest things, how he pleasured me like he already knew my body and we were fit for each other. He opened up to me, acting interested in more than a quickie, but it was all a lie.

Maybe Chase is his alter ego.

The pleasant version of him.

It hurt when he acted like he didn't know me at the barbecue, like I meant nothing to him.

Our night together meant nothing to him.

Maybe one-night stands are the norm for him but not for me.

Rich. Cocky. Handsome.

The perfect trinity for an asshole who breaks your heart.

Archer Callahan is a man who screws women and then leaves them notes as a thank-you.

He made a full damn asshole circle.

Does he not feel bad?

Was I just some disposable fuck to him?

Fuck him.

Fuck one-night stands.

Fuck dudes who leave you don't worry about locking up *notes after* they banged the lights out of you all night.

CHAPTER TEN

Archer

Six Months Later

"WE DID IT, MAN." Cohen slaps me on the back, a bright-ass grin on his face.

"We fucking did it." I stand tall in pride. No bright-ass grin from me.

After six months of finances, hard work, and Georgia-dodging, we're open. The Twisted Fox is finally open for business and ready to serve drinks. Shockingly, it took only minutes for us to come up with a name. We each chose a word.

Mine was Twisted—since it's how my brain feels.

Cohen's was Fox—after his last name.

We purchased the old restaurant building two days after the showing, then gutted it, remodeled, and created a bar. There were no complaints from me on the location. Anchor Ridge is the small town where Cohen lives and is twenty minutes from my house.

Cohen brought in his friends and Georgia to help, so I sent Kiki, who now has a new job but at least waited until the bar was complete, to do most of my bidding while I handled the behind-the-scenes financial aspects.

The less time around Georgia, the better.

Also, the less I feel guilty about what I did.

When I see her, I'm reminded of how I let her go because I could never have her.

Because it would've been nothing but problems before shattering altogether.

She hates me now, and I fake hate her.

My plan is to make her hate me more.

If she despises me, there will be no temptation.

It's opening night at the bar, and so far, everything is rolling smoothly. Thanks to Silas, there's been talk about the opening. A small radio station is in the parking lot to promote us, and he somehow convinced a few athletes to show up and post their location on social media.

It worked.

It's insane how busy we are.

We created the perfect sports bar with walls of TVs, top-shelf liquor, and an enjoyable atmosphere. I want someone to walk in and feel like they can sit and have a couple of beers with their friends—not caring about a dress code, or bottle service, or a large cover.

The suckiest part is I have no one to celebrate this achievement with. Sure, Cohen and our friends are here but no family. No Lincoln. I would've invited my mother, but she'd have felt out of place. Country clubs and black-tie parties are more her scene.

"I guess congratulations are in order."

I look up to find Georgia slide onto the stool across from me at the bar. It's been a while since I've looked at her—*really looked at her*—since I evade any eye contact, in fear she'd try to start a conversation.

"Yep," I say.

Be a dick.

Make her hate you.

"How does it feel?"

Pretty damn good.

I shrug. "It is what it is."

"All right," she groans. "Having a conversation with you is so much fun." She stands and joins me behind the bar.

"This is an employee-only zone." I narrow my eyes at her.

Shrugging, she snags a bottle of vodka, pours two shots, and hands one to me. "It seems you're only nice when you're drinking, so drink up."

I push the drink away and walk backward. "I'm good."

"I don't get it." She knocks back a shot and sets down the glass. "Shouldn't I be the one pissed at you?"

"Look, Georgia," I sneer, "was I nice to you during our first two run-ins?"

She shakes her head. "Well ... no."

"Don't you find it weird that the *only* time I was nice to you was when I was drinking?" I pause to better make my point, to sharpen the knife I'm about to jab through her heart. "And wanted to get laid."

Her eyes widen and then turn cold.

I tap my temple. "Put two and two together."

Her jaw drops. "Are you serious?"

I shrug.

"You listened to me pour my heart out about my father and how hard that day was for me." Her hand holding the shot glass shakes. "You shared your personal demons. All because you wanted to screw me?"

"What can I say? Hennessy goes straight to my dick."

"I regret ever letting you touch me," she hisses.

"You did, though." A sadistic grin passes over my lips. "And if I remember correctly, you liked it."

She gulps down the other shot, drops it, and ignores the glass shattering at my feet. "Wrong. You were the worst sex I've ever had, and your dick is small."

I run my hand over my chin. "Not what you were saying that night. Something along the lines of, *best sex I've ever had* and *biggest cock ever.*"

"I was faking it. My brother never told you I wanted to be an actress?"

I scoff.

"You know, I came over here to congratulate you, to mend fences, since we'll be around each other a lot."

"That's cool. Say hi. I'll say hi. We don't have to be friends."

"Okay then."

Her face falls, and I inwardly cringe at how I'm treating her.

I reach out to stop her when she turns to leave but immediately come to my senses and drop my hand. Shame washes through me as I clean up the broken glass.

"Dude, it's opening night," Silas calls out from the other end of the bar. "Smile."

I fake a smile before dropping it, and then I drag my finger to my lips and flip him off.

I play it off well, as if this were no big deal, but inside, it's a different story. I'm on top of the world. I own a business—*my own* business. No one can take it away from me or run shady shit through it.

As I take drink orders throughout the night, I can't stop myself from sweeping my gaze over the bar on the hunt for her. A knot forms in my throat when I finally spot her at a table with Grace and Lola. I overfill a beer when a group of guys stops at their table. As I grab a towel to clean my mess, a man has his eyes set on Georgia. Her grin lights the room on fire, and he stops the waitress, gesturing for Georgia to order a drink. She's bubbly as she recites her order, and I wonder what she ordered.

Cognac?

I'll be making the drink, so I'll find out soon enough.

I grit my teeth, remembering the high of being the man buying her a drink and holding her attention.

Don't give it to this guy.

Don't give him what you gave me.

I crack my knuckles. No way can I stomach this night after night. My hope is that she becomes too busy with her job and classes to hang out here frequently.

I can't let this affect me.

I have to pretend not to care.

When she casts a glance in my direction, she runs her hands through her long hair and warily stares at me before mouthing, "*I hate you.*"

I give her a thumbs-up.

The rest of the night flies by in a blur. I make a drink, search the room for Georgia, see what she's doing, and then go back to work. Over and over again.

When the night ends and my work is done, she's gone.

Cohen and I share a celebratory drink after the bar closes.

I don't mutter a word about breaking his sister's heart.

CHAPTER ELEVEN

Georgia

One Year Later

"I'M SORRY, but we have to let you go."

What a shitty way to start the day.

I wince, taking in my boss's words. "What? Why?"

"Eighty percent of our profit derives from online sales." My boss —*old boss*—Francine shoots me an apologetic smile. "It's just not cost-effective to have a physical store barely dragging in revenue while paying rent and payroll."

I've worked at Boho Doll Boutique, a small shop owned by Francine and her husband, for three years. The pay isn't anything that'll bring me riches, but I get discounts on clothes, and they work with my school schedule.

"Can I help with online orders?" I ask, scrambling for ideas.

She shakes her head.

"Social media? I'm pretty skilled at creating quirky little posts." I poke my finger through the air with the last three words.

"We'll give you two weeks' pay while you look for another job." She reaches out and squeezes my hand. "I'm sorry, Georgia."

———

I COLLAPSE onto a barstool at Twisted Fox and cover my face in defeat.

"What's wrong, sis?" Cohen asks.

I move my hands, a frown on my face. "I lost my job."

"What happened?" He swoops a towel over his wide shoulder.

"They're going exclusively online."

His eyes soften. "I'm sorry. Any ideas where to go next?"

I inhale a deep breath.

He won't like my answer.

"A couple of clubs in the city are hiring."

Those soft eyes darken in disapproval.

"You banked when you bartended in clubs, and it'll work well with my school schedule."

"You're not working in a club in the city."

"You're not going to tell me what to do. I have bills to pay."

"Work here then."

"Really?"

He nods.

"If I recall, you shot me down last time I asked for a job."

"I'd rather you work at my bar than anyone else's." He points at me, his tone turning authoritative. "As long as it doesn't interfere with your classes."

"It won't. I promise." I've pulled all-nighters before and still aced tests the next morning. I got this.

"Cool. You start Thursday."

I jump up from the stool and clap my hands. "Can't wait!"

That night, the reality that I'll be working with Archer hits me.

I smirk.

Let him see me all the time.

Let him see me make his life hell.

Let him see what he's been missing.

Let him see what a mistake he made that morning.

———

"REPORTING HERE for my first day of duty." I salute Cohen when I walk into the bar.

"Reporting for *what?*" Archer asks, stone-faced.

Cohen jerks his head toward me. "I hired her."

"Hired her for *what?*"

"To sell golden chickens on the black market." I roll my eyes. "To work here, idiot."

Cohen gives me a *shut your mouth if you want this to go smoothly* look. "She'll wait tables, bartend, whatever we need her to do."

"Except clean urinals," I say with a shudder. "Sorry, but I'm not cleaning urinals where drunk dudes piss."

"We don't need her to do anything," Archer argues. "We're not hiring."

"Destiny quit last week, so we're short an employee." Tension breaks along Cohen's face. "She'll fill that void."

"Call me the void-filler," I mutter, resulting in another glare from Cohen.

Archer works his strong jaw. "You can't hire people without discussing it with me."

Cohen has hired plenty of employees without Archer because Archer prefers not to deal with it. His tantrum is because he doesn't want *me* working here.

Cohen's voice deepens. "She's my sister. She's working here. End of discussion. Be pissed all you want."

"This is bullshit." He shoots me a death glare before sweeping his hand toward the back of the bar. "My office."

———

THEY SPEND a good twenty minutes discussing if my ass will get canned before returning to the front of the bar. Archer's pissed, and Cohen is annoyed.

"Don't mess up shit," Archer snarls while passing me.

Cohen nods to Trina, a waitress. "You'll train with Trina for a while, familiarize yourself with waitressing duties, and then I'll have you work with Archer and me behind the bar."

"She'll work *with you* behind the bar," Archer corrects.

My next two hours are spent with Trina, and when my time with her is done, I skip over to Cohen. Waitressing isn't bad, but the real fun is behind the bar.

Cohen holds up his hand, stopping me from being loud, and points at his phone. "Sylvia." He walks toward his office at the back of the bar.

I nod, stand in the corner, and watch Archer work. When a woman hits on him, I cringe. Not that I blame her. It's a hot sight. Watching him move around the bar, making drinks, is hypnotic. He gives the woman attention yet doesn't. I'd think he went home alone every night if Cohen hadn't let it slip that he has his fair share of late-night hookups.

Jealousy pricks my veins at the thought of him giving women what he gave to me.

"Sylvia has a family emergency and needs to leave," Cohen says when he returns, referring to Noah's babysitter.

"Uh-oh," I mutter at the same time he calls out Archer's name.

Waving Archer over, he points at me. "Finish training her. Noah's babysitter had to bail."

Archer doesn't spare a glance in my direction, as if I weren't here. "Have Georgia cover for the babysitter, and you stay here."

Cohen shakes his head. "The faster she finishes training, the faster she'll be put to work. It's only for a few hours. No way am I having her train on the weekend. It'll be too chaotic. Let her shadow you."

I perk up. "I'm a quick learner."

"Sure, whatever," Archer mutters, turning away and stalking to the other end of the bar.

"Text me when you get home," Cohen directs me. "Or if you need anything."

I give him a thumbs-up. "I got this. Now, get to Noah."

Cohen leaves at the same time Archer tosses a drink book to me. "Study this."

I play with the book in my hands. "Study this?"

"It's the drink list."

I set it on the bar, flip through the pages, and hold it up. "I'm more of a hands-on learner."

"Whatever," he grumbles. "You don't learn shit from that book anyway."

"Yet you told me to study it."

He's already setting me up for failure.

"Why do you hate me so much, Archer?"

I need the answer. This bickering is a never-ending game with us, and it's getting out of control. Over a year has passed since we hooked up. This rivalry, enemy shit needs to end. All it'll do is ruin company morale and drive a wedge between him and Cohen. If it ever came down to me or Archer, Cohen would choose me.

Archer silently stares at me, working his jaw as though he doesn't owe me an explanation.

"How about a truce?" I thrust out my hand toward him.

"Sure, whatever." He ignores my hand and walks past me. "Now, study your book."

I grab his elbow, stopping him. "You're going to train me, or I'll tell Cohen you wouldn't."

He jerks out of my hold. "Really?"

At his movement, sharp hints of his cologne—a light sandalwood —drift up my nostrils.

It's all man.

Like taking a hike on a crisp autumn day.

"Really." A deviant smirk flashes on my lips. "I was quite the tattletale growing up."

That's a lie. My mother's absence didn't provide much opportunity to have someone to tattle to.

He jerks a glass from a stack and points at me with it. "Have you ever made a margarita?"

I shake my head. "Not professionally, but I've drunk a few." I've also purchased the frozen ones in bags and enjoyed them during our girls' nights. "I tend to drink alcohol in red Solo cups, poured from a keg or cheap vodka." I'm a college student on a budget.

"You were drinking Hennessy at Bailey's," he deadpans.

My breathing slows. *He remembers.*

"You were buying." I grin. "I planned to have the drink and then go home."

"Yet you didn't go home." His eyes turn hooded. "You went home with me."

I nod timidly. "I did."

Something shifts in him, in the mood, and he reaches out. Our gazes meet, his eyes unreadable.

"Georgia." My name is said in a tight whisper.

I close my eyes.

"Bartender!"

My eyes flash open, and Archer pulls back.

"We need to get our drink on!" an obnoxious man shouts. "Which means, we need drinks."

I glare at the jerk.

How dare he interrupt us.

For once, since our night together, Archer gave me something other than anger.

His vulnerability screamed his truths.

A moment when he stopped pretending.

Archer clears his throat and swings his arm toward the guy. "He's all yours."

Thankfully, after being here with Cohen so much, I know my way around the bar and where everything is. I know all the menu items since I helped create it.

After I take the man's drink order, I drift to the group of college-aged guys waving me over. "What can I get you? Forewarning, I'm a newbie, so nothing complicated, please."

A guy with bright blue eyes and blond curls grins. "You know how to make a Can I Have Your Number?"

I chew on my lip.

Is he asking for a drink or hitting on me?

Dozens of drinks have sexual innuendos as names. Sex on the Beach or Screaming Orgasm, to name a few.

"I'll be right back," I say.

Archer is pouring a beer when I go to him, but his attention is pinned on the guys I was helping.

"Do you know how to make a Can I Have Your Number?"

He furrows his brow. "A what?"

"A Can I Have Your Number?"

"Who ordered that?"

I jerk my thumb over my shoulder to the curly-haired dude.

Archer slides the beer to the customer and walks around me, and when he reaches the guys, he towers over them. "What's in that drink?"

Curly's face pales. "It's not … a drink."

"What is it then?"

"I was"—Curly's gaze angles to me—"asking for her number."

I smile.

Archer snarls.

CHAPTER TWELVE

Archer

GEORGIA WILL BE the death of me this shift.

This job.

Hell, my damn life.

How, out of all people, did I manage to hook up with the sister of my business partner?

Just my luck.

I almost told Cohen I quit for the night if I had to train her. If he wasn't leaving for Noah, I might've gone through with the threat. I hate training, but add in that it's Georgia, and it's a goddamn nightmare.

Guys are hitting on her, not that I blame them.

"We don't serve that here," I bark to the guy who gave her the cheesiest-ass pickup line. "We'll never serve it. Order something else, buddy."

Georgia stares at him intently. "I wouldn't say never, just not tonight. I'm training. Maybe another time?"

The douchebag licks his lips. "I got you. How about a few Coronas for now?"

Georgia smiles sweetly. "I got you."

"Thanks, babe."

When he winks at her, I'm tempted to smash the Corona over his head.

As she turns to grab their beers, I stalk behind her and hiss, "Quit flirting with guys."

"Why?" She tilts her head to the side. "You jealous?"

I shake my head. "I'd say the same to any employee." I snatch the Corona and point at a group of women. "I'll take care of the Justin Biebers. Go serve those women."

As soon as I hand the guys their beers, I turn back to her. She's already a pro at this. Her people skills are on point. She's a smiler, someone who can make conversation with anyone, and she will be a great asset to the bar.

Not a great asset to me, though.

The death of me.

Reminder: tell Cohen I'm making the schedule now. Georgia and I will be working together as little as possible.

"Well, well, look who it is."

My back stiffens at her voice.

Clear, articulate, and one who once moaned my name.

My past is here to haunt me.

"I heard this is where you started a bar," she says when I shift to face her.

"What are you doing here, Meredith?"

"I wanted to see how you were doing." She sets down her designer bag and climbs onto a stool. "It's been so long."

Wish we could've made it longer.

"How are you?" she pushes.

I stare back at the woman who spent years at my side, who was once a part of me. She's just as gorgeous, just as put together, but just no longer for me.

"Good," I clip. "Busy."

"Oh, come on," she says with a sweet laugh. "You can't be too busy for me."

"Go back to the man you're engaged to." That should get her out of here.

We're huddled in the corner, and I hear drink orders being thrown at Georgia left and right. I need to shut this shit down and help her before everyone gets a faulty drink.

"Yeah, that engagement didn't work out."

"Looks like you still haven't bagged a husband your parents approve of."

She flinches at my harsh tone. "I couldn't love him the way I loved you, and he'd never love me the way you loved me before ... everything fell apart."

"Our relationship was never perfect."

"True." She sighs, her shoulders drooping. "It was perfect for us, though. You loved me enough to propose, to make me your wife."

"You're the one who wanted out."

"You still don't understand why I left, do you?" She scoffs. "No, you know why. You just don't care."

"Why are you here?" I seethe. "To talk about our past? We're over. Have been over for years."

"I miss you," she whispers. "Back then, I had to walk away."

"You're right. I don't blame you, and there are no hard feelings." *Now, leave.*

"Hello, Mr. Trainer," Georgia sings, sneaking up next to me. "Engaging in secret conversations in the corner isn't productive when I have so much to learn."

Meredith's eyes narrow as her attention pings from Georgia to me.

"Can I get you something to drink?" I ask Meredith, blowing out a strained breath.

She shakes her head. "No, but let's talk tonight. After you close, for old times' sake."

Georgia tenses.

I scrub a hand over my face. "Nah, I'll be exhausted."

Georgia stays, inviting herself into the conversation, and ignores my look of warning. Her employment will not go well here. She's not one to follow rules.

At least she breaks the tension by saying, "If you're staying, how about that drink order?"

"I'll have a Commonwealth," Meredith replies with a phony smile.

Georgia mocks her smile. "Never heard of it, but I'll see what I can do."

"Really?" I glare at Meredith when Georgia leaves.

"What?"

"Commonwealth has seventy-one ingredients."

"She's in training. I'm helping you out." Meredith shrugs. "She likes you," she says matter-of-factly, tapping her manicured nails along the bar. "No surprise. Even with this asshole demeanor, it's hard not to be attracted to you."

I ignore her comment and turn to Georgia. She pokes her cheek while studying the drink book before slamming it shut and grabbing every wrong ingredient.

Without sparing another glance to Meredith, I go to Georgia.

"Did you read the wrong page?"

She shakes her head, pouring random shit into the glass. "Nope, I read it right. My plan is to make her a crappy drink so she'll leave." Throwing a cherry and lemon wedge into the glass, she drops off her concoction to Meredith.

Meredith eyes the drink suspiciously. "That's not what I ordered."

Georgia shrugs. "I followed the book's directions." She forces another fraudulent smile and leaves.

Meredith eyes me, and I throw my arms up.

"What did you expect?" I ask.

The sound of glass shattering stops our conversation, and when I spin around, there's a circle of broken glass at her feet.

"You should leave," I mutter to Meredith, pushing myself off the bar.

"That was totally an accident," Georgia rushes out when I approach her.

She falls to her knees and scrambles for the broken pieces, and I notice a flicker of red before realizing blood is gushing from her finger.

"Shit, Georgia." I bend down and snatch her hand to inspect it.

It's deep but not deep enough to require stitches. I carefully grab her hand and help her to her feet. Tugging a towel from a drawer, I wrap it around her finger. She hisses when I push down on it, giving it pressure.

"Trina!" I yell, snapping my fingers to get her attention as she walks past us.

"Yeah?" she asks.

"Run to the employee room and grab the first-aid kit."

Her attention moves to Georgia before she nods. "On it."

Not caring if blood gets on me, I lead her to the end of the bar and settle her onto a stool. "Hang out here for a sec and keep pressure on this."

"Okay." She peers down in embarrassment. "Sorry, I should've been more careful."

"Shit happens." I pat her thigh before gently squeezing it.

"This is the perfect reason for you to prove to Cohen I shouldn't have this job."

I tilt my head down and wait until her eyes meet mine. "I won't use this against you."

"All right," Trina says, rushing over to us with the kit.

I give every customer who yells out a drink order a *wait for a sec* gesture and bandage her up. I inspect it when I finish. "See, all fixed. Why don't you go home for the night and let that rest?"

"Thank you, but I'm staying," she whispers before sliding off the stool and wincing.

"How about this? I'll explain each drink as I make it. That way, you can give your hand a rest."

She bites into her lip. "Okay."

I'm only doing this as an employer. I'd do the same with any employee.

At least that's what I'm fighting to convince myself.

———

"GOOD NIGHT, GUYS!" Georgia calls out, waving a hand through the air. She exchanges a glance with me. "Thanks for training me. You're always such a good time."

"You think you're good to drive?" I ask, stopping her.

She inspects her hand. "Yeah. The ibuprofen I took has helped, and it's only a short distance."

I rub at my face, not wanting her on the road this late. "Let me find Finn and ask him to give you a ride home."

"I'm fine, really. I don't want anyone going out of their way. It's late, and we're all exhausted."

I nod. "Someone needs to walk you out."

It's company policy that one of us guys walks the female employees out or they go out in groups.

Finn, who's been working the door tonight, holds up his non-ringing phone. "Call coming in. You do it, Archer."

He puts the phone to his ear and walks toward the restrooms.

I give him an *I'm going to kick your ass later* look, and he smirks.

Georgia hitches her bag up her shoulder. "If it's that much of a burden for you, I'm fine. I know karate, and Cohen taught me all the pressure points to bring a man to his knees. I might protect myself better than you would. Hell, I might be the one protecting us both."

I shove my hands into my pockets. "I'm not betting my money on a woman who can barely reach the height minimum for the Tilt-A-Whirl to protect me."

She yawns, and I trail behind her as we head out the exit without saying a word.

"Are you leaving?" she asks when we reach her car.

I shake my head. "Nah, I have closing stuff to do."

"Oh, shoot. Is that my job?"

I debate on lying, but in the future, she can't bail on the tasks. "Yes, it is."

"I can go back in—"

"I'll have Cohen show you on your next shift." I stretch out my arms. "I'm exhausted, and I think we both need some rest. I'll do a quick close tonight, and you can learn another day."

She nods. "Good night, Archer."

I nod back without returning the words.

Waiting until she pulls away, I fish my phone from my pocket while walking back inside. After Georgia's finger incident, her attitude scaled down, and we worked together well. Meredith left but was sure to leave a napkin with her number scribbled on it for me. I'm unclear what her intention was by coming here, but I don't want anything to do with her or that life. We had what we had, but it's history now.

I send Cohen a text, letting him know Georgia is on her way home so he can make sure she gets there safely. Finn is wiping down tables when I walk in, and thankfully, he shut off the TVs—an aid to my headache.

"Cohen is going to flip his shit when you fuck his sister," Finn says, no bullshit.

"We're not fucking, so nothing to worry about," I grumble.

"Not yet." He smirks. "It'll happen, though."

"We can't stand each other."

People need to believe this. It's why I put up this entire charade with her.

"You act like you can't stand her because you want to fuck her."

I flip him off.

"You'll fuck her"—he winks—"and then get your ass kicked."

Silas laughs, coming into view.

Where the fuck did he come from?

He hasn't been here all night.

"Dude, do you see the size of him?" Silas asks. "No offense to my boy Cohen, but I'd be afraid to fuck with Archer."

"You two keep that thought," I mutter.

In case you ever find out what has already happened between us.

CHAPTER THIRTEEN

Georgia

WHEN I GET HOME, I head to the bathroom to inspect my finger. It stings when I clean it and change the bandage. Nothing screams, you'll be a bad employee, like breaking stuff and bleeding on your first day.

I've been at the bar plenty of times and helped out randomly, but I've never worked there. It's more intense than what it appears from the outside. Add that chaos with working with Archer, and I'm shocked it was a glass that fell at my feet and not my heart.

It was all a whirlwind. Working with him, his possessiveness sneaking out, and the woman who showed up.

A woman who was no stranger to him.

Ex-girlfriend.

Ex-fling.

There'd been something, and from the way she stared at him, that something was still there for her. She wanted the man I so desperately want myself. Call me stupid—because that's what I am—for still loving his attention and wanting him when he's shown me nothing but hatred.

Even though he shut her down, a pang of jealousy hit me when they were whispering in the corner like two lovebirds ready to share a strand of spaghetti.

My eyes are heavy as I stroll into my bedroom and collapse face-first onto my bed. The last time I had so much one-on-one time with Archer was when I was in his bed, and our one-on-one time included us all up in each other's genitals.

My problem with hating Archer is that it's fake.

He acts like a dick, but deep down, if you dive into his soul, there's more.

I saw it that night, and throughout his time with my brother, I've caught flashes of it.

What happened?

What pain is he masking with anger?

I drag myself up, change into my pajamas, and call Cohen while crawling into bed.

"I'm home," I say around a yawn.

"How was training?"

"Super fun."

He chuckles. "I'm sure Archer was the life of the party."

"How can you be friends with him? He's so rude." I fluff my pillow out and relax into it.

"Archer has always been distant, but it got worse when his brother got locked up. He doesn't trust people, so I was shocked when he asked me to partner up with him."

"Why is he distant?"

"Not my story to tell."

"Not your story to tell, or you know nothing?"

"It's his business. If he wants you to know, he'll tell you."

I frown. "Ugh, you're no fun. You're supposed to give me the scoop."

"Be patient. Maybe he'll tell you."

"And maybe I'll grow a horn out of my head."

He chuckles.

I yawn again. "Since you're not up for a gossip time, it's my bedtime."

"Good night. I'll talk to you tomorrow."

When we end the call, I plug my phone into the charger and turn off my lamp, but I don't drift to sleep. Instead, I wonder how my relationship would be if Archer and I had never slept together. He's always a dick, but he doesn't act like Lola's or Grace's existence kills him.

What gives?

Was I sucky lay?

He had no complaints that night.

Or maybe he didn't care. He did say he went there to get laid.

I could've been a convenient vagina for him that night.

I wish I could see him as a convenient cock for me, but I can't. I'd never had sex with a guy I wasn't dating, and I threw all of that out for him.

Look where it got me.

————

I STROLL into the bar with an iced coffee in one hand and a Cronut in the other.

I'm in my last year of college, and I will soon have a master's in social work. My plan after is to become a school counselor. I want to help children who don't have a Cohen, like I did, and who need someone to talk to or help them.

It's in the middle of the day, and the bar is quiet. Regulars are lingering, eating baskets of fried food and having a drink, but the crowd hasn't made its landing yet.

Choosing a stool at the far end of the bar, I set my coffee and Cronut down before sliding my backpack off and placing it on the stool next to me. My attempt to study at home was a bust. It was too quiet, and I needed background noise. There were no open tables at the coffee shop, so alas, here I am.

I'm collecting my notes and setting my laptop down when Archer approaches me. I groan, expecting to hear a comment about me hanging out here randomly.

"What are you studying?" he asks.

I freeze, a note drifting to the floor. "Huh?"

He gestures to my notebook. "What are you studying?"

"Oh, law and social work." I bend down to pick up the fallen paper, and when I stand, he's still there.

"I minored in psychology. That shit is hard."

"Really?" I'm shocked he's sharing this with me. "Where'd you go?"

"Stanford." This isn't said with pride or with a cavalier attitude. You would've thought he'd told me he went to Barney's School for Dinosaurs.

"Why are you working in a small-town bar when you have a degree from Stanford?" Hell, I'm staring at him like he said he went to Barney's School.

"It's my father's alma mater. I graduated with a business degree and then started a business with your brother, not just some bar."

"I didn't mean it like that." I chew on my bottom lip. "What I meant was, why aren't you in some ritzy, top-floor office making six, seven figures?"

His face goes slack, a hint of hurt flickering. "That isn't the life for me. I was expected to go to Stanford, no exceptions. Now, I'd rather be here."

I take a seat. "I'm the first person in my family to graduate from college."

He smiles. "That's awesome, Georgia. It's something to be proud of."

My eyes widen in shock at the compliment. "Uh ... thank you."

Who stuck a nice pill in his coffee this morning?

A brief silence passes, and I'm thankful Silas is manning the other end of the bar, so no one can steal Archer away from me. While I have him in this ... *mood*, it'd be stupid of me not to take advantage of it.

I suck in a breath of courage and ask, "Do you not want to be around me because of what we did or because you genuinely don't like me?" Hurt seeps through my blood, outstripping the joy I had from him opening up to me. "When you said I was nothing but a screw to you that night, were you lying?"

He withdraws a step, as if my questions were a blow to the chest. "That was the past, Georgia. Time to move on."

"Time to move on."

That can't happen when only one of us is trying.

"Will you stop being a prick for a minute and act like you have a heart?" I question, waiting for him to turn around and walk away. A routine for us whenever I ask something personal.

"Who said I have a heart?" He raises a brow. "And I'm not acting like a prick."

It's my turn to raise a brow.

"This is my shining personality." He chuckles—a rarity. "You didn't know that?"

"You most definitely do not have a shining personality. You have one of the most unchivalrous personalities I've ever encountered."

"Appreciate the compliment." He tips his head down. "Although you might be alone in that opinion."

"Trust me, I'm not alone in that opinion whatsoever."

"Why don't you enlighten me with who my personality haters are?"

"My friends." *And ninety percent of Iowa's population.*

He snorts. "Of course. They know what happened between us and are taking your side."

"Someone would have to be on crack and have no heart if they didn't take my side in our situation." I fight back a smile. "Not to mention, they've seen your *shining* personality aplenty to gain their own opinion of you."

He stares at me, unblinking, before moving closer. "Want to know the truth?"

I nod.

He invades my space and bows his head, his voice sharp and low. "I never saw you as *a piece of ass.* I didn't walk into Bailey's hoping to find a fuck. I planned to get shit-faced and then take an Uber home, but then there you were, sitting at the bar, broken. I couldn't stop myself from going to you, from wanting to talk to you, from wanting to make you whole again." His cheek brushes against mine, the rough scruff like sandpaper against my skin. "It wasn't about me getting my dick wet; it was about how drawn I was to you. Then we talked, and for some damn reason, I shared more with you about my feelings than I had with anyone. You know more about my goddamn life than the woman I was engaged to, than my mother knows—"

As much as I want this moment to last, I wince and pull away from him. "You were *engaged* when we had sex?"

It takes a second for him to register my change in mood. "What? No. I *was* engaged, and it ended years before we had sex."

I nibble on the inside of my cheek and nod, waiting for him to continue. I hate myself for stopping him. His confession has my heart thumping wildly.

I want more.

More of his truths.

Of his conversations.

Of *him*.

"I don't hate you, Georgia," he says. "I just don't trust myself around you." He taps his knuckle against the bar, turns, and walks away.

———

"HEY, BABE," Grace greets when I walk into our apartment. "How was training?"

She's in our kitchen, eating sushi, with a stack of papers on the table in front of her.

We moved into our two-bedroom apartment last year. While I go to school, she teaches at a private elementary school.

Grace became my best friend when I moved to Mayview, and she was my tour guide at our middle school. We instantly clicked. She didn't care about my family's social status, which was in the gutter. The same with her parents, who welcomed me with open arms and helping hands.

Lola joined our circle during our junior year of high school. We were at a party, and after Grace turned a guy down, he called her a bitch. Lola jumped in and told him to get fucked. The three of us have been inseparable ever since.

I grab a plate and steal a sushi roll from her. "Stressful."

She drops the pen in her hand. "Cohen wasn't easy on you?"

"Cohen didn't train me."

"Uh-oh."

I nod.

"On a scale from one to ten, how awful was Archer?"

"A twelve." I grab a bottle of water from the fridge. "Check this out. I went to study at the bar today, and he was nice to me."

Her eyes widen, and she pinches herself. "I'm sorry. Did you say he was *nice to you*?"

"Shocker, right?"

"Huge shocker." She makes strong eye contact with me, her teacher face emerging. "Maybe you and he should sit down and talk. It's one thing to be around each other when we're in a group, but you'll be working directly with each other now."

"I've tried. He always shuts me down."

"I hope working there doesn't break your heart." A shade of sadness passes over her face.

I'm reminded of what Archer said to me earlier today, and chills shoot up my spine. I open my mouth to tell Grace but stop. It's fresh, and I still need to process it. After he dropped that bomb and turned around, I studied. Okay, *tried* to study. Instead of focusing on my homework, I watched him until I eventually left and came home.

"Anyway," I drawl out, "what are you doing tonight?"

"Coming to visit you on your first night at the new J-O-B."

"Second night, thank you very much." Since I'm super classy, I pick up the sushi roll with my hand and take a bite.

She laughs. "Lola and I will be there, ready to order all the drinks from you."

———

"I WAS HOPING you wouldn't show tonight," Archer says when I walk into the bar.

I curl my lips into a smile. "I see Dr. Jekyll has turned back into Mr. Hyde."

He's so hot and cold.

One minute, he's nice.

The next, he's pissed about working with me.

"What if I paid you to get another job?" He makes a show of shoving his hand into his pocket and yanking out his wallet.

I glare at him. "What if I cut off your dick?"

He holds up the wallet. "Five hundred bucks?"

"Five hundred grand will do."

"Funny," he deadpans.

I snatch the pen clipped on his shirt pocket, tap his chest a few times, and walk around him. "Working here or not, you'll see me everywhere, Archer Callahan. There's no getting rid of me."

"Yeah, you're like a bad dream, haunting me."

"A bad dream or a wet dream?"

"Jesus, fuck, Georgia," he hisses.

"What? One of us needs a personality in this rivalry game of ours, and it's not you. You have the personality of a stale piece of bread."

"You have the personality of a hamster who's been on a crack binge for days."

I tie my apron around my waist, and before I move onto the main floor, I glance back at him. "Oh, and, Archer?"

He raises a brow. "Yeah?"

"This little back-and-forth game, you know what it reminds me of?"

"What?"

"Foreplay."

He points toward the incoming crowd. "Get to work."

———

I UNDERSTAND why Cohen didn't want me behind the bar tonight.

It's a madhouse. A boxing match is on pay-per-view, so the place is flooded with people who didn't want to pay for it at home.

I take an order, scurry to Archer, recite it to him, and hop to the next table. Lola and Grace showed up a few hours ago, but I barely had time to take their orders before I was called over by another table. The plus side to the craziness is that I've already made more in tips than I did in a week at the boutique.

While waiting on drinks, I watch Archer. Seeing him work is a lustful sight. He wipes the sweat off his forehead with the back of his arm as he and Silas maneuver around each other behind the bar. At times, I feel him watching me. When I catch him, when our eyes meet, I smile. To which he immediately scowls and quickly glances away.

When the patrons start clearing out at closing, I stroll to Cohen's office, sluggish and exhausted. Waitressing really gave a girl a workout tonight. I barge in without knocking, and he peeks up at me with a smile on his face while sitting behind his desk.

"What'd you think?" he asks, rolling back in his chair and scrubbing his hand over his dark brow.

"It was fun." I yawn. "I think I did a good job."

"You killed it."

We air-five each other.

"Although I think you have to say that since you're my brother."

"I'm also your boss, and as your boss, I'm saying you killed it. You're good with people, so it's no surprise." He jerks his head toward his desk. "Let me finish this paperwork, and then I'll walk you to your car."

"Coolio. I'm going to run to the kitchen and grab a water."

He gives me a thumbs-up, and I leave his office. On my way to the kitchen, I pass Archer's office. His door is open, and I use it as an opportunity to take a peek.

It's similar to Cohen's in size, and the layout is the same, but while Cohen's is warm, Archer's is cold.

My brother's office is decorated with photos of Noah and our family, memorabilia, and cheesy souvenirs from the places we've gone on vacation together.

Archer's is passionless. There isn't a smidgen of anything that shows his character or fires off hints of the life he lives. Not on the walls, on his desk, nothing. I glance in both directions of the hall to make sure the coast is clear before inviting myself in.

A bottle of overpriced water sits next to his iMac, and a jacket hangs off the edge of his computer chair. When I travel to his desk, I pick up the pen resting next to his mouse pad. It's wood and the same one he used to write his information on the day of our accident. It appears handmade, and it's light as I play with it in my sweaty hand. I trace my fingers along the keyboard, somewhat stalker-like, and search for anything to show me who he is.

My heart doubles in speed when I spot a small picture taped to his computer.

It's a boy—my guess, early teens—and an older man on a boat.

The boy's characteristics match Archer's. He's grinning in the picture. It's wide and authentic, and you can tell he's been laughing.

I play with the photo in my hand, moving my finger over the old paper.

"Can I help you?"

I jump, my hand flying to my chest, and find Archer standing in the doorway. His arms are crossed, his stare pinned to me, and his face is red and tight.

I clear my throat and slowly return the photo to its place.

Then I do it again while scrambling for an excuse as to why I'm office-stalking him.

"I wanted to, uh …" I run my hands down my wrinkled, *smells like vodka and nacho cheese* shirt. "Thank you for training me … and for making my drinks tonight. You must've done well because I made killer tips."

He nods without saying a word.

Alrighty then.

Convos with him are still a blast.

I play with my hands in front of me before saying, "Well … have a good night." I move around his desk, overcome with curiosity, my heart now tripling in speed.

He steps away from the door, giving me plenty of room to brush past him. "Good night, Georgia. Don't visit my office again."

CHAPTER FOURTEEN

Archer

STARTING a bar was supposed to bring me peace.

Instead, it brought me Georgia.

My human version of a migraine.

My version of hell.

She's made me question everything.

The kind of man I am, the kind of man I want to be, the life I want to live.

She's puncturing my plan of living lonely.

Night after night, I watch her smile and laugh, and then I go home and think about her. Things have been tense since I found her poking around my office. My pulse sped as I watched her stare at the photo of my grandfather and me. Having the photo in my office is a double-edged sword. I love the memories of hanging out with my grandfather on my father's side growing up but despise the one of his death. I should've never taped it to my computer.

Anger stormed through me, and as soon as she left, I slammed the door shut, plucked the photo off my computer, and slipped it back into my wallet. Had she been anyone else, I would've ripped their head off for snooping through my shit.

She moves around the bar, practically skipping, and all eyes are on her. Her black shirt, branded with the bar's logo, is tied in a knot at the base of her back, right above her ass, and her short-shorts have me remembering what it felt like to be between her legs. She wanders around, throwing smiles at customers and being the sunshine she is.

While I'm standing in the darkness.

What is it about this woman?

It could be the connection we shared that night. We bonded over sex, secrets, and our hate of the people who'd hurt us. I'd never opened up to anyone like I did with Georgia.

Not my mother, not Meredith, not Lincoln.

Only her.

Why can't I stop thinking about her?

Solution: find a woman to take my mind off her.

Not one to date.

One to screw until I forget about her.

"Hi. You're hot. Want to fuck?"

My attention slides from Georgia to the woman in front of me. She plants her elbows on the bar, leaning in closer, and licks her bottom lip while waiting for my answer.

It's as if God had heard my thoughts and sent her to me.

Or possibly the devil since I'm not sure how keen God is on one-night stands.

"My friends dared me to come over and ask you." She grins and winks at me. "I'm newly single, looking for no-strings-attached sex, and there's no ring on your finger." She eyes my hand for a moment as if double-checking. "You game, sexy?"

I hesitate in answering and stare at her. She's gorgeous—plump red lips, dark hair, huge tits. Unfortunately, I'm not sure if my dick would even get hard for her after watching Georgia all night. My new type is apparently a woman who is short, snarky, wears the weirdest damn clothes, and braids her hair too much for someone her age.

I start to decline, but Georgia speaks over me, "I need two margaritas, stat, bartender! No time for talking while we're this busy."

The woman shoots Georgia a death glare.

I whip around and start on her drinks at the same time Georgia rushes behind the bar. She dodges Silas, who's holding three beers in his hand, and storms in my direction.

"Don't think I didn't hear her little dare with her friends," Georgia seethes as I grab the tequila. "She's lying. She told her friends she could do it, not the other way around. She just wants to bang you and thought that'd be the perfect pickup line."

I continue making the drinks. "Why do you care if it's a dare?"

Her face reddens. "Do you want to bang her back?"

"Bang her back?"

She nods.

"You mean, do I want to fuck her ... like I did you?"

She slides in closer, her waist bumping into mine. "I don't know. Do you?"

I stay quiet, wishing I could tell her I want to fuck *her* again.

Wishing I could tell her I didn't give a shit about that woman.

"Even if you tried, it wouldn't be as good it was with me," she adds with a smirk.

I don't smirk back. "Take your drink orders, Georgia."

"If you sleep with her, I'll be disgusted with you."

"Is that anything new?"

"Yes."

I raise a brow.

"Right now, I just think you're an asshole."

I hand her the margaritas and return to the woman, saying, "I get off at three."

Unable to stop myself because I'm a mean bastard, I glance at Georgia. All playfulness has left her, now replaced with pain ... and disgust, like she said.

The woman grins wildly. "I'll be here."

For the rest of the night, Georgia barks out her orders to me with no emotion and not one extra word muttered in conversation. I even catch her calling out orders to Silas to avoid speaking to me. When her shift ends, she asks Finn to walk her to her car, not sparing me one look.

"So," Dare Girl asks, "your place or mine?"

"Your place or mine?"

The same question I asked Georgia.

My stomach churns at the memory. I've had doubts about going home with this woman all night, hoping she'd leave without waiting for me, but as she stares at me in expectation, I shake my head.

"You know what?" I wipe my hands on the towel. "I changed my mind."

———

"THIS IS a collect call from the Oxford Correctional Facility," the recording says after I answer the call.

It pauses, allowing my father to cut in and say his name, before the automation picks back up.

I decline the call and toss my phone to the side.

Twenty minutes later, it rings again. Same number, but this time, after listening to the recording, I accept the call.

"Hey, brother. How are you?" Lincoln asks.

"Same shit, different day." I rub my forehead with the base of my palm, sprawl out on my couch, and tip my head back while leveling the phone against my ear with my shoulder.

He chuckles. "I feel you on that."

"Counting down the days until you're a free man?"

"More along the lines of trying to stay positive. Am I excited? Fuck, yeah. It puts a damper on shit when I think about Dad not coming with me, though."

"He should be in there longer than you." I grind my teeth, hating that he still cares about Dad after what he did.

After the situation he put him in.

After he fucked up his life.

Noticing the tension, Lincoln clears his throat. "*Anyway*, how's everything at the bar? I can't wait to see it."

His subject change is a good one, and our conversation takes a more positive turn as I tell him how well the bar is doing. We talk for twenty minutes before we're kicked off. I toss my phone down and groan—hating that I can only talk to my brother via collect calls with a time limit.

CHAPTER FIFTEEN

Georgia

I'M FINISHING off a strawberry Pop-Tart when there's a knock on my door.

"Coming!" I scrape the crumbs off the table, pile them in my hand, and drop them into the trash can on my way to answer it.

As soon as I open the door, a wave of dizziness hits me, and I release a sharp breath as we stare at each other.

I'm not sure how long it's been.

Seven, eight years maybe?

Sometimes, when I walk down the street, I ask myself if I'd recognize her if we passed each other. My question is answered, only we're not passing each other. She's on my doorstep.

Seconds pass as neither one of us mutters a word.

"Hi, Georgia," she finally whispers.

Anita Fox.

My mother.

I strengthen my grip on the doorknob, questioning if my next action should be slamming the door in her face.

I can't.

I can't because I'm hit with the reminder of when I showed up at my dad's house, only to be rejected. I'd never hurt someone like that.

It's not in my heart.

Not in my soul.

She moves from one foot to the other.

"Come in," I rush out, waving my hand forward and widening the door to give her room.

Her face registers shock as she digests my words. That clearly wasn't the reaction she expected, and she takes slow steps into my home.

Did she expect me to be a monster like my father?

"Can I get you something to drink?" I ask, shutting the door.

Please don't say alcohol.

Or crack-laced water.

She clears her throat. "I'll take whatever you have."

"Tea? Water? Coffee?"

"Water would be nice." She bows her head. "Thank you."

She follows me into the kitchen, where I pour us two glasses of water. I hand her one before leading us into the living room, and it's quiet when we both sit—me on the couch and her taking a seat on the chair.

I have so many questions.

Why is she here?

Why didn't she come all those years before?

There's no holding myself back from asking, "Why are you here? How do you know where I live?" My tone isn't angry, yet it's not friendly.

Just because I didn't shut the door in her face doesn't mean I'll get my hopes up or that I'm elated she's here. She's visited Cohen a few times at his house or his job, begging for money. He helps her, and then she disappears in the middle of the night until she needs help again.

One time, I asked Cohen if he thought she was dead. He said no, that he checked on her regularly—whatever that meant—and that I had nothing to worry about. I never knew if he was telling me that to make me feel better or if it was the truth.

Her hand shakes, causing the glass to rattle. "I was in rehab with a woman whose brother is a private investigator. I asked him to look you up because I wanted to see you."

"Why?" I take a small sip of water.

"I'm clean now and getting my life together."

I stare at her skeptically. "How do I know that's true?"

Her shoulders slump. "You don't, and I understand you might not believe me. I'm here because I'd like to prove to you that I am."

I lean back on the couch and take her in, searching for any signs that she's using. She's aged, which is normal, given it's been years since I've seen her. She doesn't look healthy, but she doesn't look strung out either. She was ... or possibly *is still* an addict, and her abuse shows in her every feature.

Briefly, I wonder what she would've looked like had she never become an addict.

Would she look more like me?

I see our resemblances—her chestnut-brown hair, her height, even her eccentric style.

I glance down at my phone when it rings, and Cohen's name flashes on the screen. I could answer it, tell him my situation, and ask him what I should do. He'd tell me to ask her to leave, or he'd drive here and do it himself.

I ignore the call and focus my attention on her. "You'd like to prove it to me? How?"

———

"WHAT'S on your mind over there?"

I peek up from my computer. "Huh?"

"You're zoned out," Archer replies. "Everything okay?"

I sigh. "Yes." Another sigh. "No."

The bar has weirdly become my new study sanctuary. Who would've thought I could concentrate better when people were drinking and cheering on sports around me? I move to different sections, different tables, and different ends of the bar to switch it up. Archer doesn't seem to mind, and at times, we make small conversation.

I questioned whether to come in today. We haven't seen each other since the night he went home with Dare Girl. For the first time since I started working at Twisted Fox, I considered quitting. It was one thing to hear about him being with other women or him being an asshole, and another to witness a woman waiting to go home with him. I was lucky enough to be her waitress for the night and had to listen to her brag about him going to her place later.

She couldn't wait to fuck his brains out, wondered how good he was in bed, and made bets with her friends on how big his cock was.

That night, I couldn't leave the bar fast enough. I slipped Trina a twenty to do my closing responsibilities and peaced out.

Archer circles the bar, pulls out the stool next to me—causing me to nearly fall off mine—and sits. Clasping his hands together, he rests them on the bar. "Talk to me, Georgia."

I can't with him today.

For once, I'm not in the mood for nice Archer.

For conversation with him.

It feels tainted now.

All I can think about is him touching her, kissing her, screwing her.

"I don't want to talk about it," I grumble, avoiding eye contact. *It's mommy issues this time.* "Trust me, you don't want to hear about it."

"I wouldn't have asked if I didn't." He chuckles. "You know, I'm not one to stir up conversation mindlessly."

I can't go to Cohen about this.

Not yet at least.

He'd tell me to haul ass away from her, automatically assuming she had shown up to use me.

I downcast my gaze. "My mom … She showed up at my house today."

He stays quiet before saying, "Your mother, she left you too?"

"She didn't leave per se, but she wasn't there either."

He nods in understanding.

"She's an addict. Or was an addict. I'm not exactly sure on what tense I should use at the moment."

Why am I opening up to him?

Just like the night at the bar, it comes without thinking, without hesitation.

He can draw the truth out of me by simply sitting down and talking in that deep, smooth voice of his.

How this man can make me hate him and confide in him at the same time is beyond me.

"What'd she say?" He scratches his cheek. "Did she seem clean?"

I shift my weight on the stool. "She said she's in a sober house, and she didn't look strung out or anything."

"Do you believe her?"

I shut my eyes, replaying my conversation with her in my mind. "I do."

"Then follow your gut. If you believe her and think she's changed, give her the opportunity to prove it to you. Put your toes in the water but don't go all in." His voice thickens. "Do not hand all your trust over to her. Don't let her hurt you."

"Don't let her hurt you."

What about the times he's hurt me?

I struggle to yell at him, to scream that he's just as bad as her and my father.

Making me feel unwanted and unworthy, like the rest of them.

It's become a trend in my life, I guess.

To be unwanted.

"Georgia," he breathes out, "I'll never forget how you looked that night at Bailey's—not just your beauty, but also your heartbreak, the pain of rejection that'd blocked out your light."

He grips the seat of my stool and rotates me to face him. My eyes water at his words, at what today has been, at what this week has been, and I slip him a guarded look. When our eyes meet, a single tear drops down my cheek, and I shiver when he runs the pad of his thumb over my face, brushing it away.

I shut my eyes, savoring his touch, and he drags my stool closer to cup my face in his strong palm. I say nothing, just stare at him, his touch a comfort to my pain.

"Just trust your gut but protect your heart," he whispers, dropping his hand down to curl around my knee. He squeezes it tenderly before resting it there.

"Protect your heart."

My eyes flash open.

"Protect your heart."

That pertains to him too.

The thought of him sleeping with that woman storms through me.

Did he touch her with the same hand he's touching me with?

Did he use those fingers to pleasure her?

I shiver, disgust climbing up my throat.

How dare he.

How dare he do this again—play the savior when, behind his walls, he's really the devil.

I drop my hand down and peel his fingers off me, one by one.

"Don't touch me again, Archer," I snarl, pushing him away and sliding off my stool. "Go call the woman you fucked."

"Georgia."

He attempts to grab my hand, but I swat him away and stick my finger in his face.

"No."

He pulls back but calls my name one last time as I leave.

————

"HI, SWEETIE."

I peek up from stocking the beer fridge to find a woman plucking a pair of designer sunglasses off her face.

With a gorgeous Chanel handbag hanging from her shoulder and no doubt a monthly Botox budget, she's crawled straight from *The Stepford Wives* movie. The opposite everything of our everyday customer base.

Our regulars don't sport cashmere.

Don't have rocks on their fingers that cost more than it would to feed a small village.

Either she's lost—or from Archer's world.

"I'm looking for Archer," she states, her tone polite.

Cougar alert.

How many more of Archer's women will I have to deal with?

I can't stop myself from snapping, "Why?" I take a step back with a cringe, wishing I could backtrack my response.

A week has passed since I told Archer about my mother showing up at my apartment.

A week since I told him to keep his hands off me.

A week since I told Grace to punch me in the face to knock some sense into me if I looked at him with googly eyes again.

Archer and I have switched roles.

I'm now the one avoiding any run-ins, conversations, or contact with him.

"Uh-oh." The woman laughs, holding out her hand. "I'm Josephine Callahan, Archer's mother."

Well, shoot.

Plot twist.

I pull myself together, embarrassment hitting me, and clasp her hand in mine. "Oh."

Can I climb into a hole now?

She grins. "How long have you been dating my son?" She shakes her head with a tsk. "I swear, he hides everything from me."

A blush creeps up my cheeks as I pull away. "The never day of never."

My response doesn't deflate her smile.

"I see he's being his difficult self," she says. "Difficult, but under that hard exterior is an incredible heart. It's just overgrown from hiding so long." Her smile widens. "It'll be like hitting the jackpot when you make it there, I promise. Don't give up."

My mouth drops open as I scramble for a response. Even with her uppity appearance and barely moving forehead, she's nice. The problem is, she doesn't know my history with Archer. He doesn't want me to find his heart. He doesn't want *any* woman to find his heart. He wants her to find his cock, and then he discards her. I haven't seen Dare Girl since the night he banged her—a clue he most likely played morning-ditcher with her as well.

"We don't exactly get along," I tell her. "That won't be happening."

"My son can be complicated."

"Yes, he can also be a jerk, rude, and inconsiderate—no offense." I slap my hand over my mouth at my outburst, but she doesn't seem fazed.

"None taken." She sighs.

I flash her a genuine smile and point toward a door with an *Employees Only* sign "His office is through there. Down the hall, second door on the left."

"Before I hunt him down, how about a glass of your best wine?"

Uh-oh. If she drinks liquor like Lola described her husband did, our *best wine* will taste gross to her.

"Of course." I twist around and eye our wine options. I'm not much of a wine connoisseur, so I pick the one ordered the most. Grabbing a glass, I pour her a glass of pinot blanc.

"He's working through healing," she adds when I hand over her drink. "I promise, he has a big heart."

"That heart seems to shrivel up more and die when we're around each other."

She takes a sip, her face scrunching up as she swallows it down. "Thank you. Don't give up on him, okay?"

CHAPTER SIXTEEN

Archer

"KNOCK, KNOCK."

I hear my mother's voice seconds before she barges into my office without knocking.

"Please ask the cute spitfire employee out on a date," she says, shutting the door behind her.

"Hello to you too," I grumble.

She grins. "Hi, sweetie."

Why is she here?

My mother doesn't visit the bar frequently. The few times have been when I didn't answer her phone calls and she was worried. It's not her scene, and I understand. Some feel comfortable in sports bars, others in clubs, and galas if you're Josephine Callahan.

She points toward the door. "That spunky little thing behind the bar? I like her, and she likes you."

Spunky little thing?

She has to be talking about Georgia.

I toss my pen onto the desk and sink back in my chair. "She doesn't know what's good for her."

She straightens out her knee-length white skirt and sits down in a chair—her posture prim and proper, back brace–style. "You should pick up dating again. Ask her to dinner."

"She's my partner's sister. Not happening."

Her liking Georgia isn't surprising. They might be from two different worlds, and Georgia doesn't wear designer clothes, but people fall in love with her personality.

Even if Georgia isn't your cup of tea, you can't *not* like her.

I've tried like fucking hell not to.

"What's the plan for your life then, huh?" she asks. "Stay single forever? Work in this bar and sulk while everyone else gets married and has children? You can't hide forever, Archer. Eventually, you'll need to step up and work through your"—she searches for the appropriate word—"grief."

There isn't a right word.

"I have," I seethe. "I face it every damn night."

"No, you *regret* it, not face it. Those are two different things, honey. You can think about those issues all day long. Facing them takes a different type of strength—more work, harder initiative—but the payoff is better. There's a deeper cut, but it's easier to heal without slapping a Band-Aid on it or constantly thinking about it because the scar is what remains."

"I'll work on that," I lie.

She crosses her legs and places her folded hands on her lap. "Your father is shutting down the company."

I wince. "What?"

"He's closing Callahan Holdings and selling all the real estate. He owes restitution, as does Lincoln, and the money will go toward that." Her shoulders sag, shrinking the prim-and-proper posture. "You refuse to work there, and given their felonies, neither Lincoln nor your father can." She squeezes her eyes closed, processing her words.

Her dream life isn't a dream after all. It's a nightmare of fraud and schemes.

"Finally, someone makes a good business decision."

Is my response rude?

Absolutely.

But it's the truth.

I rub the tension on my neck before moving it from side to side.

My ears are ringing, and my chest tightens.

Her tone softens. "It's breaking your father's heart."

Mine too.

It's time it happened, though.

Too much damage has been done.

My grandfather's legacy is going to be sold to the highest bidder. The company he built from the ground up will be reduced to ashes from his heirs burning it down.

We're pathetic.

We don't deserve it.

I lean forward to settle my elbows on my desk and throw out my hands. "I hate that it has to end this way."

She flicks away a tear falling down her cheek. "Which brings me to our next conversation."

I shake my head. "One conversation a day is your max. Come back tomorrow."

"Lincoln will be released soon."

"I know this," I reply with a nod.

"Did he talk to you about working here?"

I flinch at her question, my stomach dropping. "No."

"I figured. He's worried you'll say no."

My body tenses. "You have to understand, he's a felon, and this isn't only my business."

If it were only my ass on the line, I'd say yes in a heartbeat.

But it's not.

"Companies won't hire him," she rushes out. "He'll be seen as too much of a liability. Please, Archer. At least until he gets on his feet."

"I'll help with any money he needs."

"It's more than that."

"I'm not the only one who makes business decisions here."

"You know your brother would never bring any harm to your business."

"I trust him. The problem is, I don't want the bullshit, the drama, any of that."

"Think about it. When he's released, he'll need to lean on us. His time away has been an eye-opener for him." Another tear drops down her cheek, and she hastily sweeps it away. Josephine Callahan is also not a public crier. "He's not the same man he was before."

I grind my teeth. "I'm well aware."

Lincoln is smart, a human calculator, and he would be an asset anywhere.

"Everyone makes mistakes," she adds.

"I'll talk to Cohen. The decision isn't only mine."

"Yes, but he's family. And Cohen hired his sister."

"His sister hasn't done time in prison."

CHAPTER SEVENTEEN

Archer

Five Years Ago

"ARCHER, HOW DID THIS HAPPEN?"

I barely make my mother's question out.

My hands shake, my jaw throbs, and I lick my lips to taste the caked-up blood in the corner while staring at my mother.

I open my mouth.

Shut it.

I have no words.

The answer, it will kill them, kill *me,* as it seeps up my throat and out of my mouth.

Fall from my lips, as if I were spitting up poison.

Not that it matters.

It's already assumed that I'm to blame. The accusatory stares and glares of disappointment have been my view for the past hour. It's narrowing down some, thanks to people leaving and one of my eyes now swelling shut.

"Those Callahan boys, wild as can be," I heard someone whisper in the background.

"I can't even look at you," my father snarls, spit flying alongside his fury. "You disgust me."

I welcome the verbal assault, flinch as each word lacerates deeper into my veins, aware the agony will forever be embedded inside me.

I welcome it because I deserve it.

"Dad, stop!" Lincoln yells, pushing forward to separate him from me. He hooks his arms around my father's, saving me from another face blow.

My father stumbles back, and my mother sobs harder.

"Honey," she cries out to him, grabbing his arm before he attempts to deck me again. "Calm down. *Please* calm down!"

Following my mother's lead, Meredith captures my clenched fist. "Come on, baby. You need to sleep."

"Fuck sleep," I grit out, pulling away from her.

Her touch isn't welcome.

Only pain is.

"Listen to your girl and go the fuck to sleep," Lincoln demands, shoving his finger in my face. His eyes are glossy, and his lower lip is trembling.

"I don't need goddamn sleep!" I roar, roughly shoving my palm into my chest.

There'll be no sleeping for me tonight.

My brain can't shut down—can't shut down the adrenaline, the disgust, or the shit I snorted up my nose earlier.

I tip my head up to the sky and scream for a release that'll never come. A single tear—the first I've had in over a decade—slips down my cheek.

"This is all my fucking fault," I whisper into the night, admitting my truth.

CHAPTER EIGHTEEN

Georgia

"STOP SUCKING on your Popsicle like that."

"Huh?" I peer up at Archer, and the expression on his face confirms he didn't mean to say that out loud.

He waves to the Popsicle in my mouth.

"What? I was concentrating." I grin and perform a long, dramatic, R-rated suck. "Why? Does it bother you? Are you turned on?"

"It's turning on everyone in here," he hisses.

I do a show of glancing around the bar. "Really? It doesn't seem like anyone *but you* is looking at me."

A few weeks have passed since I told him to keep his hands off me. We've played the *avoiding* game, tiptoeing around each other and only speaking when necessary. He's strictly followed through with my hands-off demand, not even brushing by me when we're working behind the bar, almost as if he's terrified to touch me now.

But as per usual, it's always for awkward reasons that our conversation strikes back up. No regular talks in the soap opera of Georgia and Archer. Nope, it's always super-fun discussions like parent issues, arguments, and debates on me sexualizing my grape Popsicle.

"Just ... suck on it like a normal person," he grates out.

I don't.

He should've never made a comment.

I suck on it theatrically this time. "How exactly do I suck on it like a normal person?"

I wrap my tongue around the tip, sucking hard before pulling it away. His eyes narrow as they ping from my mouth to my eyes.

I grin, slide my tongue over my bottom lip to capture the juices, and hold it out to him. "Want to show me how normal people suck it?"

"Knock it off, Georgia," he fumes.

The air in the bar grows thicker. It's noon, so it's not busy, and I've been studying while sucking on my Popsicle. Archer is bartending alone tonight, which is typical for a weekday. Weekends are when they tend to double up.

I wave the stick in the air. "You don't have to fake it not turning you on, Archer. There isn't anyone around who can overhear you admit this makes you wonder how it'd feel if I were sucking your cock instead."

"Jesus Christ," he hisses underneath his breath.

I grin.

I'm in a mood.

It started off in a *let's annoy Archer* mood.

Now, it's a *please take me to the back and bang me* mood.

"Quickie in the back?" I raise a brow.

I let out a *humph* when the stick is snatched out of my hand. Archer finishes it off, taking the last bite, and throws it in the trash. I stare at him, wide-eyed and slack-jawed.

"I told you to stop," he clips.

I grin. "But not stopping is more entertaining."

———

"CAN YOU WORK TOMORROW NIGHT?" Cohen asks, stepping in from the back of the bar.

I'm counting my tips and finishing off a basket of cheese fries after my shift.

Silas and Finn are here, shooting the shit.

Archer is cleaning up behind the bar.

I stack my dollar bills in a pile and shake my head. "I have plans."

"What kind of plans?" Cohen asks.

"A double date with Lola." I shove all my cash together and slip it into my purse.

"That's fucking trouble," Silas says, a smirk on his masculine face.

"At least it's not a double date with Grace," Finn comments with a booming laugh and a gleam in his eyes.

"I'd prefer it to be with Grace," Cohen inputs. "Grace dates respectable guys who wait until marriage to have sex."

"Boring," I sing out, rolling my eyes.

Guys are dumb. They see Grace—strawberry-blonde hair, innocent smile, closet full of denim overalls and summer dresses—and think she's some Virgin Mary. Grace doesn't openly talk about sex, but it doesn't mean she *doesn't* have sex.

Lola, on the other hand, they see as the opposite—straight black hair, deviant smile, closet full of leather jackets and ripped jeans. She openly talks about sex, will give pointers, and creates play-by-plays on the best sex positions, if asked.

Cohen gets a phone call, holds his finger up, and make a beeline toward his office.

"Who's the guy?" Finn asks, stealing one of my fries and shoving it into his mouth, cheese hitting the edge of his lips.

"A friend of the guy she's dating." I shrug.

Don't know. Don't care.

I'm not going for the guy.

I'm going for the distraction.

We're going to a club, so it won't be an intimate affair. A group of her friends from work is going, and I'm tagging along because my life is dullsville. I've become a rat on an endless wheel in the dating game. I swear off men, but then I go on these dates even though I'm not interested, nor do I have the time for a new relationship.

Again, the distraction.

The distraction from the brooding dude behind the bar.

"I suggest you ditch the date and work," Archer says. "That's what a responsible adult would do."

I twist in my chair and glare in his direction. "Not everyone is all work, no play, and dull as ditchwater."

"Whoa," Silas says, smirking. "How dare you lie and say Archer isn't fun?"

"We have no one else to work," Archer fires back. "Cohen can't. Silas requested off. You want to go on a date that'll be lame. You lose."

"First, it won't be lame," I argue. "And you have Trina."

He's stopped his cleaning, and I've stopped my eating. We're staring each other down as we throw digs at the other.

"Trina is terrible behind the bar," he points out. "Not to mention, if I stick her behind the bar, we're down a waitress. How does that help?"

"You say *I'm* terrible behind the bar." I twirl a strand of hair around my finger and raise a brow.

"Not as bad as her." He clicks his tongue against the roof of his mouth before pointing at me. "You're working. Cancel your little date," he says, the last sentence turning more mocking with each word.

"That's not fair," I whine and then cringe at how childish I sound.

Archer throws his strong arms up. "Life isn't fair, sweetheart. Consider this a life lesson."

"Too bad you're not my boss." I grin and pop a fry into my mouth.

"Shots fired," Finn calls out in the background, his hands cupped around his mouth.

Archer doesn't oversee me in anything. Everything goes through my brother. Therefore, my brother is my boss and can tell me when I can and can't work.

"I'm not your boss, huh?" His face darkens in frustration. "Who owns this place?"

"You *and* my brother. I consider him my boss. Not you."

"Let me get this straight. You want the bar to be short-staffed so you can do who knows what with some random asshole?"

He taps the side of his cheek, over his stubble, and my legs squeeze together. Even after all this time, I remember what the scruff felt like, rubbing along my inner thighs, marking me.

I cross my arms, hyperaware all attention is glued on us. "Are you mad because I can't work or because I'm going on a date?" I turn to Silas. "I'm sure you're taking off to hit the clubs."

Silas holds up his hands and retreats backward. "It's my brother's bachelor party, babe. We're hitting up Vegas."

I switch my attention to my next victim. "Finn?"

He shakes his head. "Working the door."

"Looks like it's you and me," Archer states flatly. "See you tomorrow—and that's from *your boss*."

A soulless smile crosses his lips, setting me on fire. When he steps around the bar and stalks toward his office, I'm hot on his heels. He doesn't peer back at me, only makes his strides longer. He opens the door, walks into the room, and sits behind his desk.

"I know why you're doing this," I hiss, slamming the door shut behind us.

He leans back in his chair and spreads his arms out. "Oh, do you?"

"Can you make up your mind on how you feel about me?" I cross my arms. "Anytime you hear about me being with another guy, you act like a dick."

Okay, he *always* acts like a dick.

His mood is on steroids when it involves another man and me.

He pinches the bridge of his nose. "I think you're mistaken."

"Really?" I snort. "When I met a guy for drinks here, you randomly charged over to the table and said I needed to work ASAP because we'd gotten slammed out of the blue, which was a lie."

"This is the place of your employment, not a chance to meet and date guys."

"Like you don't meet women?" I shake my head. "Double standard much?"

"Whatever I do, I do it *privately*. I don't speak about it, don't flaunt it—"

"Whoa," I interrupt, simmering with frustration. "I don't flaunt anything."

"You do." His voice is flat. "You bring guys you're not interested in around to make me jealous. Here, barbecues, when we hang out with friends."

"Don't flatter yourself."

It's true.

For someone who's sworn off men, I do a crappy job of the swearing part.

Swearing off men means swearing off Archer.

I'm fighting to replace him with someone else, but nothing moves past the first date because he takes over my mind.

"This is such bullshit." I advance around his desk to his side. "Admit it."

"Admit what, Georgia?"

"Admit you don't want me with other men because it makes you jealous."

He turns in his chair to face me, and a twinge of exasperation laces his voice. "I don't like you being around other guys. I get jealous." A pained stare clouds his features. "Does that make you happy? Does that make our working relationship any less messed up?"

I dig my nails into the edge of his desk to prevent myself from falling, his words nearly knocking me on my ass.

His words.

His tone.

His anguish.

I hit buttons I never knew existed.

And from the looks of it, he never knew they existed either.

I wasn't prepared for that truth bomb.

His confession is a high before the low.

Excitement but then devastation that he'll never do anything about it.

"Yet"—my throat thickens with heartache—"you don't want to be with me."

He lifts his hands, curling them around my waist, and stares up at me. "We can't be together, Georgia."

The anguish is gone.

Vulnerability in its place.

"Why not?" I choke out.

"It's too complicated." He gives my hips a rough squeeze. "You're my partner's sister. You're too young. You're my employee. I don't do relationships." He shakes his head. "A long list of additional reasons as well."

"You don't do relationships, yet you were engaged?" I shake my head. "That doesn't ... it doesn't make sense."

"My failed engagement is what taught me that I don't do relationships." He slides his hands up and down my waist, his touch setting me on fire. "We have enough problems as it is. Us *being together* would create more tension when it fell apart. Our friends would know, and so far, we're finally doing a halfway decent job of being civil toward each other. Think about how that'd go back to hate." His hands shift to my thighs, gripping them. "If something were to happen in this office, if I took you to my bed again, if I fucked you again ..." His voice trails off.

I shiver in his arms.

"It'd lead to nothing but problems."

"Do you want to fuck me again?"

"Every time I look at you, I want to touch you. I have to clench my hands to stop myself. I have no right to be jealous, and I'm working on that, trust me."

He drops his head, his forehead against my stomach, and I massage his scalp, running my hand through his hair.

"What if I'm willing to take that risk?"

He expels a long breath when he pulls away. "Georgia, half the time, we can barely stand to be in the same room."

"Because we're running," I say, my voice trembling. "We're failing ourselves in fear. My brother, he'd understand—"

"It's not only about him, Georgia. I'm fucked up in the head. I've done fucked-up shit."

"We all have, Archer." I cup his face in my hands. "We're human."

He repeatedly shakes his head.

I fall to my knees, causing his hands to slide up underneath my armpits, so we're level. "Talk to me."

"You're too pure, too happy to be dragged down with me. You deserve better."

"What if I don't want better than you?" I blink away tears, unable to stop a few.

He drops his hands, smooths his palms over my cheeks, erasing them, and catches my chin between his thumb and forefinger. Silence envelops his office as his gaze explores the features of my face.

"Trust me," he whispers, "you do."

"Archer! Dude, we need you!"

I gasp, jumping, when someone knocks on the door.

Archer kisses my forehead and then the tip of my nose. "If you want the night off, you can have the night off."

There it is.

This conversation has ended us.

"No," I say, my chin trembling. "It's okay."

"Archer!"

We should stand.

Separate.

"Give me a fucking minute!" he barks, rolling back in his chair.

I gasp at the loss of his touch, at the loss of his warmth.

Silas barges into the room, stopping as we come into his view. "I didn't see shit." He slowly backs away, the same way he did earlier. "But seriously, we need you. Wrap this shit up. There's a guy losing his fucking mind in the parking lot demanding to see our camera footage because his wife left the bar with another man."

"Great," I mutter when Silas turns and leaves the room.

Archer stands before holding his hand out. "He won't say anything." He sighs, kisses the top of my head, and walks toward the doorway.

"I'll be here tomorrow," I say before he exits.

He nods. "See you then."

CHAPTER NINETEEN

Archer

"I TOLD you something would happen between you two," Silas says in warning. "Your relationship with Cohen is about to get messy as fuck."

"It's not what you think."

"It sure looked like what I think. She was on her knees in front of you—"

"Whoa, she was not about to suck my—"

"Not where I was going with that. The look on her face, the sadness—there's something there. That hate game you play is a bunch of bullshit. I know it. Lola knows it but won't share anything with me because she would never break the girl code. Finn knows it. The only one who's blind is Cohen. Hell, he probably knows it but is trying to convince himself otherwise."

"Just don't say shit."

"I'm keeping my motherfucking mouth shut. When this shit all blows up, don't you dare say I knew."

"It won't blow up."

"It will, and Silas knew nothing."

"ABOUT YESTERDAY," Georgia says when she gets to work.

Her voice sends a chill up my spine. She's all I've thought about since yesterday happened.

Instead of being honest, I lie, "There's nothing about yesterday."

"Archer."

I stop and turn. "You want to know the truth? Let me lay it on you. The day I brought you home and fucked you, I liked you. The day I saw you at the cookout, I knew I was screwed, but once I figured out our only communication was at the bar and a few outings where I could keep my distance, I was relieved. Then you started working here and fucked everything up for me."

"Wow," she says.

"Had this been another time in my life, our situation might be different."

"Had this been another time in your life, you'd probably be married."

"Possible. I don't know." I run my hand through my hair. "But it's not another time in my life. This is now, and now, I'm not the man for you." I gesture between the two of us. "As much as we want this to happen, it can't."

"It's embarrassing, you know, having someone say they like you but not want to be with you. You start to wonder why, you know? Is it because I don't come from money, like you do, that you don't feel like I'm good enough for you, that I'm only your type in bed or physically? You know, it's probably worse that I learned your truth. At least in the past, I thought you hated me. Now, I know you don't hate me; you just don't see me as worthy enough to take a chance with, to be with me, to show me I'm good enough. Yes, my father ran off on my family; yes, we were poor; and yes, my mother was an addict, but that doesn't define who I am."

"This has nothing to do with stature or you and everything to do with me." I smack my chest. "Me and my fucked-up life, my fucked-up family."

"At least you have a family!"

"Look, whatever you have in your head about us, kill that thought.

Fucking slaughter it. We work together. That's it. All I will ever see you as is an employee."

"Jesus, you give me a headache from your whiplash of emotions."

"Georgia, move on. Be with someone else!"

She throws a glass down. "I can't because you don't want me to! You stop me."

I only nod and walk away.

————

SHE ISN'T the same Georgia for the rest of the week.

Somehow, it's like every feeling she had for me is gone … except for the hating part.

I'm an asshole for being sad that she doesn't want me anymore since I'm the one who turned her down.

That night in my office changed everything between us.

It wrote in stone that we're done.

Over.

Nothing.

And never will be.

I grab the most expensive bottle of alcohol from my kitchen and throw it across the room. I wish I were a different man, one who could give her what she wanted, one who wasn't fucked up in the head.

One who wasn't responsible for someone else's death.

CHAPTER TWENTY

Georgia

"HOW ARE YOUR CLASSES GOING?"

My mom glances up from her plate at my question. We're at the Moccasin Diner, where she works and the place we meet at once a week. It's not the best diner in Anchor Ridge. The checkered floor tile is dingy, the silverware is always bent, and it's a trucker hot spot. Every time I leave, I cross my fingers I don't get food poisoning.

I don't come for the food. I come for her.

To cheer her on, so she never turns to drugs again.

So far, the ride to developing a relationship has been smooth. It's nice to finally have a mother. Even though it's only halfway, it's still better than nothing.

It should've happened sooner, though.

She should've been there since day one.

I'm working hard not to hold that resentment toward her, but it hasn't been easy. Cohen was the one there for me—when my period started, after my first heartbreak, during my first hangover, preparing me for college.

Not my mother.

Not my father.

Not two people who were meant to be my biggest supporters.

Cohen.

Every week, I struggle to put it aside, knowing we'll have to talk about it eventually.

People make mistakes.

Drugs make people selfish.

That's why I haven't fully thrown myself into a relationship with her—in fear of her disappearing. Cohen refuses to see or talk to her. He passes off my visits as something that will only break me in the end.

The thing with me is, my heart survives a beating.

It can get fractured in every way possible, nearly destroyed, and I'll still pick up every piece. I'll gather them one by one and then hand them over to someone even more reckless.

Sometimes, my heart is too good for me.

Sometimes, it's too bad for me.

It's also why I am who I am and why I love so hard.

In the end, I can say I tried—tried with my mother, my father, Archer.

I gave every single one of them an opportunity. What they chose to do with it was up to them.

She smiles at me from across our booth, one nestled against a window. "Good. I'm attending them every night I don't work and have been saving up my money to get my own place when I leave the halfway house."

Her cheeks are sunken from the drug's long-term effects. She's gradually gaining weight, and her halfway house drug-tests her every three days. She's missing two bottom teeth, and the others aren't in great condition—another side effect from the addiction. Her plan is to save enough money for dentures.

"That's awesome! Congratulations." I reach out and grab her hand, squeezing it tightly before pulling it away and taking a sip of my strawberry milkshake.

"How are *your* classes going?"

"Good. I'm ready to graduate and forget about midterms and papers and exams."

"I'm so proud of you." She places her palm on her chest over her heart. "My daughter, a college graduate."

I blush.

"All on her own … without a mother."

I open my mouth to tell her it wasn't all on my own. I had Cohen, but she sniffles and keeps talking.

"I'm so sorry, Georgia. For failing you, Cohen, our family." She wipes at her eyes. "My apology will never make up for my absence, and I'm not asking for a pass. You and Cohen will never forget my neglect, but someday, I hope you can forgive me for it."

"I understand," I reply with silent tears.

Her love for the drug was stronger than the one for her family.

I pray that's changed.

That her yearning for forgiveness is stronger than her love for a high.

CHAPTER TWENTY-ONE

Archer

WHAT'S HARDER?

Hating someone or acting like you hate someone?

Forcing yourself to push them away?

Georgia stares at me from across the bar.

Every inch of me craves her.

Before she car-blocked her way into my life, I was who I wanted to be.

Who I deserved to be.

Callous. An asshole. Heartless. A loner.

It's who I was.

Enter Georgia Fox.

Coming through with warmth, softening my callousness.

It's unfair to her, us arguing.

Silas calls it foreplay.

I tell him to shut the fuck up.

We haven't touched again.

But that doesn't mean she hasn't touched me in other places. That she hasn't climbed her way into my thoughts and affected me in ways to make me a different man than who I am.

———

"DON'T FORGET, tomorrow is my birthday, bitches," Silas says, sucking on a lollipop.

Finn slaps his back as he walks by. "I'll be there."

"I'll think about it." Lola smirks, her plump lips bright red.

Silas stops behind her stool, wraps his arms around her shoulders, and nuzzles her neck. "You'll be there. Don't forget my present, my little hellcat."

She tips her head back, staring up at him. "I'll be sure to purchase a value pack of condoms from Costco."

He kisses her forehead. "That's my girl."

"Rule number one," Finn says, sitting down on a stool at the pub table. "No one tells Archer that Georgia is coming."

"I can hear you, dumbass," I grind out, approaching the table. "I promised Silas I wouldn't bail. I'll be there."

I wish *she'd* bail, though.

Georgia perks up in her stool. "I'll be on my best behavior."

Finn snorts and motions to Georgia and then me. "You'll have at least one spat before the night ends."

"Who even says *spat*?" Georgia asks.

Finn shoves his thumbs into his chest. "Fuckers like me."

I want to go to the club like I want to hang out with Lincoln in his prison cell. Silas bribed me into going when I asked him to cover a shift for me. I'm a man of my word, so I'll stop through, have a birthday drink, and then slip out.

Why Silas has his birthdays in clubs is beyond me. Dude is sober and drinks seltzer water at parties. Still a better time than me, though.

Silas has never shared why he doesn't drink. It's been brought up a few times, but he shuts us down—only sharing, "It's not my thing."

As a sober man, he still kills it as a bartender and as our liquor purchaser. Lola has a lot to do with it. She tells him what to buy, and he listens to her every word.

That's why it's no surprise that he invited the girls.

He invites her to everything.

With Lola comes Georgia.

With Georgia comes my aggravation.

With Georgia comes my frustration.

With Georgia comes everything I can never have.

———

THE CLUB IS PACKED.

Club Soho is the best club in the city.

Once, I lived for this shit.

The loud music, expensive alcohol, drugs.

Now, when I take a seat, I cringe.

"Private tables are the bomb dot com," Georgia says, walking into our VIP section with Grace and Lola. She straightens out her button-up denim skirt and collapses onto the white couch.

Why did she come looking like that?

To torture me?

Short skirt. Low-cut white top. Black suede boots hitting her knees.

Adorable woven into sexy.

I drink her in as if she were the drink that'd get me through the night.

Instead of the club being my high, it's her.

That blond hair—I've dreamed of it tangled against my pillow.

I had her as a brunette, wild and in my bed.

Now, I need the other.

Tonight, it's our small group—Georgia, Lola, Grace, Silas, Finn, and me.

"It's not hard to get the VIP section when you're the shit," Silas replies, smirking around a blue sucker.

"You mean, it's not hard when *I* set it up," Lola says, elbowing him. "Happy Birthday, asshole."

He points at her with his sucker. "True, *but* it's also easier when you're banging the owner of the club. You got me beat on that one, babe."

Lola flips him off.

"Jealous she's hooking up with him and not you?" Georgia asks—because she's Georgia and she always has to talk some shit.

"Lola knows I'm always jealous of who she's sleeping with." He winks at Lola. "My services are available anytime she wants."

Lola laughs. "Whatever. Everyone knows it's stupid to screw your best friend."

"Love you." He kisses her cheek and drags her onto his lap.

"Hey!" Grace says at the same time Georgia says, "Oh, he's your best friend now?"

"Best *guy* friend," Lola corrects.

"Can I be offended by that?" Finn asks. "I thought we were friends."

"Your best *girl* friend is Grace," Silas answers before squeezing Lola's knee as she squirms in his lap. "Stay away from mine."

"Kinda feeling left out over here," Georgia mutters.

Silas jerks his head toward me. "Then there were two. Looks like it's you and Archer, babe. I know Archer is up for some BFF bracelets."

"Pfft," Finn says. "They hate each other."

"Do they, though?" Silas asks, leveling his eyes on me and stroking his cheek.

Finn is oblivious to his insinuation. Grace and Lola share looks before peering at Georgia.

Georgia raises a brow, her gaze meeting mine. "Do we hate each other, Archer?"

I lick my lips before taking a long draw of my Jack and Coke. "You tell me. I think you've moaned how much you hate me aplenty."

"*Moaned* it?" She cocks her head to the side.

I nod.

"Wrong." Georgia delivers a devious smile. "You know what name I do like to moan?"

I shake my head. "Hard pass."

That devilish smile widens. "Chase."

Grace spits out her drink.

Lola shoves her face into Silas's shoulder to hide her laughter.

"What am I not getting?" Finn asks the crowd before focusing on Georgia. "You have a new boyfriend?"

"Gross." Georgia exaggeratedly shudders. "Chase was some douchebag I had a one-night thing with." She's answering Finn but staring at me. "Totally didn't deliver bedroom-wise, if you know what I mean."

"Keep that from your brother," Finn says, all brotherly like. "He'll lose his shit if he hears about you hooking up with some random dude."

You have no idea.

With music blaring around us, I take in the club. Dancers are hanging from the ceiling, doing acrobatic shit. We're on the top floor, a balcony-like layout, overlooking the sea of people dancing to the electric music the DJ is bumping. We talk—I randomly throw in comments—and suck down liquor.

Our waitress returns with a glowing tray of drinks and shooters in her hands and drops them off. Silas slips her a hundred, and she blows him a kiss. Lola and Georgia grab a shooter, and Georgia holds one out to Grace.

She waves it away and yawns.

The girls knock their shots back.

"I'm exhausted." Grace glances at Silas, pouting out her lower lip. "Do you mind if I leave early?"

"You go ahead, Teacher Grace," he replies. "Teach those brats their ABCs."

She rolls her eyes and smacks his arm.

Georgia lifts up, and her ass points in my direction when she slides her phone from her back pocket. "I'll book us an Uber."

My back stiffens, though it shouldn't.

Don't leave yet.

Her presence, sipping on her drink and laughing with our friends, has been my entertainment for the night. I'm not ready to end that yet.

Not ready to go home to an empty bed and think about her.

Grace stops Georgia from unlocking her phone. "Nope. Finn is driving me home. He has to leave early, and his house is on the way to my parents'. Stay and have fun."

Silas snorts. "Almost your bedtime, Finn?"

"Hell yeah," Finn says with a nod. "I need my beauty sleep."

"Are you sure?" Georgia asks Grace, chewing on her bottom lip. "I have no problem with going home."

If she leaves, I'm dipping.

Grace shakes her head. "I'm going to my parents' for the night anyway."

"Okay. Make sure you text me when you make it there, okay?" Georgia says.

Grace nods, and she and Finn say their good-byes.

"And then there were four," Silas says, relaxing in his seat and throwing his arm over Lola's shoulders.

"Oh my God! Archer?"

My back stiffens as my name is yelled over the music.

Here we go again.

I swallow and raise my chin to find Meredith and her two friends walking toward us.

Keep walking.

Pretending I don't see them, I lean forward and make myself a drink. As I do, my gaze sweeps to Georgia, who's giving Meredith a death glare.

"Can we join you?" Meredith asks.

"We're pretty full over here," Georgia replies at the same time Silas shrugs and says, "Sure, whatever."

Georgia's icy stare shoots to Silas.

Silas, confused, sends me a curious glance, raising a brow.

We're all looking at each other, not knowing what the fuck is going on.

Meredith chooses Silas's answer and gracefully strolls into our section.

Georgia slides off the couch. "I just remembered, Lola and I have cute guys to meet on the dance floor."

She bumps into my knee while walking toward Lola. Lola stands and grabs her hand, and my eyes are glued to them as the only reason I haven't left disappears through the crowd.

I down my drink, but it doesn't help the dryness in my throat.

So I make another drink.

Meredith sinks down next to me. "Uh-oh," she coos, sliding in too close for comfort. "Looks like Little Miss Jailbait is still crushing on you."

"Jailbait?" I tighten my grip around my glass. "You know she's not jailbait."

Silas signals back and forth between Meredith and me. "How do you two know each other?"

Meredith holds up her bare ring finger. "Archer used to be my fiancé."

"Holy shit," Silas says, pointing at me with his water. "You were engaged to this heartless bastard?"

"He didn't used to be so heartless," Meredith says, brushing her hand along my thigh and resting it there.

I pluck her hand off me as if it were toxic, and Silas arches a brow.

"Wow," Meredith rasps, her mouth slackening.

I bow my head and lower my voice, "Nothing will happen here, Meredith. Give up on that dream. It'll turn into nothing but a nightmare for you."

CHAPTER TWENTY-TWO

Georgia

SWEATY AND ANNOYED with men copping feels of my ass, I walk off the dance floor. Heading in the direction of our table, I freeze, remembering Pageant Barbie is there with Archer.

I clamp my eyes shut and release a deep breath.

There are so many reasons I hate the woman.

Archer gave a relationship with her a chance.

Loved her.

Proposed to her.

That's more than he'll ever give me.

And from the way she looks at him, she wants that back.

I dart toward the bar with the urge to drink, to get so inebriated that I have no idea who they are when I look at them.

Become strangers I don't give a damn about.

As I order my vodka cranberry, a guy slides between me and the person at my side, barely cramming himself in.

"I got this," he tells the bartender. "Add one on there for me too."

The bartender nods and walks away.

Shifting, I smile. "You're in my psych class."

"Georgia." He says my name matter-of-factly, no questioning himself or throwing out a guess in an attempt to please me.

I nod.

He's attractive with short black hair and bright blue eyes that remind me of the sea, and his blue shirt nearly matches them.

He's the ocean. Happiness.

The opposite of Archer, who's a hurricane over that ocean.

Blowing out a nervous breath, he runs his hand over his head. "Don't judge, but I've been trying to muster up the courage to talk to you for months. Looks like tonight is on my side." He laughs; it's friendly and authentic—something you don't find much from men who ask to buy you a drink at a bar. "Unless you're about to tell me to kick rocks, and in that case, it definitely isn't on my side."

A blush rises up my cheeks. "Nervous to talk to me?"

His shyness is a breath of fresh air, but for some damn reason, Archer comes to mind—the memory of how he was the night he bought me a drink.

No matter what, my thoughts always lead back to him when I should be running like hell away from them.

Focus on this guy, Georgia.

He's not hanging out with his ex. He's talking to you.

"Hell yeah," the guy says. "You're gorgeous, and you seem chill as hell." He holds out his hand. "Logan."

When I shake it, chills run up my spine as he runs his thumb over the top of my hand.

"You here alone?" His question isn't creepy; it's more concern over me hanging out solo in the club.

I shake my head. "I'm here with friends, but I had to take a break from the dance floor before I kneed a dude in the balls."

"Ah, dudes can get creepy over there."

"Tell me about it," I say. "They know nothing about personal space."

"What about a dance with me?" He presses his hand to his chest. "I swear not to be creepy, and if I am, I give you full permission to knee me in the balls."

I glance down, biting into my lip as another blush hits me. Maybe Logan is the answer to getting over Archer. We can dance, drink, and exchange numbers at the end of the night.

My thoughts of moving on with him crash and burn when Archer steps behind Logan, his tall body towering over him. My back stiffens, and the bartender drops off our drinks.

"She'll pass," Archer says, his jaw clenching. Pulling out his wallet, he plucks out a few bills and slams them onto the bar in front of the bartender. "I got her drink." He smirks down at Logan, who's curiously staring at him over his shoulder. "Since I'm crashing your little party, I'll pay for yours too."

I am going to kill him.

Murder his ass.

Then he won't get a chance to have a relationship with anyone.

Logan's attention returns to me. "He your boyfriend?"

"Hell no," I rush out. "He's my older brother's friend."

"Ah, so a bit overprotective." Logan slips closer to me and then turns to face Archer.

I'm not sure if it's worry that Archer will rip his head off or so he can get a better look at him.

"Swear to you, man," Logan tells him, "I'll be on my best behavior."

Archer doesn't spare Logan a glance, as if he weren't there, and pins his gaze on me. "*Just* your brother's friend?" He offers a self-satisfied smile. "You're not going to tell him we slept together too?"

My breathing labors, and I gape at him, speechless.

With his piercing eyes not leaving me, he draws out a fifty from his wallet and retreats a step. I wait for him to leave. To run off the guy and then run off himself—the typical Archer and Georgia storyline.

Typical damn Archer.

Wanting no one to have me yet not taking me for himself.

Just as I'm about to grab Logan's hand and lead him to the dance floor, Archer taps a girl on the shoulder.

When she turns in his direction, a giddy smile covers her face.

He shoves the fifty in her hand and motions to Logan. "Dance with this guy."

"What the hell?" I snap, tempted to throw my drink on him.

"Okay," the girl chirps, making eyes at Archer. "*Only if* you save me one for later."

"Yeah, sure, whatever," Archer mutters, not giving her a second glance.

Logan hesitates, his gaze pinging between me and the girl. "No, you really don't have to—"

"Scram," Archer barks. "Or you won't have any legs to dance with." He grabs another bill, as if he were a damn cash cow, and thrusts it into Logan's hand.

Logan smiles apologetically, hands Archer the hundred back, and walks away, deciding I'm not worth the hassle. Not that I blame him. We haven't even danced, and he's already being threatened. I sigh, guilt tripping through me and then annoyance. He didn't take the money. He was a good guy, and Archer ran off him.

Leaving me with Satan himself.

Archer stumbles back, caught off guard, when I push his shoulder.

"You can't just shove your wealth and size around to scare people," I snarl. "I wanted to dance."

He crosses his arms, moving closer into my space, giving me a whiff of his cologne. "I can do whatever the fuck I want actually."

I inhale again, searching for a hint of perfume, of Meredith.

Nothing.

I cross my arms, mirroring his stance. "News flash, Archer: everything doesn't revolve around you." I invade his space, standing on my tiptoes, struggling to be eye-level with him. Even with my heels, I'm nowhere close. "What is wrong with you?"

He peers down at me with a mocking grin. "Nothing is wrong with me."

My body is tense. My mind scrambling. Anger firing through me.

I jerk my arm out toward the crowd. "I wanted to dance, and the guy seemed nice, unlike half the creepy guys out there. Of course you had to ruin that like you ruin everything else—fucking me up in the head more and more while you pull shit like this." I shove him again, and his arm hits my drink, spilling it. "Go be with Meredith and leave me alone."

He looks at his arm, grabs some napkins, and wipes up my mess. "Why?"

"Why what? Why do I want to dance?"

He nods, wiping down his arm.

"Uh, it's fun, unlike being at our table and watching you and Pamela Anderson get your flirt on."

He shakes his head, his face unreadable. "Never flirted with her."

I scoff. "She basically sat down on your lap."

"I don't want her, Georgia."

"Do you want *anyone*? Or do you only prefer random women you can screw for a night, and that's it?" It's as if we are alone, the chaos around us fading, and I'm hyper-focused on him.

"I'm selfish, to be honest."

I flinch at his honesty. "So, what? You don't want anything to do with me until a decent guy grabs my attention. Then you stalk over here, all caveman-like, and run him off. I want a boyfriend, and I want someone to fucking dance with!"

This isn't about dancing.

Or a boyfriend.

This is me no longer tolerating his ups and downs.

"And that's what I'm going to do."

I turn to leave, but he reaches out, grabbing my arm, and stops me.

He shoves me into his chest. "Looks like we're fucking dancing then."

I stumble back into him, nearly tripping over his feet. "Wait, what?"

"You want to dance? We'll dance."

His hand captures mine, his grip tight as if he's scared to lose me, and he leads me through the crowd. My heart spirals, pacing as fast as the electronic music playing. Since all Archer and I do is fight, with the exception of orgasm night, I'm clueless on *how* to dance with him.

Does he know how?

Does he think this will be some ballroom shit?

My dancing is *so not* ballroom dancing.

More Lil Jon & the East Side Boyz.

Lola is dancing with Silas, and she waves me over to them. Her eyes widen, and she smacks Silas, pointing at us when she notices Archer is with me.

"Welp, this is a new development," Lola says, her eyes piercing Archer in warning.

To clear my head, I start dancing, ignoring Archer as he awkwardly stands behind me.

Why is he even here?

A pair of masculine hands grip my waist, a strong body behind me, and just as I'm about to swat the person away, I hear, "Relax. It's me."

Archer.

I shut my eyes, relishing the weight of his body pressing against mine, and he drags me in closer. We dance, my ass pushing against his waist, and lose ourselves to the music.

To each other.

I shiver when his lips go to my ear, and his words are a rough whisper. "I shouldn't want you like this."

"But you do," I return.

One of his arms is wrapped around my waist, keeping his hold on me, and the other sweeps over my stomach. "The things I want to do to you …" His voice trails off, as if he's stopping himself from being vulnerable.

"Then do them," I whisper. "Do whatever you want."

"I can't."

"You can."

"You'll hate me more."

I grind into him, his erection growing against my ass.

If he asked me to go home with him, I'd blurt out yes without hesitation.

Be in his bed in a heartbeat.

Archer touching me like this, his honesty slipping from his lips, is the biggest turn-on.

Emotions, honesty, vulnerability are what I'm attracted to.

If a man can screw me well, that's a plus, but he can be taught to do that.

Pouring himself out to me? Revealing his heart?

That can't be faked. That can't be taught. It has to be all him, ready to open up.

I gasp when his fingers feather over the waist of my skirt, gently and barely lifting my top up to allow him better access.

"More," I whisper.

He hesitates.

I squirm against his ass.

He tilts my head to the side, his face falling into the crook of my neck, and his cold breath blows over my skin.

"More." My tone is demanding.

A long sigh bellows from my lungs when he swiftly pushes his fingers underneath my skirt, which allows his large hand hardly any room, and into my panties.

"Look at you, wet as the alcohol you were drinking," he says into my ear, pressing a finger to my clit, adding pressure torturously. If his free hand wasn't gripping my waist, I would've fallen at his feet. "I remember this—how wet you got for me before. I wonder if you taste the same." He flicks my clit, his lips traveling down my neck. "Do you ever think about me inside you?"

I nod.

A gasp.

Another.

A moan.

Until finally, I'm able to say, "Do you think about being inside me?"

He licks up my neck, grinding against me. "All the time. When you scamper around the bar, when I jack off in the shower, when I hear your voice."

I shiver. "Tell me more."

"I remember how good my dick felt inside you, how your pussy was perfect for me in every single way." He sucks on my earlobe and runs his finger through my wetness. "Come home with me tonight." His voice turns pleading. "Please."

"Okay." I tilt my head back, allowing it to fall along his shoulder, and his mouth dips down to mine, our lips touching.

"I will make you feel so good," he says against my lips, slowly gliding his fingers out of my panties.

He turns me around, staring down at me, with heat and need in his eyes.

I nod, a silent go-ahead, and he captures my hand in his.

"Let's go."

"Let's go," I repeat, my throat raw.

"Okay, you cool kids," Silas says, karate-chopping our connection, causing my hand to fall from Archer's. "Time to break it up."

Lola stands behind him, her arm and chin resting on his shoulder, and she stares at me with curiosity and worry.

Excuse them?

What do they think they're doing?

Archer's face falls, and he steps away from me.

Reality hitting him.

We got lost together—forgetting our hate, how he'd hurt me. All we wanted was the other.

That moment is gone.

Archer's face is pained, and everyone follows him off the dance floor.

"I have to head out." He steps in closer, his mouth lowering so only I can hear him. "I'm sorry, Georgia. That won't happen again."

My hand covers my lips as he walks away. I'm unsure if I'm holding myself back from screaming at him, crying, or vomiting up my humiliation.

"What was that?" I ask, chasing Lola as we return to our section, which is thankfully Meredith free.

"That was me saving you," she says, glancing back at me.

"Saving me? Saving me from what?" My tone is harsh.

Finally, Archer and I were going to take that step again.

Finally, I was going to get what I'd wanted from him all along.

"You guys were in a moment," she explains, worry in her tone. "Archer doesn't deserve to touch you like that, not until he proves he'll do better than the last time he did."

"What'd he do last time?" Silas asks, raising a brow.

"None of your business," Lola answers, her piercing stare sliding to him. "Whatever you heard and saw stays between the four of us. Got it?"

"Yes, boss woman." He wraps his arms around Lola's waist and kisses her cheek. "Let me hunt down Archer and make sure he gets a ride home before he kicks someone or something."

As soon as he disappears, Lola shoots straight into question mode. "What the hell happened? You were practically screwing on the dance floor. I'm sorry, but Silas and I had to stop it. That rat bastard knows how to play with your head, and I refuse to watch you get hurt. To prevent that from happening, my ass will be lurking around and pulling you away from possible Archer-screwing."

"You're right." I sigh, my stomach twisting as I take in the reality of her words. "You ready to go?"

"Yes." She gives me a hug. "Operation I Will Kill Archer is now in full effect. Let's steer clear from allowing him to have his hand in your panties again. Capisce?"

"Capisce," I mutter, swiping a tear off my face.

CHAPTER TWENTY-THREE

Archer

TO CANCEL.

Not to cancel.

Never has a decision had my brain scrambling so hard.

If only I hadn't let my emotions get the best of me.

If only I hadn't touched Georgia when I didn't deserve to.

I'm not worthy of touching her.

I'm unworthy, yet I still stop another man from having her.

Like the selfish bastard I am, I ruined it for her.

And fucking Meredith.

Had she not strutted in and invaded our night, Georgia would've never left. Had she not, I wouldn't have created more problems for myself—for my relationship with Georgia.

There was so much raw tension—sexual and emotional. I was thinking with my dick and not what was good for us.

What was good for her.

Silas played the question game when he met me outside, and I told him to tell the girls I was leaving. Had I not walked away, I wouldn't have cared what Silas or Lola said. I would've begged Georgia to go home with me. I was that desperate for her. Our friends were at least smart enough to stop it.

When I got home, my cock was still hard as a rock. I showered, punishing myself for my stupid decision and holding myself back from stroking my cock and thinking of her.

Unfortunately, I lack restraint when it comes to thoughts of Georgia.

In my head, she was in the shower with me.

Wet. Soaked for me.

I held out my hand, filling it with water, and stroked myself faster. Her name is what slipped through my lips as I came.

Choosing not to be selfish, I pull into the parking lot of the ski resort at the same time as Silas. Ski North is one of the tackiest places I've ever been to, but I'll be here for the next two nights, celebrating Noah's birthday with everyone. It's a small resort, known for its faux snow, where people can ski and snow tube.

I locate my cabin, unload my bag, and meet the gang. Unlike most of them, I rented a place to myself. The girls are sharing a cabin, Finn and Silas are taking another, and the last one will be Jamie, Cohen, and Noah.

Jamie is Heather, Noah's mother's, younger sister. After Noah's birth, Heather ran off to Vegas, and Cohen moved a town over to steer clear of her family. For years, it worked. Until Cohen took a feverish Noah to the hospital, and Jamie was the doctor on duty. After Jamie begged him to allow her to have a relationship with Noah, he finally agreed. Now, they have somewhat of a divorced-couple-visitation like situation. Well, they *did* have that type of relationship. Lately, they're getting closer. I have a feeling their little arrangement is starting to evolve into something more intimate.

Everyone is gathered in the ski shop, where racks of skis and poles fill the room, selecting their rental equipment. They're circled around Jamie and arguing whether she'll die while skiing.

"Whoa," Finn says. "No one expected you to show."

"Why?" I grumble, tucking my skis into my side since I brought my own.

"You bail on half the shit we do."

"It's Noah's birthday. I wouldn't miss it."

The little guy is cool as shit, and his birthday means the world to him. He handmade everyone's invites.

I move farther into the room, and Georgia freezes when I come into her view. We've avoided each other since the club.

"I'm shocked you're here," she warily says when I stop behind her. "You've been avoiding me—no shocker."

"I've been busy."

"Bullshit," she grits out, shaking her head. "Good thing our friends stopped me from doing anything stupid with you."

I flinch.

"Nothing would've changed between us."

She turns away from me and tells Jamie she's not getting out of skiing.

———

YOU SHOULDN'T WANT *to break a ski instructor's neck.*

Yet why do I want to?

Maybe not break his neck but kick him far away from Georgia.

I grind my teeth and tap my foot, watching him flirt with her— clueless that she's my obsession. She smiles, one that's brighter than anything she's ever given me.

I shut my eyes, listening to her laughter.

Watching them is a sucker punch to the throat.

A sucker punch that I deserve.

"Want to share a lift?" he asks her when we walk outside.

I step forward to join their conversation. "Nah, she's riding with me."

Georgia narrows her eyes at me. "I think Finn needs someone to ride with." She jerks her head toward the line waiting at the gondolas. "Ready to go?"

He nods, and his palm rests on the curve of her back as he leads the way.

Lola smacks my stomach as I follow them. "Unless you want to admit your feelings for her, quit cockblocking, asshole."

"I'm not cockblocking shit," I seethe.

"You are, and it isn't fair to her. Georgia deserves someone who wants to be her number one, who wants her to be *their* number one. I don't know what your deal is, but it needs to stop."

Silas laughs, jogging to us, and wraps his arm around Lola's shoulders. "That's my girl. I love her spitfire attitude."

I stay quiet.

"You good to ride with Finn?" Silas asks Lola as they walk alongside me.

"No, I'm riding with you," she answers.

He turns and whispers in her ear.

She rolls her eyes and playfully shoves him. "Fine, whatever. I'll tell Finn he's riding with me. You jerks enjoy each other's company."

She joins Finn in line, and not much time passes before we load into our gondola. When Silas settles next to me, I know he didn't make that decision for shits and giggles. I ignore him and keep my attention on Georgia and Ski Instructor Boy three gondolas up from mine.

"You know, Cohen probably wouldn't care if you and Georgia dated," Silas says. "He knows you're a good dude. We all do. We wouldn't be friends if you weren't. Cohen is being a big brother, but deep down, if he thought any of us would be a threat to her, he'd never allow us around his family."

Every muscle tightens at his comment.

How much does he know about Georgia and me?

He and Lola are close, but Lola's loyalty is as strong as Lincoln's. She wouldn't share Georgia's business unless it was cool with Georgia.

I nod in agreement.

I'm not scared of Cohen beating my ass.

It's that him hating me is the best excuse I have.

The reason I give to hide my own truth.

———

SILAS: *We're having drinks in the lodge's bar. You game?*

I'm fresh from a shower and drying my hair when I see Silas's text.

Skiing yesterday was a nightmare. Georgia, who seemed like she was a regular at Ski North, didn't need any instructing. Yet the instructor—who I later learned was Calvin—stayed by her side the entire time.

Who did need Calvin's help?

Jamie.

She rolled down the hill, Humpty Dumpty-style, and sprained her ankle.

Today, we had Noah's party, and now, everyone is doing their own thing.

I snatch my phone, ready to ask if Ski Instructor Boy will be there, but then I stop myself. Georgia and I need to talk, to hash out what happened. And what better time than when she might be with another man?

Me: I'll be there.

Silas, Lola, Georgia, *and* Calvin are seated at a table in the back of the bar. It's not a dive like Bailey's or a sports bar like Twisted Fox. It's quaint with piano music thrumming in the background and people casually sipping drinks while conversing.

The only open chair at the table is next to Georgia, and Calvin is on her other side. I slip past everyone and drop into the chair. Calvin scoots closer to Georgia, eyeing me suspiciously, knowing damn well there's a chance I'll shove a dagger into his game tonight with Georgia.

Sure will.

He won't be sticking his dagger anywhere near her.

Georgia twists in her seat and glares at me, tilting her head to the side. "Can I help you?"

I lean in closer, the same way Calvin did, only looming over her more. "We haven't had a chance to talk since the club."

"You could've solved that problem days ago." She sighs, a twinge of hurt flashing along her face. "Our friends were right to stop us. It would have been a mess had it gone any further."

I nod, hating her honesty. "You're right."

I'm hot and cold.

I don't blame her for finally walking away.

For being done with my ass.

It's what I wanted from day one.

Isn't it?

It stings me, but it'll be good for her.

She turns her back to me and starts talking to Calvin.

This is it.

When another man steals her away.

I order a drink, and when the waitress delivers, I move my cup in circles, studying the liquor as it splashes along the rim of my glass. Everyone talks, and as usual, I'm on the outside, listening.

"You coming, man?" Silas asks me as the night grows later.

All eyes are on me as everyone stands.

I shake my head. "Nah, I think I'll stay back."

As they clear out, I grab my glass and stroll to the bar, taking a seat. The hairs on the back of my neck stand when Georgia approaches me.

"Stay back and do what?" she questions.

I raise my glass and take a swig as my answer.

She chews on her lower lip. "Stay back and wait for another woman to sit down before taking her back to your cabin?"

"To drink." I fasten my attention to her, hoping she sees the sincerity. "I'm not worried about a woman."

"Why not?" She does a sweeping gesture of the bar. "This is a similar scene to what happened before we slept together. Did you forget about that?"

"I'll never forget." My answer is barely audible.

"Should I stay back and drink too?"

"If you stay back, it'll lead to trouble. Your ski boy is waiting for you." I dismissively flick my hand through the air. "Run along."

She gapes at me. "Fingers crossed he doesn't leave me a *see yourself out* note."

"Georgia," I say her name in warning, hating the thought of her with someone else even though it's what I tell myself I want.

Never in my life have I been so fucking confused.

So frustrated.

"Archer," she says, mocking my tone, a hint of a slur in her voice.

"You're wasted."

"Not wasted. Tipsy."

"Same difference." I gesture to the empty stool. "Have a seat if you need proof I'm not leaving with anyone tonight."

"Do you want me to stay?"

"Georgia!" Lola calls us. "Let's go, babe."

Georgia throws me a questioning glance.

Say yes.

Beg her to stay.

I tip my glass toward her. "Have a good night."

"Don't go home with anyone," she whispers, her voice strangled.

I keep quiet.

"Promise me." Her eyes squeeze shut in pain.

"I'm not promising anything to a woman who's about to leave with another man."

"Georgia!" Lola says again.

Her eyes open, she nods, and then she turns away to be with fucking Calvin.

———

SITTING *at the bar by yourself is a lonely venture.*

I witness it regularly at Twisted Fox.

The brokenhearted who drink away their feelings, positive their lives will never go back to normal.

Tonight, I'm that guy.

My loneliness calls out to me, and I can't stop myself from grabbing my phone. Taking a deep breath, I unlock the screen and hit Georgia's name.

It rings, and as if fate knew what was coming, it goes to voicemail at the same time Cohen slumps down in the seat next to me.

"Damn, dude, you definitely look like you need a drink." I set my phone down next to me. "A motherfucking strong one."

He slides my glass off my napkin and wipes his hand with it. "I need a few of them."

Before answering, he orders us a round of Jack and Cokes. A pained expression is on his face, and his entire body is tense.

"What happened?" I ask. "You and Jamie finally fuck?"

He stays quiet.

"Is that a yes?"

The bartender drops off our drinks, and he mutters a quick thanks. Tonight, I'm seeing a different Cohen, one I've never seen. Cohen is the most grown-up of our group and usually put together. He doesn't make drastic decisions and never allows his emotions to get the best of him.

"How was it?" I push.

Damn, he's pulling a me with the not opening up.

Is this how people feel when they try to get an answer out of me?

"We didn't fuck," he finally grinds out.

"Something happened, though."

He doesn't deny anything.

"How was it?"

"Fucking wrong. That's what it was."

"Wrong because there was no connection, or wrong because of who she is to you?"

He shoots back his drink, slams the glass onto the bar, and calls over the bartender for another.

"Wrong because of who she is to you, I take it."

"She's my son's aunt." He works his jaw. "Hell, he doesn't even know she's his aunt. She's my ex's sister. Her family attempted to take my son away from me, and now, I'm fucked. If Noah loses her, it'll break his goddamn heart. All because of my stupidity."

I refrain from asking what happened.

From asking for the details.

Sure, I'll give advice, but I won't make you pour your heart out to me to get it.

"What are the reasons it could be right between you two?"

"Nothing."

"Yet you still hooked up."

He glares at me.

I shrug, grab my drink, and take a sip. "You're attracted to her. There's something there. Go for it."

If only I'd take my own advice.

I'm a goddamn hypocrite.

"Attraction doesn't always mean it's a good idea."

I tip my glass his way. "True." *Hear, fucking, hear.*

My phone rings, and I gulp when Georgia's name flashes across the screen. I quickly silence it but not fast enough.

He side-eyes me. "Why's my sister calling you?"

I shove the phone into my pocket. "Who knows? Probably to yell at me or ask me about work."

I called her because I can't get her out of my head.

I called her because I'm just as confused about my feelings for your sister as you are with Jamie.

"I didn't know you had each other's numbers."

"We work together." I gulp down my drink. "Look, you're my friend. The situation you're in is weird, and I don't blame you for not crossing a line, but I can't tell you what to do." I poke his shoulder. "Only you know how far you want to take it, how much you want her, how fucking broken you'll be if you lose her. Whatever your choice, just remember, it's on you. Either way, I'll support you, but in the end, I hope whatever you choose makes you happy."

Practice what you fucking preach.

My phone rings again, vibrating in my pocket, and I ignore it, hoping my guilt isn't clear on my face.

The bartender returns with another round, and we knock them back together. When Cohen decides to finally head back to the cabin, I tell him good-bye and good luck.

Then I sit there and run the advice I gave him back through my head.

How can I tell one person to do everything I should be doing myself?

Time passes until I can no longer take it. I drag my phone from my pocket to text her.

Me: Can I stop by?

Three bubbles appear underneath my message.

Then disappear.

Then appear again.

Georgia: Sure.

I stand from the stool and walk to her cabin.

CHAPTER TWENTY-FOUR

Georgia

"WHAT ARE YOU DOING?" Lola asks when I stand from the couch, grab my shoes, and slip them on.

"I need a breath of fresh air," I lie.

"A breath of fresh air?" she slowly repeats my words. "I call bullshit."

I sigh. "Archer is outside and wants to talk."

"That's trouble," Grace whispers from her chair, snuggled in her blanket.

"Babe, you need to be careful," Lola says. "I love you, and I don't want you to get hurt."

Grace nods. "Agreed."

My heart seemed to freeze when I read Archer's text, asking to come over.

At the bar, when we'd talked, it was hell for me. My stomach dropped as I pleaded, fighting to hold back tears, for him not to bring a woman back to his cabin. Meanwhile, Calvin was standing in the doorway, waiting to come back to ours. The thing was, Calvin coming back to my cabin didn't mean anything. I hadn't wanted him, and twenty minutes after he got here, I told him I was tired, and he left.

I shrug, as if my head isn't spinning. Archer never goes out of his way to be alone with me. It's always been forced, at work, or when we're with friends. Never anything like this, but then again, until the club, he'd never danced with me while his hand was down my skirt. Our relationship is shifting. Whether it's for better or for worse, I have no idea.

"Fucking Archer," Lola grumbles. "I swear, the guy is the coach of mixed signals."

"Yeah, always giving me the red light," I fire back.

"I'd say it's more yellow with you," Grace inputs.

Staring down at my pajamas, I frown, pulling at the bottom of my Nap Queen tee—complete with crown-printed pajama pants. Most definitely not a hot look when meeting the guy you've been lusting over. I peek over at Lola, taking in her black lace romper, and contemplate asking her to do a tradesie. With the way she's staring at me like I have a horn growing out of my head, I doubt she'd be up for it.

"It's one in the morning," Lola continues. "*Are you up* texts are booty-call texts. Remember what he pulled last time. *And*, might I add, this will be harder. Last time, you didn't have feelings for him like you do now."

"Sheesh, Negative Nancy," Grace mutters.

"Not negative, nor am I trying to sound like a bitch." She blows me a kiss. "I just love you, is all."

"Let's just see what he says. Give him the benefit of the doubt," I say.

"No matter what, don't you dare go to his cabin," Lola says. "Even if he confesses his undying love for you, don't. It could be the alcohol talking."

"I got this," I say, expelling breaths before repeating, "I got this."

"And she most definitely doesn't have it," Grace says commentary-style as I head toward the door.

My hand is sweaty when I grip the knob and walk outside onto the porch. There's a bite to the wind, and I cross my arms, scanning the lot. The cabins are set up around a cul-de-sac layout, so you can see all of them from yours. It's quiet outside, everyone in their bed, snug as hell and not waiting for the boy they're obsessed with to come to their porch.

I shiver when Archer comes into view.

Even after everything, I can't stop my face from lighting up. He comes closer and stops at the bottom step of the porch. His heavy-lidded eyes meet mine underneath the dim light.

"Hi," I whisper.

"Hey." He kicks the top of his shoe against the step.

My stomach turns as I take a good look at him.

He smells like a distillery.

There's a hint of desperation in his puffy red eyes.

His stare is pained.

My throat thickens, my heart kicking into my chest, as reality hits me like the bitch that she is.

This is *the talk.*

The conversation that will change everything.

All of our arguments, flirting, sexual tension has led us to tonight.

His drunken lips are about to speak his sober thoughts.

Am I ready to hear them?

When I build up the courage to speak, my voice is weak. "Did you need something?"

It takes him a moment before he says, "No."

That's it.

I wait for him to continue, but he stays silent.

I swallow down the sick feeling in my throat. "Why are you here, Archer?"

He shrugs, as if he doesn't understand my question. "I don't know."

For fuck's sake.

"*I don't know* yourself out of here then." I motion toward the street and point at a random cabin. "Either be honest or go."

"I'm a liar," he states clearly with no bullshit.

"A liar?" I stare at him intensely. "About what?"

"I do need something."

I remain quiet, waiting for him to continue, but in Archer fashion, he only silently stares at me.

"Jesus Christ!" I finally snap, anger rolling through me, causing me to jump down the stairs and step to him until we're inches apart. I swing my arms out, and my voice rises, filling with edge. "Be honest! For once, in this messed-up friendship, relationship, complication-ship we have, please just be honest." The edge in my voice shatters to brokenness. "That's all I'm asking for. It's not that hard."

"You want my honesty?" He runs his shaking hands through his thick hair, tugging at the roots, and his tone is as chilly as the air. "I wanted to see you. I always want to see you." He reaches out, his hands freezing as they cup my face. "You're in my head, in my heart, living inside me, Georgia. No matter how hard I fight, there's no getting rid of you, and it's fucking breaking me. How much I want you and can't have you but other guys can—it tears my goddamn heart out."

Every word of his is a sucker punch to the gut, and I jerk out his hold, my blood on fire. "Is that why you're here? You thought I was with another guy?" I throw out my middle fingers to him. "Screw you! You don't want me, but no one else can have me either?" A strong sigh escapes my lips, and I groan, fighting to restrain my tears.

He winces at my truth, and with hesitation, he comes closer. I shiver as his thumb tenderly brushes my cheek, ridding me of the tears I'm fighting to stop.

"You're beautiful." His voice cracks, the stench of whiskey escaping his mouth. "So damn beautiful and pure, so fucking full of light." He squeezes his eyes together. "I'd kill that inside you, do you hear me? I'd burn you out, be another person in your life who failed you— something you never deserve." He caresses my cheek, moving down to my jaw before tipping his head down and kissing a tear away. "I wish I were a better man for you," he says against my skin. "Someone who'd help you shine, but all I'd do is put you out."

I wrap my hand around the back of his head, holding him in place, and he rests his forehead against mine.

"Why are you so convinced you'd put me out?" I whisper. "That you wouldn't be good for me?"

"I destroy everything. It's who I am."

I pull back, and this time, it's me cupping his face, his scruff abrasive against my palms. "Whatever it is, I can deal with it. I will deal with anything for you."

"You can't." He shakes his head and releases a heavy breath before pulling away, causing my arms to fall limp at my sides.

As I peer up at him, I read his eyes, and they tell me everything I need to know.

He's not here to be with me.

I take a step back and hold out my hands. "No, this isn't fair to me anymore."

"Georgia," he says around a sigh.

"It's not fair!" I scream. "You can't keep showing up when I'm trying to move on! Stop railroading your way back into my heart, only to crush me over and over again."

"I'm sorry," he whispers.

"You're sorry?" I snort, shaking my head. "That's rich. Tell me your truths, tell me what has you so shaken up that you're afraid to open up to me, to give us a chance?"

He stares at me, more defeated.

I scoff, now staring at him in disdain. "Enough. We've played this game for too long. I'm done." A hard sob escapes me. "Just set me free! Let me go!"

"Georgia," he pleads, stepping closer. "Come back to my cabin with me—"

My hand connecting with his face echoes through the empty street.

His eyes are shut as he processes what happened, but he doesn't flinch.

Doesn't feel his face as if it didn't faze him.

"Really?" I shout. "You came here for a booty call? Do you think I'd ever do that again after what you did?"

"I'm sorry," he says, pained.

"You're not," I hiss, pushing him away from me. "You're never sorry, Archer. From the beginning, you've done nothing but play with me. Fuck you." *Shove.* "And your games." *Shove.* "And your bullshit." *Shove.* "And your lies."

"Georgia. *Please*," he begs.

"No." I dash up the stairs and turn to face him. "I'm done."

He's saying my name as I swing open the door and walk in, tears pricking at my eyes as I lock the door behind me.

Grace is waiting and pulls me into her arms as I sob into her shoulder. She leads me into the living room, and I collapse on the couch.

Lola walks in, holding a bottle of vodka. "Time to drink away those feelings for him, babe."

I take a shot, wishing it'd erase him from my brain.

I take another, wishing I'd never parked and blocked him in.

I take another, wishing I'd never asked him to leave the bar with me.

CHAPTER TWENTY-FIVE

Archer

"SET ME FREE."

"You're never sorry."

"I'm done."

I shut my eyes.

Georgia's words have been replaying in my mind.

Haunting me.

Rubbing guilt inside the wounds already inside me.

It's what I wanted all along, right?

For Georgia to decide she was done with me.

When I'd made the mistake of asking her to come back to my cabin, I'd succeeded in doing what I'd wanted to do when I found out she was Cohen's sister.

Make her never want to see me again.

The problem is, what I wanted then isn't what I want now.

While that moment helped heal her wounds, her scars of us, it only stabbed mine deeper.

I fucked myself over that night—ruined us. My words and actions were a reality smack in her face.

Since then, she's steered clear of me. Our conversations are only work-related or when we're out with our friends. She makes friendly conversation, only if necessary, but that's it.

Hardly any bickering.

And, goddamn it, I miss it.

When we were arguing, at least there was *something*.

Getting nothing from her is worse.

She cut down her hours at work, blaming it on school, and helping with Noah.

That sure went down as a shitshow with his baby momma.

I shudder, thankful I'm not in that mess.

Cohen slaps his hand on the bar. "Don't forget Georgia's graduation party next weekend."

"I'll be there," Finn replies.

"Thanks, guys," Cohen says. "She's ecstatic to graduate."

Silas waits until Cohen is out of earshot before turning to me. "You going?"

I shrug. "Probably best I don't."

"Something has changed between you two."

"She got smart and realized I wasn't worth it."

———

"I CAN'T BELIEVE I'm getting out soon. It seems surreal."

I smile at Lincoln's words.

It does seem surreal.

"You'd better have a party ready for me," he says around a chuckle.

"I'm not throwing you a *congrats on getting out of prison* party."

He groans. "You suck."

I lean back in my office chair and kick my feet onto my desk. "What's your plan when you're released? Staying with Mom?"

"Hard pass." He laughs. "She'll smother me and make sure we brunch like it's our damn jobs. I've been cooped up for a while. Going back to Mom's will drive me insane."

"You want to crash at my place?"

"That's exactly where I'm crashing. It's nice of you to finally offer."

He lowers his voice, his words clearer. "Did you talk to Cohen about me working there?"

"If you want a job here, you can have a job here."

Cohen can be pissed, but this is my brother.

I trust Lincoln.

———

I KNOCK on Cohen's office door with my knuckles and wait for him to yell, "Come in," before opening it. Unlike most people around this joint, I wait for people to reply before barging into their offices.

"I need to talk to you about something," I say, walking in.

"What's up?" He tosses his phone to the side to give me his full attention.

"My brother is being released."

He grins. "Sweet! I'm happy for you, man."

I thrum my fingers against my cheek before scratching it. "He needs a job."

His smile drops. "I hope you're not asking me what I think you're asking me."

"I'm asking what you think I'm asking you."

I bite my tongue, stopping myself from saying I'm not *asking* shit. Lincoln needs a job, and I want to hire him. Cohen hired Georgia without consulting me. I can do the same.

"I know he's family, but he's a felon. He was in prison."

"For embezzlement, not murder."

"*Money* embezzlement." He slams his finger onto his desk, his brown eyes widening. "We deal with *money* here."

"Let me correct myself." I hold up a finger, and though I'm not trying to be threatening, there's no stopping my voice from rising. "He went to prison to protect my family. You can't fault him for that shit. You'd have done the same. Give him a shot. If he fucks up, I'll fire him myself."

"No." He stands.

"I'm not backing down on this, Cohen. I don't demand much

around here, but my brother needs someone to give him a chance, and he needs a job. And that'll be me and *here.*"

"If anything happens, Archer—"

"Nothing will happen," I interrupt. "You have my word."

CHAPTER TWENTY-SIX

Georgia

"YOU SEEM DOWN TODAY," my mom comments in her smoke-cured voice.

I stare at her from across our booth and shift in my seat. "Boy problems." I take the last bite of my cherry pie, lick my lips, and drop my fork onto my plate with a *clank*.

Archer problems.

Ten thousand times more complicated than just *boy* problems.

Heartless-jerk problem.

Her face falls. "Oh, no."

My relationship with my mother has been getting better and better. She hasn't shown one sign of using again, and next week, she'll be moving into her own studio apartment. I watch as she shoves her last bite of apple pie into her mouth, noticing the changes in her. She's gained weight, and her natural style is showing through. Her clothes scream the '80s—denim vests and pants with bright and over-the-top makeup. I don't have the heart to tell her Smurf-blue eye shadow is definitely out.

Since I've been consumed with midterms and graduation, it's been easier to busy myself and keep my mind off Archer. My game of dodging him has gone well. There have been times he's tried to stop me and attempt to strike up conversation, but I scurry away before giving him the chance.

The night at the cabin was finally my breaking point. When I'd walked outside, in the pit of my stomach, I had known it'd change us.

No longer will I allow Archer Callahan to play with my heart. Every minute we were outside was a kick to the stomach, harder and harder with each word. My brain, finally growing some balls, kicked my heart to the side. It was time I let go.

I tried, begged, for a piece—*anything*—but got zilch.

He slipped up that night. *For once*, he allowed his vulnerability to step out before shoving it back in. He almost showed me his truths and where I stood with him.

He had feelings for me. The pain on his face confirmed it. Someone can be in love with you all you want, but that doesn't mean they know how to love you right.

The worst part, what hurt the most, was him asking me to go to his cabin for a booty call as though that was all I was good for. Never had I been so furious. Never had I slapped, shoved, and screamed at someone so irately. And he gave it to me. He allowed me to give him all my anger. I should apologize, but anytime I start, the memory of his behavior sweeps through me, stopping me.

I cried that night, full of tears, as I remembered his comment from years before.

"Don't you find it weird that the only time I was nice to you was when I was drinking? And wanted to get laid."

Nothing said to me has been more hurtful.

"A hot chocolate refill," our waitress says, placing the steaming mug in front of me.

"Thank you," I reply with a smile. A smile that doesn't reach my eyes.

I've decided to be done with Archer, yes, but that doesn't mean all of me is happy about it yet.

My mom wipes her lips with a napkin and sets it next to her empty plate. "I'm no expert on men—or heck, even life in general, but my advice is to always trust your gut. Throughout my years, my gut has screamed out to me, begging me to listen, but I allowed what I believed was love to blind my rationality. If I'd thought with more than just my heart, it would've saved me from a lot of heartbreak ... and making wrong decisions that were destructive to my well-being, to my life, to my children's lives." Her gaze falls to her plate, regret staining her features, and she plays with the pie crumbs between her fingers.

She has a point.

I listened to my gut to form a relationship with her, and she hasn't let me down.

She peers back up at me. "What did he do?"

An ache forms in my throat as I squirm in my seat. "It's more along the lines of what he refused to do."

"If he won't fight for you, then it won't work. A relationship can't have only one person fighting for it. Nothing good in life can be one-sided."

I stare at her, unblinking, soaking in her advice.

"That, or show him what he's missing." She winks and waves the waitress over for another slice of pie.

———

MY STEPS ARE slow as I make my way to Cohen's office.

He never calls me into his office. Normally, I just barge in whenever, so I feel like a kid seeing the principal.

I knock and slowly open the door when he yells for me to come in. He peeks up at me from his desk, a thin smile on his face, looking almost keyed up.

I rack my brain for reasons he'd be this tense.

Does he know about Archer and me?

Is Archer dead in his office?

Come to think of it, I haven't seen him all day.

Lately, Archer's mood has been as grumpy as Red Forman's. While Archer and I crumbled on the ski trip, Cohen and Jamie came together. Unfortunately, their happily ever after was happily ever short-term since they've already crashed and burned.

He scratches his neck. "I need to talk to you about something."

"Okay?" I shift from one foot to the other.

"Archer's brother is being released from prison." He frowns. "He's going to work here."

Phew.

"Cool." I shrug.

From what I've heard about Lincoln, minus the whole prison vacay, he sounds cool.

"You're not against the idea?" He squints at me harshly as if he's waiting for me to object.

"Nope." I crack a smile.

He blows out a stressed breath. "You should be."

"Oh, big bro." I collapse onto the chair across from him, sitting on it sideways with my feet dangling over the armrest. "Convicts are actually my cup of tea. If he doesn't have a teardrop under his eye, I will be severely disappointed."

"Funny," he grumbles. "For real, if you're not okay with it, tell me."

"I'm cool with it."

"He was *in prison.*"

"What's your beef with second chances?"

He massages the space between his brows with two fingers. "It's kind of hard for me to be gung ho on second chances now that I have my son's mother trying to wedge herself into our lives while I'm falling in love with her sister, and it's been a nightmare."

"That sounds complicated." I chew on the inside of my cheek before clicking my tongue against the roof of my mouth. "Have you tried eating a Snickers or something?"

He grabs a piece of paper, crumples it up, and tosses it at me.

I laugh while dodging it, and the sheet falls to the floor.

———

IT'S TIME.

Time to break my Archer-dodging, and what a better way than to give him shit?

"Is your brother hot?"

He peeks up at me before looking at each side of the bar, unsure if I'm speaking to him. "Excuse me?"

"Is your brother hot?" I repeat as if I haven't been avoiding him and we're good ole buddies, ole pals.

"Georgia," Cohen warns, his voice sharp as he walks around me.

I frown. Cohen wasn't supposed to join this game. He was supposed to stay in his office and sulk.

"I'm not asking *you*," I tell Cohen. "I'm asking him." I jerk my head toward Archer.

A confident smile is plastered on my face when I train my attention on Archer. "Well, is he?"

Archer pins his stony stare at me. "I take it Cohen told you about my brother working here?"

I nod, my grin nearly taking over my face. "Yep, and I love myself a bad boy."

"Georgia," Cohen warns again.

"What?" I tilt my head to the side and keep my attention on Archer. "I'm in need of a boy toy."

Archer tightens his jaw, and Cohen is shaking his head when I walk away.

CALL ME GEORGIA FOX, M.S.W.

After six years of busting my ass, I finally have my master's in social work.

I stroll through Cohen's backyard with my graduation cap on. Congratulatory gifts for yours truly cover one table, and the other is lined with a taco bar. There's a cake with my face on it—Jamie's idea—alcohol, and food galore. My stomach growls as I snag a plate, ready to eat my weight in tacos.

Even after graduating, I don't have a full-time job yet. What sucks is that jobs want you to have experience before hiring you, but if no jobs will hire people without experience, then how the hell are we supposed to get experience? Luckily, there's a possible job opportunity at the school where Grace teaches. Their guidance counselor is retiring, so until she does and to see if I'll be a good fit, I'm "shadowing" her.

After a heated argument with Cohen, he agreed—with Jamie's persuasion—to let my mother come to his house. She timidly waved to him when she walked in, but he turned around and walked out of the room. We haven't introduced her to Noah yet. I'm still working on convincing him it's a good idea. I bought him a book on forgiveness and left it on his desk last week, only to find it in my book bag later.

Cohen and Jamie finally got their heads' out of their asses' and are in a relationship. Not *only* are they in a relationship, Jamie is also pregnant with his baby. To say they're over the moon is an understatement, and I can't wait for the little one to come.

I open gifts and visit with everyone, and as it grows later, the small crowd clears out. The tacos gave Jamie the gift of heartburn, and Cohen went to check on her, leaving me alone outside for some much-needed quiet time. I toss my cap onto the table next to my green apple Smirnoff wine cooler. Stretching out my legs, I tilt my head back and relax.

"Congratulations."

I slowly raise my head at the same time Archer takes the chair next to mine. My heart beats like a drum as his gaze locks on me.

He sets a black gift bag with *Congrats, Graduate* scrawled across it in gold glitter.

"Thank you," I whisper, a flush spreading up my neck.

It's easier to talk shit to him when we're at the bar.

Harder during our one-on-one talks.

He stares at me, his masculine face with his strong chin unreadable as the sun sets around us. "How does it feel?"

My gaze falls, and I play with my hands in my lap, fighting a shy smile. "Incredible."

"That's a huge accomplishment, and you worked hard for it. Be proud of that."

I peek up at him, that blush creeping up my cheeks, and repeat, "Thank you."

He signals to the bag. "Open it."

I silently nod, slowly grab it, and shake the bag, like I do with all my gifts, silently guessing what it could be.

It's heavy. Something rattles.

I have no guesses.

With Archer, who knows?

It could be a bomb, and I wouldn't be surprised.

My smile widens as I pull out the gold tissue paper. I peek into the bag before pulling out a liquor bottle.

A bottle of Hennessy.

I play with the bottle in my hands, moving it from one to the other. "Cognac."

"Cognac." He nods, a smile flicking on his lips.

I hold it out toward him. "A reminder that we should never drink this together again?"

"That's not what the gift means." He jerks his head toward the bag. "Keep going, babe."

I bite into my cheek and start withdrawing the rest of the items—a gift card to the coffee shop where I blocked him in, a beginner's guide for driving handbook, and a jewelry box ... a blue Tiffany's jewelry box.

Random.

"What's all this mean?" I ask.

He gestures toward the gifts. "We met at the coffee shop. You forgot how to drive and slammed on your brakes—"

"To prevent a murder," I interrupt.

"To apparently prevent chipmunk murder." He chuckles, waiting for me to open the jewelry box.

"What's this mean?" I ask, holding up the box. "From what I remember, we didn't rob a jewelry store."

He scratches his cheek. "We didn't, but those gifts weren't enough."

You being here is enough.

I inhale a deep breath, and we fall silent, the only noise me popping the box open. Gasping, I carefully remove the necklace, holding the chain between my fingers as I take in the gorgeous piece. Two charms with engravings hang from the chain—a long bar with my name and a small circle with *M.S.W.* Next to the charms is a small, sparkling diamond.

"What ... what is this?" I stutter, admiring it.

"A necklace," he states.

"I know that," I say with a laugh. "This ... this is beautiful."

And so thoughtful.

This isn't something he purchased for me at the last minute.

He planned it, had it custom-made—from Tiffany's.

"Thank you, Archer," I say, clasping the necklace in my fist and holding it to my chest, warmth spreading through it.

He subtly nods. "You're welcome." He slides his chair back and stands.

My mouth drops open.

Is that it? He came to drop off the gift and bail?

He holds out his palm. "Here."

Relief rushes through me, and I'm hit by a sudden giddiness.

A soft breeze whirls around us, and loose pieces of tissue paper blow across the table. I hand over the necklace, and my palm returns to my chest, hoping to settle my raging heartbeat. He stands behind me and sweeps my hair off my shoulder, bunching it along one side of my neck. His hands are cold, and my breathing turns ragged when he fastens the necklace.

He brushes his fingers along the nape of my neck.

"You're back to your natural hair color," he whispers, grabbing a strand of my hair and curling it around his finger.

"I needed a change."

Rather, I needed to go back to who I was. I've spent hundreds of dollars and made multiple visits, and I am in the ombre stage of returning to my natural hair color.

"It reminds me of our night together." He gives my neck a gentle squeeze and returns to his chair, turning to face me. "You're beaming."

Even if I wanted to hide my smile, I couldn't. "It's been a good day, and your gift, I can't thank you enough. Seriously, this was so thoughtful."

"You're welcome." He thrums his fingers against the table. "I tried to get here earlier, but it was visitation day for Lincoln, and I was running behind. I came as soon as I could because I didn't want to miss the chance to give you that. It looks beautiful on you."

Who is this Archer, and where can I get him full-time?

"Want to stay?" I blurt out, shocking both of us. I scramble to grab the Hennessy bottle and hold it up. "Hang out and have a drink, for old times' sake?"

His jaw clenches. "I think we both know that'd be a bad idea."

We do, but I don't care.

"So?" I ask, feigning innocence. "Why?"

He licks his lower lip. "From the way you're staring at me and how you look tonight, our night would end the same as our night at Bailey's."

I scan the yard, making sure we're still alone, and lower my voice. "What if that's what I want?"

"It can be what you want, but it's not what you need."

"How do you know what I need?"

"I know what you *don't* need—someone who can never give you what you deserve. I'm that guy."

I sweep my arm over the table, where the gifts are, before running my hand over the necklace chain. "Why show up here with the gifts then?"

"I didn't buy you those gifts so you'd sleep with me. I bought them because you deserve that and more." He briefly slams his eyes shut and bows his head, and his voice is half-whispered. "There are times I wish I could be the guy to make you happy. I might be a heartless bastard, an asshole, but when it comes to you, I stop myself from being the man who crushes your heart."

"Yet you are crushing it," I croak out.

"Babe, trust me." Slowly, he rises to his feet, kisses the top of my head, and says, "Good night, Georgia."

I don't get a chance to say a word before he leaves.

CHAPTER TWENTY-SEVEN

Archer

"THANKS FOR LETTING ME CRASH HERE," Lincoln says, tossing his bag on my guest room bed. "Guarantee this shit is more comfortable than what I was sleeping on."

It's the first time my guest room has been used, but since he's been sleeping on a concrete slab for years, I wanted him to be comfortable here. Like the rest of my family, Lincoln grew up with the finer things in life: family trips on yachts, disposable money to blow on whatever we wanted—a lot of times it was blow—and nice-ass bedrooms. I can at least give him the last one of the three.

"I got you," I say behind him, stopping in the doorway and leaning against the door. "How's it feel, being a free man?"

He's four hours free, and damn, it's been a long day. I learned prisons are in no rush to release inmates. My mom and I waited six hours before he stepped out of the building. Our first stop was his favorite restaurant, where he ate his weight in steak and lobster.

I yawn, and my eyes are heavy as he spins and takes in the bedroom. It's almost midnight, and I worked until three this morning. Had I known his release day would be as long as it takes for people to land on the moon, I would've left early and had someone cover for me.

"Damn good," he mutters with a hint of a frown. "Sucks Dad

wasn't released with me." He slumps onto the edge of the California king-size bed and hangs his head low, shaking it. "I offered to take a longer sentence to shorten his, but the assholes wouldn't allow it."

He did what?

This is the first I'm hearing about his little act of stupidity.

I clench my fists. "Why in the living hell would you do that?" There's no masking the aggravation in my tone.

"He's family," Lincoln points out, peeved, exhaustion overplaying his features. "That—loyalty to our family—might not mean as much to you as it does to me, but Dad's older, and he has heart problems. He doesn't need to be in there."

I unclench a fist and slam my hand against my chest. "Are you saying I have no loyalty?"

"You have loyalty *to me*, sure. To others? Not so much. This stupid game you and Dad have played for years is draining to everyone around you. What happened that night—"

"Don't," I warn, cutting him off. "Don't play that. Whether that happened or not, I still wouldn't be Dad's puppet to his bullshit."

"You threw away your life!" He starts naming off a list on his fingers. "Your job. Your friends. Your family. The woman you were supposed to fucking marry. All because you couldn't get the fuck out of your head and deal with reality." He shakes his head. "I'm not a fucking puppet. I'm living—unlike you."

I didn't plan on us being at each other's throats his first night home. I knew there'd eventually be a conversation about Dad and some back-and-forth shit, talking about loyalty, but nothing this early.

"Oh, piss off," I mutter. "Get off your high horse."

"High horse? I took the job intended for you. You always do what's best for Archer without giving two shits about anyone else. *You* get off *your* high horse and take a look around. Everyone else is living, not staying in the past, but you won't even try. Hell, I've been in prison for nearly two years, and I still hold no grudges as strong as you."

"What about you?" I seethe. "You sat back while Dad shit all over Grandpa's *legacy*. Where was your loyalty to him? To our name, huh?" I raise my voice. "Where was that goddamn loyalty?"

"What else was I supposed to do, huh?" He rubs the back of his neck. "I took my salary, nothing extra. Did I know what Dad was doing? Yes. I got time because I knew, because I wouldn't turn on my family. Loyalty runs through my blood."

"Your *loyalty* landed you in prison."

If I hear loyalty *one more time, I'm going to throw myself out that damn window.*

He stands, plucks his bag from the bed, unzips it, and starts unpacking.

"Look," I say, blowing out deep breaths to calm myself, "it's your first night home. Let's not talk about shit we'll want to kill each other for."

He holds up his arm and flexes his muscles. "Admit you don't want the smoke from these guns."

Lincoln is buff, gym-built buff, unlike me, who'd have a large frame whether I worked out or not. He worked out constantly during his stint in prison and is in the best shape he's ever been. Still doesn't have shit on me size-wise, though. While I got more of my father's size, Lincoln is between my dad's and my mother's.

I tap the door with my knuckles. "Unpack. Get some rest."

"Mom's having a party tomorrow night, and you're coming," he rushes out before I leave.

"No, I'm not."

"Yes, you are."

I shake my head. "You have fun with that."

———

I CAME FOR LINCOLN.

I'm drinking for my sanity.

There's nothing like celebrating your freedom and being around the fake friends who talked shit when you were arrested, calling you a criminal on the down-low. My mom handled the guest list, and Lincoln, knowing this as well, has steered clear of those people. He insisted my mom have something small, but the seventy-five-plus people in attendance is far from that.

The party is too much for me, and I have to stop myself from bursting out in laughter. There's a harp and piano playing as tonight's entertainment. A fucking harp and piano for a *get out of prison* party. Caviar, Kobe beef, *costs more than my bar makes in a week* champagne.

My mother does not know how to read the room for shit.

I climb up the spiraling staircase at my grandparents' mansion, using the railing as my guide since my tunnel vision isn't doing a great job of leading the way. I walk, weaving from side to side in the hall, until I find the guest room I'm searching for. I slam the door, lock it, and collapse onto the bed as if I hadn't slept in years.

Lincoln decided to crash here after my grandparents offered to have their chef whip up his favorite breakfast in the morning. Considering I told him his ass would be having Lucky Charms at my place, he went with their offer. I might as well do the same.

As soon as my head falls onto the pillow, Georgia comes to mind.

Like my asshole self always does, I shoved myself back into her life. I couldn't show up *without* a gift; that would've been more asshole-like.

At least, that's my excuse.

As I brainstormed gift ideas, I didn't want to give her a generic-ass gift card or a *Congrats!* picture frame. More thought needed to be put into something for her big day.

"Screw it," I groan, reaching across the bed and grabbing my phone from the nightstand. I play with it in my hand while scrambling for the best excuse to call her.

Not that there is one.

I shouldn't.

It's too late.

A bad idea.

Selfish.

Selfish or not, I don't stop myself from unlocking my phone and scrolling down my Contacts until I reach her name.

"You selfish bastard," I mutter to myself when I tap it.

Ringing comes alive on the other end, and excitement crawls through my inebriated mind when she answers.

"Hello?" Her voice is cloaked in confusion.

"Hey," I croak out.

"Is, uh … everything okay?"

"Yeah." I'm wasted, in bed, and talking to her. Everything is happy-go-fucking-lucky over here.

The line goes mute for a moment until she finally asks, "If everything is okay, why are you calling?"

Good question there, woman who's crept her way into my heart. I wish I knew the answer too.

I tighten my hold on the phone. "I wanted to check on the bar." I tap myself on the arm for my genius answer, too lazy to do the actual *clap on the back* motion.

"Huh?"

"I had the night off, and you worked. I'm calling to confirm everything ran smoothly." Another pat on my arm for me.

"When have you ever called, asking if the bar ran smoothly?" she asks, no bullshit. "Call Cohen if you want to talk *about the bar* while slurring your words."

"Not slurring my words," I reply, slurring my words.

"Where are you?"

I hold the phone between my shoulder and head while dragging my shirt over my head. "A party."

"Archer Callahan, president of the I Hate Parties and Fun Club, is at one? Voluntarily or did someone force you?"

"Hell no, not voluntarily. It's for my brother, and I would've looked like an ass if I hadn't come."

"How is that any different than what you look like on the regular?"

"Funny," I grumble.

She releases a long breath. "Why are you calling me?"

"You're on my mind." The room starts spinning at my confession.

"I'm always on your mind when you're drunk," she deadpans. "You only want to talk to me when alcohol is flowing through your system. But you know what? I refuse to be your tipsy toy."

"Tipsy toy?" I wet my lips. "The fuck is a tipsy toy?"

"Someone you only want to play with when you're drunk."

I swallow hard. "You're not my tipsy toy, and you're wrong. I'm only stupid enough to tell you how much I think about you when I've been drinking."

My drunken brain is the only one that allows me to open up to her.

"I hate this cat-and-mouse game we play," she whispers.

"Me too."

"Then quit playing it."

With that, she hangs up.

I SCRUB AT MY EYES, my head taking my over imbibing last night out on me this morning, and yawn.

"Cohen, Lincoln. Lincoln, Cohen," I mutter, signaling between the guys.

Lincoln arrived at the bar fifteen minutes ago. We talked before heading into Cohen's office to introduce him.

"Don't forget about me," Georgia says, strutting into Cohen's office and collapsing into a chair. She presses her hand to her chest. "I'm Georgia, and you're hot."

She peeks over at me for my reaction, and I narrow my eyes at her in warning. It's all a game to her. She's paying me back for all the times I've fucked with her head. My eyes widen as I fight a smile trying to make its way to my lips when I spot the necklace around her neck. She's worn it every day she's been here since I gave it to her.

Lincoln rubs the side of his mouth, no doubt imagining Georgia naked. "Ah, I already like you. Appreciate the compliment, sweetheart."

Oh, shit.

Cohen's back stiffens.

"Can I be on training duty for him?" she asks, her voice perky. "I need to practice training, and it'll be the perfect opportunity for me."

"You won't be training anyone," Cohen says with a scowl. "You don't even work tonight."

She cups her chin with both of her hands and dreamily stares at Lincoln—showing off her dramatic acting, apparently. "I'll pick up an extra shift for him."

"How about you pick up yourself and leave my office?" Cohen says, raising a brow and glaring at her as hard as I am.

"All right, all right. Non-training Georgia is out of here." She stands, presses two fingers to her lips, and blows Lincoln a kiss as she passes him before leaving the office.

"Motherfucker," Cohen mutters underneath his breath while I clench my fists.

Cohen points at Lincoln. "My sister is off-limits."

Lincoln's eyes widen. "Oh shit, that's your sister?" He holds up his hand. "My bad, my bad. I really appreciate you giving me a chance, man. I won't let you guys down."

"Archer's family is my family," Cohen answers.

His words are genuine. Sure, he gave me hell when I approached him about hiring my brother, but Cohen knows I wouldn't bring trouble into our bar. He won't mind the extra help since Jamie is close to popping out their baby.

Jamie is good people.

I'm glad Cohen found her.

Found love.

And Noah loves her.

I rub my hands together and jerk my head toward the hallway. "Let's go to my office and get your paperwork started, brother."

He presses his hands together and tips his head toward Cohen. "Thanks again, man."

We walk to my office, and as soon as he shuts the door, he says, "You and the smart-ass sister have something going on, you sly fucker, you."

I stand at my desk, focusing on my computer as I open the folder for the employee documents. "I don't know what you're talking about."

He smirks. "Georgia. Is something going on between you two?"

I drag my finger along the trackpad and hit print. "Hell no."

"That mean she's available?"

"Hell no."

He chuckles, rubbing his hand over his strong jaw. "There's something then."

"There's nothing."

"When she walked into the room, your eyes followed her every move. You were ready to rip my head off my shoulders while she flirted with me. And then you went back to wanting to decapitate me when I just asked if she was available."

"Do you want to get fired before you start?" I level my dark gaze on him.

"I'd prefer not to be."

"Then shut the hell up."

"Cohen seems like he just tries to be intimidating. Ask her out. It'd be good for you. She'd be good for you."

A knot forms in my stomach. "I'd ruin her."

CHAPTER TWENTY-EIGHT

Georgia

I'M NEVER HAVING a gender-reveal party.

These things are stressful.

No way could I wait to find out the sex of my baby, but Cohen and Jamie have been patient.

Spoiler alert: I peeked at the cake.

They're having a girl.

After they find out and I get them alone, I'm requesting Georgia at least be thrown in as her first or middle name.

I planned the party with Jamie's best friend, Ashley, but Cohen and I have been planning an additional surprise. He's popping the question to Jamie today, and we set up for the perfect proposal.

A baby-bottle piñata and blue and pink streamers hang from the trees in Cohen's backyard. Games and food are spread along the tables, and the party is half-catered, half-Cohen grilled. He insisted no one but him was grilling his burgers. Friends and family are scattered around the backyard—sitting at tables, playing games, conversing with each other.

Cohen caved again and allowed our mother to tag along with me. After I swore on my life that she'd changed, Jamie and I convinced him that it was time for Noah to meet her. He did, and it only created more sparkle in her eyes. Maybe that's what she needs—a support system, a family—to help her stay sober.

All our friends are here, including Archer and Lincoln. My sleep has been crappy and my stress high since the night of my graduation party. I'd never had anyone gift me something so sentimental. Since then, we've had a few side conversations, but with him training Lincoln and getting Lincoln situated into normal life, we haven't had much time to talk. Not that I'm sure he would talk even if I cornered him.

The man drops bombs and then walks away as if he didn't ignite my feelings for him. I've considered asking Jamie for whiplash medicine because the boy is confusing me with his back and forth.

He's back and forth.

His *I like you, but I'm no good for you.*

His *let me be sweet but make you hate me at the same time.*

When I went home that night, I decided to take my mom's second piece of advice—make him see what he's missing. That's why I've taken on the pastime of flirting with every man Archer can see. Lincoln, guys at the bar, even the man who delivered our beer shipment yesterday.

If you can't beat 'em, might as well create some jealousy.

Strolling through the yard, I spot Lincoln relaxed in a chair, a water bottle in his hand. "Lincoln, Lincoln, Lincoln," I call out, walking over to him before plopping down on his lap and wrapping my arms around his neck. "When are you going to take me out on a date?"

Lincoln wraps his arms around my waist, glancing down at me with a smirk. "Whenever you're available, babe." His lips go to my ear. "Keep making him jealous. It's working."

Lincoln shares some similarities with his brother: chips on their shoulders and not one for small talk, but he's more easygoing than Archer.

These Callahan boys.

Handsome men ready to destroy everything in their paths.

We flirt, but I've never crossed a line with him. Nor will I ever. Even with Archer being a jackass to me, I have more respect for him than that. I have too much respect for Lincoln to use his heart as a pawn. I'm also not so keen on having sex with brothers.

That's my brother's thing ... but with sisters.

Sorry, Cohen, totally kidding.

I love Jamie, love how she's fixed my brother, and she's a chill chick.

"You ready, guys?" I hear Ashley yell. "Cohen! Jamie! It's time!"

All eyes are on Jamie and Cohen, and I prepare myself for my fake surprise face—like I didn't cake-peek and I have no idea what's about to happen. Their hands are wrapped around a balloon string, and they have pins in the other.

We count down, and as soon as we say, "One!" they pop the balloon.

Pink confetti rains down on them. The crowd jumps to their feet, cheers, and grabs pieces of the confetti while yelling at them in congratulations.

"Oh my God!" I gasp, my hand on my chest over my heart. "I can't believe this! I so didn't think it'd be a girl."

"You peeked, didn't you?" my mom asks with a smile.

I smirk. "Maybe just a little."

She laughs, shaking her head.

Now comes my other job. I rush into the house, grab a black balloon, and am nearly out of breath when I reach Jamie and Cohen.

Reminder: get your ass to the gym.

I hand the balloon to Cohen, my face in a sappy grin, and walk backward to give them their moment but not wanting to miss a second of this.

"Oh my God! Are we having twins?" Jamie asks, eyeing the balloon.

Cohen hands her a pin. "Pop it."

She does, black confetti fluttering to the ground, and everyone else glances at each other in confusion—not noticing what's lying at Jamie's feet.

"Holy shit," she whispers.

"Cuss word!" Noah calls out, making the crowd laugh.

Cohen drops down to one knee and delivers a speech no one can hear.

Lame.

She says yes, the celebration continues, and that's my cue to grab the cake.

"I cannot wait to eat, like, ten slices of you," I say to the cake as it sits in the fridge. "Do not let me down with your buttercream frosting, please and thank you."

As I go to take it out, my hand is snatched, the fridge is closed, and I'm being tugged down the hall and led into Noah's bedroom. It happens so fast, and though I don't see who it is, I know it's him.

I feel him.

His presence.

Have memorized his scent, as if it were the perfume I wear daily.

He slams the door shut and turns me to face him. "Stop flirting with my brother."

And today, we are getting mad-at-the-world Archer, ladies and gents.

Well, at least mad-at-Georgia anyway.

There's no patience in his eyes as he stares at me with disdain.

"What?" I ask, dramatically fluttering my eyes. "I don't know what you're talking about."

"Don't bullshit me," he seethes. "You're flirting with him to fuck with my head."

I'm fucking with his head?

Me?

The one who's been straight up, who's begged him not to fuck with my head.

My flirting dies and resurrects into anger.

"Screw you, Archer," I snarl, poking him in the chest, my nail creating a wrinkle. "Maybe I like your brother. Maybe I'll go on a date with him, and I'll kiss him. And you know what? I might even fuck him too!"

"Don't say that shit," he grinds out.

"Why? Do you think that because you fucked me, you can tell me what to do now? You lost that right a long damn time ago."

When the door swings open, I jump, and Archer flinches.

Cohen is standing in the doorway.

"What the fuck?" he yells.

Silence stretches through the room.

It's like time stands still.

My embarrassment skyrocketing.

Archer's patience dwindling.

Cohen's anger building.

This is mortifying.

I knew there was a chance Cohen would find out what'd happened between us, but I never wanted it to go down like this.

At his party.

One of my brother's happiest days.

I've ruined it for him.

For Jamie.

Cohen's face is red, and he snarls his upper lip as he stares at his business partner, his friend, the man he found out had screwed his sister. "She's my fucking sister!"

Luckily, Jamie saves the situation and stops him from going Mike Tyson on Archer.

"Nuh-uh," she says, grabbing his arm. "This isn't happening right now."

"Oh, it's happening," Cohen snaps.

My attention repeatedly pings from Cohen to Archer, back and forth, waiting to see who will make the first move.

Will it be with punches?

With words?

Archer holds up his hands. "I'm out of here. You can rip me a new asshole tomorrow."

He's leaving?

Oh, I'll be ripping him a new asshole for leaving me stranded with these question-askers.

Archer sends me a sympathetic glance, lazily mouthing, *"I'm sorry."*

I reply with an infuriated stare.

Do not walk out of here.

Jamie pulls Cohen back, giving Archer room to exit Noah's bedroom, their eyes locked in anger.

Tears slide down my cheeks—at the hurt, the humiliation, the anguish.

He left, left me to deal with this, and I hate him for it.

Tears are in my eyes when Jamie and Cohen stare at me in question.

"Nope." I sniffle, shaking my head. "Today is about you two. Any dramatic conversations about my life will wait until later."

I leave the room, brushing past them, and rush to the bathroom. After fixing myself, I return to the party, good as new.

One thing my non-relationship with Archer has improved is my pretending skills.

I'm a pro at pretending nothing has built between us, that I'm not stupidly in love with him.

Acting like I'm this happy-go-lucky woman while my heart is cracking with every conversation I have with him.

It's time I stop pretending he isn't crushing my heart and stop allowing him to do it.

CHAPTER TWENTY-NINE

Archer

"WE NEED TO TALK," Cohen says, stepping into my office without knocking.

I nod, tossing the pen in my hand down. "We do."

Cohen had the weekend off from the bar, so we had time to cool off before having this conversation. He's my dude, and not saying he's a wimp, but he'd be stupid to fight me.

I should've never gone to the party. Every time I say I'm going to keep my distance from Georgia, I go and do stupid shit like call her while I'm drunk, buy her custom Tiffany's, or show up at a damn party where damn streamers are hanging from the trees.

Watching her flirt with Lincoln was a stab to the throat. They had started flirting on his first day—both of them doing it to fuck with me. At first, I wasn't worried, but the more they did it, the more Lincoln got to know Georgia, the more terrified it made me. Lincoln might think it's a game now, but if he sees the Georgia I do, he'll fall in love with her too.

Jealousy doesn't care who the other man is. All it sees is someone having what you want.

Cohen isn't happy about their flirting either. When I demanded

Lincoln stop, he muttered something along the lines of, "Then make your fucking move on her."

I shouldn't have followed her into the house.

Georgia isn't mine.

After leaving the party, I called and texted her, but no answer. I'd been wrong to walk away, but if I'd stayed longer, the chance of punches being thrown between Cohen and me would have been higher.

Cohen sits, his face unreadable. "Georgia's told me some."

I nod, unsure what *some* is.

"She said you slept together before I introduced you, that it was a one-time thing, hasn't happened since, and you mutually agreed to keep it private between yourselves."

"That's true." I wait for him to tell me what a piece of shit I am for bailing on her the next morning.

He doesn't.

She didn't tell him.

"Is that why you two constantly argue?"

I shake my head and laugh. "Nah, we have conflicting personalities."

"Not conflicting enough to not sleep together."

I stay quiet, worried of saying the wrong thing.

"Archer, you're a good dude. If you like my sister, I'm okay with it. I'm not jumping over the moon, given if you hurt her, it'd fuck up our business relationship. I care about you both. I'll leave you two to handle your business and make your own decisions without worrying if I'll be mad. I know I talk a lot of shit about my friends staying away from my sister, but I'd never allow someone I thought was a terrible guy to be my friend."

I don't tell him I can't date his sister.

I don't tell him that if I try, I'll break her heart more than I already have.

When Lincoln got home that night, we had it out. He was pissed that I'd ditched him and texted him later, telling him to quit flirting with Georgia and to find his own damn way home. It was a dick move, but I'd had to get out of there. The next argument came when he told me to stop throwing my life away.

Cohen slaps his hands onto his legs and brings himself up. "That's all I needed to say. Whatever you do, that's on you."

When he leaves, I grab my phone and hit Georgia's name, hoping she answers this time.

Me: We need to talk.

I'm surprised when it beeps thirty seconds later.

Georgia: I don't think that's necessary.

Me: I do.

Georgia: I don't.

Me: I'm coming over.

Georgia: I'm not letting you in.

Me: I'll stand outside all night then.

Georgia: Bring a sleeping bag then, stalker.

Me: I'll be there in 15.

Georgia: I won't be waiting up.

I grab my keys, leave my office, and head to Georgia's place.

———

GRACE ANSWERS THE DOOR, wearing the dirtiest look she can manage, which is laughable.

"What do you want, Archer?" she snaps, resting her hand on her waist.

"Is Georgia here?"

"Yep." She taps her foot, her stare cautious.

"Can I come in and talk to her?"

"One moment, please." She slams the door in my face, and I hear her yell Georgia's name before saying, "Asshole Archer is here."

She opens the door again, steps out of my way, and points down the hall.

It's my first time in their townhome. They recently moved into Jamie's place after she moved in with Cohen. It's nice, but I'm too preoccupied to take a good look around. Making shit right with Georgia is my objective, not admiring the fucking wallpaper.

Georgia is standing in her doorway, her hip nudged against the doorframe, with her arms crossed. "Why are you here? I told you not to come."

"And I told you I was anyway."

I stand a few inches from her, not wanting to creep too much into her space yet. She hesitates, staring so hard at me, as if she's attempting to read my soul. Her hair is down with two messy pigtail-looking buns on the top of her head, and her sweatpants are so large that I'm positive they're Cohen's. At least, that's what I want to tell myself and pretend there's no way they could be another man's.

I'm surprised and grateful when she steps to the side and waves me into her bedroom.

Backing up, she falls onto her bed, grabs a bright purple shag pillow, tugs it against her stomach, and sits cross-legged. "Why are you here?"

I walk deeper into her bedroom. "You're seriously fucking asking me that?"

"I'm seriously fucking asking you that."

"We haven't spoken since the party."

"That's a problem?"

"Jesus, Georgia. Yes, that's a goddamn problem. What we were afraid of happening—Cohen finding out—happened, and you're acting clueless as to why we should talk."

She tightens her hold on the pillow. "I'm well aware of what happened." She taps her chin. "You left me there, by myself, to clean up the mess. I was already worked up after you demanded you have a say in who I can and can't sleep with." She shifts her finger from her chin and points at me. "Then Cohen walked in, and you bailed. I had to force a smile and go back to the party because, unlike you, I don't run away like a scared bitch when problems arise. I put on a brave face and handle it."

Guilt seeps up my throat. If I could go back in time, I'd stay. I'd stay, and poor Noah's room would have some damage to it. In my head, I was thinking about Cohen. He needed time to calm down before we talked. I should've thought more about Georgia and how it would affect her.

"I've been putting on a brave face for years, Georgia." My honesty shocks us both. I sit on the edge of her bed. "I came here to apologize. What I said and how I acted was wrong. Hell, after all these years, all the shit I've done and how I've treated you is wrong."

I fucked us up.

Fucked up everything.

Fucked her up.

At that moment, I realize I've been selfish, doing all this to her.

I should've made it clear in the beginning that there was never a chance for us. Instead, I sent mixed signals.

Fucked with her head and her heart.

"I appreciate the apology," she says gently and genuinely.

"This should help with the tension, Cohen knowing."

"Mm-hmm." She nods in agreement. "Does this mean you'll stop acting like I'm the plague you want to steer clear of?"

I wish things were different, wish that I could apologize with more than words. That I could lay her down and ask for forgiveness with my lips, my tongue, my body. I'd slide into her and whisper how much she meant to me.

How my dead heart can't stop pounding against my chest when she's around.

How, even with her arguing, she's kept me going more than she'll ever know.

How she's helped heal me without even knowing about it.

I nod. "I want the bullshit, the games, to stop."

She raises a brow. "Is that you saying you want to be friends?"

"I guess so." This is us settling—something that's necessary but also hurts.

"Friends?" She holds out her hand.

I shake it. "Friends."

One word.

One word I hate when it comes to her.

We'll try, but we'll never be able to go back and start fresh.

CHAPTER THIRTY

Georgia

FRIENDS.

The word hurt when it left my mouth.

I've never been friends with Archer.

We've been one-night lovers and enemies.

But never friends.

We will never be just friends.

Always people who shared an extraordinary night together before one crushed the other.

I've never seen Archer as a friend—only a man who broke my heart and never let me break into an inch of his.

I inhale a deep breath to stop the tears from surfacing. "Friends it is."

There's an uncomfortableness in the room.

Like the air even knows we're lying.

Archer and I have two emotions, two sides to our relationship.

Anger and lust.

Arguing and wanting each other.

No friendship qualities there.

Even though we're calling a truce, I know friends isn't much of an option for us.

I can try.

I can pretend.

It'll be the same as we've been since our morning after, changing my life.

My heart.

Any relationship I have had and will ever have.

"As your new friend, can I ask you one question?" I half-whisper, pulling fuzz off my pillow, unable to meet his gaze.

He slaps my bed. "Shoot."

"Why'd you leave that morning?" I hug the pillow tight. "What did I do to deserve that? To make me feel worthless, like some trash that you were done with?" I hate that a single tear runs down my cheek, and I use my arm to cover it, masking the hurt, as I've done all along.

Masking it with anger.

With sarcasms.

With *I hate you*s.

I tense, preparing to hear that I was a bad fuck, that it was all his drunken dick wanting me, all the reasons he's thrown at me.

"I never planned to leave that morning," he answers, his voice raspy. "If there's anything I wish I had done differently, I wish I'd never taken you to my bed that night."

I wince. "Is that supposed to make me feel better?"

"You deserved better than what I did. You deserve better than me."

"Why'd you leave that morning, Archer?" My tone turns harsh and demanding.

"I was out of coffee, so I went to the coffee shop and picked up some doughnuts. You were sleeping when I got home, and then my mother called in hysterics." He drums his fingers along my comforter. "The reality of my dad being locked up had finally hit her. She'd been holding on to hope that it wouldn't happen—that he and Lincoln would go free because we had expensive lawyers with great records. She'd taken an extra mood stabilizer to help, but it did the opposite— causing her to have a complete meltdown. I had to leave to be with her. I almost—*al-fucking-most*—went to wake you up to tell you I had to go, but when I walked into the room and saw you sleeping, I knew you deserved better than me—a guy who was questioning whether he should ditch you. And even if I had stayed or woken you up, I'd never be the man for you—the kind of man a woman like you deserves."

My voice is hesitant when I ask, "How do you know what I need?"

"Someone who isn't an asshole, who doesn't, for one moment, think about leaving you the next morning."

"Archer, it was for your mom." That doesn't make his excuse acceptable, but I hate that he had to endure that—to see his mother broken.

"The kind of man for you would've woken you up, explained the situation, and given you his number." He scoots forward, toward me, and stretches out his arm, wiping tears from my cheek.

Here we go with the damn tears again.

I need to learn to get control over these damn things.

"I'm sorry for everything," he croaks out, his hand massaging my cheek. "I have a lot of regrets in this fucked-up life of mine, one of them being what I did to you, how I broke a heart so big—broke a woman who didn't deserve it. For that, along with everything else, I'm sorry."

"Why didn't you just tell me?"

"It's embarrassing. I'd be dragging someone into this life, a depressing fucking ditch, and I never want to do that. You deserve someone to shine light into your life, like you will theirs, and that's not me. I'm not a fucking ray of sunshine like you."

I pull away from him and level my eyes on his handsome yet desolate face. "Are you kidding me? Do you remember how broken I was that night? You provided light for me then, one of the days when my heart was broken more than anything. *You.* You have no right to tell me what will and won't provide lightness in my darkness."

"I'm glad I was there for you then." He blows out a breath and takes a look around. "I like your room. It screams you."

Nice change of subject there, ole buddy, ole pal.

"Thanks." I smile timidly.

I haven't finished decorating my room, but I hung strands of white lights behind my bed and a stardust tapestry on another, and I completed the look with a rattan mirror. My bedding is white and covered in bright-colored shag pillows.

"I'll stop bugging you now." He claps his hands and rubs them together.

No, wait!

Stay!

Stay to make up for when you didn't.

Stay and tell me that you don't hate me.

"Good night, Georgia." He kisses the tip of my nose, shocking me, and stands. A short wave is his last move before he leaves my bedroom.

For so long, this man has denied himself, has denied me, of any type of intimacy.

Friendly, romantic, anything.

Just the brush of his lips against the tip of my nose lights me up.

I love this man, and now, I have to be friends with him.

———

"GEORGIA," Lincoln asks when I walk in the bar and head toward the exit after picking up my tip outs. "Have you seen Archer?"

"No?"

Why's he asking me?

I'm the last person Archer would report his whereabouts to.

A week has passed since he came into my bedroom and delivered his truths, and we declared ourselves friends. We've been civil at the bar, tossed a few jokes around, but I don't see us trading friendship bracelets anytime soon.

Friends.

Ha.

That was a fake-as-fuck declaration.

"No one can get in touch with him," Lincoln continues, holding up his phone.

That's odd.

Archer never misses a day or calls off.

"Do you have any idea where he could be?" he asks, his tone bordering frantic.

"No idea. He's, uh … not that open with me, if you haven't noticed."

"He wasn't always that way, you know."

"Are you talking when he was, like, six months old, when he couldn't call people names and stomp around because someone had stolen his pacifier?"

"No, it's just … sometimes, shit happens that changes you."

"Like what?"

"Not my story to tell, babe. Not my story to tell."

I nod, accepting the answer I expected. "Maybe he's taking a nap?"

Lincoln slumps in his stool. "Nah, I doubt he'll be sleeping much today. It isn't a good day for him … for our family."

"Why?"

He shakes his head, not answering me.

"If I hear from him, I'll let you know."

He smiles sullenly. "Thank you."

I call Archer when I get into my car.

No answer.

I turn the ignition, and it hits me.

I know where he is.

CHAPTER THIRTY-ONE

Archer

IF THERE WAS a day I could kick out of the calendar, it'd be today.

Every year, it haunts me.

I've attempted different ways to handle my regret.

Sleep.

Booze.

Sex.

No matter what, there's no escaping my conscience.

Tonight, I've chosen booze.

"Fancy seeing you here."

My heartbeat kicks up a notch at the familiar voice—that sweet, silky voice of hers. The stool next to me is dragged out, and Georgia casually drops onto the seat.

Recollection of the last time we were here zips through my blood —a diversion from my shame.

A recollection of when we attempted to booze through it.

Then sex through it.

I knock back my Hennessy before saying, "What are you doing here?"

Her voice is soothing as she answers, "Thought I could use a drink."

I lick my bottom lip, the taste of warm spice on it. "Lincoln send you?"

She shakes her head. "No, but he is looking for you."

"Does he know I'm here?"

She shakes her head. "I took a guess that you'd be here, but I haven't told anyone."

"Go home, Georgia, and don't tell Lincoln where I am. This has been my perfect hiding spot for years. I don't feel like finding another."

"Your secret hiding place is safe with me." She hums. "Just return the favor if I ever go MIA."

"Go home," I repeat, biting out each word.

In typical Georgia style, instead of listening, she signals to the bartender. "I need a drink." Her attention returns to me after she orders a Coke. "I'll go home when you go home."

I whistle, catching the bartender's attention, and hold up my glass. He nods in understanding.

"Prepare to stay here all night."

"I'd better order some nachos to go with my Coke then, huh?"

This might be what I need.

She might be who I need.

Not screwing her but talking to her.

She blows out a breath. "What's going on, Archer?"

"Why does it seem like this is our place?" I ask, in need of a subject change.

"Talk to me."

And she doesn't take the bait.

"Even if it's small, talk to me."

"Once upon a time, there was a princess who lived in a castle—"

She shoves my shoulder. "Funny. Why are you here, and what is today to you?"

"Go home." I have a feeling I'll be saying that a lot tonight.

"Not happening." She smiles when the bartender delivers her Coke, and she orders nachos. "You came to me when I was here. Consider this me returning the favor."

"Does it end the same way?"

"Negative." Her comforting gaze tugs at my heart. "Lincoln said this was a rough day for your family. Why?"

"How did my telling you to leave lead you to believe I'd spill my heart out to you?"

"You're wasting your breath, telling me to go, because you know that won't happen."

I stay quiet.

"Your brother ... all of us ... we're worried about you."

"Tell him ... them ... *you* that I'm fine."

She talks to herself. "Archer said he's fine even though he's most definitely not fine." She pulls out her phone. "I'm at least telling him you're okay."

I eye her suspiciously. "Don't tell him where I am."

"My lips are sealed." She does a zip motion over her mouth. "I don't want anyone knowing about this place either."

"Oh, so is this your place now too?"

"Apparently so." She bumps her shoulder against mine. "I think there's room for the two of us."

She unlocks her phone, her fingers jabbing letters on the screen, and I hear a *swoop* sound when she hits send.

Sliding the phone into her bag, she gives me her undivided attention. "Lincoln knows you're okay, and I told him I'd keep an eye on you."

"I don't need a babysitter."

"Consider me ... less of a babysitter and more as company." When the bartender drops the nacho bowl in front of her, she smiles and thanks him. "I'll sit here silently and devour these nachos." She slides the bowl over to me. "Want some?"

I shake my head as she grabs one, shoving a chip in her mouth before licking the cheese off her fingers.

She eats, offering me nachos every three minutes, and drinks her Coke.

I sulk and drink cognac.

I'm not sure how much time passes before she wraps her hand around my arm.

"Come on. Let's get you home."

I shake my head. "Nah, I'll stay the night here."

"Stay the night here?" Her eyes widen as if I'd lost my mind. "Where are you going to sleep? On the bar?"

"My car."

"Yeah, not happening." She sweeps her hand over the bar. "This isn't the best neighborhood, and you don't do yourself any favors, driving around in that ridiculously expensive car of yours. You'll be a sitting duck, waiting to be robbed." She wiggles her fingers toward me. "Keys."

I tuck my hand into my pocket and slowly drag them out before stopping. "What about your car?"

"Someone would probably pass over a car that resembles a ladybug. I'll drop you off at home and then Uber back."

"I think the fuck not. No way are you taking an Uber that late and coming here. We'll leave my car, and I'll contort myself to get into yours."

"Whatever you say. My goal is to get you out of here. Whether it be in my car, in your car, or on Rollerblades, you need to get home."

I pay our tabs and slide off my stool. I'm not wasted, and I can walk on my own, but watching her help me to her car is comical. I've never been in a car so damn cramped. My head is inches from hitting the top.

She peeks over at me. "Do you want me to go in and grab you a water or something? Please do not puke in my car."

I shake my head before tipping it back on the headrest. "Today is the anniversary of my grandfather's death, and it's my fault he's dead."

CHAPTER THIRTY-TWO

Georgia

HIS WORDS SHOCK ME.

My keys fall from my fingers and onto my lap, and I stare at him, mouth dropped open. "What?"

He angles his head to look at me, not lifting it from the headrest. "It's my fault my grandfather died."

I knew Archer was suffering through an emotional agony, and for years, I racked my brain on what it could be. I didn't expect that.

Questions rapidly hurtle through my brain.

"What?" I stutter. "How?"

His head shifts, so he's no longer looking at me, only blankly staring out the windshield. "He died because I was a selfish prick."

"Can you elaborate on that?"

I want to turn on the light, grab his head, and force him to look at me, but I'm scared he'll stop. Maybe in the dark is the only time he'll open up to me. If I have to stay in the darkness for him, I will.

He sucks in a deep breath.

Exhales.

Deep breath.

Exhales.

"My grandfather was my hero, growing up," he says, his voice thick with emotion. "I was closer to him than my father. The summer after I graduated from college, I moved into his pool house. One night, we got into an argument. He thought I wasn't taking life seriously and was partying too much. To be a little dickhead, I threw a big-ass party at the pool house to spite him. I got drunk, coked out, so fucked up that I didn't care what damage was done." He stops, his voice trailing off, and I wait for him to continue.

Another deep breath.

Another exhale.

I situate myself on my knees, moving in closer, and rest one hand on the center console while using the other to run my hand down his arm, praying he takes it as a touch of comfort.

Deep breath.

Exhale.

"He came home during the party and started cleaning the mess." His voice cracks, nearly shattering me. "He tripped, hit his head, fell into the pool, and drowned."

His shoulders slump, his body slouching in my passenger seat, as he breaks down.

We go quiet, and I process his confession.

"Archer," I finally whisper, moving in closer. "I'm so sorry."

He drags his hand through his hair and tugs at the roots. "He probably screamed for help, but the music was blaring. He wasn't found until hours later, and by the time help came, he was already gone. My father blamed his death on me, and he's right. Had I not thrown that party, been a selfish bastard, that wouldn't have happened. After that, I pulled away from everything in my life—the drugs, money, parties, social life. I wanted nothing to do with it. I was disgusted. It was what had killed my grandfather, and he died, knowing I didn't give a shit."

I move his hand and replace it with mine, dragging my fingers through the strands—an attempt to soothe him. "Archer, it sounds like it was an accident."

"An accident that could've been prevented. He died because of my party."

When he finally looks at me, there's fire in his eyes. I gasp as he grabs my waist, pulls me onto his lap, and smashes his lips into mine.

He grips my face, claiming me, as I wrap my arms around his neck. He kisses me like his life will end if our mouths part. I moan into his mouth when he slides his tongue inside mine, our tongues curling together, and I slowly rock against him.

"Georgia," he moans, his cock hardening underneath me.

I rock faster at the feel of him.

"Georgia," he says, pulling away, and we stare at each other, catching our breaths.

He's breathing heavily while staring up at me. "Georgia, you need to take me home and drop me off, and if I beg you to come in, don't."

My head is still spinning from his kiss. "What?"

"If you come home with me, I will fuck you. I will use you to forget what today is. Don't you dare allow that to happen."

Nothing kills a mood more than the guy saying he'd be using you.

"Well then," I mutter, doing the crawl of shame off his lap. I fetch my keys that fell onto the floorboard and shove one into the ignition, the smell of lust lingering in the small confines of my car. "Can you plug your address into a GPS, so I know where I'm going?"

The last time we left from this bar to go to his place, it was in an Uber. I'd been drinking, and his hand was up my dress, so it was kinda hard to pay attention to when we turned right and left.

He nods, grabs my phone, and punches in his address.

"Thank you," I whisper.

Our ride is silent, our mood somber, while I drive to his penthouse.

How did we go from dry-humping to hardly muttering a word to each other in minutes?

I shift my car into park when we reach his place. "I can't leave you alone."

"Lincoln should be here."

I pull out my phone and text Lincoln.

Lincoln: Hold tight. I'll be right down.

He turns to look at me, his face inches from mine, before he comes closer and nudges his nose against mine. "I'm sorry, Georgia."

We jump when my passenger door swings open, and Lincoln stares down at us.

"How the hell did you manage to get in this car?"

CHAPTER THIRTY-THREE

Archer

"COME ON, MAN," Lincoln says, helping me out of the car before glancing at Georgia, who's next to him. "Thank you."

She smiles, and it lights up my drunken ass before I step out of the car. "Of course."

I stabilize myself and swat Lincoln's hand away. "I can walk."

The last thing I need is my doorman thinking I'm a hot mess and complain about me to the building manager. They're strict about that shit here. I'm straight as I walk in and step into the elevator, and we land in my penthouse.

"You got him?" Georgia asks Lincoln while I grab a water from the fridge.

Lincoln nods. "I'll take good care of him."

I point at Georgia with the water bottle and drag my drunken ass toward the couch. "Pretty sure you'd take better care of me."

Her cheeks turn a bright red, and I can't stop myself from smiling when I see the evidence of my beard rubbing against her face.

We touched. We kissed. I had her in my arms again.

As much as it killed me, I had to stop her.

She deserves better than coming home with me and having drunk sex again.

If I ever get the luxury of touching her again, I need to be clearheaded.

Lincoln turns to Georgia. "Thanks for taking care of him, babe. I appreciate it."

I snarl at him calling her *babe*.

"You're welcome." Georgia's attention slides to me. "Good night, you guys."

"Night," I say, my voice tight.

Don't go.

It pisses me off further when Lincoln walks her down to her car and not me.

I fucked up.

I'm fucked up.

I hang my head low and raise it when Lincoln returns. "Don't flirt with her. Don't call her babe again," I hiss.

Lincoln halts in his steps. "What?"

"Georgia. She's not your *babe*."

He looks at me like I've lost my mind before shaking his head. "Nope. I'm not taking that bait so that you have someone to argue with. My feelings toward Georgia are strictly platonic."

"Good, because she's mine."

"Yours, huh?" He walks farther into the room. "You sure don't seem to claim what's yours. If she's *yours*, why do you keep pushing her away, the only woman who seems capable of putting up with your miserable ass?"

"Fuck you," I snarl.

"Fuck me?" He releases a cold laugh. "I was worried sick about you. I called Mom, the police, even the hospital. You were too selfish to even tell anyone you weren't dead."

"I needed space. I'm tired of people thinking they can fix me every year on this day."

"You sure didn't need space from Georgia," he mutters before catching himself. "Look, I don't even give a shit if it's not me you want to talk to, but a heads-up that you're alive would be nice."

I let out a wicked laugh. "Lincoln, always the martyr of the family."

"Don't start that shit."

"The dude who put his freedom on the line for his family. Who makes sure his brother is alive. Who still attends his mother's parties."

"Don't pity yourself. It's a bad look."

"You doing a stint in the pen isn't a bad look?"

"I'm going to act like you didn't try to throw that shit in my face because you're drunk and hurting. Sue me for being loyal."

"That loyalty put you in prison!" I scream.

He shakes his head and lowers his voice. "It did, and *here we go* with this same bullshit conversation. I went to prison. You blame Dad. I'm out. It's time to move the hell on."

I work my jaw. "Do you regret it?"

"I don't blame anyone but myself. I'm a big boy."

"He played your ass," I release around a snarl. "Straight played your ass."

The more shit I talk, the redder Lincoln's face gets, his patience dwindling.

Good. Let him sucker punch me like Dad did that night.

It's what I deserve.

He stands tall, crossing his arms, and anchors his attention to me. "This beef between you and Dad needs to end. No one played me. I wasn't innocent. I knew about the transfers and the offshore accounts. I didn't participate, but I warned him."

I drop my head into my hands, shaking it. "I hate being fucked up in the head."

Lincoln collapses on the opposite end of the sectional. "Everyone is a little fucked up in the head. It's what makes us who we are."

"You're a good brother." I remove my hands, one by one, and stare at him with affection. "A good son."

"So are you."

I shake my head and scoff. "I'm a shit brother, a shit son, a shit person."

"You and Dad need to talk."

"Nothing to talk about. I will never forgive him for blocking me from attending grandfather's funeral, for throwing it in my face day after day that it was my fault he'd died, and drunkenly saying he wished I were the one who had died."

Lincoln shuts his eyes, the memory paining him. That was a tough time for our family, and Lincoln always played referee. "I think it's time you see him."

"You're right."

———

I'VE MADE the drive countless times.

The difference is, I'm visiting someone new.

Someone I swore I never would.

The process is the same—show ID, get searched, walk through a metal detector, wait, and then enter a room filled with inmates until you spot who you're looking for at a table. One advantage of being in a low-security federal prison is, they aren't as strict on you.

My father stares at me from his chair with folded arms and raised eyebrows. Gone is the wealthy and confident man I once knew. His face has aged, his hair peppered with gray sprinkles and thinning, and the suit he's sporting is no longer designer. While Lincoln came out of prison fit, my father isn't in that same boat.

"This is quite the surprise," he comments as I take the chair across from him.

I clear my throat before speaking, "Trust me, even with the long drive to process it, I'm shocked I'm here."

He strokes his chin. "Why'd you come?"

I tap my foot. "It's time we clear the air."

He nods. "Agreed."

I get straight to the point. No use for small talk until we come to terms with our issues and work them out. "Why do you keep asking Mom for me to visit? Why do you keep calling?"

He pinches the skin between his eyebrows with two fingers. "Even before my sentencing, we hadn't held a conversation in years. No matter what, I'm your father, and you're my son."

His son.

"The son you blamed for murdering your father." My jaw clenches.

"You banned me from his funeral, wouldn't allow me the opportunity to say good-bye to my own grandfather."

"Archer." He releases a long breath. "You have to understand my anger."

"I do. You lost someone you loved, but so did I."

"He died because of your negligence, your selfishness."

"Like father, like son then, huh?" I scoff. "You didn't kill someone, but you put your son in prison."

He winces. "Lincoln and I are working through our issues, and it doesn't concern you. You can't compare prison to death."

"Do you really ..." My voice trails off momentarily. "Do you honestly think *I* killed him?"

He works his strong jaw before replying, "Did you push him into the pool or hold his head underwater? No. But your actions resulted in his death. I'll never go back on that, go back on the truth."

"Wow." I shake my head, planting my palms on the table. "Coming here was a mistake."

He nods in agreement. "You didn't come here to make amends. You came to argue, to vent out your frustrations since his anniversary was a few days ago."

I stand. "Go fuck yourself. Don't call me. Don't speak to me again."

"Archer—"

I turn around and leave.

CHAPTER THIRTY-FOUR

Georgia

"I DON'T CARE what anyone says, no one serves margaritas and queso like La Mesa," I say, shoving a chip dripping with queso into my mouth.

"I swear, you'd think I raised you in a barn," Cohen comments from across the table, eyeing me from over his menu and shaking his head.

Noah stares up at him, blinking. "You raised Aunt Georgia in a barn?" He frowns. "Why can't we live in a barn? I love barns because that's where they have horses!" He shakes his chip in the air, shoves it in the queso bowl, and tosses it in his mouth.

Like aunt, like nephew.

Cohen didn't raise no queso haters.

The older Noah gets, the more he reminds me of Cohen. His chestnut-colored hair has grown out and is spiked up with gel, and he's sporting his *Single & Unemployed* shirt—a gift from me. He has the sweetest smile, which cons me out of cupcakes like crazy. Every time I babysit, the kid needs his cupcakes. To which I gladly oblige.

"Oh shit, look who showed up," Finn calls out.

"Language," Grace warns in her teacher voice, jerking her head toward Noah.

"Archer!" Noah shouts, throwing up his arms and swinging them in the air.

At his name, I glance up and train my eyes on Archer and Lincoln approaching us. My mouth waters for more than a margarita. The Callahan men are a sight for sore eyes.

Archer's broad shoulders are covered by a black tee and his hair pulled back into a loose man bun. The man bun isn't a frequent style for him, and I never thought I'd be attracted to them before Archer came along.

Archer has switched up my type.

Shitty attitude.

Allergic to fun.

Plays mind games.

Scruff and man bun.

I scrunch up my face.

He's been a total fuckboy, but after our night at Bailey's, I've grown more understanding of him. It's not an excuse for his behavior, but I know where his pain comes from now.

"How the hell did you convince him to come?" Finn asks, resulting in a playful elbow nudge from Grace. "He's turned us down for Taco Tuesday for years."

Lincoln chuckles, rubbing his hand over his strong jaw. "I told him it was either we come here or I was inviting you over to his place."

"Suckered," Grace says, laughing.

Today is my first time seeing Archer since the night at Bailey's. He texted me an hour after I left, thanking me for taking care of him, and I texted him the next morning to check on him. Neither one of us mentioned the whole *dry-humping in the car* event.

It all finally makes sense.

Why Archer is the way he is and why his family claims he hasn't always been this way. I can't imagine the pain he had when it happened, the guilt he lives with day after day. It makes me want him more, makes me want to help heal him.

That night, when I slid into bed, all I thought about was his mouth on mine. The taste of his tongue. His hands on me. His secrets he'd given to me.

Surprising everyone, Archer takes the chair next to mine. He smiles and doesn't seem fazed that everyone is eyeing him as though he's lost his mind.

"I think motherfucking hell has frozen over but granted me with tacos for some good deeds I did," Finn says.

Grace slaps his shoulder. "Really?"

"Nah," Silas says. "Last I heard, they don't serve tacos in hell."

"Can you guys please stop cussing in front of my kid?" Cohen says in his best dad voice.

"It's okay," Noah says. "I know cuss words, like *shit* and *fu*—"

Jamie cups her hand around his mouth. "Enough of that talk."

"Jamie," Lola gasps. "What are you teaching him?"

Cohen drags his finger down the table, motioning to us. "It's all of you that have no filter."

They start arguing about what words Noah learned where—most of them probably coming from me—and I stare over at Archer.

"How have you been?" I ask, keeping my voice down.

He bows his head, his tone just as low. "Better. Not good, but better."

I offer a small smile. "I'm glad."

"Thank you for being there for me, Georgia." He shuts his eyes and blows out a breath. "My night would've ended a lot worse had you not hunted me down and stayed with me."

"You're finally realizing that no matter what, you can't get rid of me?"

He chuckles. "This is easier, you know. We went about it all wrong."

"What's easier?"

"Us not pretending to hate each other."

"It is, isn't it?"

He gestures to the table. "So this is Taco Tuesday, huh?"

"See what you've been missing?"

He laughs—something I've rarely heard from him. It's deep and husky and manly, and it shoots straight into my soul.

When I glance away from him, I notice everyone's attention is pinned in our direction, even Noah's. Our friends know *something* happened between us, but the only ones who know the full story are Grace and Lola. I doubt Archer is telling people he ditched me that morning. Lola says Silas pressed her for details, but she wouldn't budge. Then Silas brought his interrogation to me, which I ignored. He didn't even bother taking it to Archer.

"Carry on," Archer says, and they return to their different tasks—dipping chips into salsa, studying the menu, grabbing their phones—pretending we're not their chosen entertainment.

As much as I want to ask him a hundred questions about our night at Bailey's, I hold back. This isn't the place for that convo.

"How annoying was Lincoln to get you here?"

"On a scale from one to ten, a good fifteen."

I smile. "I like your brother. He's good for you."

"I'm glad he's home." He opens the menu. "What do you suggest?"

"Uh …" I chew on my bottom lip. "The margaritas are to die for."

"Not much of a margarita man."

My hand dramatically flies to my chest. "Have you ever had a margarita?"

He doesn't answer.

"Shut up." I slap his arm. "You've never had one, have you?"

"Again, do I look like a margarita man?" He gestures to himself.

"You are tonight." I call over our waiter. "Top-shelf margarita for my man over here."

"Nah, I'm good," Archer argues.

"He's good to order one." I smile at the waiter. "Make that two. One for him. One for me."

"Look at Georgia, bossing Archer around like she's his babysitter," Silas says. "I never thought I'd see the day."

"Aunt Georgia is the best babysitter ever!" Noah chimes in. "She buys me extra cupcakes and lets me have sugar in my Cheerios."

Cohen narrows his eyes at me.

I shrug, ignoring Cohen's dirty look. "They don't make it sweet enough."

The waiter drops off our margaritas, and I wait for Archer to take a drink before touching mine. It's almost comical, watching him tip his head down and suck the margarita goodness from the straw.

He swallows it, his face puckering. "Sweet as hell, but not too bad."

I smile. "Don't lie. You love it."

He chuckles.

I laugh.

And I wish we'd had this all along.

———

"YOU KNOW he's in love with you, right?" Lincoln says, stealing Archer's chair after he leaves for a restroom break.

"What?"

Did he say that, or were the margs stronger than what I thought?

He jerks his head in the direction Archer headed. "My brother. He's in love with you."

I snort. "Yeah, right."

He leans back in his chair, tents his hands together, and holds them to his mouth. "Archer Callahan is here for Taco Tuesday. You think that's the norm for him?"

"Well, no," I answer softly, chewing on my bottom lip. "You told him it was either come here or there'd be a party at his place. It's no surprise he chose here."

Archer has feelings for me; there's no denying that.

But *love?*

That's on a completely different level.

That's on *my* level.

He chuckles. "Come on. You know Archer would kick each one of you out if he didn't want you there. He's here because he thought I'd flirt and then fall in love with you too. He's pissed I call you babe."

I'm silent, processing Lincoln's claim.

Lincoln squeezes my shoulder. "Give him time, Georgia. He's opening up to you. Hell, he talked to you about our grandfather's death—something he hasn't done with me, my parents, or his ex. You're someone to him, and the closer you two grow, the clearer it gets."

———

I'M IN BED, tossing peanut M&M's in my mouth and catching up on *Schitt's Creek* when my phone vibrates. Setting my snack to the side, I stretch across my bed and snatch my phone off my nightstand.

Lincoln: Can you do me a favor?

Weird. Lincoln never randomly texts me.

Me: Depends on what it is. No, I won't have your baby. Yes, I will let you buy me a new car.

Lincoln: I know it's late, but can you go to the bar?

No smart-ass response. Not good.

Me: Okay ...

Lincoln: Go see Archer there. It's important. I'll explain later.

Me: Give me 15.

Lincoln: Thank you.

I jump out of bed, slip on my shoes, and snatch my M&M's container for the road. Lincoln's text caught me off guard, and my stomach knots harder with every mile I get closer to the bar.

I swerve into the back parking lot, scurry to the door, and let myself in. The bar is silent—no shocker since we're closed—and I stroll down the unlit hall. When I reach Archer's office, the light is on, and the door is cracked open.

I knock.

No answer.

Holding my breath, I peek through the opening. Archer's shoulders are hunched forward in his chair, and his head is in his hands.

"Archer, are you okay?" I ask, hesitating before tiptoeing into his office.

I gasp when he lifts his head.

His face is red.

Tearstained.

"Archer," I repeat, "are you okay?"

I've seen this man resentful—the night his father went to prison.

I've seen him sad—the anniversary of his grandfather's death.

But this is different.

This is broken.

I creep closer.

"My dad is dead," he states with a restrained stare.

I halt. "What?"

"He had a heart attack. He's dead."

I tense, my hand clutching my chest. "Oh my God. I'm so sorry."

His chest rises and falls with rapid breaths. "I visited him for the first time in prison last week. It didn't go well. The entire time he was locked up, I ignored his calls. We hated each other." He slams his hand onto his desk. "He died in prison. We'd argued, and I'd told him to go fuck himself." He bitterly scoffs. "I argue with someone, and then they die. I'm the goddamn angel of death."

He keeps his vacant stare forward when I stand next to him.

"Archer," I whisper, "that's not true."

"Appreciate you trying to make me feel better, but it is."

"Look at me."

He spins in his chair, and his gaze cuts to me before he rises. I gasp when his lips crash into mine—hard and needy and desperate. He slips an arm around my waist, yanking my body to his, and his tongue slips into my mouth. I taste him while he devours my mouth—the flavor of his booze drawing me in. Picking me up, he steadies me on the edge of the desk, my ass slightly slipping off. He parts my legs and settles his large body between them.

"I need you," he groans into my mouth. "I need to be inside you."

Reaching down, he roughly tugs at the drawstring of my sweats, and just as he's shoving his hand down them, I push him back.

"No. I refuse to be your distraction or how you cope with your loss." I shake my head. "You're not releasing your pain by screwing me."

"Let me eat your pussy then," he pleads. "Let me suck on your clit. *Please.*"

It's tempting.

There's nothing I'd love more than his hands, his tongue, getting me off.

He retreats a step when I slide off the desk and tie my sweats.

"I'll be here for you, but I'm not sleeping with you." I hold out my hand. "I'll drive you home."

"Nah, I'm sleeping here."

"You're not sleeping here." I snap my fingers. "Let's go, or I'll call Lincoln to come get you."

Speaking of Lincoln ...

How's he doing?

He captures my hand, his grip tight as though I'm his lifeline. Not a word is spoken while I lead him out of the building, lock up, and we walk to my car. I assist him into it, but he moves my hand when I try to buckle the seat belt and clicks it himself.

"Have you talked to Lincoln?" I ask, turning out of the parking lot.

"He's with my mother."

"Do you want me to take you there?"

He shakes his head. "She asked to be alone. I asked to be alone. Lincoln understood my request but was worried about Mom, so he's there with her."

He scrubs at his eyes with his knuckles and tips his head back, not muttering a word during the drive.

When I reach his building, he shifts and settles his gaze on me, torment in his eyes. "Will you stay?"

My eyes widen, and I shake my head.

"Not for sex. To keep me company, so I don't lose my goddamn mind."

"I thought you wanted to be alone?"

"It's different with you. I like to be alone or *with you*. You put me at ease, giving me a peace I've never experienced." He reaches out and strokes my face with the pad of his thumb. "Stay."

"I told you—"

"I'll sleep on the couch; you can have my bed. Just stay with me." Silent tears fall down his cheeks.

"Okay, I'll stay."

His shoulders relax, and after parking, we walk into his building. Swinging his arm back, he snatches my hand and leads me to the penthouse.

I drop his hand when we walk in. "I need to text Lincoln and let him know you're okay."

He nods, kisses my forehead, and heads into the kitchen.

Me: He's home, safe and sound. I'm so sorry about your dad.

Lincoln: Mom popped an Ambien and is sleeping. I can come home.

I join Archer in the kitchen and read him the text message.

"Tell Lincoln to stay his ass there."

I follow him into the living room, and he collapses on the couch as I'm replying to Lincoln.

Me: He said to stay your ass there.

Lincoln: Not surprising.

Me: I told him I'd stay.

Lincoln: You're amazing. Thank you, Georgia … for everything.

My next text goes to Cohen. I tell him the news and ask him to cover Archer's shift tomorrow night. Archer might not like it, but he needs time to heal.

Sex, working too much, locking up your pain—it will only last so long. Archer has reached his breaking point.

"Can I get you something to drink?" I ask.

"Shit, sit down, Georgia." He shakes his head and rubs at his eyes with the heels of his palms. "Here we are again, you coming to my rescue when it should be the other way around." His voice cracks. "Do you see it now? Why you're too good for me?"

I settle in the space next to him. "Archer, everyone has their issues. Right now, yours are more intense than mine, but I'm sure, somewhere along the road, I'll need you too."

His stares at me vacantly. "Lincoln is crashing in the guest room, so you can have my bed."

"Okay," I whisper, not pushing.

Now isn't the time for relationship talk. He needs time to grieve. Despite his relationship with his father, he's hurting. His wet eyes, broken voice, and desperation are clear.

He stands and jerks his head toward a hall. "I'll show you where it is."

Not that I need the tour.

I've been here before—in this home, in his bedroom, in his bed. The massive bed has a new duvet cover, going from white to black, but everything else is the same.

"Do you need something to sleep in?"

I shake my head. "No, this is fine."

He awkwardly stands in the doorway, his face slack. "Watch a movie with me? Hang out for a minute? Stay with me longer."

I nod and walk out of the bedroom. He rests his hand along my back as we return to the living room. As soon as I sit on the couch, he's dragging me into his arms.

"My last words to him were *fuck off* and *don't speak to me again*," he whispers into my ear, settling my back to his chest.

I reach up, gripping the back of his neck before massaging it. "You didn't know this would happen. You were angry and thought you would have time to make it right, to cool off."

"Did I, though?" He relaxes into my touch. "I told him never to talk to me again, and now, he's gone."

My chest trembles as the man behind me struggles to hold in his hurt, his body shaking behind me—shaking my heart into despair because he's experiencing this pain, this hurt, and just like with this grandfather, he's depositing blame onto his shoulders.

We don't watch TV. I stay with him.

Our breathing is the only noise until he says, "I'm sorry ... for everything I've put you through." He squeezes me tight, as if pushing his apology so far into me that he can never take it back. "Now, I know the power of my words, and I'll never do anything to hurt another person I care about."

I drop my hand and rest it over his arm on my stomach. As I stay tucked in his hold, we drift to sleep. I yawn, my eyes sleepy, when he wakes me hours later and carries me to his bed.

———

IT'S ROUND TWO.

Round two of waking up in his bed.

My stomach twists at the reminder of why I'm in his bed, my heart aching for him all over again. I shift when I hear a light snore and find Archer asleep next to me. He's over the covers—as if he wanted to keep distance between us—on his back, and fully dressed.

Our second time in his bed.

Our first morning waking up together.

What he did that morning was inexcusable, but as time passes, my forgiveness for him deepens. It could be the optimist in me, my big heart that seems unwilling to yield to hard resentment.

I shut my eyes, casting my thoughts to his anguish and apologies last night. Kissing two fingers, I press them to his cheek, hoping I don't wake him, and I slide out of bed. Yawning, I stroll to the bathroom, use my finger to brush my teeth, and throw my hair into an even messier bun than I did last night.

As I pass him, it hits me that he'll wake up the same as I did that morning. The only difference is, he'll still be in the house, and I'm too exhausted to go hunting for doughnuts. I pad into the kitchen and realize I'll need to go coffee-hunting since Archer has none. As I grab a water and search the cabinets for breakfast food, the door clicks open.

"Oh, hey, Georgia," Lincoln says, walking in with heavy eyes and a face that screams exhaustion.

I smile gently. "Hi."

He glances around. "He still sleeping?"

I nod. "I think he needs it."

"Agreed." He holds up his phone. "I'm ordering coffee. Want some?"

"I thought you'd never ask."

He walks into the living room. I recite my order to him, keeping my voice as low as I can, and he punches it into his phone.

"How are you doing?" I ask, hugging him, my heart breaking for their family. "How's your mom?"

"Not well." He pulls back. "She lost my father to prison, and now, he's gone for good. My grandparents are with her now, so I could run here for a change of clothes and to check on Archer."

"If there's anything I can do to help, I'm here."

"You're too good to us."

"You're my friends, and friends take care of their friends."

"I'm glad you're in his life. You're one of the best things to happen to him."

"Archer?" I ask even though I already know the answer.

He nods. "When he told everyone to leave him alone last night, I knew he meant everyone *but you*. When our grandfather died and his girlfriend tried to comfort him, he only pushed her away. They had been together for years, and he never let her in like he does you—never let *any of us* in."

I swallow a few times before replying, "People say I'm easy to talk to. It's what I want to do for a living—talk to people and help them through their struggles."

"Georgia, the best psychiatrist in the world couldn't get Archer to do the shit you do. It's not that."

Our conversation is interrupted by Archer coming into view, rubbing at his eyes and looking like he'd been run over, then stomped on, and then run over again.

Lincoln envelops Archer in his arms, giving him a tight hug. Archer squeezes him back, patting his back a few times before pulling away. Their eyes are red, their emotions showing through their usual hard, masculine demeanors.

The doorbell rings, and I answer it, grabbing our coffees.

Lincoln wipes his eyes with the back of his arm before taking his coffee and looking at Archer. "I'm heading back to Mom's."

"How's she doing?" Archer asks.

"Handling. We're trying to keep her mind off it. One good thing that came out of this prison mess is, she's not living in the same house as she did with Dad, where she would have been surrounded by memories of them."

He nods in agreement.

Lincoln packs his bag, tells us good-bye, and leaves.

Archer's attention moves to me.

"Coffee?" I ask, holding mine up. "I can share mine with you, but it's on the sweet side. If you don't mind waiting, I can order you something and have it delivered."

He yawns and shakes his head, now wearing shorts and a tee. "I'm good right now." He yawns again.

We maybe slept for three hours, max.

"You might need to go back to bed," I say when he yawns for the third time.

Another yawn, this one longer.

"You might be right." He tips his head toward his bedroom. "You want to stay? You look like you need sleep as much as I do."

Since yawns are contagious, I do it twice. "Maybe a few more hours would be good for us."

I follow him into his bedroom.

"I know I said I'd sleep on the couch last night," he says, slipping under the blankets. "And forgive me, but when we crashed out on the couch, I knew we'd be more comfortable in here. I never touched you since you told me no last night, so you have nothing to worry about."

"It's fine," I say, joining him but keeping plenty of space between us.

In minutes, his breathing turns heavy, and he's back to sleep.

————

ROUND THREE OF waking up in Archer's bed.

I shut my eyes.

What'll it be this time?

I shift from my back to my side, facing him, and my heart beats wildly when my gaze meets his. There's no shock on his face, no disdain. I blink, my brain playing a guessing game of what's in that unpredictable mind of his.

He's flawed perfection as he returns my stare—his eyes hooded, his face unreadable.

I clear the sleepiness from my throat. "How long have you been staring?"

"Not long." He grimaces, as if struck with a sudden pain. "I fucked up."

I tense, doubt charging through me.

Round three is about to get messy.

I slip him a guarded look. "What?"

"I fucked up." His teeth clamps on his lower lip. "This is how we should've woken up that morning, not you in here, alone."

The rejection I expected escapes my thoughts. I'll never forget what he did our first morning, and there will always be a twinge to my heart at the memory, but I'm starting to grasp his reasoning.

"You look perfect here," he says. "Like it's where you belong."

"I feel like this is where I belong," I reply honestly. "It's where I've always wanted to be."

With you.

In your bed.

In your heart.

The bed shifts when he eases closer, and a comfortable warmth fills the air.

"How can you be like this?" he rasps.

"Be like what?"

"So good to me when I've been nothing but a dick to you."

"There's more to you than your anger. You hide behind your pain."

"Not so much with you though, do I?"

Chills spread across my skin when he reaches out to stroke my cheek.

"You're too good to me and too good *for* me."

I tilt my head to the side, into his touch. "That's my decision to make."

His hand drops to my neck, and he captures the necklace he gave me, playing with the charms between two fingers. "I love seeing this on you."

I enfold his hand in mine. "Someone who didn't care, who I was *too good for*, would've never gifted something so meaningful."

He shuts his eyes, and his voice thickens when he drops the necklace. "Georgia, do you still want me?"

My breath catches in my throat, and I repeat his question in my head, as if I misheard him. My heart skitters before battering against my chest.

He stares at me with intent.

Desire radiates between us.

Longing whispers in the air.

His breathing labors as I creep closer, the sheets soft against my skin, until we're inches apart. His breath is chilly against my cheek.

"Always," I answer before brushing my lips against his.

He groans into my mouth.

Our kiss starts slow.

Gentle.

His tongue darts into my mouth.

His heavy hand cups my face as we make out like teenagers, him devouring me.

Everything changes when I grind against him. Long gone is the light kissing, now replaced with an urgency.

"Shit," he hisses into my mouth, wrapping his arm around my waist to tug me close.

Another groan escapes him when I hitch my leg over his waist, and all hell breaks loose. The spark has been lit, and the fire is starting. I'm rolled onto my back, and he climbs over me, our mouths staying connected. I part my legs, giving him access to everything I wish he'd take as his—*make* his. I gasp for breath when he pulls away and stares at me with lust-filled eyes.

"Last night, you said you didn't want to be used to heal my pain, which I understood," he says. "That's not what today is—hell, it wasn't even what last night was. I want you, Georgia—not just intimately— and if you want me to stop, say the word."

"Don't you dare stop." I raise my hips and rub against him.

He groans, throwing his head back, while his hand tugs at the drawstring on my pants. I lift my butt, allowing him to slip them and my panties off me. After he tosses them onto the floor, his eyes flick to me in question, and I nod. Sliding down the bed, he parts my thighs with no hesitation and settles his body between them. His eyes stray, peeking between my legs, and I've never felt so exposed in my life.

Yet I don't feel shy.

My legs are shaking as he sweeps his hands along the inside of my thighs.

"Georgia," he says, staring up at me, "let me make up for the time I should've been doing this, should've been pleasuring you, loving you, showing you how much you mean to me. Let me make up for my stupidity."

I gulp, nodding, and he grips my legs, holding them still. Without wasting a second, he slides the length of his tongue between my folds. My back arches toward the ceiling, and his delivery isn't what I anticipated.

I've had guys go down on me before, but it was nothing like this.

Archer sucks on my clit, shoving two fingers inside me, and I squirm beneath him. He raises my shirt and shoves his hand underneath the cup of my bra, exposing my nipple.

"Please," I beg as he pinches it before squeezing my breast.

I want this to last the rest of my life, but with his fingers and his tongue and *him*, there's no hope for me. When he adds a third finger, I fall apart.

"Yes, come for me, baby," he groans against my core.

I'm still coming down from my high when he lifts himself, his palms slapping on the bed on each side of my body, and claims my mouth.

"See how good you taste?" he hisses between my lips. "I've missed this taste. Have been craving it since our first night together."

Heat rips through my body, begging for another orgasm, and I moan when he peels off my shirt, tossing it across the room. His hand moves to my back, lifting me to unhook my bra. I'm exposed to him, every inch of my body on display.

"Archer," I pant, "I need you inside me."

He stops to shake his head, his eyes meeting mine. "This is for you to feel good. Not me. I don't deserve you yet."

"Your cock inside me will feel good."

He freezes.

I whistle and point at the apex of my thighs. "Your cock, inside me now."

He smirks. "Give me another orgasm, and I'll think about it."

I throw my arms out. "Orgasm me away then."

He chuckles before whispering, "You're beautiful," and runs his hands up and down my thighs. "Perfection," he adds.

And I lose all thoughts as he rains kisses down my body, worshipping every inch of me.

His tongue licks me up and down.

He teases my clit.

I've never been so turned on.

Never wanted someone so desperately in my life.

My need for him is stronger than our first night together.

"Archer," I moan, "please fuck me."

"Say it again," he demands, his voice hoarse.

I tilt my head, all orgasmed/confused out. "Please fuck me?"

"No, my name, say it again."

"Archer."

His name falling from my lips while I'm naked in his bed sets him on fire.

He falls back, shrugs off his tee, and shoves down his shorts, exposing his thick cock. My eyes widen and dart to my parted thighs.

He chuckles. "It'll fit. I promise." Without warning, he shoves two fingers inside me, twisting them. "You're so wet for me, baby. I'll slide right in."

He glides off the bed, kicks off his shorts, opens his nightstand, and grabs a condom. Ripping it open with his teeth, he slides it over his throbbing cock and rejoins me. I gape in anticipation when his heavy body hovers over mine.

He fastens his hands around my wrists, pulls my arms over my head, and tugs them together. "I'm going to take care of you, baby." His lips brush over mine. "Show you that my bullshit will be worth it in the end. Leave these here."

He drops his hands from my wrists and tilts up my waist, and when he slides into me, it's heaven.

Perfection.

Worth the wait.

He wastes no time before pounding into me, and I meet him thrust for thrust, moaning his name. We're sweaty and sticky, and my legs ache.

I'm close to reaching my brink for the third time when he groans, "You feel so damn good. No pussy, no woman, has ever been better, has ever taken my cock better, fucked me better, shown me love better."

His words set me off.

Pleasure shatters through me, and a few pumps later, he shoots his load into the condom.

CHAPTER THIRTY-FIVE

Archer

"I HATE that you have to go," I groan.

Now that I have her, I want to keep her.

In my bed. In my arms. In my life.

"Trust me"—she peeks over at me, shyness in her eyes—"I'd love for us to stay in bed and forget everything, but we can't." She turns onto her stomach and rests her chin on my chest. "You need to go see your mom."

"Thank you," I whisper. "For being there for me."

She plants a quick peck to my chest. "Thank you for opening up to me, showing me the real you, letting me in, *and* for all the orgasms."

That's Georgia.

Thanking me for showing her the real me—that's all she wants from me.

Oh, and the orgasms.

Coming from my world, that's irregular.

Meredith came with a long list of wants, and her thank-yous came after she received Chanel bags, trips abroad, diamonds.

All it takes for Georgia is a goddamn apology and explanation of why you acted like an idiot.

"It took you long enough to realize this," she adds.

"Yeah, yeah, yeah," I grumble. "We can't all be Georgias."

"The world would be a better place, though." She winks.

"And we'd have more terrible drivers on the street."

I run my hand down her bare back. Waking up next to her this morning was what I'd never known I needed. As I stared at her sleeping, it hit me.

She's changing me.

This spitfire of a woman makes me want to be a better man.

The man my grandfather, my father, wished I were.

It's too late to prove it to them, but I'll prove it to myself.

To Georgia.

To my family.

To my friends.

The first time I slept with Georgia, it was lust.

The anniversary of my grandfather's death, I was falling in love with her.

Now, I'm positive, no doubt in my mind, that I'm in love with this woman more than I've ever loved anyone, more than I love myself.

This broken life led me to her, to a woman who accepts every damn chipped piece of me—imperfections, flaws, despairs. All of them.

I slam my eyes shut and hold in a breath. When I leave this bed, it'll be time to face reality. Earlier, in bed and inside Georgia, my worries faded away, all my thoughts consumed by her.

Us together, making love, owning each other.

She rises, taking our sheet with her, and starts hunting down her clothes, leaving me exposed to all my glory. Good thing she brought the sheet with her because I'm getting hard by the scene in front of me. If she were nude while bending over to grab her panties, we wouldn't be leaving this room for another hour.

She turns around and smirks. "Quit staring. You need to get going."

"Join me in the shower?" I raise a brow.

"Nope." She snaps her fingers and points at the bathroom. "Quick shower and then to your mom's. I know you're not looking forward to it, but she needs you."

I nod. "I know, and I want to be there for her. It's just hard for me … expressing myself."

"No one is asking you to wear your heart on your sleeve. Sometimes, all you need to do is wrap someone in a hug and let them know you care."

I stand as she pulls her sweats on and wrap my arms around her waist. "Will you come back tonight?"

She frowns. "I wish I could, but I told Grace I'd sleep at home tonight, *but* you can stay at my place."

I brush her messy hair away from her face and kiss her. "I might take you up on that offer."

———

BETTI, my mother's housekeeper, gives me a quick hug with tears in her eyes, when I walk into the house. "Your father might've made some mistakes, but deep down, he was a good man."

I stiffen, wondering if she's mistaken me for the wrong brother. Yes, I'm always nice to Betti. She makes the most bomb-ass grilled cheese sandwiches, but I'm not the friendly Callahan brother. Lincoln is the hugger. I'm the avoider.

Lincoln is waiting for me in the foyer, his eyes tired, holding an energy drink in his hand. "You and Georgia, huh? Can we talk about how cute you two look?"

I glare at him. "Swear to God, if you say *how cute you two look* again, I'm smacking you."

He slaps my back, yawns, and chugs the drink. "Don't worry; I'll let you off the hook for now, but I'd bet the fifty dollars the Feds left in my bank account that you'll have a girlfriend soon."

Ignoring him, I glance around the foyer. "Where's Mom?"

"Showering, but she'll be down any minute."

I follow him through the formal dining room, taking in the table blanketed with bouquets, cakes, cookies, pies—all the *sorry for your loss* shit people send. He strolls into the kitchen, opens the fridge for another energy drink, and offers me one. I shake my head and reach around him, grabbing a Coke.

"Does she know I'm coming?" I ask, opening the can.

He nods, and we head back to the foyer.

"How's she doing?"

"Better than I thought she would, but she's Mom. She can smile to our faces and then break down when she gets to her bedroom."

I nod in agreement.

Us Callahans can't stand showing our emotions.

After kissing Georgia good-bye, I showered, dressed, and drove to my mother's, nausea growing in my stomach with every passing mile. My mother is one of the strongest women I know, but she has her slipups. She slipped when my father was sentenced to prison, and that's nothing compared to death.

I hear her heels tapping against the handmade Italian tiles before she comes into view. On the surface, she's not displaying one sign of a grieving widow. Her white pantsuit and heels are all a front.

I see who I get it from, Mom.

Like Lincoln said, the world won't see Josephine Callahan break down—only us.

I take long strides in her direction and wrap my arms around her. She stiffens before relaxing into my hold and shoving her face into my shoulder, breaking loose, that emotional wall she put up crumbling.

Georgia's words ring through my mind. *"Sometimes, all you need to do is wrap someone in a hug and let them know you care."*

All along, who would've thought that holding my mother tight was all she needed to let her guard down? Georgia did it for me. I'm doing it for her.

Mascara runs down her face when she pulls away, and she stares up at me in shock, as if I'm a different person, a different son.

"My Archer," is all she says before cupping both hands around one of mine, raising it to her lips, and kissing it. "My Archer is coming back to me."

———

IT'S after midnight when I get into my car to leave my mom's house.

Lincoln and I spent the evening with her, and it was one of the strangest nights of my life.

Growing up, we hadn't spent much time with our parents. They were off doing their black-tie parties and traveling with their country-club friends. Lincoln and I were off blowing their money on partying and drugs. We had been too busy for family time.

We convinced her to eat pizza we'd ordered from the local joint in the city, and from the look on her face, you would've thought we'd asked her to give up her Louboutin collection.

We'd never ordered pizza when we were younger. Ours had been made by our chef with premium, organic, no-bullshit, no-fun, no-greasiness ingredients.

Tonight, she ate three slices before admitting she *sort of* liked it.

Us stubborn Callahans.

After gorging ourselves with pizza, we spent the next four hours in the theater, watching chick flicks she'd selected. They were lame as hell, but as I watched, they reminded me of shit Georgia would like. I sent her a picture of the screen during one movie, and she replied with laughing emojis that it was in her top ten favorites.

We texted throughout the day. Her asking how we were doing, me asking about her day. As I sat there, half-paying attention to the movie, I wondered where we'd go from here.

Will we start dating?

Does she want to date me?

My eyes are heavy when I drag my phone from my pocket and text her.

Me: I'm leaving my mom's now. I know it's late, and I don't want to wake you in case you're sleeping.

I don't want to be a dick and wake her, but I also don't want to be a dick and make her think I've forgotten about her or that I wasn't serious about everything that I said today.

I was serious about every word.

The only times I'd lied to her was when I said I didn't have feelings for her. It was easier to lie than reveal my truth—that I was falling hard for her every single damn second of the day.

The night of my father's death, it hit me. I said cruel words to him, thinking we'd talk again.

The same with my grandfather.

There was a chance that could happen with Georgia. I could lie to her face and make her feel unwanted by me and then possibly never see her again.

It had been a reality check for me.

No more hiding my feelings.

She needs to know every emotion running through my body for her.

My phone rings, and her name flashes across the screen.

I smile.

My lips are probably shocked as fuck since smiling is a rarity for me.

"Hi," I answer.

"Hey," she says around a yawn.

"I woke you up."

"Nope."

"You lying?"

"Yep." She yawns again. "How'd everything go?"

"As good as it could have, I guess." I relax in my seat and massage my forehead, the pain of losing my father hitting me. "We tried distracting her, but the doorbell constantly ringing with sympathy gifts didn't help."

"Poor thing. That has to be hard on her heart."

"She's struggling but working through it well. It helps that Lincoln is here too. Had he still been locked up, it would've been harder on her … on both of them since he couldn't have been here for her or attended our father's funeral."

"I'm glad he's back for you and your mom. You make a good team."

"Me too." I rub at the tension at the back of my neck. "Is the offer to come over still open?"

I don't want to go back to an empty house, and Lincoln is staying with our mom for the next few days.

"Always," she answers with no hesitation.

———

GEORGIA PRESSES her finger to her soft lips when she answers the door before waving me inside.

I texted her a few minutes ago, letting her know I was here, so I wouldn't wake up Grace by ringing the doorbell. As soon as I walk in, I envelop Georgia in my arms, holding her tight. When we pull apart, she grabs my hand and walks me through the dark hallway to her bedroom. The only light comes from a lamp on her nightstand, and her bed is in disarray.

When she turns to face me, my mouth waters as I eye her up and down, taking in her short-shorts that show off her tanned, sleek legs and an oversize tee that I'd guess was once Cohen's.

At least that's my hope and that it's not some other dude's.

I pull at the bottom of the shirt. "Where'd you get this from?"

She peeks up at me. "Cohen, I think?"

"You think?"

She shrugs. "My brain is too tired to remember."

And I'm too tired to stress the question for answers.

Her eyes fix on me as I strip out of my jeans and tee, leaving on only my boxer briefs. I wait for her to get into bed before sliding in after her.

When I stretch out, half my body is off the bed. "Remind me to buy you a larger bed."

"Hey!" She smacks my arm. "What's wrong with my bed?"

"Baby, have you seen the size of me?"

She bites into her lip. "I have definitely seen the size of you."

I shake my head. "What am I going to do with you?"

"Anything." She yawns loudly, causing me to do the same. "But make that anything in the morning because I can't keep my eyes open."

I kiss her lips, then her nose, and then her cheek before whispering, "Good night."

She curls against me, her back relaxing against my chest, and her legs tangle between mine. Draping my arm over her waist, I make myself comfortable and spoon with someone for the first time in my life.

———

I WAKE UP, half my body dangling off the side of Georgia's bed, and her leg is hitched over my waist.

Her T-shirt rises, exposing the bottom curves of her breast, and my mouth waters.

She's finally mine.

Finally, I got my head out of my ass and did the right thing.

I stopped hurting her.

Stopped holding myself back from happiness.

Georgia is the best thing that's ever happened to me.

Through all my sadness, all my bullshit, and my grief, she's been by my side, no matter what.

I sweep my gaze down her body and glare at the tee, remembering no one knows where the hell it came from.

It needs to come off, just in case it didn't come from Cohen.

Thrown in the trash.

Burned.

She stirs when I grip the bottom of the shirt and drag it up.

"You said you don't remember where you got this shirt?"

She stares up at me with tired eyes, taking a moment to process my words.

"Off it goes."

She nudges herself up onto her elbow, assisting me in whipping it over her head, and I throw it across the room.

"This is a better view anyway," I say, rolling her onto her back and hovering over her on all fours.

"That's my favorite nightshirt." She pouts.

I bow my head to nuzzle my nose against hers. "You can raid my closet for a new favorite."

She gasps when I slip my hand between her legs, slide her panties to the side, and plunge two fingers inside her.

"Or just don't wear one at all."

To see all of her, I flip the blanket off us and slide her boy shorts down. I groan, crawling down her body, parting her legs, and lick her clit, swirling my tongue around it before sucking on it hard. She moans as I tease her.

"More," she begs.

"More of what, baby?"

"You. Your tongue. Fingers. Mouth. Cock. Whatever you have for me, I want more of it."

"More of this?"

She gasps when I add a finger inside her without warning.

"Yes, please. Definitely more of that."

Her back arches as I finger her pussy and suck on her clit, loving the sounds of her whimpers.

"Do you want my tongue?"

She spreads her legs wider.

"Answer me," I grind out, pulling my shorts down and releasing my aching cock, slowly stroking it.

"Please, please, please," she gasps.

Her pleas have me parting her folds and diving into her pussy. I love eating her out—tasting her on my tongue, her thighs squeezing against my face, her writhing underneath me.

All the time, at the bar, when she pranced around, I'd remember how she'd let me taste her once and how she was sweeter than any drink I could make.

"Condom," she rasps, pointing at her nightstand. "First drawer."

I ignore the sinking feeling of her having easy access to condoms, snatch one, and cover my cock with it.

"I love your weight over me," she moans as I thrust inside her.

"Yeah?" I ask, edging up onto my knees, changing the direction of my strokes.

"Yes."

"I love being inside you."

I pound into her, resting her thigh along her shoulder, and when I flip her on all fours, I slam into her, causing her headboard to slam into the wall.

———

GEORGIA AND I EAT BREAKFAST, and we kiss good-bye. I go home, shower, and drive to my mom's.

We have an appointment to plan my father's funeral arrangements.

CHAPTER THIRTY-SIX

Georgia

I CAN NAME the number of funerals I've attended on one hand.

Lola and Grace are next to me when we walk into the packed cathedral. Finn, Silas, Jamie, and Cohen are behind us. We weave our way around people in the aisle with polished wooden pews on each side of us. Archer is standing at the apse with his mother and Lincoln, surrounded by people making conversation with them. As if he senses my presence, he glimpses in our direction.

It's an Archer I've never seen before. He stands tall in his black suit, tailored to perfection on his body.

His eyes meet mine, and I shyly wave to him. He whispers something into his mother's ear before kissing her cheek and stalking in our direction. We shuffle to the side, allowing people to pass us. As Archer walks through the crowd, a few people attempt to stop him for conversation, but he brushes past them.

His face is blank.

His guard is up.

No shocker.

He won't show these people what he shows me.

"Thanks for coming, guys," he says when he reaches us. "I really appreciate it."

If this were anyone else—Cohen, Finn, Silas—the girls would've already hugged them, but this is Archer.

A man who isn't a hugger.

Who isn't a talker.

Jaws drop, and a gasp falls when he smooths his lips over mine.

"Holy wow," Jamie says as Archer's attention rests on me.

He grabs my hand in his, draping his free one over our connection, and guides me to where his mother is standing. I hear the guys throwing questions at the girls behind us.

"Grandma, Grandpa," Archer says.

An older couple turns to face us. The man's hair is gray, not one strand of color, and he's wearing a pair of thin gold glasses. Archer's grandmother is the opposite—her hair a dark brown and curled out— and there's a Chanel brooch on her black dress.

Archer squeezes my hand. "This is my girlfriend, Georgia." Another squeeze. "These are my grandparents, Evie and Sanders Eubanks, and you've met my mother."

Sanders gives me a head nod while Evie says, "It's nice to meet you, sweetie."

Archer's mother, whose arm is around Lincoln's, steps closer, and I see a timid smile underneath her mourning veil.

"You too," I say, my hand resting on my chest, hoping I don't look bug-eyed and close to passing out—because that's how I feel. "I'm so sorry for your loss."

I stand at Archer's side as his family talks and people approach us —all of who he introduces me to as his girlfriend. When the service starts, he asks me to sit with him. As I take my seat, I notice the photo of his father atop the closed casket. Archer bears a striking resemblance to him. While Lincoln takes more after his mother, Archer looks more like his father.

I peek back at our friends. Cohen stares at me like I'm in a different world, and Jamie's eyes tell me she'll be questioning me about Archer's kiss later. Just wait until they hear him tell people I'm his girlfriend.

That'll really shock them into next week.

Before the service ends, the priest calls for Lincoln to come up to say a few words. Lincoln stands, and as he walks to the podium, I want to smack the bitches behind me as they whisper about his *prison time*.

I squeeze Archer's hand again, dragging my nails into his skin, and hold myself back.

Who talks shit at a funeral?

Lincoln is confident as he gives his father his good-bye. He ignores the whispers as he lays himself bare—telling us how he looked up to his father, the kind of man he was, and how much he'll be missed.

It's heartfelt.

Beautiful.

Brings me and those around me to tears.

Including Archer, who's fighting like hell to hold them back.

———

SINCE THERE WASN'T room for me in the car and I felt his family could use a good bonding moment, I told Archer I'd ride with Lola and meet him at his grandparents' home, where his father's wake is being held.

The back seat door flies open, and Jamie, who rode to the funeral with Cohen, jumps into Lola's car.

"Whoa, what the …?" Grace says next to her.

Jamie pushes her top half forward to ger her head between Lola in the driver's seat and me in the passenger's, her baby belly not making it easy. "How about you tell us how long you've been keeping you and Archer a secret for?" she says, intrigue on her face.

"It's fresh," I reply. "I didn't want to say anything until everything calmed."

"Apparently, Archer didn't share that sentiment," Lola says with a snort. "He strode right through that church and claimed you as his. It was hot. I know I've talked shit about the guy, which he fully deserved, but Jesus, what did you do to him, Georgia?" Lola starts the engine and follows the procession line of cars pulling onto the road.

Jamie falls back to buckle her seat belt. "She gave him time to open his eyes." She cups her hand over her chest, and a tear slips down her cheek. "It was beautiful."

"That's the pregnancy speaking," Lola says.

"It is," Jamie says. "I think it's sweet, but these damn hormones had me crying over a Cheerios commercial this morning."

Fifteen minutes later, we're pulling up to a gated entrance, where a man wearing a suit is waving cars in.

"This house is gorgeous," Jamie says as I stare at it in awe.

Sure, Archer's penthouse is expensive but nothing like this. His is more subtle, and this castle-appearing home is far from subtle.

We drive around the circular driveway before getting out of the car. Lola drops her keys in the young valet driver's hand, and we walk next to manicured hedges to the front door.

The expansive entryway is flowing with people chatting with finger foods and drinks in their hands. I look around and spot Archer sitting next to Lincoln on a sofa.

He stands when I reach them, tugs me into his arms, and kisses my cheek.

"Your girlfriend, huh?" I ask.

He peers down at me, his brow rising. "Is that not who you are?"

Fine and dandy with me.

"Does that mean you're my boyfriend?"

"Is there something else you'd rather me be?"

"I mean …" I bite into the edge of my lip.

"Georgia, if you're all in, I'm all in." He kisses my hand before holding it on his chest over his heart. "I'm done being scared, being an idiot, because who knows how long I'll have to be here with you?"

It's been five days since we spent our first night together, and I haven't slept alone since. He's either in my bed or I'm in his. It's been nice in our own little world. Lincoln knew, of course, along with Grace since she heard me moaning Archer's name. At first, she thought I was taking myself to pleasure town until the headboard started banging. She slipped on some headphones and then texted Lola to deliver the tea on my new relationship.

"I'm all in," I whisper.

"Looks like we're boyfriend and girlfriend then, huh?"

"Looks like it."

Holy hell, Archer Callahan is my boyfriend.

———

"FOR ONCE, my son listens to me."

I'm sitting in the gazebo with our friends, surrounded by bright-colored flowers and beautiful shrubs, when Archer's mother settles next to me on the bench. He went on a bathroom-slash-refill trip a few minutes ago.

"Huh?" I ask, glancing over at her.

"My son. I told him to ask you out when we met at the bar. It took him forever, but I'm glad he finally came to his senses."

He didn't exactly ask me out.

"Me too."

A few times, the worry of not being good enough for his family, of not being *rich enough* for them, caused me some insecurities. Like when I noticed Meredith as Archer led us to the gazebo. She was chatting with his grandparents, and she looked like she belonged in their world.

Josephine clasps her hand over mine. "Thank you for bringing him back into the light, Georgia. You are the only one who could've taken on a task that large. My son loves you, and thank you for loving him."

CHAPTER THIRTY-SEVEN

Archer

AT LEAST I was allowed at his funeral.

I stop myself from that thought, working on not holding that grudge.

I owe my father that.

There's nothing like a good support system. When my friends showed up, reality kicked in with a force. These people cared about me —the dick me, the brooding me, the me who hid. Even the girls, who'd never been my biggest fan after what I did to Georgia, came. All along, I'd thought I was this lonely, isolated bastard, but I was wrong. I had family, friends, a business partner, a woman I loved.

I'm headed back to my friends, Georgia's water refill in one hand and mine in the other, when I'm stopped.

"You've changed."

I shift to face Meredith. "I have."

"You love her, don't you?"

"I do."

She cringes before pulling herself together. "As much as I hate that it wasn't me who brought you back, who makes you happy, I'm glad you found yourself."

"You'll find someone." I stare at her, noticing the differences between a woman I thought I loved and the woman I do love.

Who would've ever thought, instead of this woman with her designer dress and David Yurman diamond cuff, the one who saved my heart would sport pigtail buns and sandals that laced up to her knees on the regular?

She swings her arms in the air. "I had a lovely conversation with your mom, and she thanked me for leaving you."

I arch a brow. "What?"

My mother loved Meredith and was devastated when we broke off our engagement.

"She thanked me for leaving you and said had I not, you would've never started to find happiness, where you belong." She tips her head toward Georgia sitting in the garden. "That girl, she's who you need, and your friends over there, they care about you. I'm jealous." She kisses my cheek before squeezing my hand. "I'm happy for you, *but* if it doesn't work out, you know my number."

Not happening.

"Thanks for coming," I say before heading back to where I belong.

———

I TOOK a week off from the bar.

Not by choice.

When Cohen heard the news about my father, he had my shifts covered. As much as I hate being away from the bar, it's given me time to grieve and be with my family—something I steered clear of with all my might before.

I stare at Georgia from across the table of the coffee shop. "You have this weekend off, right?"

Now, there's a happy sense of nostalgia whenever I come here. If possible, I park in the spot where we met and she turned my life upside down.

She shakes her head. "I work Saturday night."

"Can you find someone to cover?"

"Sure." She raises a brow. "What's up?"

"We're scattering my father's ashes at my grandparents' vacation home on Jackson Lake. It's a few hours away. Want to come?"

"Will your family be okay with that?" She plays with the straw in her iced coffee. "I don't want to intrude."

"My mom already asked if you were coming."

So did my grandparents and Lincoln.

Her face brightens. "Really?"

If it were anyone else, I'd feel weird asking them to attend something so personal for my family, but I want her there. She's the calm to my storm.

My mother has already mentioned an engagement, wedding, and children with Georgia. Even with the few interactions they've had, Georgia has won her over, like she always does with people. I've accepted my mother's comments and recommendations—though I don't follow through with most of them—because it takes her mind off my father's passing.

I nod. "Really."

"I'll be there."

I lean across the table, grip her chin, and kiss her.

———

LINCOLN SLAPS me on the back. "You good to go, brother?"

I nod. "Good to go."

My mother grips the gold urn in her shaking hands, and there's silence as we make our way out of the house, down the stone steps, and to the dock. This was my grandfather's favorite place and then my father's when they needed a breather from the corporate world. When the Feds began seizing my father's assets, my mother's parents purchased the lake home, so our family wouldn't lose something so cherished.

The last time I was here was when we scattered my grandfather's ashes. That day, I refused to stay away, and my father and I went at separate times to avoid contact. He'd already prevented me from saying good-bye to my grandfather at his funeral, and it wasn't happening again.

Lincoln is next to my mother.

Her parents behind them.

Georgia and me following.

My father didn't have much family.

The Callahans are one cursed bunch.

My grandmother passed when my father was young. When my grandfather remarried, she died a decade later. He gave up on marriage after that. The female companions he had later in life were all decades younger and regularly recycled.

Lincoln and I are the only ones to carry the Callahan name.

My mother sobs as she carefully places the urn on the dock and opens it. My stomach turns as a morbid chill hits me.

That's all you're reduced to when you die.

Ashes or a body in the ground.

You live your life, only to have your loved ones stare at your urn and weep.

Georgia stands at the front edge of the dock to give us space while we take our turns with the urn and then scatter his ashes.

We hang out on the dock for an hour, sharing memories, and then my mom and grandparents leave. Last night, Lincoln had asked if I wanted to stay at the cabin overnight, for old times' sake, so we stay behind.

Now, I'm seated upright against the leather headboard of the bed in my old room.

My mouth waters, my cock stirring, when Georgia circles the bed, wearing one of my baggy tees, and my heart races when she climbs into bed with me. As soon as her knees hit the sheets, I bend forward and pull her onto my lap, and she straddles me.

Caressing her cheek with one hand, I use the other to knot her hair around my wrist, pulling it away from her face. "Thank you for coming, baby."

She smiles down at me as she reaches forward to massage my tight shoulders, easing the constant tension. "Thank you for inviting me to something this special to you."

Jerking her head to the side, I drop kisses along her neck.

"You look so good in this bed." I gently sink my teeth into her skin before sucking hard.

She drops her head back. "You're going to give me a hickey."

"Exactly my goal." I lick up her neck and then suck harder. "I want to mark you everywhere."

She moans. "This used to be your bedroom?"

"Mm-hmm," I mutter into her neck.

I give no shits about talking about this room.

All my focus is on her and how I'm going to spend the rest of the night pleasuring every inch of her body.

"Did you sleep here a lot?"

"Sometimes."

"Did you have other girls in this bed?"

I freeze. *This is where she was going with that.* "Not the time for us to have that convo."

"Why not?"

"I don't want you mad at me, but I'm also not going to lie to you." I raise my hand, slipping it under her shirt, and trail my fingers up and down her spine. "Look at it this way: you'll be the only one here with me from now on."

She frowns, staring down at me, her hands now stationary on my shoulders. "I don't like that answer."

"I don't like that question." I lift my hand and tug on her bra. "Let's get this off."

She gently rocks against me, her thin panties the only barrier between her pussy and me. When she starts pulling up her shirt, I stop her. The sight of her in my clothes is nearly enough to have me busting in my gym shorts.

"Shirt stays on. Lose the bra and panties." Slipping my hand into her panties, I groan. She's soaked, dripping down my fingers. I sink a finger inside her with no warning. "Never mind. I can work with the panties on."

She unsnaps her bra, slightly lifting up to her knees, giving me a better angle to pump my fingers inside her while also pressing my thumb to her swollen clit. As she unshoulders her bra and moves into my touch, her breathing quickens.

"Pull my dick out," I demand. "Fuck what's yours. *Only* yours."

She crawls down the bed, her face at my lap, and she licks her lips before untying my shorts. My back arches when she cups me through my shorts, sliding her hand up and down my hard cock.

"Take it out, baby," I groan.

She tilts her head to the side. "And then what?"

"Jerk it. Suck it. Fuck it. *Anything.*"

"Hmm." She taps the side of her mouth. "Which one should I select?"

"Baby," I rasp. "If you don't take off these goddamn shorts soon, I'm going to *select* it for you by pushing you onto your back and fucking your face."

"Am I not supposed to want that?"

When I rise at the waist, she shoves me back against the headboard. In seconds, she's dragging my shorts down my legs and tossing them off the bed. My knees lock up when she swallows my entire dick into that sweet mouth of hers.

"Fuck, that mouth," I moan.

I used to think all it did was talk shit, but she sucks my dick as if her mouth were made to do it. I've never had to lead Georgia, show her how I like to be sucked; she already knows what sets me off. I wrap her hair around my wrist again, pulling tight, and watch her suck me, her cheeks hollowing out.

"Shit, stop," I grind out when she massages my balls. "Your mouth isn't what's going to take my come tonight."

She smiles. "Then what will?"

She yelps when I haul her back onto my lap, and she wastes no time before grinding against me, her pussy rubbing against my hard cock, which is coated in her saliva.

Her lips go to mine. "We need to be quiet."

I slide my tongue into her mouth.

"Lincoln is in the next room," she says, pulling back.

"Lincoln is the last person I'm worried about hearing us." I jerk my head toward my nightstand. "Condom."

With no hesitation, she stretches across the bed, opens the drawer, and snags one.

"Put it on me."

I hold in a breath when she opens the wrapper and pulls out the condom before slowly sliding it over my erection.

Gripping her waist, I lift her before slamming her onto my cock. Her pussy sinks around my dick perfectly, making us one. She grips my shoulders as she starts riding me, giving my cock the best pussy it's ever had—the only pussy I ever want to have. The more of herself she hands over to me, the more addicted to her I become.

I throw my head back, rotating my waist underneath her. "I could stay inside you forever."

She's biting her lip as she grinds against me, holding back her moans, her groans, the way she gasps my name as my cock fills her.

"Say my name," I moan into her mouth, playing with her clit.

She rides me harder. "Archer."

"Again."

She rides me deeper. "Archer."

"A-fucking-gain."

This time, she moans out my name while falling apart. I keep her still, my fingers pressing into her hips, while I pound inside her until I'm the one groaning her name.

CHAPTER THIRTY-EIGHT

Archer

"YOU SURE YOU'RE ready to be back?" Cohen asks, walking into my office. "If you need more time off, I got you."

I shake my head. "Nah, being here is what I need."

Today is Lincoln's first day back too. Like me, he's ready for something to take his mind off losing Dad. It's worse for him, though. Not only was he closer with our father but he also doesn't have much of anyone now. I have Georgia and my friends, but he spends his nights either in the guest room of my penthouse or at Mom's. I need to get my shit together and be a better big brother.

Tonight will be the first night I sleep without Georgia next to me since my father's death. My stomach hollows at the thought. Tomorrow is her first day of working at the school, and I don't want to wake her up after my shift.

Cohen crosses his arms and rests his back against the bare wall. Unlike his office, there are no chairs for visitors in mine—a great preventive measure. If there's nowhere for them to get comfortable, they won't stay longer than necessary.

Cohen kicks his shoes against the floor. "You and my sister, huh?"

I nod, leaning back in my chair, flipping a pen in my hand. "Me and your sister."

Cohen waits for me to elaborate.

I don't.

Dating Georgia won't change everything about me. Yes, I'm coming around more, but I'll always be closed off to everyone but her.

"I forgot about how you talk so much." He shakes his head. "Dude, you need to learn when to shut up."

I shrug. "Mr. Social over here."

He shoves his hands into his pockets. "Is it too soon to ask a favor?"

"Depends on the favor."

"It's a favor for Maliki."

"Yeah?"

Maliki is Cohen's best friend who worked with us before moving home. He owns Down Home Pub, a bar in Blue Beech that's been in his family for decades. Down Home is in the next county, and before Cohen agreed to buy our building, he double-checked to make sure it was okay with Maliki. Cohen didn't want him to see us as competition. Maliki didn't give a shit, of course, and ripped Cohen's ass for thinking he would.

"Sierra's sister needs a job," he says.

I raise a brow. "A job here?"

He nods.

"Sierra is engaged to Maliki, and he owns Down Home Pub. Why doesn't he hire her sister there?"

"Not sure of the full story, but it seems she needs to get out of town for a while."

I shrug. "Fine with me."

"Cool. I'll schedule an interview for her to come in."

"Sounds good."

He turns to walk out, but before he does, he stares at me over his shoulder. "I'm happy for you. You and my sister deserve it, man. Be good to her."

———

"DUDE, do I even have a roommate anymore?" Lincoln asks, stepping behind me at the bar.

I throw my arms out. "You see me standing here, don't you?"

He flips me off. "Will you be at home tonight or snuggling with your girlfriend?"

I've spent most of my nights at Georgia's—even though I complain about it and offer to buy her a new bed every night I'm there. For some reason, she says Grace doesn't like staying by herself. The nights Georgia has stayed with me is when Grace is at her parents' or siblings' houses. She won't explain why Grace doesn't like shit that goes bump in the night while she's home alone.

"Home tonight," I answer.

"Guess you'll have to watch movies and feed me strawberries instead of Georgia then."

"Funny," I deadpan.

I text Georgia throughout my shift until she tells me good night with a row of kissy-face emojis.

At the end of the night, I close the bar and go home. When I sluggishly walk to my bedroom after work and dive into my bed, I miss the heat of her body next to me. Setting my alarm, I only sleep for a few hours before dragging myself out of bed. Knowing I'll regret it later, I take an energy shot, pick up Georgia's and Grace's favorite coffee, and grab them breakfast sandwiches before heading to her townhouse.

My tired eyes dart open when Georgia answers the door.

"Damn, can I be a student?" I whistle, giving her a once-over and licking my lips at the sight of her in a black pencil skirt and white button-up top. My dick stirs.

She looks sexy and sophisticated. Even with her professional attire, Georgia puts her style into it with her earrings—two hoops with a moon hanging off one and a sun on the other and bright pink heels.

She laughs, slapping my chest, and steps to the side to allow me access into the house. "What are you doing here? You should be in bed."

I drop the coffee and food onto the kitchen table. "Sleep can wait. It's your first day. I came to see you and kiss you good luck." Bowing my head, I give her a quick peck on the lips before wrapping my arms around her waist and dragging her into me. "But now that I've seen you, how about a good-luck orgasm?"

"I wish," she grumbles, resting her chin against my chest as she peeks up at me. "Miss me already, huh?"

My eyes soften as I stare down at her. "You have no idea how lonely I was in my bed. Our sleepovers all week have spoiled me."

She grips my wrist and holds it up to read the time on my watch. "You've only been off work for three hours."

"And those three hours were miserable."

She stands on her tiptoes, her heels still not bringing her to my height, and presses her lips to mine, smiling against them. "I missed you too." She laughs. "Although it did feel nice not to have you hog the bed."

"That's why you should let me buy you a new one." I drop my hands to her ass, grabbing a handful, and pull her closer to me—my cock hard just from the view of her and this conversation. "You're coming over when you get off work, and I'm going to fuck you in this skirt."

She shivers in my arms.

My lips go to her ear, and I know I'm punishing myself by getting us worked up when we can't do anything about it. "When I push it up, do you want me to finger-fuck you or eat your pussy?"

"Oh my God," she groans. "You need to stop before my excuse for being late is that I had to ride my boyfriend's cock."

"Gross, ew," Grace says, walking into the room while shoving a sparkly pink laptop into her bag. "As if I don't already hear enough of your banging at night."

Georgia turns to face her, and I drag her ass against me, hiding my erection from Grace.

"Hey, he did buy you those noise-canceling headphones."

Grace grabs her curly strawberry-blond locks and pulls them up into a smooth ponytail. "Do you know how hard it is to sleep with bulky headphones on your ears?"

I jerk my head toward the coffee and food on the table. "I at least brought you breakfast and coffee."

Grace, who can't hold a frown for longer than three seconds, grins. "Why couldn't we have had this Archer all along? You are becoming a decent part-time roommate with our coffee and food."

I shrug and kiss Georgia's forehead. "It just took time ... and the right person."

Grace smiles. "I guess so."

We say good-bye to Grace. I walk Georgia to her car, kiss her with a little tongue, and go home to crash for half the day.

————

"WILL THIS BE WEIRD?" Georgia asks, playing with her hands in her lap.

She's been distant all morning. When I asked her what was wrong, she waved off my question and insisted it was nothing.

Parking in Cohen's driveway, I glance over at her. "Why would it be weird?"

"We've never exactly been nice to each other at one of these."

I shift the car into park. "We were nice on Taco Tuesday. At the funeral."

"Nice to each other while people know that we're"—she pauses, as if searching for the appropriate word—"dating."

I frown. "Do you want us to be mean to each other?" My voice turns playful, and I hope it perks up her mood. "Role-play?"

She side-eyes me. "You know what I mean."

"It'd make for some hot sex later."

Her frown tips up into a smirk. "How about we ditch the party and go have sex?"

It's my turn to frown. "You want to bail on your brother's birthday?"

This isn't like Georgia. Unless she's had work or class, she's never missed a party or barbecue at Cohen's house—definitely not on his birthday.

"No." She shakes her head as if she's trying to rid it of her thoughts.

"Baby," I say, my chest tightening, "what's wrong?"

She's quiet, chewing on her bottom lip.

"Talk to me."

"I'm scared," she whispers.

"Scared of what?"

She avoids eye contact and plays with her hoop earring. "We've been in our own little world, and with the exception of Grace, we haven't shown our friends how serious we are. If it doesn't work out between us, I'll be humiliated."

"Humiliated? Humiliated over what?" Uneasiness stirs in my stomach.

"The guys, they don't know how deep my feelings for you are. If something happens to us, then it'll be embarrassing. If they think it's casual for us, then it might not be—"

I wince, her words a smack in the face. "Whoa, you think we're *casual?*"

A flush fills her cheeks. "I don't know what we are."

"You shitting me?" Disbelief cracks through me.

"I'm worried I'm a ..." She trails off.

"A what?"

"A distraction," she blurts out. "I'm worried I'm a distraction ... from everything happening in your life."

"A distraction?" I repeat slowly. "You're scared that I'll use you and then discard you after my life isn't shit?"

"A little, yes." She shakes her head and clutches the door handle. "Forget it. It's stupid."

"Whoa, you can't throw that out there and then say *forget it.*" I stop her, my head pounding. "Do you really think that I'm not all in with us?"

"I know how you are when you're in pain," she says softly. "You've used me before."

"You've used me before."

I squeeze my eyes shut and force down a sick feeling. "I've introduced you as my girlfriend. I've confided in you in ways I never have with anyone. I brought you to spread my father's ashes with my family. You think that's casual?"

"That's why I said, forget it," she grinds out.

She turns to open the door again, but I speak before she does, "Georgia, look at me."

There's a delay before she does, and my head pounds harder at the uncertainty on her face.

I caress my thumb over her cheek, my stomach twisting at the tears simmering in her eyes, and level my voice. "I'm all in. Every piece of me is in this with you. You're not a distraction. You're the woman I've wanted for years—*years*—and I'm finally done *distracting* myself with other shit to avoid my feelings for you."

She relaxes into my touch, my confession slightly putting her at ease. Three words are at the tip of my tongue. Just as they're about to slip from my lips, Georgia jumps when someone pounds on her door.

"Come on, kids," Finn says as he passes us on his way to Cohen's backyard.

I'm kicking his ass.

She wipes her eyes. "What better way for our first *public appearance* than for me to have red eyes?"

"Georgia," I rasp, "I swear on everything, I will never embarrass you."

She sniffles.

"Come here, baby." I wipe tears off her cheeks and nudge my nose along hers before kissing her. "This is not casual for me. You will never be casual with me. I'm nine thousand percent in this with you."

"Okay." She nods. "I just …"

"I don't blame you for doubting me."

Our lips brush again, longer this time, and I run my tongue along the seam of her lips. She opens her mouth, curling her tongue into mine, and I pull back.

"I don't know if our first public appearance should involve me dragging you onto my lap and fucking you right before we see everyone."

She traces my lips with her tongue. "That would be a great way to start it out."

I place a kiss on her forehead. "Let's get going."

She turns to grab Cohen's gift bag from the back seat, and I interlace our hands as we walk into the backyard. It's a Monday night

—the only day everyone in the gang could get off work. It's hard for us to get together on the weekends since at least one of us needs to be at the bar when it's busy.

To me, it doesn't seem weird. Our friends have been around us together. Hell, Grace has heard us fuck and seen us playing house— eating, watching movies, snuggling on the couch.

Far from goddamn casual.

"Well, well, if it's not the happy couple," Lola says when we come into view. She jumps up from her chair and hugs Georgia. "I feel like I need to move in with you and Grace to see you." Her eyes shoot to me. "*Or* be Archer."

I shrug, holding back a shit-eating grin as Georgia's shoulders relax.

"Girl time," Georgia says.

"You're going to be talking about me, aren't you?"

"Definitely not," she says.

I kiss her cheek while she sits with the girls, and I head over to the guys standing around the grill, drinking beers. We bro-hug each other, and no one acts any differently about Georgia and me. It's as if it's natural, and we've been walking around holding hands for years. I'm sure there's been some talk when we're not around, though.

"Maliki, my man!" Cohen calls out.

I turn around to find Maliki; his fiancée, Sierra; and his daughter, Molly, along with a blonde walking in our direction. As soon as Molly sees Noah and Jamie playing on the swing set, she darts toward them, yelling Noah's name. I'd bet my money those two will date or some shit by the time they hit high school.

"Who's Blondie?" Finn asks.

"Sierra's sister," Silas answers.

"She's cute," Finn comments.

She's young and on the skinny side, and she reminds me of Sierra —pretty, rich, and trouble. Maliki was like me—a loner, not giving two shits or looking for a relationship. Enter Sierra, who kept sneaking into his bar when she was underage. And somehow, they're now engaged. I don't know the full story since I mind my own business.

When he said it took the right one, I snorted.

Now, I get it.

"She's the one we're hiring?" I ask Cohen.

"Hiring where?" Silas asks.

"At the bar," Cohen replies.

"Twisted Fox?" Finn questions.

Cohen nods.

"Why not work at Down Home?" Finn continues.

I have a feeling that will be a frequent question.

"She got into some trouble. Maliki didn't tell me the entire story because he hardly says shit," Cohen replies. "If you want in on any gossip, Sierra is the one you go to."

Georgia, Grace, and Lola trade questioning looks. They're cautious, and they've banned us from bringing random women to the barbecues after one of Finn's flings showed her ass. I didn't give two fucks about the ban since I didn't have random flings I dragged around my friends. When Sierra came with Maliki the first time, they were accepting of her. It could've also been because none of them wanted Maliki.

Since Grace loves Finn.

And Lola and Silas have some weird type of relationship.

Thirty minutes later, we're finishing dinner, and Georgia declares it is cake time before rushing inside. I don't know how she always ends up being the cake-getter.

Deciding we need some alone time, I jog across the yard and wrap my arms around her, dragging her into my side before raining kisses down her cheek and neck.

She laughs, pushing me away, before freezing. "Holy shit, is that my mom?"

CHAPTER THIRTY-NINE

Georgia

WHAT THE HELL IS HAPPENING?

My jaw drops as my mom slowly walks through Cohen's backyard, gift bag in tow. My attention zips to Cohen, as I'm nervous for his reaction. I didn't invite her since it's his birthday, and when it's your birthday, you get to make the guest list.

Did Jamie?

Cohen drops a kiss to Jamie's shoulder, shoves his phone into his pocket, and waves to my mom. His strides are long as he meets her in the middle of the yard. They smile at each other—hers gentle, his inviting.

"Oh, wow," I mutter when he hugs her tightly.

"You want me to grab the cake while you …" Archer asks, jerking his head toward the scene I'm focused on.

I nod. "Good idea."

"On it."

I wait, keeping my distance, while Cohen and my mom make small talk. I've been begging Cohen to talk to her, and my heart flutters that he finally is, that he's opened up the forgiveness pocket of his heart. The man who doesn't believe in second chances is giving her one.

Taking her hand, he leads her to Jamie and Noah, and when they exchange hugs, my eyes water.

"Got the cake," Archer says, stopping next to me. "Who the hell chose this?"

"Noah." I laugh as I take a look at the Scooby-Doo cake that says, *Happy Birthday, Dad!* "He cons Jamie into letting him make all the decisions."

Archer carries the cake as we approach them.

"Hi, Mom," I say, masking the shock on my face and hugging her.

"Hi, baby." She squeezes me tight.

"Cake is here," Archer says before placing it on the table. He slides his arm around my waist and kisses my cheek.

My mom raises a brow.

"Mom," I say, "this is Archer."

"Hi there," she says skeptically and waves, recognizing his name from the few times I've confided in her.

Her motherly instincts have started kicking in as our relationship grows.

As though he can read her mind, Archer steps forward, and says, "I stopped fucking up."

My mom smiles. "I'm glad to hear that."

Everyone digs into the cake, and when I see Cohen is alone, I pounce.

"You invited Mom?" I ask.

He nods.

"Wow, what am I missing? Are we in an alternate universe?"

"It was time I got my head out of my ass." He runs his hand through his thick brown hair. "Archer's dad's death didn't only help open his eyes; it did mine too. It was time I quit holding a grudge against her. I'm having a little girl, and I'd love for her to have two grandmothers. She's been in the picture with you for a while now, and she hasn't given you any reason to doubt her."

I grin. "I'm happy you and Mom are reconnecting."

He jerks his head toward Archer, who's talking with Maliki. "After all this time, I kept telling myself that you two just hated each other."

"Were we that good at acting?"

He shakes his head. "I think I was good at turning a blind eye to it because I didn't want it to start drama, but then I sat back and thought, you two dating isn't shit compared to the situation I'm in."

I laugh. "True dat, big brother. Your baby momma's sister is over there, preggo with your next baby."

"Okay, don't make it sound so Jerry Springer-ish."

"Why? It's so much fun."

"Man, you're a pain in my ass," he says, laughing while hugging me.

I take a look around the yard, noticing everyone and everything that's happened.

Everyone around me is taking risks.

And I love it.

———

"I'M SORRY," I say, stretching myself out on Archer's bed, "for what I said about us being casual."

I was nervous.

Scared.

Our relationship had turned serious so fast.

No dating. No foreplay. Just diving straight into each other.

In the car, Archer flinched when I said *distraction*, as if the word was a slap to his face. I was happy with him, on top of the world, but scared. Archer's way of handling stress is by running, drinking, and fucking. I can't be blamed for worrying that he was using me to get through his issues and then would discard me later.

He stands at the foot of his bed—in a pair of gym shorts, shirtless, showing off his buff chest.

His face softens, and he gently smiles. "Baby, don't be sorry for expressing that. My job is to change your mind from feeling that way."

"I mean, I was in a mood—"

"And I'm in the mood to prove to you that this isn't casual."

Leaning over the bed, he grips my ankles in his rough hands, and I shriek when he tugs me down the sheets. My ass is half off the bed, and before I catch another breath, my panties are ripped down my legs. Parting my thighs, he drops to his knees and stares at my bare pussy, his attention riveted.

I gulp, never feeling so on display before.

"Uh … everything okay down there?" I ask before inching my legs closed.

Call me awkward for never having my vagina on display like the *Mona Lisa.*

He stops me. "I'm admiring you."

"Can you, uh … stop admiring and start …"

He peeks up at me, a hungry look on his face. "And what, baby?"

I wave my hands in the air in a *hurry up* gesture.

He chuckles, and anticipation flickers through me when he rains kisses down my thighs and legs and then back up.

My heart pulsates, my body tingling with my need for him.

All of him.

Every damn inch of this guy—mentally, physically, emotionally.

I want him to be my forever.

I want to be his everything.

Without warning, he plunges two fingers inside me.

Laps his tongue around my clit while fingering me.

The attentiveness this man gives my body is like no other.

I've never had a man work to pleasure me like Archer does.

His tongue. His fingers. His mouth. His groans between my legs.

"Come for me, baby," he says.

I arch my back, raising my hips, and he keeps me in place, finishing me off while I ride out my orgasm.

I throw my arms out, catching my breath as my body shakes. He grabs my waist, and I yelp when he tosses me farther up the bed.

He drops his shorts, his cock hard, and slides on a condom. I part my legs, welcoming him, and he kisses me. Darting my tongue in his mouth, I suck on his, and he groans. I wait for him to settle between my legs and thrust into me, but he doesn't.

Instead, he tortures me, cupping my breasts before squeezing them together, sucking and pulling and teasing at my nipples.

Proving this isn't a quick fuck.

That we aren't *casual.*

"I want your cock. So damn much."

He ignores me, sucking on my nipple.

I change direction. "I want you," I croak out. "I want you so damn much. Show me how this isn't casual."

My words set him on fire, and he pulls away, his eyes searching mine. Maintaining eye contact, he situates himself between my legs and eases in and out of me slowly.

Torturously slow.

Unhurried.

Fucking me in a way he's never fucked me before.

His gaze not leaving my face with every stroke until he's close.

He slams his eyes shut, his thrusts rougher and faster, and just as I'm there, he stops and collapses onto his back, rolling me with him to keep our connection so I'm now straddling him.

"Ride this cock you wanted," he demands, his palm cupping my ass before he gently smacks it.

My body tingles with excitement, and I rock my hips, pushing him farther into me.

Heat courses through my veins as I allow him to guide me how he wants it. I ride him hard, and his hips lash forward, meeting mine.

Our sweet fucking has turned into heated fucking.

The sound of my ass slapping into his thighs.

We moan.

We moan each other's names.

My sweat drips down my body and hits his chest.

"Oh my God, Georgia." He throws his head back, slowing his movements. "I love you so fucking much, baby."

I stop.

He gasps, his eyes wide as he stares at me, unblinking.

I'm panting, unsure of where to go from here.

He said ... he said the L-word.

He knots his hand in my hair. "Why do you look so shocked?"

"Was that ... it was a heat-of-the moment love devotion, right?" I shake my head. "Totally overthinking that."

I grind against him, but he stops me.

"I mean, yeah, I love when you're riding my cock, but I also love *you*."

I freeze again. "What?"

His eyes search mine, and his voice is rough when he says, "I'm in love with you, Georgia."

My thighs shake, and he grips them under his large palms as a tear slips down my cheek.

"Shit," he hisses. "I'm sorry. I know it's early."

I press a finger to his lips. "I think we both already know that I'm in love with you."

Grabbing my hair, he pulls my mouth to his, and then he flips me over, so he's on top again.

"Mine. So fucking mine," he groans as he thrusts inside me.

I wiggle underneath him. "Yours. All yours."

Archer kisses me. "Never leave me."

"You'd have to kill me first."

CHAPTER FORTY

Archer

"I LOVE YOU."

Before today, other than my mother, I've only said that to one other woman.

Meredith.

It was part of the natural progression of any relationship.

Date. Fuck. Profess *I love yous*. Get engaged. Marry.

That was the course for all relationships in our circle.

In my case with Meredith, it was fuck and then date—which also seems to somehow be the norm for me. It's easier for me to give someone my cock before giving them my heart.

Sure, I thought I loved Meredith.

I liked her enough to propose to her.

But now that I have Georgia, I know I didn't love her.

Love is when you want to wake up every single day and prove to the other person that you'll work on being a better person than you were the day before—a better lover, a better friend.

Georgia is my girlfriend, the woman I love, but she's also been my best friend and the only person I'm comfortable confiding in.

I glance up at the knock on my office door, and Georgia walks in, closing the door and clicking the lock behind her.

"Our first shift together as a couple," she says.

I nod.

She licks her lips and walks around my desk. "Should we celebrate?"

I turn in my chair to face her, my cock stirring as I take in her short-shorts and V-neck shirt that shows off her cleavage. "What'd you have in mind?"

God, I want to suck on her tits right now.

Dropping to her knees, she pulls out my cock, and without warning, she wraps her lips around my length, taking in every damn inch as if she'd been doing it her entire life. She hasn't given me many blow jobs—mostly because I like to come while my dick is inside her pussy, not her mouth.

My knees buckle, my balls draw up, and my hands grip the back of her head.

"Yes, suck me just like that," I groan. "You own my cock."

I stare down at the view of her perfect, plump lips moving up and down my cock.

And as usual, I stop her, wanting to bust my nut inside her pussy.

"Take off your shorts and your panties—and make it quick, so we don't get busted."

She bites into her lip and does what I said.

I bend her over my desk, spread her legs wide, and run my finger through her folds.

"Look how wet you got from sucking my cock," I say into her ear. "You love sucking it, don't you?"

"Yes," she moans when I plunge two fingers inside her.

"Love fucking my cock, don't you?"

"Love it more than anything."

She plants her palms on my desk, knocking shit over, and arches her back as I slide into her.

"Then take it."

I fuck her hard.

One hand gripping her waist, another one over her mouth to mask her screams.

I love this woman, and I pray to God she never leaves me.

———

"I'M a little worried that that's my replacement," Georgia says, signaling to Cassidy when she walks into the bar for her first day of training, wearing cutoff jeans and a crop top.

She's lost her goddamn mind if she thinks she has anything to worry about with another woman. I never wanted anyone to have my heart, but Georgia did the unthinkable. She pushed, she punched, and she shoved her way straight into me, to where she's so deep that I'll never be able to drag her out.

Sure, Cassidy is cute, but she's not Georgia—and that gives every woman a disadvantage when it comes to me.

"Don't even think for a second that I'd be interested in anyone but you," I say, leaning forward to kiss her neck.

We're at a pub table, having a quick bite to eat before our shifts start.

"God, I take back all the times I said Archer needed to get his head out of his ass. You two are gag-worthy," Lola comments, sliding out a stool at the table and sitting.

"I think there's a rule against kissing in the employee handbook," Silas adds, coming into view and stealing the seat next to Lola.

Behind them, I see Grace and Finn, and they join us.

Seconds later, Lincoln is standing behind me.

It's like one big, happy damn family.

"They're cute," Grace says, her voice calm and polite.

"I think it's so cute too," Finn adds, resting his arm over Grace's shoulders. "The bastard has grown a goddamn heart."

I use both of my hands to flip them off as Georgia laughs, finishing off her sandwich.

"Nah. Archer is still the grumpy dick, just not to Georgia," Lincoln argues.

"She's the only one who doesn't deserve it." I stand, brush the mustard off her lips, and kiss her. "Let me know if you need anything."

She returns my kiss with another peck.

"Swear to motherfucking God, I love you two, but this is a

working zone," Lincoln says. "Don't be messing up my tips while you guys run around each other with hearts sticking out of your ears."

Georgia laughs, scrunching up her face. "What does that even mean?"

Lincoln shrugs. "I heard the expression on TV once. They don't give you many channels in prison."

I cover my face, shaking my head. "Jesus, you guys are fucking nuts."

This might be the longest conversation I've had with our friends at one time, and damn, does it feel good. I never thought that I could be this way again—sitting and shooting the shit, forgetting about my troubles, being happy and joking around.

This is what I've been missing all this time.

Instead of torturing myself, I could've had this.

A woman who I love.

Friends who are goddamn crazy.

And a great relationship with my brother.

Georgia brought me back to life.

If I didn't have her, especially after my father's death, I don't even know if I'd still be around here.

She's what I needed when I thought I didn't need anyone.

Even when I was shaken, fucked up inside, she took a chance on me.

The woman changed me.

She gave me life again.

Lincoln slaps my back, and we walk to the bar, getting ready for the Saturday night chaos. I'm thankful Cohen didn't give me too much of a hard time about hiring Lincoln. Like with me, I think this bar and these people are also bringing him back to life.

The extravagant parties, the stuck-up and fake friends, the fast chicks—that's not the life for us anymore.

This is.

CHAPTER FORTY-ONE

Georgia

I WAVE over Cassidy when she comes into view after she's filled out her paperwork with Cohen. I'm training her tonight.

"Hey, girl," she says with a bright smile—now wearing a black shirt with the bar's logo on it.

Cassidy will do well here. She's gorgeous, outgoing, and smart. A people person, like me.

She sits down at the table with us, and I go through her training packet while my friends make side conversations around us—me having to hush them a few times for being too loud.

When I'm finished, I shut the employee handbook and clap. "You ready?"

"I think so." She holds out a finger to stop me before moving it to the bar. "Who is he? I want him for breakfast, lunch, and dinner."

The table falls quiet as everyone follows the direction of where she's staring with starry eyes … straight to where Archer is standing.

I inhale a fast breath, ready to storm into Cohen's office and tell him to train this girl himself—or better yet, fire her goddamn ass. She was at Cohen's party. Archer didn't make it a secret that we were together.

Grace drops her fry.

Lola leans back in her chair, crossing her arms, her eyes narrowing in on Cassidy.

Silas laughs—it's one covered in edge and warning. "You might be eating those meals through a straw if you keep talking about Archer like that in front of Georgia."

At least someone said it for me.

"Archer?" Cassidy's attention flicks to Silas, shaking her head. "Not him. We met at the barbecue. I'm talking about the guy next to him."

Everyone's gaze returns to the bar, and the tension leaves the table.

My heart settles.

Grace snags a fry.

Lola no longer looks ready to throw her drink on Cassidy.

"Lincoln?" Silas asks. "Archer's brother?"

"If that's the man next to him, then yes," she replies, her eyes following Lincoln as he moves behind the bar. "Is he single? Can I have him? What's his favorite breakfast, so I can make it for him on our morning after?"

Damn …

This girl is confident.

Silas scratches his cheek. "Be careful, newbie. We have a strict *no relationships between employees* rule around here. Too much drama."

Cassidy glances at me. "Aren't you and Archer dating?"

"They're the exception," Lola inputs.

"Maybe I can be an exception then too," Cassidy says with a smile.

Oh, she's going to be shaking some stuff up at Twisted Fox; that's for sure.

Probably why Maliki sent her our way—so he wouldn't have to deal with her.

"All right," I drawl out, taking a quick sip of Lola's drink before standing. "Time to get this training party started."

"Have fun, you cute kids, you," Lola sings out, and I smack her shoulder while passing her.

I train Cassidy—instruct her on our policies, show her around, and introduce her to the other employees.

"You met Archer," I say—even though I doubt Archer said two

words to her at Cohen's party. "And this is Lincoln. They're our bartenders for the night."

Cassidy's eyes shine as she licks her lips and stares at Lincoln. "Hi, I'm Cassidy. Your future wife."

I snort, ready for this mini show, and Archer rubs his forehead, as if he doesn't have time for this shit.

Lincoln laughs. "You're working here? Are you even old enough to legally buy a drink?"

"Obviously, or they wouldn't have hired me," Cassidy fires back.

Lincoln whistles and takes a step back. "I stand corrected." He winks. "I'm the fun bartender." He jerks his head toward Archer. "He's not."

Archer's brows furrow, and he looks at Lincoln with a *stay away from her* look.

Lincoln shrugs with a smirk.

Cassidy is eating up Lincoln's flirting.

Oh well.

She can flirt with Lincoln all night long, and I'd give no fucks.

Archer slaps my ass with a towel before kissing me on the lips. "You go train away, baby."

I smile, all giddy and flirty, and blow him a kiss as we walk onto the floor.

"So … why aren't you working at Maliki's bar?" I ask Cassidy as she follows me around.

For the first time, Cassidy seems shy, and she rubs her hands up and down her arms. "I got into some trouble, and we decided I needed to get out of town for a while."

"What kind of trouble?"

"Just stupid stuff that got me kicked out of college."

"Oh, I'm going to get that story out of you sometime."

———

TRAINING ON A SATURDAY night has been a catch-22.

Since the bar is slammed, I haven't had much time to train

Cassidy, but it's nice having the help. It'll also prepare her for the hectic shifts. I give her the two-top tables to make it easier on her.

"Dayum, sexy," a guy—my guess, early twenties—calls out when I approach his table. His tongue darts out and slides along his lower lip while he eyeballs me.

A little too friendly.

A little too aggressive.

Great, these tables are always so super-duper fun.

This asshole is going to ruin the Archer high I've been riding the past few days. I already know it.

Ignoring him, I sweep my gaze around the table, irritated. "What can I get you guys?"

"Your number," one answers with a smirk.

"Dude, back the fuck off," Original Creep—who I'll call OC—says, a sure-of-himself expression on his face. "I called dibs on her."

Feeling a headache coming on, I tap my pen against my notepad. "Seriously, your order, or I'll come back."

"Now, that's some bad customer service," OC says with a tsk. "Don't make us get your boss."

I hold back a snort. I always love when people threaten to tell my *boss.*

These are the times I'm happy that I work for my brother and that he's a good guy. Some bars have that *the customer is always right* mentality. It's a bunch of bullshit because a drunk person isn't always right.

Hell, a drunk person is rarely right.

As a person who works in a bar, I said what I said.

Thank God I didn't give Cassidy this table. My jerk reader must have been alive and well when I saw them sit.

But I did give her instructions on how to deal with customers like him. Tell Finn or one of the other guys and steer clear of the creeps. The problem is, I don't always follow my own instructions. To avoid conflict, I brush off advances, cheesy pick-up lines, and offensive slurs. If I go to Finn and ask him to throw a guy out, he'll tell Cohen—who I don't want to get in trouble for defending me.

I cringe as he scoots closer.

"What do you suggest?" he asks, reeking of booze and weed. From his bloodshot eyes, I'd put my money on more drugs than weed being in his system.

I tense and jump back when his hand scoots up the back of my thigh and up toward my ass.

Swatting it away, I shove his shoulder. "Touch me again, and your ass is out of here."

He smirks deviously. "Speaking of asses, you have a nice one, baby. How about you give me some of that?"

He reaches for me again, but I push him away, my back bumping into his friend, who's just as touchy as him.

"That body is just screaming for me to touch it, lick it, fuck it." He dramatically makes a sucking noise with his mouth.

"That's enough," I say. "Give me your order before I have our bouncer come over and take it for me."

"Oh shit, Chad, she's threatening you," another jerk says.

Chad runs his hands through his curly blond hair. "Nah, she's playing hard to get, but we all know she'll be on her knees with my cock in her mouth by the end of the night."

"All right, you need to leave."

"That's enough."

I peek up at the husky voice to find a guy who's stayed silent until now.

He strokes his chin and smiles at me. "Give her your order and shut the fuck up about her ass."

I release a long breath and send him a smile full of gratitude. He answers with a jerk of his head. As long as he keeps these douchebags in line, I'll grab their orders and ignore their comments the best I can.

"Fine, fine. You're no fun, Brad," Chad grumbles. "We'll have a round of Jäger bombs, and I'll also have a vodka and Red Bull." He smacks his hand on the table. "And keep the bombs coming, baby."

I take their orders and rush away. We don't get too many assholes, but it's a bar, so it's bound to happen.

"You good?" I ask Cassidy as I pass her.

"Yep!" she chirps with a smile while delivering drinks to a table.

My hand is clenching my pen so hard that I break off the clip. I'm scatterbrained as I walk toward the bar and drop my notebook on the way.

"God," I grumble, scrambling to pick it up.

"You okay?" Archer asks, staring at me with concern from behind the bar.

I nod, nearly out of breath. "Just busy."

"Are you getting overwhelmed?" His eyes meet mine in concern. "I'll get someone to help you."

I wave off his offer. "No, it's fine."

"You look like you're on the verge of tears," he snaps. "What the hell?"

"Nothing," I rush out. "Drunk people. They just suck sometimes."

His nostrils flare. "Is someone fucking with you?"

"No, it's just …" I shake my head and start rattling off my drink order.

He makes them, and before handing them over, he says, "If something happens, you run your ass over here. You hear me?"

"I hear you," I croak out.

My heart is racing when I deliver their drinks, nearly spilling one, and then I rush away from their table. As I run around, helping other customers, I feel their eyes on me.

———

"HEY, bitch, you're taking too long on our drinks. I shouldn't have to hunt you down," Chad hisses in my ear, fastening his hand around my elbow and jerking me toward him before I could walk away from the bar, toward another table. "I said to keep 'em coming."

I pull away from him. "Go to your table, and I'll grab them for you."

He blinks rapidly while staring at me. "You afraid to get in trouble, baby?"

When he grabs my arm again, a drink topples off my tray, shattering to the floor.

"You bitch!" Chad snarls, holding out his shirt to examine the bright red blotches—courtesy of the vodka cranberry that was on its way to table fifteen. "You ruined my shirt."

I guess that's my thing with assholes.

I spill drinks and mess up their shirts.

Serves them right.

I don't pick up the glass. No way am I bending down in front of his waist. I can only imagine what the creep would try.

"You okay, Georgia?" Cassidy yells over at me.

I nod, giving her a thumbs-up, and force a smile at Chad. "I'm really sorry. Your drinks will be on me tonight."

Chad smirks. "How about *you* be on me tonight to make up for it?"

Cassidy's question must've caught Archer's attention because I hear him calling my name from behind me.

"Look," I breathe out, "go to your table. I'll get your drinks, okay? I'm really sorry about your shirt."

He laughs manically. "Sorry won't cut it, sweetheart. Sucking my dick will, though."

I swallow down the nausea seeping up my belly. "Go back to your table before I tell my boss you're harassing me, and he kicks you out of here."

"Harassing you?" He snorts, his voice slurred. "Baby, this is harassing you."

When he grabs my ass, I drop my tray, every glass breaking, and push him with all my power. He stumbles back, hitting a few people and knocking down a chair.

I smile, proud of my badass self.

"What the fuck?" I hear Archer roar.

When I peek back at him, he's jumping over the bar and storming toward us, venom in his eyes, as the crowd parts, providing a straight line to Chad.

"You motherfucker!"

Knowing this won't end well, I turn and scurry in front of Chad just in time. "Archer, no!"

"Fuck that shit," Archer snarls, emphasizing each word. "Move, Georgia." His hands tighten into fists as he levels his gaze on Chad.

Everyone's awareness is on us now. Since it's a small-town bar, they know that Archer is an employee here. The main bartender. A few know he's also the owner. The last thing the bar needs is talk that an owner beat the shit out of a drunk guy. I've already spotted three people recording us.

I hold up my hand. "He's drunk. Let Finn kick him out."

"Nah, I'll take the trash out myself."

My breathing hitches as I straighten my back.

Relax.

When Lincoln appears at Archer's side, there's a hint of that relaxation. I exhale another breath when Finn stops next to me, his eyes shooting back and forth between Archer and Chad.

"I got this," he says.

Then Chad stupidly decides to make things worse. "Oh, look, the assholes are coming to her rescue."

"Georgia, goddamn it, move." Every muscle in Archer's body goes rigid.

We're in a standoff, and I can't believe I'm standing between my boyfriend and a man who grabbed my ass, asking my boyfriend to let it be.

There isn't one person in the bar who isn't looking at us, and panic charges through me when Cohen joins us, his gaze bouncing between me, Archer, and Chad.

Archer doesn't look at Cohen or Finn for backup.

His glare is fixed on Chad, waiting for me to step aside so he can unleash his rage.

"No," I say, my voice shaking. "He's drunk, and I don't want you doing anything stupid."

"He fucking touched you!" Archer screams. "Don't fucking defend him!"

"What do you mean, he touched her?" Cohen yells, tapping in and ready to play sidekick to Archer's ass-kicking.

"Cassidy," I call out, my voice pleading, "tell his friends they need to take him home." They've been watching the scene, but so far, none of them have come to his rescue.

Cassidy nods and scrambles toward his friends. With groans and looks of annoyance, they get up.

Chad tilts his shoulder in a half-shrug, and now that he knows his friends are coming, he grows braver. "She's been asking for it all night. You should've seen the way she was looking at me, practically drooling for my cock."

My hands are shaking in anger as I attempt to tune out Chad's words. I whisper Archer's name, struggling to grasp his attention.

Look at me.

Only me.

Chad pounds his fist against his chest and stares at Archer mockingly. "You want a piece of her pussy too? I'll share after I've had my fill."

His words light a match underneath the fire that is Archer, and there's no stopping him. Archer swings around me to reach Chad.

I fall, and everything goes black.

CHAPTER FORTY-TWO

Archer

I SHOULD WALK AROUND with a D on my chest.

A scarlet letter kind of way.

A signal that says, *If you love me, prepare for death.*

Guilt spreads through my chest, as if an infection, controlling my every thought.

This is all my fault.

I was on too much of a high—a high where I thought my life could be different.

That I could be happy.

That'll never be me.

I'm a curse.

Poison to the heart.

Unlike my grandfather, everything I touch doesn't turn to gold.

It turns to black.

Into flames.

Obliterated.

If only I'd walked away from that fight.

If only I'd listened to her.

After Georgia fell, everything became a fog.

The man who'd groped her became the least of my worries. I

should've been paying more attention, but the fury I had toward the guy consumed me. He needed to get his ass kicked.

For hurting her.

For touching her.

For the vile shit he was spitting from his lips.

She took a hard blow to the head and was bleeding. Her eyes were shut, and she wasn't speaking, like she was in a deep sleep. She was breathing but not lucid. I desperately yelled her name, gently shook her shoulders, snapped my fingers in front of her face until Cohen pushed me to the side and did the same.

Someone called 911, and she was rushed to the hospital. Chad and his friends ran out of the bar, and since our attention was on Georgia, no one tried stopping them.

I hate myself.

I veer into the first open spot I find in the hospital's parking lot and slam my fists against the steering wheel. Cohen rode with Georgia in the ambulance, and I followed them. Lincoln and Finn stayed behind to work the bar until someone could cover for them.

My head is bowed in shame when I step out of my car and rush into the emergency room.

I ignore other patients, ignore the workers at the front desk, and say, "I need to see Dr. Jamie Gentry."

Name-dropping Jamie is the fastest way to get to where I need to be. She's the doctor on shift at the hospital tonight, and Finn called, giving her a heads-up to expect Georgia. The woman behind the counter surprisingly nods, and the double doors electronically open. The scent of antiseptic invades my nostrils, and I rush over to Jamie, who's talking to a nurse.

"She wasn't waking up," I say, my voice quivering. "She wasn't waking up."

Never have I felt so vulnerable around someone other than Georgia.

Jamie's face is professional, her look both serious and packed with concern. "She's awake. Well, she's conscious but sleeping. She's going to be okay." Her voice is soothing. "We're thinking it's only a mild concussion."

I shake my head and repeat, "She wasn't waking up."

Just like the memory of dragging my grandfather out of the pool, begging him to wake up, Georgia lying on that dirty bar floor, unconscious, will forever haunt me.

Visit me in my dreams.

Reminding me of my fuckups.

Jamie steps closer and wraps her arms around me.

"Where's she?" I ask, my voice nearly a plea. "Can I see her?"

"Room four." She tips her head toward a room and takes my hand. "Just … if Cohen tries to argue, don't engage."

I nod, holding back the urge to barge into Georgia's room, sit by her side, and apologize.

When the door clicks open, Cohen's eyes narrow, looking at me to blame.

I slip my hands into my pockets and walk farther into the room. I have to see her. He can punch me, beat my ass, do all the shit he should've done the day of his gender-reveal party so that this would've never happened.

He exchanges a look with Jamie, and she stops behind him, wrapping her arms around her fiancé from the back. He runs his hand over his face, shielding his silent tears.

"I'm sorry," I tell him, taking the few long strides to Georgia.

Cohen massages his temples. "It's not your fault. It's that asshole's fault."

"Archer, it was an accident," Jamie says.

Thanks for trying to make me feel better, but you're wrong.

Cohen stands. "Can you sit with her while I use the restroom?"

"Yes."

"They'll be coming and getting her for a CT scan," Jamie says. "We want to check for internal bleeding on the brain. She's on pain medicine, so she'll be groggy."

I scrub my hand over my forehead and nod.

Cohen tips his head down and leaves the room with Jamie, giving me the alone time I so desperately need.

"Baby," I say, stepping to her side, wiping my watery eyes and my face with the back of my arm.

A white bandage is wrapped around her head, covering the wound she wouldn't have if I was able to control myself.

Her eyes slowly open, brimmed with confusion, and she fights for them not to close again. I reach out, running my hand along her sweaty forehead, and my chest aches.

"I'm sorry," I cry out in a whisper.

This is why I didn't want to get close.

Her voice is hoarse, and my name comes out in a long breath. "Archer." She looks down, noticing the IV in her arm, and winces when she touches her head. "What am I doing here?" She scans her body, as if it were foreign, inspecting her hands and arms.

"You fell." I clasp my hand over her clammy one. "You hit your head, but you'll be okay."

She struggles to keep her eyes open, and I tip my head forward, drawing closer.

"Get some rest." I caress her face, as if it'll never happen again, my goal to lodge it into my memory, never forgetting the perfection I had but ruined.

She relaxes into my touch, her head resting against my palm. "Will you be here when I wake up?"

"Always," I say, squeezing my eyes shut, my pain clutching my throat. "I'll always be here." I brush my lips against hers, lingering for a moment, and then I pull away and press one to her forehead. "I love you."

There's a gentle knock on the door, and a nurse walks in. "Hi there, I'm here to take her to her CT scan."

Georgia's eyes are heavy as she whispers, "I love you."

My shoulders hunch forward as I take one last look at her, aware I'm losing everything again.

Walking away is what I should've done.

Not invite her into my bed, into my heart, only to fall in love.

This time, I need to stop being selfish and do what's right for her.

CHAPTER FORTY-THREE

Georgia

"I'LL ALWAYS BE HERE. I love you," are the words I remember when I wake up.

As the woman wheeled me away, I noticed there was a deep pain on Archer's face.

My eyes are heavy as I open them, and Jamie is standing over me.

"Hi, Georgia."

"Hi," I say in hesitation around a scratchy throat.

My gaze darts around the room as questions ram through my aching skull, so fast that I can't keep up.

"Do you know why you're here?"

I hear her voice, but it's as if she were speaking to me from across the room. I shut my eyes, thinking back to earlier.

"A little. I hit my head?"

It's obvious *something* happened to my head. I've never felt a headache so throbbing, so powerful, and if I had a choice at the moment, I'd rip the damn thing off my shoulders and throw it across the room.

"Headache?"

"Like no other," I grumble.

"Sleepy?"

"I could sleep for the next month."

I shut my eyes and listen to people talk around me.

"No internal bleeding on the brain. No vomiting, slurred speech, or seizures," Jamie says. "It's a concussion—a hard hit to the head—and we want to keep an eye on her, but she'll be okay."

"Thank God for that," Cohen inputs.

"Can someone help me sit up?" I ask, feeling like I have no control over my body.

"Of course," Jamie answers, but it's Cohen who's at my side to help.

His face is red and puffy. There have been few instances when my brother has cried. He's always the strong one—the shoulder you cry on, the one who assures you everything will be okay.

I hiss a few times in pain as he helps me, and I take deep breaths as I scan the crowded room. Lola, Grace, my mother, Silas, and Finn are scattered around the room, standing or sitting in chairs.

My mother's face is splotchy.

Lola's and Grace's faces are red.

Worry creases Silas's forehead.

Finn's muscles are strained, as if he wants to kick someone's ass.

I'm thankful they're here.

I'm just missing one person.

My stomach churns, as I'm expecting the worst, when I ask, "Where's Archer?"

He should be here, right?

Maybe he went for a restroom break?

Grabbed a coffee?

Nervous glances are shared around the room.

No one says a word.

Cohen, noticing the panic, says, "We think he went home."

Untruth is plastered on his face.

I know my brother too well.

"You think? Can't you ask Lincoln if he's home?"

"Sweetie, he might be napping," Jamie says, coming to my brother's rescue.

"Jesus, be honest with her," Lola snaps, standing and walking to my side. "Head injury or not, she deserves for us to be up front with her."

Lola, always the one to give no bullshit.

The one who will give you the ugly truth to save you from harder heartbreak later.

"Babe," she says, taking my hand in hers, a doleful expression on her face, "Archer is MIA."

"Lola," Silas snaps.

Lola holds her palm toward him, not looking in his direction, her face falling as she delivers the blow. "I know it's not what you want to hear, but from your face, I know you wouldn't have stopped asking questions until someone told you anyway."

"What ..." My hands tremble. "What do you mean, *MIA*?"

She shakes her head in disappointment. "No one can find him, and he's not answering his phone."

"He was here earlier. Maybe he's sleeping or something." I gesture to Cohen as nausea consumes my stomach. "Can I have your phone, please?"

"Georgia—" he starts.

"Your phone!" I shriek frantically. "Someone give me a phone, *please*." My voice breaks; my heart breaks.

Cohen shoves his hand into his pocket, fishing out his phone. He unlocks it and hands it to me. I go to his contacts, hit Archer's name, and listen to it ring.

And ring.

And ring.

No answer.

I call Lincoln next.

"Do you know where Archer is?" I ask without offering a greeting.

"No clue," he replies. "Sorry, Georgia."

"Don't lie to me."

"I wouldn't. No one knows."

I ignore the IV in my hand, the sound of beeping machines next to me, the fact that I don't even know the full story of why the hell I'm sitting in the hospital as I break down and sob.

"I hate him," I cry out, my gut already telling me he's gone.

"You don't hate him," Silas says. I've never heard his voice so gentle. "Maybe he's taking a breather."

"He's gone," I say, no doubt in my voice.

No hesitation.

No being an optimist.

I fall back asleep, and when I wake up again, he's not there.

He walked away as if I was nothing, as if I meant nothing, as if our relationship meant nothing.

Just like the first time we'd slept together.

CHAPTER FORTY-FOUR

Archer

I CAME HERE to clear my head.

I tried my penthouse, but I knew that was the first place they'd look.

Every single friend has called me, even the girls.

After the hundredth call, I shut off my phone.

"How'd I know you'd be here?"

I peek back to find Lincoln walking down the long dock as I sit at the edge, my legs hanging over, the water splashing against my feet.

He groans while sitting down next to me. "Everyone is looking for you."

No one, other than Lincoln, would think to look here.

Like my grandfather and my father, I've chosen to take solace here.

I stare ahead. "You didn't tell them—"

He cuts me off, "No. As much as I like them, you're my brother."

"You and your loyalty,"

"Maybe you should try the shit for a change. Quit being a selfish dick."

His honesty is a nasty bitch slap.

"Fuck off," I growl.

"Georgia is in the hospital, man."

My voice is flat. "I'm well aware."

"That's where you should be."

"I saw her. Made sure she was okay. Told her good-bye." The last part is a half-lie. I did my good-byes, but I lied to her. While I knew it'd be my last time, she thought I'd be there, waiting for her. My stomach clenches. I hate myself.

"The fuck you mean, you *told her good-bye*?"

I shrug.

He scoffs. "You know that's a punk-ass move, right?"

I finally shift to look at him, my upper lip snarling. "You know I'm fucked up in the head. Why are you here, starting this shit with me?"

"You're not fucked up in the head. You have guilt."

I stab my skull with my finger. "Guilt makes you fucked up in the head."

"Don't walk away from her."

I don't say anything.

"She's asking for you. She's *crying* for you."

His words are a blow to the chest, delivering the truth I already knew. "She might be hurting now, but in the end, she'll be happy I did this."

"Happy you broke her heart? That's the dumbest bullshit I've ever heard."

"In the end, when she finds the right man for her, she will."

"In the end, where will you be? Alone, in your self-pity hell? You'll regret turning your back on a woman who'd fight any battle for you, who dealt with your demons as if they were her own, who was willing to walk down the darkest roads to be with you ... all while you were still playing games with her head. If you don't get your dumbass up and go to the hospital, it'll be the biggest mistake of your life."

I do what I do best—stay quiet.

He stands. "You coming?"

"Nah."

He blows out a stressed breath and nods. "Whatever, but keep in touch with me. Even if it's a simple emoji or *I'm still alive* text, I want it."

CHAPTER FORTY-FIVE

Georgia

One Week Later

"GEORGIA," Lincoln says when he walks into the bar.

I stare at him with the dirtiest look I can muster. "Unless you're here to tell me where the hell your bastard of a brother is, I'm not speaking to you."

He knows where Archer is but won't tell anyone.

There's been no word from him.

The first few days, I called and texted.

No response.

So, I stopped.

What I want to say to him needs to be said in person.

Lincoln has covered his shifts.

I told Cohen to fire his ass—even though I knew Cohen wouldn't go through it.

It's not Lincoln's fault his brother is a spineless jerk, but all I need is an address. An address to march my butt over to, so I can deliver the hardest kick in the balls my little body can muster.

Provide him temporary pain to ease my eternal hurt.

"Archer asked me to give you this." He holds out an envelope to me.

I stare at the envelope as if it's filled with anthrax. "What Archer needs to do is grow some balls, face me, and tell me why he left me."

Lincoln thrusts the envelope closer. "Archer doesn't always do what he needs to do. You know this."

"What's his plan then?" Cassidy asks, sitting back in her chair and crossing her arms. "He's just never coming back?"

"I think that's his plan," Lincoln mutters.

Cassidy's eyes widen. "What about you? Are you leaving too?"

Lincoln shrugs. "I have no idea. Now, take the envelope."

"What's in it?" I glare at it.

"He didn't say. Only asked me to give it to you." He holds up his hands. "Don't shoot the messenger."

I snatch it from his hand, and their eyes are on me as I rip it open. Papers are folded inside. I jerk them out as if they'd stolen today's coffee and unfold them, and then my mouth turns dry as I read his bullshit letter.

Georgia,

I'm sorry.

Fifty percent of the bar is yours.

Do what you want with it. Sell it to Cohen or be a partner but make yourself happy.

Archer

"You've got to be kidding me," I hiss, glaring at Lincoln. "Tell me where he is."

Lincoln shakes his head. "No can do, babe."

"Goddamn it, Lincoln!" I shriek, tossing the letter onto the table. "Forget your stupid loyalty for one damn minute and tell me where he is." I flick the letter away. "He's trying to sign over the bar to me."

"What?" he sputters out.

I jerk my head toward the letter. "Read it."

He does, slamming it down when he's finished, and exhales a frustrated breath. "He's at our grandparents' lake house."

Okay, I know where that is.

Kinda.

Not really.

I could pick it out of a line of houses, but no way can I just drive there.

I played passenger when I went with Archer and was too busy introducing him to every TLC song to pay attention to where exactly we were going.

"Address, please," I say.

He gives me a *good one* look.

"Directions."

"Fine, fine, but don't say I'm the one who gave it to you."

Cassidy chuckles. "There's no way you're getting out of this one." She slaps his arm. "Think of it as your good deed of the day."

He peers over at Cassidy, fighting back a smile. "Listen, youngster, don't you have some frat boy's heart to break or Barbies to play with?"

She flips him off. "Don't you need to go find your vitamins to keep your bones strong and pick up your Viagra from the pharmacy?"

Lincoln stares at me. "Georgia, since you might be the new part owner, fire her ass."

Cassidy throws her head back. "Lincoln, dear, the chances of you being fired are much higher than mine since you're related to the devilish heartbreaker."

Cassidy has made it her mission to get under Lincoln's skin, and as much as he tries to fight it, he always caves in, engaging with her.

Lincoln rubs his forehead. "He's going to kick my ass for this, so be happy that I like you."

"Just tell him I went through Lincoln's phone and gave it to you," Cassidy says with a shrug. The girl is a brave one, not even flinching at the possible wrath of Archer.

Lincoln shakes his head. "I'll text you the address."

Cassidy peers up at me. "You okay to drive? I can take you if you want?"

"She wants a front seat to the shitshow," Lincoln comments.

She whips around to glare at him. "Rude. I *also* want to make sure she's cool to drive."

"I'm fine. They told me to wait forty-eight hours before driving, and it's been a week. I haven't felt dizzy at all. All I need from you is for you to cover my shift tonight."

She points at me and clicks her tongue. "I got you."

CHAPTER FORTY-SIX

Archer

AS SOON AS I answer the door, papers are shoved into my chest.

"Fuck these papers," Georgia shouts, storming into the lake house. "Fuck your games. Fuck your excuses. *Fuck you, Archer!*"

The papers plummet to my feet, and stepping to the side, I slam the door shut. "Georgia, calm your ass down."

Her thick hair is wet, dripping at the ends, and her shirt is soaked to her skin from the downpour outside.

Why the hell was she driving?

Why the hell did my dumbass brother tell her where to find me, give her directions, and not give me a heads-up?

Georgia stares at me, shivering. "No, I won't calm my ass down." Her voice cracks as she continues, "You left me, Archer! You left me in the hospital."

I shake my head before laying out my bullshit excuse. "I went to the hospital and made sure you were okay."

"Then you left!"

"What did you expect me to do?" I pound my finger against my chest. "My actions were what landed you in that hospital bed. It's time you find a man who isn't a toxic son of a bitch like me."

"What did I expect you to do? I don't know ... uh, stay! I've been there for you over and over, but when it came time *for you* to be there *for me*, you ran." Tears fill her eyes, mascara running down her cheeks —pain and the rain the culprits.

My stomach knots, blistering with torment. "I'm sorry. It was the wrong way to end things, but by now, you should know that it was best for me to walk away."

"You're right." A cold smile creeps up her lips, sending chills down my spine. "I don't want to try to make it work with you anymore. You're selfish."

I stumble back a step, her words a blow to my chest.

Isn't that what I wanted?

For her to be done with my ass?

"What? You have nothing to say?" she rasps. "Of course you don't. I'm out of here."

My head spins, and I thank God I put down the bottle of Jack I'd been sipping on earlier, finally realizing it was time I quit relying on alcohol to mask my torment. Being alone in this lake house with hours upon hours to think has opened my eyes. Lincoln, Georgia, everyone was right. It's time for me to sit down, pull through my shit, and be the man Georgia deserves.

That means I have to let her go.

Who knows how long it'll take me to sort out my shit?

I teeter back when her shoulder smacks into mine on her way to the door.

Whipping around, I circle my arm around her waist to stop her. "No way are you driving in this weather."

She jerks away from me, venom in her tone. "In what?"

She shitting me?

I gesture outside. "It's dark, like a fucking monsoon out there. You're upset, and it's a long drive. You're not getting behind the wheel."

Her face burns with anger. "I'm sure as shit not staying here and hanging out with you."

"Too damn bad. You're the one who drove here, stomping and ready to kick my ass—"

"Which is fully deserved."

"I'll take that."

She crosses her arms. "Take me home then."

"*Neither* one of us is driving in this weather." I'll confiscate her keys, hide them, flush them down the damn toilet if I have to.

"This is entrapment."

"I'll let you go tomorrow."

She slips a glance at the papers on the floor, and I follow her gaze, recoiling as I stare at my handwriting, at the bullshit letter I wrote. Sure, it was a stupid move on my part, but it was what I felt was best.

Tapping her foot, she goes quiet, as if weighing her options. "Fine. Entrap me away."

My shoulders relax. "Let me grab you some dry clothes."

I wait for her argument, for her to tell me she isn't wearing any of my shit, but she doesn't. I hold in a breath while rushing into my bedroom, grabbing the first shirt and gym shorts I see, in hopes that she won't bail on my ass. Chasing her through the rain sounds like a bad time. When I return, she's on the couch, shivering and running her hands up and down her arms.

I hand them over. "Here."

With hesitation, she takes them, rises, and walks to the bathroom. I search for a blanket, raid the pantry, and pull out the instant hot-chocolate mix. She's tugging at the ends of her hair, the black blotches cleaned from her cheeks, and her bare feet slap against the floor as I stir hot-chocolate powder into a mug filled with warm water.

"Sit," I say, wrapping her up in the blanket and settling her down before handing over the mug.

She shifts, making herself comfortable. "How did we go from screaming at each other to you snuggling me in a blanket and providing hot chocolate?" She shakes her head. "Swear to God, our *whatever this is* between us is super dysfunctional."

I run my hand over my jaw and sit in a chair across from her, my legs wide. "Don't you see, that's what I've been trying to tell you?"

She raises the mug to her lips but doesn't drink. "Is dysfunctional a bad thing, though?"

I raise a brow, a *really* expression crossing my face.

"I don't mean *Sammi Sweetheart and Ronnie* dysfunctional. Let me reword it. Would you rather be boring? The few problems we have are nothing compared to others. When you're not running away, we get along perfectly. You're a great boyfriend and thoughtful. Well, you *were* a great boyfriend."

I grind my teeth at the word *were*.

"Archer, why do you feel like you can't love?"

"It's not that. Trust me, I *feel* love. I love you with every inch of my being. That's why I'm letting you go. I don't deserve you."

She pats the couch, and because I don't think and I long to be near her, I go to her.

My hand caressing her hair, I kiss her forehead. "I can never be perfect for you."

"I don't want perfect. I want *you*. When you're not acting like a jerk, we're good. Growing up, I saw bad relationships. I witnessed men treating my mother terribly. That's not you. It's not us."

"If you're okay with disappointment—"

"Jesus, you're not a disappointment." She yawns, exhaustion on her face, and takes a gulp of hot chocolate, like it'll give her a rush of energy. "I don't want the perfect man. That sounds scary, very Stepford Husband-ish."

I chuckle.

"Like you, I have issues. Daddy issues, an attitude problem, I've been called a sarcastic bitch more times than I can count, I get hangry like no other, I kill my bank account with my iced-coffee addiction, and I am stupid in love with you."

I gulp at the *stupid in love with you* comment. "All I care about is your happiness."

She squeezes her eyes shut and shrinks into the blanket. "What if my happiness is with you?" Another yawn escapes her. "I love you, Archer."

My back straightens. Hearing her say *I love you* is a knife through my heart.

She nibbles on the bottom of her lip. "It's really over for us, isn't it?"

My mouth opens to tell her yes, but I can't do it. I can't look at the woman I love and say I'm done with her, with us. I can't. As much as I tell myself I can walk away from her, I'm too weak. Selfishly, I can't let her go.

Her eyes are wet when she sets her mug on the coffee table and flips the blanket off her lap. "While I appreciate the warm drink, staring at the man who's breaking my heart isn't a good time."

"Stop."

She freezes.

"I can't." I shake my head, my voice breaking. "I can't let you go, Georgia. I thought I could, but …" I hang my head low. "Stay tonight, please. Get some rest, and we can talk about this tomorrow."

I need to find the right words, the right way to fix us, to show her I can be a changed man. In doing that, she needs her space, needs time to process everything. And like so many other times, I don't want to use her body as I attempt to cope and deal with my issues.

"I'm not sleeping with you, only for you to tell me to kick rocks tomorrow."

"Take the guest room."

She's quiet.

"I promise, it's way more comfortable than your bed."

"Always hating on my bed." She stands. "Show me the way to my room, heartbreaker."

I lead her up the stairs and down the hallway. I open the door, and when I turn, she's wiping away silent tears from her blotchy face. I clench my fist, fighting back the restraint to hold her, to drag her to my bed so she never has sadness again.

I kiss her forehead. "Get some rest."

CHAPTER FORTY-SEVEN

Georgia

THUNDER ROARS OUTSIDE, knocking me out of my sleep, and I peek around the dark room. I left the bedside lamp on, but when I lean forward to turn it back on, it clicks, and nothing happens. The power must've gone out.

With no hesitation, I jump out of bed and creep down the hallway. His bedroom door is cracked. It squeaks as I open it all the way. I tiptoe into the room, and the sheets are soft when I crawl into bed with him.

"Don't say anything," I whisper when he stirs.

He nods, wraps his arm around me, and pulls me into him.

No words are spoken, and I fall into a restful sleep.

———

I MISSED THIS.

Missed waking up next to him, his strong body warming mine, his grip on me tight. I missed the happiness of opening my eyes and having him with me first thing in the morning—this man who I've gone through so many highs and lows with.

When I stormed out of the bar and drove to his grandparents' lake house last night, I had no plan. My lack of plan also included my lack of checking the weather. I didn't expect all hell to break loose on my drive here. Even though I fought it, I was glad he'd told me to stay.

I'm in his arms, the broad expanse of his chest against my back, and I feel his light breathing.

We need to talk.

No more arguing.

Running.

Back and forth.

Whatever is happening between us needs to be sorted out.

He stirs behind me, a yawn leaving him, and I roll away from him to settle on my back. His face is unreadable, and my sleepy eyes meet him in question.

"Morning," I whisper with a nervous smile.

"Morning."

"Last night was interesting."

My heart rages against my chest while I wait for his response.

Will he want me out of his bed?

Ask me to leave?

Beg me to stay?

Push me down and do every dirty thing he did to me the last time we were in here?

He yawns again, stretching out his arms. "A gorgeous woman crawling into my bed is indeed interesting."

My stomach settles.

"Really?" I playfully shove his shoulder. "It was pouring outside, I was in a random room, and there were weird-ass noises."

"You scared of the dark now?"

"No, I actually thought you needed consoling. You were talking in your sleep, whining about monsters. So, like the nice person I am, I came in to keep you safe from them."

He chuckles. "Appreciate that, babe."

Babe.

My head is dizzy.

"We need to talk." He pulls himself up, resting his back against the headboard.

I raise myself, shoving my elbow onto the bed, and peer up at him. "Agreed."

He blows out a breath, and his voice is level when he speaks, "I was wrong. I should've never run. I should've been by your side every minute you were in the hospital."

And I only grow dizzier.

I rub at my face, telling my head to straighten the hell up so I can process this conversation. "Why'd you do it? Why'd you leave?"

He doesn't lower his gaze or try to hide the guilt on his face. The firmness in his tone confirms our talk will be filled with truths and decisions. "I was scared." No bullshit, no excuses, the words coming out strong.

"Of what?" I whisper.

"Losing you?"

"Are you kidding me?" I shriek. "You chose to lose me."

"I fucked up. I thought I was doing what was best for you."

"I'm confused as to why *you* think you know what's best for *me*."

He groans. "Do you not realize why I'm scared? My grandfather and I argued, and he died. My father and I argued, and he died. You and I argue over me kicking a guy's ass, and you end up in the hospital with a concussion."

I raise a brow. "How'd you know it was a concussion?"

"Lincoln kept me updated."

"Snitch bitch," I grumble. "He had no problem giving out my business, but it was like pulling teeth to get him to give me anything on you."

"Lincoln likes you, likes us together."

"He's the brother with the brains."

He chuckles. "You're probably right."

I slide in closer to him. "Archer, what happened was an accident. You didn't mean to hurt me, and I don't blame you."

"I know." His face drops. "As I lay here last night when you were in the other room, I questioned everything I was doing wrong in my life. Then at the time I was mustering up the courage to let you go, you climbed into my bed. I realized, at that moment, I always want you in my arms. I don't want to lose that—to lose you and being the man who makes you happy. I love you, and I need to quit telling myself that I don't deserve our relationship."

"What are you saying then?"

"I'm saying, I love you, and though I don't deserve it, I'm asking for another chance."

My heart swells in my chest. I don't want it to seem like I'm letting him off the hook too easily, but I've never doubted Archer having feelings for me. It's whether Archer is willing to take the steps to be with me. There's no way I can look at this man that I love and turn my back on him.

Archer isn't a bad man. He's just gone through some bad shit.

"I lost my way," he continues. "Thinking people only wanted who I'd been before—the guy full of life, who didn't hold guilt on his shoulders like it was a part of him he'd die without. I'll never be that guy again, and I'm realizing that's not who you want. You didn't fall in love with that guy. You fell in love with who I am now, the man I've turned into, and for that, I realize that maybe I've found who I was supposed to be all along."

"Archer," I breathe out his name, making it longer as I search for the right words. "If I let you back in, if I put my heart on the line, then you need to promise me that you won't pull this shit again."

His shoulders curl forward. "I'm not perfect. I can't promise I won't fuck up, but I give you my word. There will be no running."

"Your word doesn't mean much right now. You gave me your word at the hospital."

"I fucked up."

"I can take flaws and haunted pasts, but I won't take disappearing. If we do this, it's all in. Period. If you can't commit to that, then walk away now. You can still work in the bar, and we'll be friends."

My stomach churns.

Friends.

I hate that word when it comes to Archer.

"I'm all in. I'm so damn sorry, baby. I was fighting to convince myself you'd end up being happier with someone else."

"Never going to happen."

"I love you, Georgia, more than you'll ever know." He grabs my arm and pulls me onto his lap. "You've changed me into a better man. You're inside me. You ripped yourself into my veins, shaking every bone in my body, until my heart finally broke free."

Tears are in my eyes.

He's fighting back his own.

I circle my arms around his neck, my stomach fluttering. "You know you have some making up to do, right?"

"Oh, baby, I know."

I giggle when he rolls me over onto my back. We're undressed in minutes, he slides a condom on, and when he positions himself at my opening, he stops.

His hand spreads on my chest over my heart. "This right here, I've never seen someone have such a big heart after going through the pain you have." He moves his hand to kiss the spot and then sucks on my nipple. "Not only is this body mine, but this heart is too." He grabs my hand and presses it to his chest. "And this, this belongs to you— the woman who saved me, who gave me a life again."

CHAPTER FORTY-EIGHT

Archer

"ARCHER." Cohen is standing in the doorway of my office with a scowl on his face and his hands shoved in his pockets.

I scrub a hand over my forehead. "Why do I feel like I'm about to get grounded?"

Cohen's face is blank as he walks in. "Maybe because what you did was fucked up."

I nod, understanding his anger. "I was in a bad place."

"You still in that bad place?"

"I can't say I'm not, but I'm also working through it."

His brows furrow. "Don't disappear on me again. You left me with a brokenhearted sister in the hospital, a son, a baby on the way, and a fiancée who craves Skittles one minute and a goddamn cheeseburger the next. I don't have time for your bullshit."

Damn.

Cohen isn't fucking around today. I feel bad. I'd assured him that there wouldn't be any issues with me wanting to pull out, but then I tried to give away my half of the bar. Cohen should have looked at the plus side. He'd have owned the bar with his family.

"I got your back, man. I'm clearing out my head."

"We all get one fuckup." He holds out his knuckles.

CHARITY FERRELL

I think I've had more than one.

I bump my knuckles against his. "It won't happen again."

He gestures toward the door. "Now, come on. We have some drinks to make."

I stand, and he claps me on the back on our way to the floor. "It's good to be back."

———

"MMM, BACK THAT ASS UP," I groan, my hard cock rubbing against Georgia's ass crack.

We're in my bed, and damn, it's missed her.

She laughs, peering back at me with a smile. "What little ass I have."

I cup her backside before giving it a firm smack. "I love your ass, baby."

"You have to say that. You're my boyfriend."

"I don't have to say shit." I run my hand over one cheek and then the other. She shivers, pressing her ass into me, moving her hips in circles. "Ah, you kill me."

Hitching her leg over my waist, I find her clit, using my thumb to play with it, and she writhes against me. She shifts, and I groan at the loss of her. When she situates herself on all fours, my dick aches.

Crawling behind her, settling myself on my knees, I eye her adorable ass. "How bad do you want it, baby?" I slide my cock between her cheeks, my free hand massaging one.

She arches her back, her ass more in my face, and her grin is devious as she looks back at me. "How bad do *you* want it?"

I chuckle and lift forward to kiss her. She slides her tongue into my mouth and moans my name, knowing that's my weakness. Tilting her hips up, her ass in the air, I give it a quick slap before sliding inside her, inside heaven.

Her pussy tightens around my cock, gripping it hard, owning it.

My hands cup each cheek of her ass while I set a slow pace, waiting for what she wants.

There are times we fuck hard.

There are times we make love.

It isn't until she says, "Harder," that I slam into her with no restraint.

My bed thumps against the wall with each thrust.

My eyes are transfixed as I watch my cock slide in and out of her.

Our moans are loud.

The sound of my thighs smacking into her ass is music to my ears.

"I could stay inside you forever," I moan. "Touch yourself, baby. Play with your clit as I fuck your pussy."

I love it when she touches herself. Not as much as I love eating her pussy or fucking her, but it's pretty damn close. Just as she loves watching me jerk myself off.

"Are you close?" I groan. "Tell me you're close to coming on this hard cock."

"Yes." Her hand moves faster as she plays with her clit.

I lose myself, pounding into her until she's falling apart underneath me. Knowing her knees are about to buckle, I plant my hands on her waist, grinding into her. As I come inside her, I jerk my arm back and slap her ass. I shudder, my back straightening, and seconds later, I'm falling onto all fours. We catch our breath.

She's the first woman I've ever fucked without a condom. The first time, it was a spur-of-the-moment thing. Shower sex. It'd put a damper on the mood to walk into the freezing cold to put a condom on. She's on the pill, and so far, we haven't had any issues.

———

"I MISSED HAVING you in my bed, baby," I whisper.

Georgia snuggles into my arms. "I missed how comfortable your bed is."

"Really? That's what you missed?" I grind into her.

We had sex ten minutes ago, but I'm ready for round two.

"That, among other things."

It's been two weeks since I got my head out of my ass.

Two weeks of me proving to Georgia that I'm sorry.

Two weeks of being the happiest man I've ever been.

"What if you could do it every day?"

She winces, staring back at me. "What do you mean?"

"Move in with me." I nuzzle my face into her neck, planting kisses along her soft skin. "Wake up with me every morning. Sleep in my arms every night."

She falls onto her back, and I level my palm on the other side of her, staring down while meeting her eyes.

"That's a pretty big step … it'd make things serious."

"I want to prove to you that I'm serious about us, baby." I tip my head down to kiss her. "I want this. I want you." I slide my tongue along the seam of her lips. "What do you say?"

She opens her mouth, sucking on the tip of my tongue, and the conversation stops momentarily as I make love to her this time.

With each circle of my hips, each thrust inside her, I hope to prove myself.

Show her how comfortable life is with me, how she'd wake up every morning.

She comes. I come.

She shrieks my name. I moan out hers.

"I need to make sure Grace can find another roommate," she whispers.

"Lola?" I ask. "Cassidy mentioned looking for a place too."

"I'll talk to her about it. I can't just bail on her."

"She can't make rent on her own?"

"She can. It's just … complicated."

CHAPTER FORTY-NINE

Georgia

Two Months Later

IT'S BABY TIME.

Not mine, I should clarify.

Nor am I trying to make a little mini me yet.

I'm practically dancing in my chair while in the hospital waiting room. Anticipation has consumed me since Cohen called last night and said Jamie was going into labor. He asked us to wait until the baby was born before coming to the hospital since it'd just be a waiting game. An hour ago, he called and said there's another Fox baby in the family.

I'm over the moon for them. Jamie gave my brother the happiness he'd thought he'd never have again. His trust in people was shit, especially with a woman related to the girl who'd not only turned her back on him, but also his son. Having a woman look you in the eye and ask you to give your unborn baby up can be soul-crushing. My brother was never the same after that.

This time, it's a different experience. He's not going in, unknowing if Jamie will want their baby girl. There will be no bittersweet day when he's excited to meet his son yet scared of the agony of uncertainty if his child will have a mother.

"You excited?" Archer asks.

"I can't wait to meet her," I tell him.

He chuckles, squeezing my knee. "You're going to spoil the shit out of her, aren't you?"

"Damn straight."

I'm already guilty of letting Noah sucker me into giving him extra cupcakes and sneaking him fruit snacks that have actual sugar in them.

Not only am I riding the excitement of a new baby in the fam, but next week, I'm also moving in with Archer.

Even though Archer asked a few months ago, I didn't want to jump straight into the idea. I waited, giving Archer time. We were fresh, and my trust in him was still iffy. No way would I risk being homeless if he ran again. Our relationship has grown stronger, and I'm ready to take the risk with him.

I agreed to move in with him, and Cassidy will be taking Grace's new roomie spot.

"Hey, guys," Cassidy says, walking in with Lincoln behind her.

I smile and wave to them before leaning into Archer and lowering my voice. "Something will happen between them. Twenty bucks and fifty orgasms, they bang by the end of the year."

When we're at the bar, Cassidy flirts with Lincoln like it's her part-time job. Lincoln tries to keep his distance, joking that she's too young. Cassidy has had an easy life. Lincoln just got out of prison. They're not exactly bread and butter.

But hey, look at Archer and me.

"I'll take you up on that bet," Archer whispers. "I'll give you the orgasms no matter what, though. She's too young for Lincoln's liking."

"She's not *that* much younger than him. Their age gap is similar to ours."

"Let's just say, Lincoln likes them older."

"Older? As in cougars? Like, is his type women who need to hit their Life Alert after he gives them the D?"

He shakes his head, laughing. "Jesus, what am I going to do with you?"

"Answer the question. Now, I'm curious."

Come to think of it, I've never seen Lincoln with a woman. I stay with Archer all the time, and Lincoln hasn't gotten his own place yet. Not that I mind him being there.

Lincoln is good for Archer. Not only has their relationship grown but so has Archer's relationship with his mother. He has dinner with her once a week, and she's a frequent visitor at their place. Archer is finally realizing he doesn't have to face his problems alone.

"He's going to kill me," Archer says, keeping an eye on Lincoln. "He had a thing with one of my mother's friends." He pauses. "Two of them actually."

"You're joking."

He shakes his head.

It's not that I have a thing against age gaps. Archer is my brother's age. It's just surprising, especially the whole *mother's friends* thing.

"He can change, though," I say, having hope for Cassidy.

The girl is fun. I'd love for both Callahan men to find love.

"I'm sure you didn't think you'd end up with someone like me," I add.

He raises a brow. "Someone like you?"

"Quirky. Voice of a Valley Girl. Fun."

He grins. "Sure, but little did I know, a quirky, Valley Girl-voiced woman is who I needed."

Silas and Lola join us, interrupting our conversation.

Silas uses his sucker to signal between Archer and me. "When you two have a baby, you'd better hope it has your personality, Georgia."

I grab Archer's chin and move it from side to side. "Why? You know he has a shining personality."

"Only for you, babe." Archer winks at me.

"I think our baby will have a combination of our personalities," Cassidy says, smacking Lincoln's thigh.

"Your baby?" Silas asks. "What did I miss?"

Cassidy nods vigorously. "Hypothetical baby."

"There will be no babies," Lincoln corrects, shaking his head.

"I mean, first comes marriage." Cassidy smiles eagerly while glancing at me. "You'll be such a good sister-in-law, Georgia."

I burst into laughter.

All talk ceases when Cohen steps into the waiting room.

He rubs his hands together, a radiant grin on his face. "You ready to meet my daughter?"

———

ISABELLA GEORGIA FOX IS ADORABLE.

The middle name was a surprise to me.

I hold the sleeping girl in my arms, running my thumb over the peach fuzz on her head, and brush a quick peck to her forehead.

"She's so beautiful," I say, peering over at Archer.

His eyes are unreadable, and he smiles at me.

"Do you want kids someday?" I wrinkle my brow at the realization that we've never had this conversation.

He gulps. "I'm not sure."

I turn quiet, fighting to stop my face from falling. My face muscles hurt at my phony smile.

"You do." It's a statement. Not a question.

"I do." My body turns rigid, and I focus my attention on Isabella.

Another speed bump.

There are so many pieces in relationships. So many choices that can make or break you. Sure, you can love each other, have great sex, be happy, but when it comes down to spending the rest of your life with someone, there are conversations that need to be had, choices to make.

Where you'll live. Marriage. Kids.

Cohen's first relationship ended because his ex had decided out of the blue that she didn't want to be a mother after getting pregnant.

"Georgia," Archer whispers.

I shake my head violently, not looking at him. "Now isn't the time to have the baby talk."

"Georgia." When I don't look at him, he uses the tip of his finger to drag my chin up. His eyes meet mine, and they're gentle, warm, honest. "Don't ever feel like you have to hold back from me."

I shut my eyes before focusing on Isabella. "Then yes, eventually —*not* anytime soon—I want kids."

I peek up when the nurse walks in and starts talking to Jamie and Cohen. When she asks for Isabella, I carefully hand her over.

When Cohen was a single father and I was living with him, I helped him with Noah. I can change diapers, clean up vomit, and handle situations without batting an eye. It's why I work with children.

"Georgia," Archer says, scooting in closer to me, "you know I'll always be open and honest with you. In the past, I wasn't sure if I was mentally ready for children, but with each day I spend with you, I think about how much I want a family with you."

I grin at the thought of a family with Archer—of him being my husband and us having children running around. I wouldn't want to have one with anyone else but him. We may not be ready yet, but when the day comes, Archer will be an amazing father. I'm sure of it.

WANT MORE TWISTED FOX?

If you enjoyed Stirred and Shaken, check out the other books in the Twisted Fox series!

Straight Up
(Lincoln & Cassidy's story)
Chaser
(Finn & Grace's story)
Last Round
(Silas and Lola's story)

BOOKS BY CHARITY FERRELL

TWISTED FOX SERIES

(each book can be read as a standalone)

Stirred

Shaken

Straight Up

Chaser

Last Round

BLUE BEECH SERIES

(each book can be read as a standalone)

Just A Fling

Just One Night

Just Exes

Just Neighbors

Just Roommates

Just Friends

STANDALONES

Bad For You

Beneath Our Faults

Pop Rock

Pretty and Reckless

Revive Me

Wild Thoughts

RISKY DUET

Risky

Worth The Risk

ABOUT THE AUTHOR

Charity Ferrell is a USA Today and Wall Street Journal bestselling author of the Twisted Fox and Blue Beech series. She resides in Indianapolis, Indiana with her fiancé and two fur babies. She loves writing about broken people finding love while adding humor and heartbreak along with it. Angst is her happy place.

When she's not writing, she's making a Starbucks run, shopping online, or spending time with her family.

www.charityferrell.com

Made in United States
Orlando, FL
09 August 2022

20756536R00340